T0372160

PRAISE FOR *DANGEROUS*

'Brooding and brilliant' A.J. West

'As mesmerising and charismatic as Byron himself can ever have been. Beautifully written, accomplished in its meld of fact and fiction, this is a magnificent gothic tale of scandal, secrets and murder. I was hooked from line one!' Janice Hallett

'A plot as labyrinthine as the Venice backstreets, told in dazzling prose; suspenseful, seductive stuff' Erin Kelly

'Evokes all the grimy charisma of eighteenth-century Venice and at its brooding heart the flawed yet seductive Byron, enmeshed in a mystery as sinuous as the city's alleys and canals. I was enthralled' Elizabeth Fremantle

'Brilliant, daring writing ... a darkly delicious Venetian tale of murder and mystery with the deeply flawed, complex, but charismatic Lord Byron' Anna Mazzola

'Essie Fox expertly weaves fact and fiction in this gloriously gothic thriller, in which Venice becomes the atmospheric backdrop to Byron's daring attempt to catch a killer and clear his name' Anita Frank

'Sumptuous, entertaining, and glorious' C.S. Green

'Fox is the queen of darkly glittering gothic fiction, and *Dangerous* is an electrifying mystery inspired by Lord Byron's life – a tale so compelling I devoured it in one sitting' Louisa Treger

'Many writers have tried and failed to capture the Byronic quintessence, but the brilliant Essie Fox has succeeded admirably. She proves that the poet and rake remains fascinating because he is, indeed, mad, bad and *Dangerous*' Alex Larman

'A heady and intoxicating brew, sweeping the reader to a city of menacing shadow and melancholic splendour ... scandalously scintillating' Kate Griffin

'A gorgeously clever thriller' Amanda Craig

'A ravishing tale of murder, lust and thwarted ambition. Essie Fox's reimagining of Byron's turbulent months in nineteenth-century Venice is a sumptuous, decadent delight' Emma Carroll

'A deliciously gothic and beautifully written historical thriller starring the ultimate bad boy hero, Lord Byron' Frances Quinn

'An incredibly evocative and atmospheric book that captures the Byronic soul in all its beauty and madness' Victoria Dowd

'Perfect combination of intrigue, fun, and bad boys' Fiona Melrose

'Deliciously dark and everything I hoped it would be ... it takes what we think we know about Byron and spins it into a seductive gothic thriller where the scandalous poet is both chief suspect and amateur detective' Paul Burston

'An engaging historical mystery tale in which the dissolute poet turns sleuth to clear his own name' *Time & Leisure Magazine*

'A delicious dish of decadence ... fastidiously researched, richly imagined, full of wonderful descriptions of Venice'
Michael Stewart

'A sensuous, decadent, voluptuous read, like sinking into rich red velvet' Sean Lusk

'What a ride! Gripping and atmospheric' Caroline Lea

'Seductive and dripping in gothic ambiance. Highly addictive and original. Do not miss this' Dan Bassett

'Byronic brilliance wrapped up in dangerous devilry and murder'
The Book Trail

PRAISE FOR *THE FASCINATION*

'Makes skilful use of the tropes of Victorian gothic fiction' *Sunday Times* Book of the Month

'Essie Fox's best novel to date – one that weaves terrors with triumphs, heartache with hope ... Brava' *Culturefly*

'An inventive slice of gothic fiction, big-hearted and full of strangeness' *The Times* Book of the Month

'This is a tender, beautifully written meditation on what it meant in Victorian times to be an outsider, or to be born different' Historical Novel Society

'A scintillating cabinet of curiosities ... well worth the price of admission' *Foreword Reviews*

'A dazzling kaleidoscope of darkness and light. Disturbing and yet full of heart' Laura Purcell

'Magnificent ... a triumph' Dinah Jefferies

'Essie Fox follows in the footsteps of Angela Carter and A.S. Byatt with an adult fairy tale that delves into the darkest compulsions of human nature ... an opium trance of a novel, a vivid fantasmagoria' Noel O'Reilly

'Deliciously dark, full of twists and surprises' Liz Hyder

'A sumptuous, gothic treat that will reel you in and not let you go. Bravo!' Caroline Green

DANGEROUS

ABOUT THE AUTHOR

Essie Fox was born and raised in rural Herefordshire, which inspires much of her writing. After studying English Literature at Sheffield University, she moved to London where she worked for the *Telegraph Sunday Magazine*, then the book publishers George Allen & Unwin – before becoming self-employed in the world of art and design. Always an avid reader, Essie now spends her time writing historical gothic novels. Her debut, *The Somnambulist,* was shortlisted for the National Book Awards, and featured on Channel 4's *TV Book Club*. *The Last Days of Leda Grey,* set in the early years of silent film, was selected as *The Times* Historical Book of the Month, and *The Fascination*, published in 2023, was a *Sunday Times* bestseller. She has lectured at the V&A, and the National Gallery in London.

Follow Essie on her website, www.essiefox.com.

Also by Essie Fox and available from Orenda Books

The Fascination

DANGEROUS

Essie Fox

ORENDA
BOOKS

Orenda Books
16 Carson Road
West Dulwich
London SE21 8HU
www.orendabooks.co.uk

First published in the United Kingdom by Orenda Books 2025

A catalogue record for this book is available from the British Library.

Hardback ISBN 978-1-916788-44-2
B-format paperback ISBN 978-1-916788-45-9
eISBN 978-1-916788-46-6

Typeset in Garamond by Elaine Sharples

Printed and bound by Clays Ltd, Elcograf S.p.A

For sales and distribution, please contact *info@orendabooks.co.uk* or visit *www.orendabooks.co.uk*.

To Chris,
My own dark lord,
who still makes a fine cup of coffee.

But first, on earth as Vampire sent,
The corpse shall from its tomb be rent;
Then ghastly haunt the native place,
And suck the blood of all thy race,
There from the daughter, sister, wife,
At midnight drain the stream of life;
Yet loathe the banquet which perforce
Must feed the livid living corpse;
Thy victims ere they yet expire
Shall know the daemon for their sire.

Byron. From *The Giaovr*

THE FIRST ROLL

The Church of St Mary Magdalene
HUCKNALL TORKARD

June 15th, 1938

A lantern's furtive gleam gilds the medieval church in which the Reverend Cannon Barber peers through oily nets of shadows and recalls the golden splendour of that summer's afternoon. How sublimely had the sunshine shafted through the stained-glass windows when he'd performed an intercession, reciting prayers for all those souls entombed below the chancel steps. The poet Byron was among them, although the rumours would persist that his corpse had been removed and sold by resurrectionists – which was why Barber had decided to obtain a dispensation from the Home Office in London. To investigate the contents of the crypt and, hopefully, to lay the ghost. Once and for all.

Such a stench came rising up when the entrance stone was breached. As the builders then descended, what little light could follow down shone on haphazard piles of coffins lying one upon another, causing the oldest to be crushed beneath the weight of those above them. The splintered wood, the rotting shrouds through which the white of bones protruded conjured a setting more akin to a charnel house of horror than the sepulchre of grandeur that the Reverend imagined. But any sense of disappointment was allayed by one box in the centre of the tomb. It was draped in purple velvet. It had a coronet on top, though any jewels that once adorned it were no longer in their settings.

Was it true then? Had the crypt been invaded in the past? Hardly daring to breathe, the Reverend stepped a little closer, peering down into the gloom to watch the workmen as they prised away an outer layer of lead, after that a wooden lid, and...

What a wonder of a sight! Lord Byron had been dead for a century and more, yet who'd deny this was him? His handsome, melancholy features were quite perfectly preserved as if he'd died just yesterday, still with the crown of curling hair seen in so many of his portraits. And there! The final proof. The shrivelled foot poking out below one corner of the shroud. It was enough. More than enough.

The dead of night. Barber is back. This time he is alone. His head is cocked to the one side, listening out for any sound that might be heard above the sudden violent thudding of his heart. He's never been afraid before, not here within the house of God. But perhaps God *is* displeased at what he'd done that afternoon, what several congregants complained of on the grounds of blasphemy and desecration of the dead.

Weighed down by doubt, he now begins his own descent into the vault. There will be no other chance, not with the builders coming back to seal the entrance in the morning. Steeling his courage to proceed, he sets his lantern on a shelf beside the folded purple velvet and the damaged coronet. It takes some effort to remove the already loosened lid, and what a clatter and a crash when it falls and hits the ground. Not that Barber seems to notice, muttering as if in prayer when he gazes at the mask of sweet serenity in death – *'So beautiful a countenance I scarcely ever saw. His eyes the portals of the sun. His forehead passing from marble smoothness into a hundred wreaths and dimples corresponding to the feeling and the sentiments he uttered.'*

Coleridge, wasn't it? Or some such words to that effect, Barber ponders as he lifts one corner of the shroud and views the smooth perfection of the flesh which, in this light, could be a statue made of stone. Still, there are areas in which the embalmers' art has failed. Between the elbows and the wrists, the skin has withered, showing bone. It is the same with lower shins, though not the part that had the builders chuckling this afternoon, when one had claimed the male organ was not only still intact but quite remarkable in size. 'Like a pony!' he'd insisted, while Barber shook his head to hear such blatant disrespect. But when he sees it for himself, the noble member so engorged, he gasps aloud then swiftly pulls the shroud back up for decency.

Only then does he observe the indentation of the chest where the flesh had been incised and crudely stitched in place again. Had the heart been taken out? Embalmers did that, didn't they? Moved by a wave of sympathy, he touches the brow, as pale and cool as alabaster. His fingers comb through the hair, oddly springy, soft to touch. Silver threads among the darkness capture the glisten of the lamp. Or is that the sheen of dust?

Lost in such thoughts, he gasps anew to see the twitching of the lips. The faintest ghosting of a smile? He thinks of Polidori's *Vampyre*, based on the fragment of a story Byron composed one stormy night in the Villa Diodati, when Mary Shelley first conceived her novel *Frankenstein*, in which a corpse was re-infused with the essence of new life – *What a strange thing is the propagation of life! A bubble of seed which may be spilt in a whore's lap, or in the orgasm of a voluptuous dream.*

Is Barber also dreaming, to hear those words so clearly spoken? They might as well be from the Devil, crudely sordid and seductive. But they once stemmed from Byron's mind, and were transcribed by Byron's pen, later memorised by Barber in his studies of the man. Barber voiced them. No-one else. No other spirit in the crypt. Only the lantern's dipping flame gives the illusion of some movement.

As the bell in the tower of the church begins to chime, the first of twelve mournful tolls, Barber decides the time has come to leave the tomb and find his bed before his mind can play more tricks. With the coffin lid replaced, more of a struggle than expected, he is about to take the lantern from the shelf, when he stumbles, falling forwards and hitting his head on something solid.

Is it a moment or an hour before his consciousness returns, when he's aware of a sound, like a thrumming on the air? Is it coming from the coffin, or the echo of vibrations from the tolling of the bell? He only wishes it would stop. One of his temples is throbbing, and there's a pain in his neck from where it twisted awkwardly.

Struggling up onto his knees, he leans against the cold crypt steps and, as his vision slowly clears, notices the lantern's light gilding a large canopic jar lying inches from his feet. He reaches down, feeling compelled to peel away the dusty wax that forms a seal at the top, but then cries out in stark dismay when he discovers that one half of the vessel has been broken. Among stone shards he sees an acorn and some threadbare folds of cloth. What are those bundles of papers? Three rolls, and every one of them secured with a black ribbon. Where one binding has come loose he is able to make out the faded scrawl of sepia between the foxing of the mould that spreads across a yellowed page:

The Memoirs of Lord Byron. Venice. 1819

Is this a fake, or genuine? If real, its value is immense, could be sought out by every scholar, institution and collector in the literary world. Barber has dreamed about this church becoming even yet more famed as a place of pilgrimage once Byron's presence is established. But this!

With the rolls clutched to his breast he slumps against the cold crypt steps. As his mind begins to clear he recalls what he once read about the poet's personal papers being destroyed after his death – when a group of loyal friends met with his publisher in London and agreed that the contents were fit only for a brothel. What they'd possessed had been reduced to nothing more than dust and ashes in John Murray's blazing grate, after which whatever secrets they'd contained were lost forever. Or, had there been some copies made, and if so then who had thought to bury them at Hucknall Torkard? Was it divine intervention that led the Reverend to find them?

Steadier now, on his feet, he re-ascends into the church. As if some monkish apparition rendered in a gothic novel, he wanders restless through the aisles until he settles on a pew. For quite some time he does not move, only sits, staring down at what is cradled in his lap. Finally, his trembling fingers free one ribbon from its knot, and by the subtle radiance of the lantern at his side the Reverend Barber starts to read...

Shall I be listed with the angels, or the demons raised from Hell? You, the reader, must prepare to be the judge & so decide if I am guilty of the heinous & unnatural crimes of murder lately connected to my name.

'His thousand songs are heard on high...'

Byron. From *The Giaovr*

Oh, I am tired, & when I'm tired out comes all this & down it goes as lines of ink across a page. God only knows what contradictions this confession may contain, for I fear that one can lie more to one's self than any others, & every word I am to write may then confute, refute, & utterly abjure all those before.

These past few hours I have recalled the old bull elephant that fled from a circus here in Venice. Sitting at this very window, I heard the shouting of the keepers, who, in vain, had tried to lure it to some ark they were constructing. One man was trampled to his death. I very nearly shared his fate. Venturing out on the canal, hoping to get a better view, I saw the creature tearing up the most enormous beams of wood, which were then flung into the water & missed my gondola by inches. I do not think its mood was angry, more of a playful disposition. But later, towards midnight, it turned to one of fury & with extraordinary strength the beast rampaged across

> *the city. Musketry was employed but only proved to be in vain, until it broke into a church, where it was cornered & some soldiers fired a cannon at the beast. The first shot missed, but then the second found its mark & pierced the heart. I saw it dead the next day. Truly the most stupendous fellow. I was told it had gone mad for the wanting of a mate, for it had been the rutting month.*
>
> *The want of women is my ruin...*

Through the screeching of the gulls swooping across the Grand Canal, Byron set down his pen and muttered to himself, 'And now I'm cornered in a trap from which I fear there's no escape.'

His fingers gripped the silver base of the goblet with a bowl constructed from a human skull, once the relic of a monk who'd died some centuries before and was more recently discovered in the grounds of Newstead Abbey.

'Ah, Newstead,' Byron mused as he swallowed down the dregs of any wine still in the cup, and in his mind pictured again the dilapidated halls of the ancestral family home he'd sworn to never sell – which was another broken promise he could add to all the others.

A bitter smile played on his lips as mournful eyes caught the glitter of the candle at his side. One moment they looked blue, the next a grey, and then a violet. The whites were streaked with broken veins. The skin beneath was darkly bruised with the shadows of exhaustion as he turned towards the window where, an hour or so before, fizzing chrysanthemums of fireworks marked the end of Carnevale and lit the Venice skies with gold. Now, a dawn of rose-quartz blush appeared below black wings of night. The crumbling stones and iron grilles of the palazzos opposite loomed eerily above the veils of mist on the canal, in which the melancholy waters lapped as languid as desire.

Consumed with brooding ennui, Byron felt old. He was not old, yet in the course of thirty years what extremes of light and shade he had experienced in life. What heights of virtue, depths of vice he had discovered here in Venice, whether with whores in the brothels, or contessas in palazzos. But then, what was the local saying? *Women, they have two pockets. One for tears, and one for lies...*

Still pondering the loss of Newstead, he reached towards a silver box with the engraving of a mermaid and the ancient family crest. 'Trust in Byron,' he sighed as he lifted the lid to see a folded handkerchief with two initials stitched in silk. An acorn lay on top of it, the memento he'd once found in the grass below an oak tree where he'd kissed a lovely girl with hair as soft as burnished silk. She'd been as slender as a boy, flesh as pale and smooth to touch as any of the marble statues admired on his Grecian travels. Her name was Susan. Susan Vaughan. But Susan Vaughan had lied to him. Susan Vaughan, the maid from Wales who'd captured Byron in her spell, before she'd played him for a cuckold with another of his servants.

Why was he thinking of her now, of how she'd looked in a gown he'd brought back for her from London? Black trim of lace, like gossamer. The velvet lustre of the skirts, shimmering a forest green. When she'd worn it, who would guess at her humble origins? So fine the manners she'd affected, so pure the vowels as she'd disguised the natural lilt of her Welsh accent. And then, the night when they'd lain sated and sweat-soaked on his bed, and she'd recited lines from Shakespeare as well as any actress on the stage at Drury Lane. *'What's in a name? That which we call a rose, by any other name would smell as sweet?'*

During such moments – reckless moments – empty promises were made about inviting her to London to meet the theatre managers. But left unspoken was the truth that he preferred his pretty maid kept on his private stage of Newstead. And surely, she had known his words were spun from nought but dreams. That come the dawn all dreams must fade.

For himself, there'd come the morning when *Childe Harold* was first published and life had changed beyond all measure, transformed into a gilded palace from a children's fairy tale. Whether his palace *had* been gold, or rendered of a baser metal, he'd been subsumed into a whirlwind world of fame and adulation, besieged by women of the ton bent on offering him sex. Newstead Abbey was forgotten. So was Susan ... until now.

What had become of the girl? For a long time he stared at hands where nails were bitten to the quicks, but at last he steeled himself to dip his pen into the ink and continue the recording of more recent happenings:

> *The want of women is my ruin, and all too often it is theirs. But, more lately I am plagued by what I fear is the ambition of an unhinged & jealous man. Only last week when I attended the Countess Alfieri's salon...*

In a palazzo near St Mark's, the wealthy widow's *conversaziones* were famed for literary discussions. Usually he relished them, eager to join the busy throngs, but that night as he crossed the square leading towards her door, he felt the weight of some foreboding. Was it the sense of being watched? Nothing unusual in that. His infamy still drew attention, and on occasions he enjoyed it, affecting a persona either gregarious and charming or cold and surly in demeanour – whichever inclination was the stronger at the time. But that night he wasn't sure he was up to the charade.

Drawing the collar of his coat around his face, as if a shield, he wondered: *Should I be afraid?* So many villains with stilettos crept through Venice, sleek as rats. The sort of men who'd stab a man then push him into a canal without the slightest pang of guilt. Would he find death in such a way? A fortune-teller once predicted he would meet his final doom in his thirty-seventh year. If that was so, then he still had a good six years of life ahead. But the curse was drawing close, haunting his mind, haunting his verse: *A tall, thin, grey-haired figure, like a shade that walked the earth...*

Looking back across his shoulder he saw no old man, only a

ragamuffin child who couldn't be much more than twelve. Something familiar about him. What it was he couldn't say, but all at once Byron was taken with a philanthropic notion. 'You there! Yes. You, boy. Will you run me an errand?' Byron reached into a pocket, drawing out a leather notebook. Next, the pencil used to scribble down a message for his valet:

Dear Fletcher,
Give the boy who brings this letter some reward for his troubles. Feed him & wash him if he'll let you. Make sure to offer him a bed & if he seems the willing type, some occupation in the house.
L.B.

Tearing the page from its binding, he passed it to the beggar, also giving directions to the Palazzo Mocenigo and the name of the man to whom the note should be delivered – after which, as quick as lightning, the boy went running off, feet echoing across the bridge where Byron's gondola was moored.

So immersed had he been in watching this departure, Byron at first failed to notice when a footman appeared at the door to welcome him. Once inside the palazzo, he was slow to climb the stairs (his clubbed right foot hindered his movements, and even more so when he was weary), but at last he reached the hubbub of the salon and attempted to ignore a sudden lulling in the buzz of conversation – the way that almost every face turned to look in his direction. Glancing himself towards a servant who was offering refreshments, he declined the fragolino and the pomegranate sherbets but did accept a china thimble cup of steaming Turkish coffee. It might revive his flagging spirits.

Setting the cup back on the tray, he heard a warm and throaty voice above the strains of violins played from behind some fretwork screens – 'Ah! Here he is! The most famous of the Englishmen in Venice. The genuine Lord Byron.'

The genuine Lord Byron. Whatever could the woman mean? He turned around to see his host reclining on a velvet chaise between a pair of potted palms. Always elegant and poised, every object around her had been artfully arranged. She was a goddess come to life before an ornate painted screen on which cavorting cupids smiled from meringues of puffed white clouds. A table placed at her side held baskets of exotic fruits, though purple grapes crushed at her feet looked more like stains of crusted blood among the petals of dried flowers also sprinkled on the carpet, over which the poet limped as he focused on the garland made of pearls and ostrich feathers wreathed around her tall white wig.

How very Marie Antoinette! Byron mused as he glanced down towards the woman's full rouged mouth, although the rest of her face was concealed by a mask – which the gossips would insist was to hide the scars of pox inherited from her late husband. Not that the Countess looked unwell. She was as plump as a peach, and she exuded sex and glamour. When he bowed and took her hand there was no warning stench of rot, only the more alluring notes of her rose and civet perfume.

Byron addressed her in the English she always liked to practise, even though he was as fluent in her own Italian – 'Dearest Contessa, please forgive my late arrival. It pains me to admit to such a frailty of spirit, when I more usually philosophise and talk of nought but nonsense with the greatest of decorum, but I am suffering the effects of Carnevale's last agonies. Far too much wine and little sleep.'

'Has there been work as well as play? How we crave your latest verses. Headless bodies. Shipwrecks. Drownings. Sultans and slaves in palaces.'

'I confess I have been busy on new cantos of *Don Juan*.'

'Ah, yes! Last time we met you said the verses would be featuring a salon like my own.' Behind her mask, dark eyes were narrowed. 'Nothing scurrilous, I hope. Will you recite them for us here?'

'Perhaps,' Byron teased. Meanwhile, he was distracted by the cut-glass tones of voices drifting over from one corner. No doubt some English gentry on their European tours. Oh, how those voices pierced his heart and made him yearn for his old life. He had to force a note of mirth when he raised the raven wing of one dark brow and spoke again – 'I fear that Blackwood's magazine reviewed the work already published in a very shabby manner. I believe the words they used were "imperious and filthy" ... in light of which my newest stanzas may offend those visitors who more usually frequent the Devil's drawing rooms of London.'

The Countess's golden mask captured the dazzle of the candles in the ceiling's chandelier. They also glistened on a bracelet made of beads, an emerald green, when she pointed to the mantle on which a display of glass ornaments was kept.

'How do you like my latest treasures? Those antique goblets – do you see them? The very best Murano glass. They were commissioned for a doge over five hundred years ago.'

'Should you not keep them somewhere safer?'

'Beauty should be admired, never hidden in darkness. Otherwise, what is it for? But come ... tell me the news of your own private collection. Your menagerie of beasts.'

Byron smiled. 'Mutz, my dog, has learned the trick of drawing back the bolt of a door ... if plied sufficiently with treats. In sadder news, my badger died. But I still have the pair of monkeys, though one of them is prone to biting. There is a crow with half a beak, and—'

'And the other new addition? The little pet called Allegrina?'

'You know of her arrival?' Byron's tone became much cooler to hear this mention of the infant sent to live with him in Venice.

'This city has no secrets...' the Countess began, just as Byron's attention was diverted by some guests whose reflections shimmered grey and almost looked like apparitions in the mantle mirror's glass.

One man stood conversing with a group of doting women, and

though his features were in profile and therefore not entirely clear, the head of loose, dark curls falling across a pale brow was unmistakably his own. In a stark contrast to the fashionable brocades and peacock silks still in favour with the noblemen residing here in Venice, Byron's double also wore a plain black suit with trouser legs cut long and very full, though surely not to conceal another orthopaedic boot?

The Countess followed his gaze, 'Ah, I see you've spied your likeness?'

Byron sighed in irritation. 'It will keep happening. Only last week I was told of my appearance in Rome, where I've not been in many months. Apparently, I stood and bowed a full ten minutes at the opera. Meanwhile, another Byron was in Florence recently, at the Uffizi gallery, declaiming thoughts on Botticelli and reciting poetry.'

The Countess laughed. 'I must confess I was fooled by him at first. But only for a moment. Very soon, I realised that this man does not possess your ... oh, what is it called? The carisma? The fascino?'

As she spoke, the doppelganger chanced to glance in their direction. He made excuses to his friends and strode across the room towards them, though even with no limping gait it took some time to navigate other guests along the way.

During this little interval, the Countess rose from her chair. She was not tall and craned her neck to murmur low in Byron's ear: 'I hear he claims to be a writer and is from England like yourself ... although he looks Italian.'

Having recognised the man, Byron succinctly replied, 'Half Italian. His name is Polidori. Raised in his father's London bookshop. Qualified as a doctor at the age of just nineteen. Barely twenty when I hired him as a personal physician to join me on my travels. But his ambitions go much further than the medical profession. Polidori hopes for fame through his own works of literature.'

'And is he any good?'

'I don't deny he has some talent, but he lacks the temperament. Rarely settles to a theme and is too jealous of the successes gained by other men around him.' Byron broke off and looked regretful, 'I'm afraid that when he challenged Percy Shelley to a duel it proved to be the final straw. We reached a parting of the ways.'

The conversation ended as the younger, very slender, and altogether more Byronic-looking Doctor Polidori arrived to stand before them.

At first, ignoring the Countess, he eagerly addressed the poet: 'I'd heard this was the salon you most frequently attended, and...'

'Polly, my dear man!' Byron's voice came somewhat strained. 'What brings you here to Venice? And looking so ... like me? There are surely other ways to gain some notoriety. I do hope you have not rendered me too ridiculous with those young ladies over there.'

As he spoke, Bryon glanced back through lowered lids towards the women, who were watching them intently, some lifting palms to open mouths as they giggled in confusion at the sight of, not just one, but two Lord Byrons in the room.

Polidori's chin was tilted, and in the eyes that were not blue but a much darker, brooding brown, Byron observed the same ferocious savage silence that he'd noticed far too often in the past as the younger man replied, 'You know I've never liked that nickname. Please refrain from using it. And when it comes to my arrival here in Venice, it's because I have secured myself employment at St Giovanni e Paolo...'

'The hospital?' Byron cut in. 'Will you be working in the labs on your experiments again? Prussic acid, oil of amber, charcoal and suffocating compounds to be bubbled over flames and blown into an open vein? I must admit I never did quite see the point of the palaver – far more likely to be killed than to be cured of minor ailments.'

The flush of colour that arose through Polidori's neck and face was all too visible to see, what with the collar of his shirt being unfastened at the throat, as was the one Byron wore. When the doctor spoke again his voice was tense with indignation: 'I'm working in the morgue.'

'A detective of dissection!'

'Do not humiliate me, sir, when I seek only to admire you,' Polidori batted back. 'Though, as it happens, I have heard certain rumours that relate to *your* own business since we parted. How you and Shelley have now formed some debauched and secret sect.'

'A secret sect. Well, *that* is new.'

'The Society of Ancient Rome. Promoting your beliefs in free love and dissipation.'

'There is not and never was such a sect, as well you know. Though I'm inclined to wish there was. Oh, to act as emperors, feasting and fornicating as our empires fall around us.' Byron's lips twitched in amusement. 'Perhaps there *may* be something in it, and such excesses *do* explain my current state of enervation.' At that, he turned to their hostess. 'Forgive me, dear Countess, but I am tired, and when I'm tired I can be quite monstrous. In my absence Polidori will inform you all about his unique literary endeavours, though let us hope he refrains from recounting any horrors from his place of occupation.'

The Countess, who looked peeved to hear of Byron's departure, did soften a little when the doctor took her hand and softly muttered the words, 'Incantato di conoscerla.'

She purred her response: 'Perhaps you'd do a reading at my next conversazione.'

Hearing this, Polidori seemed to grow a good inch taller. 'I have recently completed a gothic manuscript, and—'

'Like Matthew Lewis's *The Monk?*' the Countess asked with some excitement. 'When he was here, we doused the candles. It was so very atmospheric. All those torments of the flesh and wrestling with consciences.'

Polidori replied, 'My own novel is based on the fragment of a story first conceived by Lord Byron, when we stayed at Lake Geneva and the Shelleys came to visit...'

'Oh, not the wretched vampyre tale!' Byron sighed dramatically, before explaining to the Countess, 'It was that cold, wet summer when Mount Tambora erupted, and all the world seemed to be cast in the shadow of its ashes.'

'Ah yes!' She closed her eyes and recited from a verse he had written at the time: '"The bright sun was extinquish'd, and the stars did wander darkling in the eternal space..."'

'Darkness,' Byron said, his voice both ominous and distant. 'And there was one such dismal night when a dreadful storm was raging, almost making us believe all life was at an end. Hardly the cheeriest of past-times, but we managed to amuse ourselves by reading horror stories from a phantasmagoria, after which we agreed to create some of our own. As Polidori says, mine was nothing but a fragment, and deliberately so. Though I may share nocturnal habits, I have a personal dislike of the creatures known as vampires. What little I *do* know of their affairs would not induce me to reveal any secrets. And, on that note, I'll say adieu and fly back out into the night.'

Polidori raised a hand and roughly grabbed at Byron's arm. 'Before you go, may I give you a copy of my story. It isn't overlong, and I'd appreciate your thoughts. I've sent some pages back to London. To your own publisher, John Murray. He believes ... that is to say he has informed me in a letter that my good looks and untamed spirit render me the perfect hero who might follow in your footsteps. It was he who advised I emulate your style of dress ... to set the tone, as it were. But should Murray fail to bite, Henry Colburn has expressed his own interest in the project.'

'Colburn!' Byron exclaimed. 'The wretch behind Caro Lamb's dreadful fuck-and-publish novel! Nothing but vain self-fabrication, thwarted passion and revenge, with her madman of a hero roaming ruined monasteries while howling at the moon ... not to mention willy-nilly draining the life from every woman he seduced.'

'You have read *Glenarvon* then?' Below the shimmer of her mask, the faintest smile lit the lips of the Countess Alfieri. 'All those references she makes to nibbling poet parasites, and echoes of your Newstead Abbey. Is it true the place is haunted by the ghost of a monk with burning eyes, and—'

'Must every novel nowadays include demented monks?' Byron scowled as he struggled to contain a rising temper. 'Lady Lamb is a volcano with lava flowing through her veins. Personally, I'd like her cooler, such as on a marble slab in Doctor Polidori's morgue.'

'Well, that's a little extreme, but...' With all the flair of a magician pulling a rabbit from a hat, Polidori now produced a sheath of papers from his jacket. 'I made a copy. Here it is. My dearest hope is that you might enjoy my work a little more.'

Byron was moved to refuse but having seen the desperate yearning in the younger man's expression he agreed to take the papers. Mirroring the doctor's actions, he placed them in his jacket pocket, and as soon as that was done Polidori made a bow and offered him a curt goodbye. He did not speak another word to the Countess Alfieri, only turned his back on her and marched towards the salon doors.

More than an hour was to pass before Byron could escape. Every time he tried to leave, another guest would call his name, another conversation started. But, at last, the room was emptied, the musicians stopped their playing, and though he searched to find the Countess and say goodnight a second time she was nowhere to be found.

Emerging alone on the steps of the palazzo he surveyed the shadowed square and experienced again the creeping sense of being watched. Where was his gondolier? No doubt he'd joined some revellers on the bridge's other side. Had he not been so exhausted, Byron would have liked to join them, being as happy with the whores and thieves residing here in Venice as when mingling with the gentry. How he loved the Carnevale. The painted lips below black masks. The men who dressed as Harlequins and—

A sudden cry diverted him, its ringing echo then repeated as the sound reverberated through a nearby sotoportego – a narrow passage set below the Alfieri's upper rooms, with several doorways leading off into the house's stores. However grand the living quarters, this alley stank of noxious slime. No light to penetrate the gloom, where any dangers could be lurking. But how could he ignore such a desperate plea for help – which came again, and was then followed by a horrible wet gurgle?

'Tita?' Byron called to alert his gondolier, the roguish giant of a man who came in useful at those times when he found himself in scrapes; such as when husbands sought revenge for the seduction of their wives. But tonight, the man appeared to have melted into air.

What to do? Byron returned to the porchway of the house, alerting a footman to follow him back to the passage. Moments later, a lantern carried in the servant's hand cast its light over the body of a woman on the ground. She lay unnaturally contorted – the crab-like way her arms and legs were splaying out on either side, the stark white gleam of the flesh where the fabric of her bodice had been torn to expose a single naked breast.

With a sickening lurch in the pit of his belly, Byron's legs collapsed beneath him. Now, on a level with the victim, he grasped her hand and tried to offer some words of reassurance, though he doubted she could hear them. Behind the tell-tale black mask worn by Venetian whores, dark eyes rolled up into her head, only the whites still visible. And then, the horror of her throat, where butchered flesh was curling red like the petals of a rose. And from that wound her life was ebbing, trickling between the cobbles.

'Don't die!' Byron cried, tearing the coat from his back, throwing it over her for warmth. While doing that, he heard her sigh. The barest fluttering of breath. But any breath was proof of life, and any sign of life was hope. Newly enthused with urgency, he brushed away the honeyed hair that fell across one of her cheeks. He pressed his mouth against her own to blow some air into her lungs. He did it once, and then again, was so intent upon the task he was entirely unaware of the audience of two who watched the tragedy unfold.

When Byron finally looked up, he was unconscious of the blood smeared across his mouth and hands. His eyes were dazzled by the lantern. He only vaguely saw the silhouetted form of the man who held it in his hand, and then the glisten of the mask worn by Contessa Alfieri, her mouth an open 'O' of shock before she crossed herself and gasped, 'My God, what have you done?'

Two

The sun went down, the smoke rose up, as from
A half-unquenched volcano...

Byron. From *Don Juan:* Canto X

Byron awoke late in the day to see the creeping grey of dusk leaking through the bedroom windows. Rain whispered soft against glass roundels. The sedation of the black drop he'd imbibed some hours before crawled like spiders in his mind, spinning webs of sticky glue through which he struggled to recall what had occurred the night before.

He closed his eyes, and images streaked like lightning in black skies. He saw anew the final moments of the woman in the alley, and how together with the footman he had dragged her lifeless body to a store below the kitchens. They'd laid her down on sacks of rice. Byron had wiped his bloodied hands on the rough weave of the hessian. Too late to fear what the Alfieri kitchen staff would think when they chanced upon those stains. Worse still, to find a corpse!

For then, the servants were abed. The house was steeped in oily silence, only broken when the Countess turned to mutter to her footman, 'Never speak a word of this. If the scandal should be spread. Death! At my own door.'

Now holding the lamp, the woman's trembling hands caused its light to throw black shadows juddering around the walls. The dizzying effect left Byron feeling nauseous as he replied, 'But Countess, we must send for a doctor. We must report the crime.'

'It is too late for any doctor,' the woman hissed at him. 'Tongues will wag – think of the gossip. Not just for me, but for yourself!'

'You surely don't assume I was in any way involved? You—' He broke off in disbelief. But one thing was true enough. The victim was already dead, for even now he could see the pallor mortis was extreme, her flesh the colour of white marble, striated here and there with rusted smears of drying blood.

Her cheeks last tinge, her eyes' last spark ... the tresses of her yellow hair. As the lines he had composed in his poem, *The Giaour,* rose unbidden to his mind, much like Doctor Polidori in the salon earlier, he turned his back on the Countess and walked away, without a word.

Emerging from the alley, he was relieved to see that Tita the Prodigal was back. In the soft illumination of the lamp fixed to the prow of the tented gondola, the giant of a man could well have been another Neptune, with the paddle in his hand taking the place of any trident. Sensing his master approach, the gondolier turned with a smile, and Byron froze to see the stain of something red smeared on his cheek.

'What's that?' he asked abruptly, raising a fingertip to touch it.

'Ma che sta facendo?' What are you doing? Tita's breaths blasted hot and were tainted by wine as he lifted his own hand, touching a finger to the stain and squinting down through narrowed eyes before he chuckled, then exclaimed in a gravelly deep voice, 'Ah, the proof my sins!'

'*Your* sins?' Byron said, his heart rate quickening again when he considered Tita's absence, around the time he had first heard the woman calling from the alley.

'Branded by the pretty lips I've been kissing this past hour, after I saved the saucy bawd from the villain who'd been hoping to filch her evening's takings. I grabbed the purse out of his hands, boxed his ears and sent him packing. It was out of gratitude she offered me a thank-you fuck.' The big man shrugged and offered Byron an inebriated grin. 'Well, I'd seen the other guests leaving the Alfieri party, and with no sign of you among them I assumed you'd be delayed. Didn't think you'd mind that much if I got lost in a quim of my own to pass the time.'

'There is no affaire de coeur between the Countess and myself,' Byron replied in cooler tones, at the same time wondering if Tita lied, or told the truth. Still in a state of discomposure, he held the finger that had touched Tita's cheek to his nose, inhaling scents of rose and almond. Common enough ingredients that many women used as paint to dab on faces and lips. Nothing like the iron tang of what had coated Byron's hands but a little time before, the proof of which – had Tita been somewhat less addled in his mind – could still be seen around his mouth as he stepped past the gondolier to make his way onto the boat.

So much blood, Byron sighed while gliding over jet-black waters. Would the Alfieri footman think to return to the alley and wash the evidence away, or had the Countess changed her mind and reported the crime? Or – this he thought most probable – being wary of a scandal happening on her own doorstep, had she ordered her man to throw the corpse in the canal, where it would rot or be dragged up like any other poor drowned soul? Didn't it happen all the time? The dampness of the city's air left pathways slimed and treacherous. An easy thing to lose one's footing and slip headfirst into the water, to find a welcome in the arms of any sea nymphs down below.

Back in his chambers, Byron feared himself another drowning man. His fingers clutched the marble mantle while dying embers in the grate glowed a vivid red. He fumbled to remove the bloodied clothes from his body, then roughly scrubbed his face and hands in the bowl upon the stand. Naked but for his drawers and shivering with cold, he made his way towards the bed and opened up a drawer in the cabinet beside it. The one in which he stored two pistols and a copy of the Bible.

Byron was not a man of faith, but this had been a gift from his sister Augusta at the time of their last meeting. How he missed his dearest Gus, the sweetest and the kindest of the women he had known. The only one with whom he'd shared a true affinity of spirit. Between its covers might he find some consolation for the horror he'd just witnessed in an alley?

Flicking through the flimsy pages, his eye was drawn to a line in the Book of Revelations: 'And they had hair as the hair of women, and their teeth were as the teeth of lions.'

'What does this mean?' he'd muttered gruffly, placing the book back in the drawer, reaching instead for a small bottle lying underneath his pillow. Deftly pulling out the cork, he'd swallowed down a hefty dose of the sticky, dark-brown liquid, hoping the drug would do its work and bring a sleep devoid of dreams. And it had – for a while.

But now, awake again, the nightmare of last night was still too vivid in his mind. Why did he feel such pangs of guilt for the woman he'd found dying, as if he grieved for a friend? Perhaps it was the velvet mask that marked her out a prostitute, which meant their paths may well have crossed during the month of Carnevale. Perhaps they'd fucked against a wall? In a sedan? Under a table? Perhaps he'd kissed her mouth when it had still been warm and pink, before the hue of it had faded to the phantom grey of death?

The woman's hair, as pale as straw, put him in mind of the wax model he'd once acquired while in Rome. Displayed in the window of a shop on plush red velvet, it was as peerless to behold as any Botticelli Venus. With glass blue eyes, pearls round its neck, and a tiara to crown a head of golden hair, the female form seemed to embody both the human and divine, as much at home in a bordello as in the guise of a Madonna at the altar of a church.

On the day it was delivered to his palazzo here in Venice, his valet had been out, running some errand or other – which was probably as well. Fletcher was sure to disapprove of the extravagance incurred, being enough to pay the staff of the palazzo for a year. But Tita was on hand, helping Byron to remove the effigy from the box and then assisting in arranging it on Byron's study chaise. But, in the midst of the manoeuvre, a panel in the model's abdomen creaked open on its hinges and revealed the inner organs, and how they'd glistened red and purple with the varnish used to seal them. Indeed, they'd looked so realistic, Byron would not have been surprised to see the heart begin to throb, and for his Venus to have yawned and blinked her eyes, or even smiled. Meanwhile, he'd stared at Tita, and Tita had stared at him, until the two of them agreed that the model was *too* life-like, sure to offend any guests of a more nervous disposition. Byron's Venus was returned to her bed of straw and fleece, and Tita carried her away to the palazzo's lower floor. Out of sight and out of mind.

What had the Countess Alfieri done with the murdered prostitute? The thought continued to nag as Byron pushed away dark curls that fell across his eyes, then freed his limbs from tangled sheets to kick his legs across the mattress. Limping towards the bedroom window he looked beyond the half-drawn curtains to see the dripping lions' heads protruding from the house's walls. In the fast-encroaching darkness, the chill March rain, the sleet and fog could barely be distinguished from the waters below. Such a malodourous stench rose to linger in his nose. And what was that? That other smell?

His eyes now fell on the boots and crumpled clothes he'd left discarded on the oriental rugs and cold terrazzo of the floor. He was about to pick them up and throw the lot in the canal, when he remembered what was hidden in the pocket of his jacket. The papers he extracted were in places also stained with the blood that must have seeped from the murdered woman's wounds. But, on the whole, the ink survived, and as Byron spread the pages on the surface of a table, he saw the neatly looping hand he knew of old as Polidori's.

'Very well,' he said aloud, dragging on a dressing gown then blowing warmth into his hands. 'I am in need of some diversion to elevate my dismal mood. What has the doctor produced?'

Although the fire was alight – his valet must have crept into the room to make it up while Byron was still sleeping – he now arranged more logs on top. Newly fed, flames hissed and crackled as they cast their pretty flicker over the brocade and velvet curtains draped around his large four-poster, over the crimson of flocked paper and the gilding of the plasterwork of ornamental covings. Upon this stage, which so resembled rooms he'd loved before at Newstead, Byron selected the first pages and then settled on the sopha where he started to read...

Three

The Vampyre

Polidori

It happened that in the midst of the dissipations attendant upon a London winter, there appeared at the various parties of the leaders of the ton a nobleman, more remarkable for his singularities, than his rank. He gazed upon the mirth around him, as if he could not participate therein. Apparently, the light laughter of the fair only attracted his attention, that he might by a look quell it, and throw fear into those breasts where thoughtlessness reigned. Those who felt this sensation of awe, could not explain whence it arose: some attributed it to the dead grey eye, which, fixing upon the object's face, did not seem to penetrate, and at one glance to pierce through to the inward workings of the heart; but fell upon the cheek with a leaden ray that weighed upon the skin it could not pass. His peculiarities caused him to be invited to every house; all wished to see him, and those who had been accustomed to violent excitement, and now felt the weight of ennui, were pleased at having something in their presence capable of engaging their attention. In spite of the deadly hue of his face, which never gained a warmer tint, either from the blush of modesty, or from the strong emotion of passion, though its form and outline were beautiful, many of the female hunters after notoriety attempted to win his attentions, and gain, at least, some marks of what they might term affection: Lady Mercer, who had been the mockery of every monster shewn in drawing-rooms since her marriage, threw herself in his way, and did all but put on the dress of a mountebank, to attract his notice:—though in vain:—when she stood before him, though his eyes were apparently fixed upon hers, still it seemed as if they were unperceived;—even her unappalled impudence was baffled, and she left the field. But though the common adultress could not influence even the guidance of his eyes, it was not that the female sex was indifferent to him: yet such was the apparent caution with which he spoke to the virtuous wife and innocent daughter, that few knew he ever addressed himself to females. He had, however, the reputation of a winning tongue; and whether it was that it even overcame the dread of his singular character, or that they were moved by his apparent hatred of vice, he was as often among those females who form the boast of their sex from their domestic virtues, as among those who sully it by their vices...

Byron sighed. He groaned. He muttered, 'Pedestrian and pessimistic! Polidori is deluded if he thinks this will be published. And yet...' A tickle of unease was creeping down his spine, for there were aspects of the story that were eerily compelling, even before admitting to parallels between himself and the vampyre of the title.

At least the story did not delve into the ancient melodramas still at large in the Levant. Scenes he'd referenced in *The Giaour,* inspired by meeting with some villagers in Greece who spoke in terror of creatures known as vroucholachas – monsters that feasted on the flesh and the livers of their victims, and then existed in a state in which they might appear as dead, and yet they were 'undead'. They were unquenched, unquenchable. The only way to stop the plague was to bury them in graves with millstones placed on heads or chests. If not, it was said they would rise to feed again.

The villagers had also told him of the fates of several children who had suffered from a fever, becoming pale and lethargic, wasting away until they died. News of the tragedy soon spread, with the doctor overseeing an official investigation, requesting that the corpses be exhumed and the deaths proved to be natural in cause. But all were shocked to discover that not one of the bodies showed any signs of decomposing. Some had fresh blood around their mouths, and their flesh was plump and pink. In addition to this, the hair and fingernails had grown just as they would have done in life. But, worst of all, the corpses shrieked as if in agonies of pain when stakes were thrust into their hearts. The act was merely a precaution. The doctor scorned old superstitions and suspected there must be a scientific explanation, but...

What was that? A piercing scream? Right here! In his own house?

Once he'd gathered his composure Byron wasn't that surprised. His servants often took to brawling, not to mention the antics of the toddler of a daughter who'd so recently been sent to live with him in Venice. Meanwhile, a good deal nearer, his chamber door gave off a creak, and there he saw his old brown mastiff with its eyes like yellow glass – which many strangers feared must indicate the fiercest temperament, while in reality the dog was as timid as a mouse.

Loping in to join its master, the beast's attention was diverted by the crumpled mounds of clothes left discarded on the floor. It stopped to nose and sniff around them, making the strangest whining sounds. Neither a growl, nor quite a whimper, yet uncannily disturbing.

'Leave!' Byron commanded.

The dog obeyed without objection, wagging its tail and

drawing near to rest its chin upon his knee. Byron smiled as he caressed the softer fur that grew in tufts and formed a ruff at Mutz's neck. The tactile pleasure often soothed and cleared the worries from his mind. But that day the thought of corpses being impaled within their graves, mouths opened wide in yawning terror – the awful visions would not leave him. And when the hinges of the door let out a second creak, he was startled to see the face and flaxen hair of the valet he'd employed for more than twenty years as if the man had been a stranger.

'So, you're up then.' Fletcher's voice held the warmth of northern tones, more commonly heard in any staff employed at Newstead.

As Byron offered no reply more than a vacant-looking gape, the valet carried on:

'I did look in an hour before, but you were sleeping like a babe. These topsy-turvy hours you keep! You've missed your breakfast ... and your lunch, so I dare say you're feeling hungry. I've brought your tea, pertikuler to the way you claim you like it. Not a trace of milk or sugar to give a flavour to the brew. A dish of broth, and fresh fried scampi, and the vinegar you always like to swill it down with.' Fletcher pulled a gargoyle face. 'How you imagine this can keep a body and soul together ... it's a mystery to me. Who could hope to comprehend your abstemious regime?'

Byron, the slender homme fatale, had now returned to his full senses and replied with a smile, 'Ah, but when I come to die, how beautiful I'll be, while if I ate as much as you I would by now have metamorphosed into the ursine sloth at the Exeter Exchange.'

Fletcher scowled at the insult, which was one he heard too often. Now well into middle-age, he was still moderately handsome, although compared to Byron's paleness his complexion had grown ruddy and was coarsened by their years of exposure to hot climates. In addition to this, the man's once muscular physique had gained substantially in weight during the time they'd been in Venice, mostly due to an addiction to the creamy pasta dishes.

Why, of late he'd even voiced his intent of one day going back to London and investing in a factory producing macaroni for the masses. He was convinced he'd make his fortune, 'once the English got a taste'. Fletcher himself could carry on delighting in the 'finest food created on God's earth' – but without the daily torment of the damp Venetian climate.

Damp permeated all of Venice. Fabrics rotted. Plaster bloated. Stonework crumbled into dust, and servants of a certain age were often plagued by arthritis. Indeed, the valet's wincing movements caused the contents of his tray to rattle like a tambourine, almost succeeding in erasing Byron's thoughts of gothic fiction, in which a vampyre in the guise of a handsome English lord sought his amusements by seducing and then sucking the blood from every woman of the ton.

'First Caro Lamb, now Polidori!' Byron tutted to himself, exasperated once again by these crudest of allusions to the scandalous affairs that had driven him from London. Combined with the effects of the black drop he'd imbibed, the insult caused his head to throb as he snapped at the valet, 'Won't you hurry up and put that tray down on the table? The jangling will drive me mad.'

Fletcher delivered his own judgement: 'I move as fast as I can, but patience is a virtue, and one I fear in short supply where MyLordship is concerned! Then again, if you will burn the midnight oil with no thought for your own health and constitution, we must expect some crabbiness.'

What had Coleridge once said when he'd been visiting at Newstead – that Byron and his valet bickered like a married couple? Well, that was taking things too far. It was true they shared a bond that, now and then, led to a lapsing of the natural social order, but after all these years Fletcher had grown quite immune to his lord's acerbic tongue, and little Byron did or said could cause the man surprise – until that day, when he saw the blood-stained garments on the floor.

Fletcher breathlessly proclaimed, 'Oh bless my soul. That harridan. That vicious Margarita Cogni! Has she been in here as well? I did my best to try and stop her when she came storming through the kitchen, snatching the knife out of Cook's hand and waving it at the poor nursemaid ... though for what sin I could not say, except the girl is young and pretty and therefore likely to entice you. And now, *you've* been attacked as well? Are you hurt? Has she gone?'

Fletcher, his vision far from perfect, squinted around the shadowed room for any sign of an intruder. Meanwhile, Byron calmly answered, 'I have not been attacked. But I did hear the disturbance. I should have guessed who it was.'

'Who else would it be?' Fletcher shook his head in a despairing attitude.

His master sighed at the thought of the lover he'd imagined gone for good now reappearing to drag more chaos in her wake.

At last Byron spoke, 'Whatever she's been doing with the servants in the kitchen, that's not my blood staining those clothes. Regretfully, when out last night I chanced to come across a woman who'd been stabbed and left for—'

'Dead? Was she dead?' the valet interjected in a state of wide-eyed shock.

Knowing how squeamish he could be, Byron concluded with a curt, 'Yes, she was. But I'd rather not discuss it at this moment. The event was too depressing.'

'Very well,' Fletcher said, leaving another lengthy pause as if unsure how to go on. 'We'll launder what we can, and—'

'Burn them. Burn them all!' Byron said dramatically as Fletcher stooped with a groan and bundled up the clothes, which he then placed down on the table. There, the valet's swollen fingers probed the pockets of the suit, from which he drew some carte de visites, a set of keys, several loose coins, a pencil and a notebook. Seeing that book, Byron recalled the beggar boy again, wondering if he had ever shown his face at the palazzo.

But, before he could ask, Fletcher picked up what remained of Polidori's manuscript, screwing his nose in consternation as he asked, 'And what is this? It's not your hand. Is this more blood smeared across the paper?'

'It is unfortunate, but the ink's still legible,' Byron replied while deciding not to mention Polidori as being the author of the story, for much like everybody else who'd shared his household when the man had been employed as his physician, Fletcher had taken a dislike, insisting Polidori was the queerest, coldest fish he had ever come to know, being so prone to churlish moods and always taking great offence at slights that never were intended, or indeed were never made.

Rather than hear it all again, Byron swiftly changed the subject. 'If you could just make up the fire and then bring in a glass of claret. And, *if* Margarita Cogni is still rampaging through the house, will you ensure she understands I am busy with my work and do not wish to be disturbed. Not for the next two hours at least.'

'By which time, if we're in luck' – Fletcher sounded optimistic – 'she will have tired of the waiting and decided to go home. I have to say, the way she queened it, giving orders, causing upsets in the kitchen earlier, it reminded me how calm our lives have been since she departed. Please, MyLord, do hold your nerve. Keep your urges in restraint. Whatever happens, don't encourage La Fornarina back again.'

Four

From infant's play, and man's caprice:
The lovely toy so fiercely sought
Hath lost its charm by being caught...

Byron. From *The Giaovr*

'Oh, Margarita!' Byron sighed when the valet had gone. How on earth had his affair with such a whirlwind of destruction been allowed to continue over the course of several months? But did he really need to ask? She was as practised as a whore but also pious as a nun, often stopping in whatever carnal act they were engaged in to cross herself and mumble prayers whenever church bells started ringing. There were a lot of bells in Venice. Much coitus interruptus. But, added to the clangings were objections from the staff who the woman terrorised.

It had been hard to let her go, the mistress nicknamed La Fornarina, because she looked so like a portrait by the artist Raphael in which a lovely dark-haired girl with knowing eyes and naked breasts posed as if a courtesan. Raphael's La Fornarina was said to be a baker's daughter, whereas Byron's Margarita was the wife of such a man; and being married he'd assumed she'd be less likely to oppress him with demands than women in the market for a husband. Another point in her favour was that she couldn't read or write, and therefore hadn't been inclined to send her lover endless letters of devotion or regret. Neither had she given him a lock of her hair. (Over the years he'd lost all count of the number of such trophies and was ashamed to admit that at times he had replied by sending back what he'd scissored from the tail of his dog – which was perhaps a little wicked but it saved his head from baldness.) But the greatest appeal of his Venetian Harlequina was her gift to make him laugh, a powerful aphrodisiac, though as the weeks turned into months she grew more like a porcupine – prickly if rashly touched. And then there came the evening when he'd asked some friends to dine, and she'd appeared upon the staircase like the vengeful goddess Hera after discovering that Zeus had been unfaithful with Lammia. On that occasion it was not the kitchen knife she chose to brandish, but a priceless Turkish sabre from the wall beside his desk. Poor Lady Hoppner, who'd arrived on the arm of her husband, the British consul here in Venice, was horrified to find herself faced with such violent jealousy. It was like a scene from Bedlam, but at last Byron succeeded in wrestling the weapon from La Fornarina's hands.

Luckily any wounds he'd acquired were superficial. Quick to heal, leaving no scars. But it had been the final straw for their tempestuous affair. Soon afterwards came the night when she'd been lying in his bed, and he'd confessed (in fact he'd lied) that his physician said his health had grown so frail he must abstain from all exertions that produced the slightest strain upon his heart. There had been hours of remonstrations, sufficient in themselves to cause a cardiac arrest and only ending when he'd promised her a settlement of money. She'd seemed content enough with that. Her reign of terror met its end, and in the morning, off she went, back to the floury and accommodating arms of her husband.

Until today, when she'd returned. Byron winced to hear more shouts amid the sounds of breaking china, swiftly followed by the beat of running footsteps over marble, before the doors into his room were both flung wide, and there she stood.

What an Amazonian! How could his spirit not be moved? But whatever was she wearing? Unlike her usual peasant garb, which he had always found appealing, she'd decked herself in a red hat, with netted veils and long black plumes, all somewhat drooping from the rain. A matching dress with dragon tail was also splattered black in mud from being swept about the streets, the sodden fabric hissing loudly in her wake as she flounced in.

Over the low, vibrating warning of the growl in Mutz's throat – the dog was never overfond of any women Byron bedded – came the sing-song local accent, which, when its owner was not riled, was irresistibly seductive: 'My love, I have come back. How do you like the way I look?'

'You look ... expensive, and quite formal. Also, a little soggy.'

'I used some of your money to buy myself new clothes. Am I not dressed like the greatest of the ladies from your London? Now you will never be ashamed to have me walking on your arm, and I shall always be polite to any guests invited here. To this, I swear on any Bible. No more jealousy or curses from your La Fornarina's lips. Only the kisses of her mouth. Only the kindness of her heart as she cares for her sweet Georgio and nurses him to health.'

'I wish I could believe it,' Byron muttered to himself with no small vestige of regret. But, more than that, he realised that the ruse of his poor health had only given Margarita this excuse to return. It must be quashed, immediately. 'If your temper is controlled then pray do tell me who was screaming like a banshee in the kitchens? You'll never change, Signora Cogni.'

He saw her flinch, and realised his words had cut her to the quick; the way he'd used her married name when they'd once been so intimate. But she recovered her composure just as soon and fired back, 'Yes, it's true. I am not changed, and I know I am a bitch. A bitch who is on heat, always for the want of you. But I miss you, Georgio. I miss your lips. I miss your cock. You could betray me and bring back five hundred lovers to your bed and I would *never* give you up. Anyway,' her smile was sly, 'you know I am the best. I can prove it ... if you like? I promise to be gentle. Nothing to strain your heart.'

He watched the woman raise her arms, her slender fingers seeking out the silver pin that held her hat in its position on her head. As she threw it to the floor, black hair cascaded round her shoulders. She was magnificent and wild, and Byron felt a pang of longing. How he wished to touch that hair. How he ached to remove her ridiculous new clothes, to see anew the perfect splendour of the body underneath them. But he *must* resist the bait, or it would only lead to trouble. Trouble of which he'd had enough. And what on earth would Fletcher say?

He drew a breath and forced himself to speak as sternly as he could. 'We have discussed all this before. I can't have you or *any* lover living here in my palazzo. I need a calm environment in which to write my poetry. It was enough to bear the constant interruptions back in London. A nagging wife. A crying baby. Bailiffs knocking on the door through all the hours of day and night, and—'

'And now,' she interrupted, 'you have run away to Venice, only to find another baby abandoned on your doorstep. Well, you can let your English wife have the one you left in London, and *I* will care for Allegrina. Forget that nursemaid you employed. She is too young. Too miserable. Which is why I have just told the girl to pack her bags and go.'

'You've told her what?' Byron demanded, on the verge of an explosion.

La Fornarina tossed her head, much like a bull when it's about to make a charge at a red flag. 'She said if I'd returned she would not stay another moment. *I* said good riddance! I am here. I am the donna in this house. And now she has gone.'

'Margarita!' Byron groaned, 'You're not the mistress of this house. You must not act as if you are.'

'Well, *you* act like a fool! Where is the discipline that's needed to run such a palazzo? Fletcher is idle and a dunce, paying double what is charged to any locals for your wine. The butcher sells him stale scraps that only starving dogs would eat. Tita is nothing but a scoundrel, always leering after whores. Your cook's a drunk. The maids are blind. Why else do they not see the dust that gathers everywhere, in every corner of this house?'

It was hard to disagree. As she paused to draw a breath, Byron looked around the room and saw anew the drifts of cobwebs dangling about the bedposts. The maids *were* negligent and lazy, and he would need to deal with them, but for now his every thought was taken up with La Fornarina as her diatribe continued:

'And that nursemaid was too sour, like a lemon in the mouth. Much too strict for Allegrina. The natural mother may not want the sweet bambino in her arms, but I am here, and you know she likes me very much. Today, I bought her a doll. She was so happy to receive it. She gave me kisses. Many kisses, and—'

'Where is she now?' Byron broke in. 'Who's caring for Allegra if the nursemaid's gone away? Where on earth am I supposed to find a suitable replacement?'

Mutz responded to the tension, his growls increasing in their volume as Byron rose from the sopha, letting the papers of *The Vampyre* fall and scatter on the floor. As if oblivious to this, he walked across them while demanding, 'Don't tell me that you've left my daughter to her own devices? She is too young. She must be watched. Only last week she climbed a chair and crawled across a window ledge. If the nursemaid hadn't been on hand to stop her at the time, she could have broken her neck, or been drowned in the canal!'

La Fornarina was subdued, voice coming lower when she said, 'I left her in the nursery. She was playing with her doll. I didn't think—'

'You never do!'

'Or she may be in the kitchen, begging the cook for sugared almonds. I know they are her favourites.'

Are they? Byron thought as he went storming from the room, and realised he had no notion whatsoever of the wants and the fancies of his daughter. Oddly discomposed by that, he hobbled on along the passage, and at its end the narrow stairs that led him to the nursery floor.

Bedclothes were strewn across the carpets. Drawers were hanging from their chests, as if they'd been emptied out by someone leaving in a hurry. Could it be that the nurse had also taken his daughter? Byron's all-too-healthy heart was pounding like a drum, even more so when he heard the distant sounds of panicked jabberings and screeches that were coming from much lower in the house. The monkeys were disturbed, most likely due to La Fornarina and her earlier commotions. Or could it be the little girl? She did like visiting the pets. But not alone. Never alone. That would be too dangerous.

Still in bare feet, Byron descended the cold marble of the stairs to reach the floor of the house on a level with the water. Towards the back, where it was drier, his menagerie was kept, while rooms that fronted the canal were deemed less fit for habitation; only used for storing items not inclined to rot and perish. Despite the bitter weather the canal doors were standing open. Was it possible Allegra could have wandered out of them, then slipped or fallen in the water? Could his daughter even swim? And if she *was* in the canal, how would he see her when his vision was so blurred by the rain and the dusk's obscuring fog?

He made his way down the steps to where his gondola was moored, ducking his head below the covers in the hope she might be there. Someone was, but not Allegra. Tita's snoring bulk was splayed across the velvet couch in what appeared to be another of his drink-sodden stupors. Tutting to himself, Byron stood erect again, about to call his daughter's name, when he felt the touch of something warm and moist against his hand.

Surely this must be his child, her cherub lips pressed to his palm, a pretty habit she'd developed after seeing gentlemen greeting ladies the same way. But no, it was Mutz, who must have followed from upstairs, and now walked back towards the doors, where he paused and looked around with yellow eyes that seemed to gleam with all the knowing of a human.

Come on! Hurry up! Byron imagined the command, after which Mutz led the way below a low stone arch where the pillars either side dripped with cobwebs, studded black with diamond husks of long-dead flies. Peering through what little light still shafted through the fretwork windows, Byron inhaled the fetid odours emanating from his ark. The ferrous stench of the meat eaten by the carnivores. The ripe manure and rotting straw long overdue a clearing out. He heard the cawing of his crow. Under that, the muted whimper that *could* be a crying child. Meanwhile, one of the monkeys – how on earth had it escaped from the confines of its cage? – let out a whooping cry as it bounded down the aisle, before it leapt and landed squarely in the arms its master opened, and only in the nick of time. As Byron caught the animal, in the monkey's small pink hand he saw a hank of – was that hair? His Allegrina's hair? The colour pale, the texture silky, some of the strands stained red. With blood?

Setting the monkey on the floor, he hardly dared to imagine what might have happened to his daughter. But whatever it had been had not disturbed the sleeping fox, all four legs of which were twitching, no doubt dreaming of running through some woodlands on a chase. His pair of tortoises appeared to be entirely unconcerned with anything but the business of nibbling on a lettuce, and the hen recently hired to hatch their eggs pecked at some seed. But what about the eagle with its piercing orange eye? Perhaps the irritant was Mutz as he went plodding past the cages, although the dog remained quite placid and ignored the threats of creatures kept at bay by iron bars. Mutz's interest lay instead in the basket lined with furs, generally occupied by cats invited in as homeless strays.

Today the cats were on the prowl and the basket contained quite another sort of creature. One with a head of fine, fair curls. One that sucked on bloodied fingers as it stared through tear-filled eyes at the second of the monkeys crouching close at its side. This was the monkey prone to biting, and it was clutching what appeared to be a child's china doll. At least, the remnants of a doll, for very little of the hair stitched to the head remained intact. Clothes were torn to tattered shreds. All four limbs had been ripped off, tossed to the floor around the basket, as if some ritualistic magic had been performed to prevent any others from approaching.

Slowly, cautiously, Byron reached down to shift the monkey, but it objected with a screech and bared its teeth aggressively.

'You vicious fiend!' he muttered back, at the same time wondering if the threat had been a bluff. Perhaps this monkey only wished to defend Allegrina? Perhaps it was the other one that had drawn his daughter's blood?

Endeavouring to remain calm and not inflame the situation, Byron collected some nuts from a nearby feeding box and used the bait to lure both creatures back into their cage again. Only when the door was locked did he return to the basket from where his daughter's bright blue eyes glistened like jewels in shadowed hollows. She looked so small and very frail, a fledgling bird that had fallen from its nest and had no means of flying back to it again. When he took her in his arms, she seemed to weigh no more than feathers.

Back upstairs in his apartments, the physician Byron sent for was reassuring and insisted that he had no cause to worry. Fingers could bleed excessively, and every child got into scrapes. It was merely a deterrent when he doused the puncture wounds with a concoction made of vinegar, black aniseed and alum, saying the mix was sure to sting but would hopefully prevent an infection setting in.

If it did hurt, Allegra suffered all with smiling bravery, clearly delighted to have been at the centre of attention, before her eyelids fluttered closed and she slept in Byron's arms, which was an intimacy he'd never once experienced before. It was also at that moment when he felt the weight of guilt, recalling what the child's mother had once written in a letter:

> *How I wish I could come to you with my daughter in my arms. Alas, I know there is no hope of such a dream becoming real. Were I to drown in the canal and then go floating past your house, I believe you would look down and blithely say, 'Ah voilà!'*
>
> *But then, would you, I wonder? Would you really be so cruel if you were with me today ... if you could see the way our daughter nestles close against my breast as we lie here in my bed, and how I listen to the rhythm of our breathing together? I love her so that I could tear my flesh in twenty thousand pieces to ensure her happiness. But she will be happy with you, and you will be a loving father. In return your darling girl will learn to crawl upon your knee and sit as pretty as a cherub in the crook of your arm. If you will only feed her raisins from your plate & perhaps a drop of wine from your own glass, then she will smile and think herself a little Queen of Creation.*

Five

Because of filthy loves of gods and goddesses ...

Byron. From *Don Juan:* Canto I

His little Queen of Creation. He'd mouthed the words to himself while in his chamber getting dressed, and then again as he'd walked along the passageway that led him to Allegra's nursery door. A maid was patting down the sheets under which his daughter lay. He could see her sleepy eyes – eyes so very like his own – staring out between the bars of her cot and back at him. Her lips were sucking on some coral. A sound that imitated kisses.

Smiling at the innocence of such a sweet domestic scene, Byron was sorry that Ada, the half-sister of Allegra, who still resided in London in the care of his wife, could not be here to meet her sibling. Deciding he must write, at least enquire how Ada was, he headed back to his study, only to find La Fornarina in the chair behind the desk, although at least with the folly of her hat back on her head, he dared to hope she'd soon be leaving.

Seeing him there, she rose abruptly and asked with concern, 'How is she? Our Allegrina?'

She is not our Allegrina! Byron bristled inwardly, but he spoke in measured tones: 'The maids are taking it in turns to keep a watch on her, and will continue doing so until I find another nurse. Someone who can be trusted. Who understands the needs of children.'

The words had been directed at himself as much as her, being ashamed to admit how little time he spared Allegra. Even so, how had he failed to see how fragile she'd become, especially when compared to the robust, capricious creature who'd first arrived at his palazzo? Had Allegra been neglected? Was she unhappy in his house? What had Byron really known about the nurse who'd been dismissed? Had she already gone when Allegra made her way down to the menagerie, or had she carried her there? Was the child so dexterous that she could open the cage, or was Tita to blame? In his drink-sodden state, had he set the monkeys free?

Greatly unnerved by these suspicions, Byron was suddenly aware of La Fornarina's pleading, 'Let me stay, and I will love you. I will be the girl's mammina.'

Byron heaved a sigh. 'We've had this out. Allegra needs a stable home. A quiet home. A—'

'Who is she? You never told me!'

'Who?' he asked in some confusion.

'The mother of your child? Does she exist, or is she dead?'

'Oh, she's very much alive,' Byron cautiously replied, determined to say nothing of the girl who had once plotted to ensnare him as a lover, even arranging a room at a coaching inn near London where the two of them could meet with some degree of privacy. Well, a man is a man, and what was one more night of pleasure after all the brief entanglements he'd relished in the past? He'd left Claire Clairmont the next morning, going home to sign the papers of his marriage separation, after which he would be free to begin another life...

La Fornarina tried again: 'Is she English or Venetian?'

What was this interrogation? No, she did not live in Venice, though she had followed him through Europe when he'd first departed England. The step-sister of Mary, she'd accompanied the Shelleys to the Villa Diodati. The house he'd leased for a summer on the shores of Lake Geneva, and where, at first, he'd assumed that Percy Shelley's belief in the doctrine of free love might have extended to a ménage à trois with both the siblings. But Claire Clairmont's only interest in scrambling eight hundred miles had been to meet with him again – to claim a poet of her own, and then announce her pregnancy.

Had she not realised the folly? A young, unmarried woman. The disgraced Lord Byron's bastard? From the public's point of view, she might as well be giving birth to the spawn of Lucifer. And though he did not lack compassion, having endured one loveless marriage how could he contemplate another? Eventually, Claire was persuaded to travel back to England, spending the months of her confinement hidden away from prying eyes. Meanwhile, Byron made plans to send the child to his sister, with Augusta promising to raise it as her own. But Claire demanded that her daughter live with at least one natural parent, and as Byron was the parent who could offer the best prospects, when the babe was old enough to endure the travelling, Shelley brought her here to Venice – leaving Claire, still less than twenty, able to carry on her life without the stigma of disgrace.

It had all seemed for the best. And yet, today, when Byron feared that his daughter had been lost, he asked himself what misery of separation Claire had suffered. Would it be kinder if he sent Allegra back to her in England, or invited Claire to Venice? But what if she resumed her old campaign of seduction? He was notoriously weak, and her fertility was proven. Would that mean another child being born within nine months? No! He could not let it happen...

Looking again at La Fornarina, Byron said, 'I'll ring for Fletcher. He'll ask Tita to take you home and—'

'So, I can't stay?' she interrupted.

'No!' He shook his head, about to call the gondolier, when he recalled his drunken state.

La Fornarina briefly nodded. But, unseen, her fury raged as she strode across the room, first spitting on his cheek, the next moment reaching up to pull the pin from her hat, coming within an inch of stabbing it into his eye. How did he manage not to flinch? How violently her fingers trembled as she hissed through gritted teeth, 'You think you are some modern Casanova here in Venice, but every lover *he* seduced adored him till their final breath. By the Madonna, *you* will die as a man who is despised by every woman you've deceived ... all the women who you treat like shit you step on in the street. You care for nothing but yourself. You are too vain. You are a devil. I'm not surprised you found Allegra in your menagerie today. Isn't that the only place she could be sure to get attention from the man who loves his lame and injured pets more than he does any human in this house?'

Shocked by the woman's vitriol, Byron finally replied, 'When it comes to my creatures, I know they love me for myself, not for my title, or my fame ... or for the gold that's in my purse. You may say *I* do not care, but you conveniently forget the diamond necklace I once gave you, only to see it in the window of a pawnshop two weeks later. You wept your crocodile tears and said the jewellery had been stolen, but we both know what really happened. You are a mercenary lover.'

He was harsh, but had she plunged her weapon in his eye it could not have been more painful than her jibe about his lameness. Slowly, with measured movements, he wiped the spittle from his cheek as La Fornarina glared at him and dropped the pin to the floor. The sudden tinkle of the metal falling against the hard terrazzo seemed to bring her to her senses. Turning her face from his, she made her way towards the doors leading to the balcony. In one moment, she'd walked through them. In another, she was hoisting her skirts above her thighs to sit astride the parapet, seemingly without a care for any storm that lashed about her.

Fletcher's arrival in the room came as her eyes were fused with Byron's, with La Fornarina crying out, 'Do you remember how we met?'

'I was in my gondola. You were on a balcony, calling my name and blowing kisses.'

'At the time I thought you'd saved me. You showed me such a dream. Now you've forced me to wake, but you must know I'd rather die than return to my old life.'

He shouted 'no', just as she jumped, disappearing from view into the waters down below. There was a loud, hollow splash, after which he turned to Fletcher, looking momentarily distraught before he airily exclaimed, 'Well, there's a chance she'll either drown or go and catch her death of cold. But then you know La Fornarina and her love of a performance.'

'Don't you think we should do something?' Fletcher's eyes were round with shock, his voice a toadish croak of panic.

'I suppose so,' Byron sighed. 'Could you go and fish her out?'

Saying this, he crossed the room and stepped onto the balcony. Screwing his eyes against the rain that stung his eyes and burned his cheeks, he looked over the balustrade to see the gondolier emerge from his slumber in the boat, and seemingly entirely sober as he dragged the half-drowned woman from the water to the jetty. There she leaned against a post, the tangles of her long black hair streaming loose about her shoulders, her flashing eyes looking up to meet his own as she screamed, 'Ti maledico ... dannato bastardo! Mille maledizioni sulla tua testa.'

A thousand curses on his head? Ah well, he'd heard much worse, and at that moment he could only think how glorious she looked. She could have been a river goddess, the waters puddled at her feet, her garments clinging wet and heavy to the contours of her body. Oh, what an operatic frenzy she'd produced for him that night, quite as dramatic as the stars who strode the stage at La Fenice.

It was indeed a fitting end to their tempestuous affair, even if her histrionics left him burning with desire; his only thought at that one moment being to quench his urgent thirst in the Venice Sea of Sodom.

Six

And the midnight moon is weaving
Her bright chain o'er the deep,
Whose breast is gently heaving
As an infant's asleep.

Byron. From *There Be None of Beauty's Daughters*

The horror he'd discovered in an alley just last night left Byron feeling more inclined to pay a visit to his favourite of the city's better brothels, rather than seeking out the whores who plied their wares on the streets. Situated near the church of Santa Mario Zobenigo, Veronica Lombardo's house was another place of worship, but reeked of sex instead of incense. Convenient as well, being a quarter-hour's walk, or a brief trip on the canals from his own palazzo doors. But, as Tita was engaged with ferrying La Fornarina back to her husband – again – and with Byron's need too great to sit and wait for his return, walking it had to be.

Arriving in a narrow street, he experienced the too-familiar sense of being watched, of someone trailing in his wake. But he refused to be concerned, not with Lombardo's burly guard standing outside the brothel door. And once admitted to the house, all fears for safety were forgotten, replaced instead by the routine that he had come to know so well from previous visits to the place. As in respectable hotels, one must take the silver pen left on a table in the hall and sign one's name and date of birth on that day's entry in the ledger, thereby agreeing to respect all expenses incurred for the duration of the visit. The lack of anonymity did raise the spectre of blackmail and must deter more wary clients, but Byron took the attitude that he'd already been accused of almost every taboo in the canon of transgression. What were Henry VIII, Caligula, or even Nero when compared to the antics of the infamous Lord Byron! A man who'd been accused by his own wife of just one year as a monster of adultery, of sodomy, and incest.

Feeling exhausted and oppressed by all the scandals of his past, he scrawled in haste across the page: *Lord George Gordon Byron, who is at least one hundred years* – which could have been the actual age of the woman who approached from behind a curtained door.

In youth, the Lombardo had been a cortigiana onesta – one of the 'honest courtesans', whose fame was based on her grace and intellectual wiles. But this votary of Licentiousness and Infidelity was less polished nowadays. Her frizzed and greying hair was drawn severely from her brow. Her face was covered in a paste, thick and white and prone to cracking, with the wrinkles underneath resembling nets of spiders' webs. Her back was hunched below the veils draped across her black silk gown, which, when drawn down gave the appearance of an abbess in a convent. But when her eyes were visible, as they were on this occasion, they still held traces of past beauty, being a brown flecked bright with amber, slightly slanting, all too knowing when she led him from the hall into a chamber hazed and sweet with the perfume of hashish.

Byron was barely through the door when the Lombardo

enquired, 'Any particular daughter of the house you have in mind? If not, there is a girl ... somewhat new, but I believe she is well suited to your tastes.'

She moved to stand below two paintings. One showed the angel Gabriel offering a lily to the Virgin during the Annunciation. But, if this was to suggest that the new girl was still a flower as yet unspoiled by other men, he took it with a pinch of salt. The other picture was a copy of Titian's *Venus of Urbino*. At least he thought it was a copy but could easily be wrong. Everything about this brothel reeked of opulence and money. As well as paintings, gorgeous tapestries were hung across the walls. Fretwork screens separated low divans with velvet throws stitched with gold and silver threads. Sprawled over one he recognised a patrician of the city, a corpulent and coarse-faced man, one heavy arm draped on the shoulders of a fair-haired prostitute. Byron knew her and he liked her, but that hair was much too poignant a reminder of the woman he'd discovered in the alley.

Meanwhile, the man drawled lazily through the smoke blown from his pipe, 'Ah, Byron. Back again? It seems that neither one of us can bear to drag ourselves away from this treasure box of jewels. Mother does have such lovely daughters. But I beseech you, let there be no squabbling tonight over which one we get to bed. That debacle last week was unbecoming of us both.'

What was he talking about? Byron answered with disdain, 'I believe you are mistaken. I haven't visited in weeks ... not since the start of Carnevale. What's more, the mere idea that I would squabble over whores is simply too ridiculous.'

'Ha! The man protests too much,' the other patron replied through his intoxicated slur. 'It was you. Of course, it was. Who would mistake the great Lord Byron? Star and Satyr of all Venice!'

Who indeed? Byron's composure was now well and truly rattled as he recalled Polidori at the Alfieri salon. Had the doctor been here too?

The other client's attention was reclaimed by a pair of pretty will-o-the-wisps who'd fluttered by with plates of oysters. An angelic pair they made, both with plumes of feathered wings tied to the back of muslin gowns. One was a boy, and one a girl. They might be ten, no more than twelve. But although there were occasions when Byron's carnal desires might be considered as perverse, to see their youth and innocence displayed in such a place only filled him with regret. Meanwhile, Veronica Lombardo poured some wine into the glass that she passed into his hand. He drank it down, and then another, despite the bitter aftertaste. Should he complain? What was the point? He only needed the heat of the grape to fill his veins, to blur away all memories of Countess Alfieri's salon ... and the thought of Polidori imitating him in Venice.

Startled by the touch of the Lombardo's hand on his, his attention was drawn back to the business of the night. What new delight did she promise? Anticipation was rising when she beckoned to one cupid and then whispered in her ear, before the child disappeared below an arch at the room's end. Almost at once she was replaced by a slender young woman who had been waiting in the wings for her call onto the stage. As an actress she was shy. Arms were wrapped across the silk that offered tantalising glimpses of a firm, unblemished body. Her face was lowered from his gaze, but wasn't this a common thing? A show of coy naivety could be appealing to some men – and led to Byron's sudden gasp, for in her stance and with her veil of long brown hair she looked so like another woman he'd once known. Susan Vaughan from Newstead Abbey.

The pangs of guilt struck him again, very near to all-consuming. The last he'd heard, she'd been in London. She'd written giving an address where she'd hoped they could meet. But with the parties and amusements, all the affairs he'd been involved in, he'd left it much too late. When he'd arrived at the hovel of a house where she'd been living, no-one knew or even cared what might have happened to the girl. Oh, his pretty, clever Susan. His little queen of Newstead Abbey. Where had she gone? He dared not think, but it was not to stand before him in this Venetian brothel.

If she still lived, Susan Vaughan would be more or less his age, whereas this girl was in her teens, and she was Turkish. Maybe Greek. The exotic sort of beauty rarely seen in Europeans. Her eyes were blackened with kohl. Rubies were wound at her throat, and golden chains around her ankles tinkled a pretty invitation, which was soon joined by the tapping of the cane he'd used that night when she led him from the room to climb the stairs to the upper floors.

Entering a chamber he'd never been inside before he was immediately distracted by more paintings on the walls. Among the usual display depicting acts of copulation, there was one canvas that he found to be intensely disconcerting. An image from a Bible story, in which a woman known as Judith cuts off the head of Holofernes in revenge for a rape. Not exactly welcoming, and any stirrings of desire were immediately reduced by an urgent sense of caution. Even when the cherub boy also entered the room to serve a tray of cakes and wine, he found it near impossible to drag his eyes from the scene.

When he did, it was to see the girl was reclining on the bed, staring blankly into space as if she hoped to make believe she was anywhere but 'there'. Trying not to be offended, he dropped his cane and poured himself another glass of wine, disappointed to discover that it tasted little better than the offerings downstairs. Whatever La Fornarina might have said about the vintner who supplied his own palazzo, it was better than this swill.

He felt a little more relaxed when the boy took up a lute. It seemed the child had some talent, the music eerily exotic. But when it came to making love, Byron preferred no audience, and having waved the child away he went to sit on the bed where ... was the girl trembling?

Could she be cold? He gently touched one of her naked arms, where flames that flickered in the hearth painted her flesh in black and gold. How beautiful she was. He told her this while offering his glass of wine for her to share. She drank it down, too greedily, which could hardly have been due to her enjoyment of the vintage; the only explanation being that she needed some Dutch courage. So perhaps she *was* a virgin. But such girls were highly sought. They would be advertised and auctioned to the brothel's richest clients. Not that any of the women in this establishment came cheap, which made it all the more surprising that he was forced to woo this one while paying for the privilege.

Well, here we are. Let's carry on and hope for the best, Byron thought to himself while removing his jacket and attempting yet again to melt the frosty atmosphere by enquiring her age.

'Sixteen,' she replied.

'So very young.' His interest piqued, he carried on the conversation. 'Your family? Are they also living here in the city? Only you do not look Venetian.'

'My parents are both dead. I have a brother still alive, but he is lost to me now. I couldn't bear for him to know…' She hid her face in her hands. 'It doesn't matter who I am, or where I'm from. The past is gone.'

'Ah, I know this feeling well. This desire to forget.'

'What do *you* need to forget?' She dropped her hands and turned his way. '*You,* who they call the Star and Satyr of all Venice?'

She must have overheard the drunken oaf he'd met downstairs. But Byron took no offence and raised a hand to stroke her cheek as he murmured his reply: 'I *do* understand the cost of losing those we love. But life has other consolations, and I am not such a devil. Is there really no hope that you might offer me forgiveness?'

Still holding his gaze, she cocked her head to one side. Her voice was serious and steady. 'Do you go to confession? Do you repent of your sins? I never did, but then I never knew the world could be so wicked.'

'I am called wicked, very often. And very often with good cause,' Byron answered, honestly, while at the same time wondering if his philandering existence should be coming to an end. Hadn't he always told himself that when he'd reached the age of thirty, he would *try* to be devout. But which cult was he to choose from when his instincts were more pagan? Considering the moral teachings, he leaned towards Confucius rather than the Ten Commandments. He did admire the Catholic sense of spiritual emancipation, of every sin being forgiven if one repented earnestly, but not so much the pope. How could he take the sacrament when he could never quite believe that eating bread and drinking wine would ever lead to him becoming an inheritor of Heaven? The only paradise he sought was the one of earthly pleasures while a body was still living, rather than risking disappointment while it rotted in a coffin.

He smiled at the girl. 'On the whole, I prefer to cleanse my soul in other ways. Why don't you lie down here beside me, and I can show you how I do it?'

The 'show and tell' did not go well. Even when they were both naked, with every touch she flinched away. As he was not a Holofernes, prone to forcing his attentions on any woman disinclined, Byron's lust soon fizzled out with, as Fletcher would have said, no lead for stiffening the pencil.

Oh well, his day *had* been exhausting – what with Allegra and the monkeys, and then La Fornarina's antics. Yet more distressing was the vision that returned to his mind as he drifted into sleep. The bloody wound on the throat of the woman in the alley.

Byron woke with a shiver. A bitter draught was blowing in through the bedroom's open door. The boy last night must have failed to close it properly. He got up to push it shut, found a pot in which to piss and then returned to the bed, where he moulded his body to the contours of the girl's. Her face was turned away from his, so instead of seeking lips he brushed his mouth against her shoulder, tracing the curve of her spine, the firm, round apples of her buttocks. This time she did not shrink away, but neither did she wake. Her breaths were slow and sounded shallow. Her skin felt cold to his touch, and so he drew the quilts up higher to cocoon her in their warmth. He stroked his fingers through the hair and whispered lines from *Don Juan:* '"*Her glossy hair was cluster'd o'er a brow ... Her eyebrow's shape was like th'aerial bow ... her cheek all purple with the beam of youth, mounting at times to a transparent glow, as if her veins ran lightning; she, in sooth, possess'd an air and grace by no means common...*"'

Surely any other whore would have responded to his touch, to the seduction of such words? Odd, the way this girl slept on. Odder still that he persisted in the hope that she would rouse and embrace him in her arms. But hopes could only go so far, and as the first pale glints of sunlight probed their fingers through the shutters he decided to get dressed and return to his palazzo.

He might come back again tonight. Yes, that was what he'd do. He'd ask Veronica Lombardo if – whatever was her name? She hadn't said. He hadn't asked – if she might somehow be reserved for his own exclusive use. It would be costly, he mused, and with no pleasure guaranteed if she persisted in acting like a nun who lived on nothing more than bread and prayer and water. But at least she might be saved from other brutes who'd be less kind.

Am I becoming a saint? Byron glanced back at the girl, and then sat up in the bed. Stroking the stubble newly growing on his chin he briefly wondered why his vision seemed to lack its more usual keen focus. Not that his nostrils were affected. All-too sharp was the odour of stale wine in the carafe. Under its sourness, something fainter. Something animal and faecal, like the civet in the perfume worn by Countess Alfieri. And then, a cloying tang of metal. Could that be the smell of blood? Would that explain the girl's reluctance? Her time of the month?

Emerging through the brothel door into the shadows of the lane, Byron's ears filled with the chimes of the morning bells of Venice. 'We are risen!' he called out, above the babble and the bustle of the waking morning city. The clouds had gone. The sky was blue. But the air still held a chill. Marketeers setting up stalls breathed out great clouds of iced white air. He inhaled the fragrant spices, then the greasier aromas of fried eels and spaghetti dished up to fishermen for breakfasts. One old beggar with a face as brown as nuts beneath his hat was holding up a battered cage that contained a parakeet. The creature looked to be diseased, its dark-grey flesh exposed in places. But then, birds did that, didn't they? Plucked out their feathers when distressed, or if removed from a mate? How could Byron think to leave it? He offered the few coins still remaining in his pockets, planning to take the ailing creature back to his menagerie. Better still, it would make the perfect present for Allegra. A pet to call her very own.

So rapt had he become in cooing at the bird, he failed to notice the buxom *bigolanti* in his path; the woman with a pole balanced across both of her shoulders, bearing the buckets of fresh water she delivered to the wealthy. They collided. Water spilled. Enough to splash across their feet, where it formed a spreading puddle. Byron apologised profusely, but had no money left with which to offer compensation. Still, feeling generous that day, he set the birdcage on the ground and took an opal from one finger. As he pressed it in her hand the woman looked astonished, open-mouthed in smiling wonder as she placed it in a purse hung on a cord around her neck. Having continued on her way for a good four yards or so, she looked back across her shoulder and called out, 'May the angels in Heaven bless your kindness – and do not worry for your future. Water carries no stains.'

Another local saying? Byron hoped it held some truth, and that he, a tarnished jewel, had been washed clean of all past failings on these city shores of Venice.

How could he know that before the day was even out, he would find himself accused of the blackest of all sins?

Seven

Sorrow is knowledge, those that know the most
Must mourn the deepest o'er the fatal truth,
The tree of knowledge is not that of life.

Byron. From *Manfred*

All is well, and all will be well ~ Byron glanced back into the nursery where he'd placed the parakeet on the floor between the cot in which Allegra was still sleeping, and the chair in which a maid was sitting, snoring by the hearth.

Heading to his own bed chamber, he stood before the stand, where the bowl contained fresh water, and began to wash and shave. The water was cold, but that helped clarify his thoughts, at that moment being inspired to write a verse about the beauty he'd left sleeping in the brothel. So urgent was the need to pen the words, he did not think to change his clothes from yesterday. But when he'd settled at his desk, his attention was distracted by several letters, yet unopened. Most of them were set aside to be dealt with later on, except for one, on which he recognised the hand of John Cam Hobhouse, a trusted friend since Cambridge days...

Dear Byron –

Please forgive this late reply to your last letter. As you know, I've been campaigning for the Westminster seat. Sadly, I failed on this occasion, but I am garnering support, and in due course I have high hopes of a career in politics.

With regard to your own business, I am able to confirm that your bankers have transferred the latest funds you requested. I am reliably informed that what remains is as exhaustless as is the horn of Odin. I know not how they weathercock it with such ease or speediness, or how you spend so rapidly! But the credit of two thousand pounds should be in your account before the month is out. Hopefully, it is sufficient to cover the demands of your latest low amour! How do you get into these scrapes?

For God's sake man, having seen the latest cantos of Don Juan, *should you not show more restraint in describing your own sordid adventuring in Venice? In this complaint I'm of a mind with your publisher, John Murray, though he's delighted with Mazeppa. (If I am right, these are the verses that describe a Russian Cossack?) He says it shows you as the first and the finest of the poets. But his main hope is that you'll write another epic like* Childe Harold. *Something more English in its tone. Something to raise your reputation and ease your way back home again. The mood has softened since you left when all was in a state of ferment. For every mouth that calls you bad, there are now ten of them or more who would be happy to make merry and to dine with you each evening.*

You are missed, my dearest friend.

Always yours truly, J.C.H

Byron set the letter down. Hobhouse was the best of men, always on hand to help with sorting out his business back in London. Especially matters of money, which were so very tedious, and yet so very necessary, what with the lease of the palazzo, and

La Fornarina's settlement. Only a temporary drain. But still, not insignificant.

Hobby's mention of Murray was a little more concerning. How could Byron be sure that his publisher was loyal when he was wooing Polidori to become the latest light in some firmament of stars? What's more, if Murray looked upon *Don Juan* as too salacious, should Byron be looking for a publisher less prudish?

His response was quickly scrawled:

Dearest H,

I am most grateful for your efforts with the bank, especially when you have had important matters on your mind. As you say, your time will come to join the corridors of power, although, for the life of me, I simply cannot comprehend this fixation you have with parliamentary affairs.

For myself, I am as well as ever here in Venice, though I confess I am exhausted by the Carnevale's exertions. In truth, I will be glad when this year's festival is over, for I grow tired of the fuff-fuff and passades & all the fucking. I hear you laugh in disbelief. But only this morning I awoke in a brothel with the absolute resolve to return to a life of being scholarly by day & ~ only now and then ~ a little dissolute by night.

Perhaps I shall retire to my La Mira summer house. It is the perfect retreat in which to write some poetry. If not that, I may return to my studies with the monks on the island of Lazzaro. I used to go there very often when I first arrived in Venice. They call themselves Mekhitarists & made the place their sanctuary after they fled Constantinople, around a hundred years ago. The first of them are now long dead, for even blessed celibates do not as yet possess the gift of conjuring the life eternal. But those remaining have constructed extensive libraries filled with antiquated books from Persia, Syria, & Greece ~ all so inspiring for my work. However, I assure you that, for friends more prone to leisure, the monastery has pleasant courtyards in which to while away the hours. You can eat oranges picked fresh from the trees grown in the gardens. You can sit & talk bad Latin with the monks for hours on end...

Byron's letter rattled on, only briefly mentioning having met with Polidori, and eventually concluding with a basic shopping list, asking Hobhouse to acquire and send along those medications not available in Venice. Magnesia for indigestion. Laudanum to aid his sleep. And a tin of the powder he liked best to clean his teeth. But it had to be the red one, definitely not the green, even if it did look gruesome, foaming up like boiled blood when it was brushed inside the mouth.

Setting his pen back on its stand, Byron rang the bell for Fletcher, asking his valet for some coffee and a plate of plain, dry biscuits. These were duly carried in, along with news of a temporary solution being found to the problem of Allegra being left without a nurse.

'That boy you sent the other night ... he has settled admirably, though what an appetite he has for such a streak of skin and bone. Still, I dare say he's worth the rations. He's very eager and he makes no complaints about his chores. He's also good with Miss Allegra. Very patient with the child, and she quite soppy over him, trailing around as if his shadow. Now, all the other maids must do is feed and wash your baby girl, tuck her up in bed at night, and—'

'Ah, the urchin boy!' Byron interrupted. 'I'd forgotten all about him.' Suddenly, he felt a chill run like ice through his veins. He'd sent a stranger to the house. Could that stranger be to blame, for having lured Allegra into danger with the monkeys?

'Not very likely,' Fletcher said, when Byron spoke his fears aloud. 'Spent the morning eating his body's weight in bread and cheese, and then a scrubbing in the tub while his clothes were boiled and dried. Hopefully to eradicate all trace of any lice.'

'You must tell me his name, this wondrous paragon of purity and cleanness in my house.'

'He says it is Nicolo.'

'Well, if Nicolo is so good at amusing my daughter, would the skill also extend to helping with the animals? Tita's too unreliable. I need somebody I can trust to keep the creatures fed and clean – and not so drunk he doesn't notice if the doors of the cages are locked or left wide open.'

Fletcher paused and cogitated. 'He gets on well enough with Mutz. But, returning again to the matter of a nursemaid, it was when he overheard me asking Cook if she might happen to know of any locals suitable for the position that he piped up about a sister – somewhat older than he is, and presently in occupation with other children of the gentry residing here in Venice.'

'That is odd, don't you think?' Byron frowned as he considered what sort of nursemaid would take care of other people's families while her own kin was left to beg or roam about the night-time streets. But then, what nursemaid was allowed to bring her siblings along to any house she was employed in? No doubt the woman did her best and gave the brother what she could.

At the jangle of the bell, and then the hammering of fists on the palazzo's main front door, Byron lost his train of thought. 'Who can that be, and at this hour?'

Looking out through the casement, he saw another gondola beside his own on the canal. Meanwhile, Fletcher, who'd already left to open up the doors, returned some moments later with Veronica Lombardo, and in her wake came the guard who Byron had last seen posted outside her brothel entrance.

'I did tell them to wait ... for me to ask if you were free.' Fletcher looked and sounded harassed, as well he might have been, for when he spoke the brothel mistress pushed him roughly to one side and briskly entered the room.

Byron stared in amazement to see the Lombardo somehow magically transposed from her domain into his own, although her dress was as pious and funereal as ever, so no risk of any neighbours whispering behind their shutters. Just as well they could not see her throwing back her flowing veils and thus revealing the frizzed and snake-like tendrils of her hair when, as a venomous Medusa, she glared at him in daunting silence.

Still with not a word, she cast her eyes about room. Did she admire the stuccoed gilding, painted silks and pompous portraits that were hanging on these walls, some of which depicted women in the ghastly style of Rubens? Probably not, for when she spoke it was to ask in disbelief, 'You like these fleshy women?'

Byron's answer was succinct: 'You know my tastes well enough. These belong to the palazzo and were here on my arrival.'

But he did personally own other items on a table that drew the woman's interest. The ossuary of bones, the dusty vases, and old carvings sourced from temples he had visited while travelling in Greece. A marble statuette of Flora, the hermaphrodite goddess which, when turned in one direction showed a pair of naked breasts, but spin her round the other way and a phallus was protruding through the folds of her gown. Next to such a daring figure of sexual ambiguity was a glass phial said to contain some ancient trace of Attic hemlock. Besides that, a large stuffed turtle, and four gilded human skulls from a sarcophagus in Turkey.

She turned to Byron again. 'You appear to have acquired many sinister mementos.'

He responded with the smile that rarely ever failed to charm. 'I've visited many tombs and ruins on my travels. I often gather souvenirs, but that is all they are to me. Some enjoy collecting trinkets. Boxes with shells, or painted fans. I like to look at skulls, to be reminded of my own mortality upon this earth.' At this, he raised the Newstead cup, as if to toast his visitor. 'Better to hold the sparkling grape, than nurse the earth-worm's slimy brood.'

'Immortality is found in the greatest literature.' She ran a finger over dust furring the gilt and leather books that had been piled haphazardly across another nearby table. There her attention was to linger on the tome the vendor claimed to have been bound in human skin, though Byron always assumed it was most probably a pig's.

'This Marquis de Sade.' She pronounced the name with scorn. '*The Misfortunes of Virtue*. Titles can be so misleading. Shouldn't virtue have been vice? For the cruelty of his lust, the man deserved to be beheaded. Did you know he liked to tie his victims down with ropes, then slice a knife into their thighs, making love as they were bleeding to their deaths underneath him? Do you not think that is obscene? The behaviour of a soul that has gone beyond redemption? It may be why' – her hand moved on to touch another vellum cover – 'I prefer the plays of Shakespeare. You have read this, I presume?'

Byron had to strain to read the gilding of the title. *Romeo and Juliet*.

For a moment he saw the face of Susan Vaughan again, heard her reciting from the play. But soon enough he replied, 'Indeed, I have. And more than once, though Shakespeare's plays are overrated. Flashes of genius, of course. But he does stand absurdly high. I believe he will go down, his work eventually forgotten, whereas—'

'Whereas *you* count yourself his better? How arrogant you are!'

Byron was shocked at her directness, more used to flattery and smiles when he was visiting her house. And, in truth his jibing comments over Shakespeare had been made only in the sense of mirth.

In an attempt to pacify, he said, 'As generations pass, so tastes inevitably change. Even the greatest of all writers will inevitably be lost to the annals of mankind.'

'It is surprising what remains ... especially of this story. There is a convent in Verona where you can visit the tomb where the real Juliet died from a knife wound to her heart. Is it not too horrible to imagine one so young, doomed to such a tragic end?'

'Yes, I have been there myself. But...' Byron's voice was strained, 'I confess I am bemused as to what brings you on this visit, and at such an early hour. Surely not to discuss the fates of Shakespeare's heroines?'

'I'm here to talk about the girl you attacked and left for dead.'

'What?' Had Byron heard correctly? Feeling more confused than ever, he stood and limped around the desk that until then had formed a shield between himself and his accuser. Once on the other side, he felt quite sure she must have meant the woman who'd been murdered at the Palazzo Alfieri. Had the news of that come out then, despite the Countess's demands that the crime be kept a secret?

'Fletcher,' he brusquely said, all too aware of the valet's flapping ears and gawping mouth. 'Perhaps you'd leave us alone. We need to talk in privacy.'

There was a pause before his man gave a nod and shuffled off, closing the study doors behind him, though Lombardo's brothel guard remained quite resolute, in place.

Attempting to ignore the brutish menace of the man, Byron turned to face his mistress: 'I believe you've been misled. The woman in the alley was already near to death. I did my best to revive her, but I'm afraid I was too late. If you have doubts, I think you'll find there were other witnesses who will support me in this statement. I assure you, Signora, it was not me who cut her throat!'

'I do not speak about the prostitutes who trade below the lamp posts, though...' Lombardo paused for a moment, her thin lips twisted with her malice. 'But, is it not coincidental? Two Venetian whores are dead, both in the presence of Lord Byron?'

'*Two* dead! You cannot mean...' His words trailed off as he recalled the oddly cold and clammy flesh of the girl he'd woken next to in the brothel just that morning.

'Save your denial for the law!'

'This is ridiculous. There was no murder in your house. It is a lie. A wicked lie.' Byron's voice was raised in anger, his thoughts awhirl as he responded, 'Is this what you do? Visit your clients in their homes to make intimidating threats? If blackmail is your game, then you should know I have no fear of any wife or family to raise complaints with regard to where I go – or what I do ... or what I spend my money on. But can *you* afford to have the reputation of your house dragged through the gutters of Venice? What happens if the law comes to investigate *your* claim?'

The woman's bodyguard stepped forwards, squaring his shoulders, balling fists as if in readiness to act should his mistress give the word.

She only laughed, a dreadful sound more like the squawking of a hen. 'Most of the men of the Venetian La Forsa are my friends. In return for their protection, I offer hospitality. But, even so, there's no insurance against the horror of the crime I have witnessed today!'

She raised a hand to her eye. Byron could see no sign of tears, but cosmetic paint was smeared and so exposed the pockmarked flesh she usually kept concealed – on less emotional occasions.

He shuddered at the thought of what disease had ravaged her. Meanwhile, Veronica Lombardo soon recovered her composure and continued with her insults.

'Do your best to deny it. Your wealth and name mean nothing to me. What place remains in history for the illustrious Lord Byron if he's imprisoned and then hanged like any other common villain? Mark my words, that is your fate, unless you offer compensation for the loss of any wealth I would have earned from that girl. This is the deal I offer you. But make sure you understand, you'll never pass my door again.'

'You think I'd visit after this!' He shook his head in disbelief. 'You make these wild accusations, but where's the proof? Upon what terms would I be threatened with arrest?'

'I see the blood stains on your shirt!'

Byron looked down and laughed. 'That's from the powder for my teeth!'

'And *still* you dare to jest! Well, perhaps you did not mean to kill the girl, only to satisfy your vile depravity. But she *is* dead, and now she lies with other corpses in the morgue at the Venice hospital. Go there and see the proof of what you've done, and then decide if you will offer me the value of her life ... or pay with your own.'

Byron felt nauseous to recall all the gossip and the scandals that had ruined him in London when those who'd hailed him in the salons and the theatres as a god turned away in disgust if they should pass him in the streets. His debts alone could have seen him locked inside the Marshalsea. But that was nothing when compared to Caro Lamb's vicious spite, or the wife who had so publicly complained of his incestuous affair with Augusta. Along with overwhelming debts and speculations of relationships with boys he'd met in Greece, Byron was left with no choice but to flee the shores of England or face a death upon the gallows for the sin of sodomy.

'You threaten me with death?' His voice was trembling.

The woman offered no reply. The only thing to be heard was the swishing of black silk when she turned to walk away – though before she'd reached the doors someone else came rushing in.

Waving her bandaged hand, Allegra's unharmed fingers gripped the handle of the cage Byron had left in her room. 'Papa! Papa! See my bird!' Her bell-like voice trailed into giggles as she showed off the parakeet. But when she saw the crow-like vision of Veronica Lombardo, she grew unsteady on her feet. Tripping on her nightgown's hems, she toppled to the floor. The flimsy cage's door flew open.

The bird escaped just as Mutz arrived upon the scene, and what a turmoil was to follow – Allegra wailing as the maid who'd been sleeping in her room came running in to scoop the child up in her arms to try and sooth her. But there was no-one near enough to restrain the snarling dog as it snapped its drooling jaws at the panic-stricken bird. The dog was quick. The bird was quicker, flying towards the open window and the means of its escape. Nothing remained but a few feathers, their vibrant green and golden colours swirling slowly in the shafts of sunlight flowing through the room.

Veronica Lombardo, who'd stood in silence as she'd watched this hectic drama playing out, began to smile with all the guile of a serpent when she said, 'What a pretty child you have.'

Remembering the children he'd seen working in her brothel, Byron could not help but shudder. As if he'd sensed the mood, Mutz's hackles rose anew, growling low as his master clutched his collar to restrain him.

Meanwhile, Veronica Lombardo hissed her final threat: 'An eye for an eye. A tooth for a tooth. You stole a prize I valued highly. The bill of my expenses will arrive before this evening. You have the grace of one week to pay the debt in full or face the consequences ... both for yourself and those you love.'

As she spoke those final words she turned to smile at Allegrina.

Eight

And the eyes of the sleepers waxed deadly and chill,
And their hearts but once heaved, and for ever grew still!

Byron. From *The Destruction of Sennacherib*

'Are you supposed to look attractive?'

The final night of Carnevale and Tita gawped in disbelief at the insipid, waxen features of a man a great deal older than the usual Lord Byron, with the subterfuge completed by a long grey wig and beard.

Stepping aboard the gondola, Byron's voice came somewhat muted through the mask tied to his face. 'I'm tired of being recognised.'

'Well, wherever you're going, there's little risk of that!'

Byron also came to doubt the need for his disguise. By the time they'd arrived at the Venice hospital there was not another soul on the cobbled stretch of square before its looming grey facade. Leaving the gondola to make his way towards the entrance doors, he suddenly stopped short, calling above the bitter wind blasting towards him from the water, 'If I'm not back within the hour, will you come inside and find me?'

'If I'm not frozen to death,' came the booming reply, while underneath the Russian fur worn on his head Tita scowled and clapped his arms across his chest.

Not for the first time that night Byron felt the sting of fear, wondering at his sanity in visiting the morgue. Some hours before, when the Lombardo's expenses were delivered – the most extortionate amount, which he would not be honouring – he'd agonised over whether or not he should report her to the police authorities, or go and see with his own eyes if the girl was really dead? But how to do so privately, without drawing more attention to the crime he'd been accused of? Polidori! That was how. Hadn't he said he was employed at the Venice hospital?

A note was scribbled down in haste to enquire if they could meet at his place of occupation, hopefully that very night, and as late as possible. Better by cover of darkness than in the open light of day when awkward questions could be asked by others working in the place. Of course, there was a chance Polidori had lied, doing little more than swanning around the city's brothels, the gambling houses and the salons, regaling any who would listen with the details of his novel. But if he had told the truth, then his novel was the key. Surely, the doctor would agree to such an odd assignation if only to discuss Bryon's reaction to *The Vampyre*. He didn't need to be told how little had been read, and in the meantime Byron's message mentioned a canto of his own that had a scene set in a morgue, and now he wished to be quite sure that his descriptions were authentic. Would *that* story be convincing?

The boy Nicolo delivered Byron's note that afternoon, and then returned with the response in which the doctor agreed to meet him around midnight. It was not possible before, as Polidori was attending the Teatro La Fenice.

Hopefully there would be no repetition of the fracas Polidori had once caused in a theatre in Milan, when he'd insisted that a man blocking his view of the stage remove his hat or else agree to face the doctor in a duel. Quite a scuffle then ensued. Polidori was arrested, on the point of being banished from the city before Byron was called in to plead his case, when he swore that Polidori was not really dangerous. He had the hot Italian blood. He was too passionate. And young.

These matters turned in Byron's mind while he was drawn, as if a moth, towards the lights of candle flames seen in the windows up ahead. What a wedding-cake concoction the Venice hospital appeared against the clouded winter night, the pale stone like sugared icing, with many ornamental arches running high above the roofs, or as decorative niches with their guards of standing lions. *Could those lions come to life?* What strange distractions in his mind – before he caught the nearby sound of someone whistling a tune. A melody he knew from Mozart. *The Libertine Punished.*

The whistling stopped. A man stepped out from the shadows of the porch. Beneath the glimmer of a lamp there was a moment when the doctor's handsome features more resembled the outline of a skull – a grinning skull that immediately recognised the poet behind the mask of an old man. But then, of course, Polidori would have seen the dragging gait as Byron made his approach. There was no hope of hiding that.

Polidori turned away to knock three times against the doors. There was but the briefest wait before a hatch was opened up, and through the gap a bleary-eyed and wrinkled doorman pushed his face as he exclaimed, 'You again? Don't you have a home to go to?'

Polidori replied, 'My friend has hurt his leg while celebrating Carnevale ... can hardly walk for the pain. I fear there may be broken bones. I need to take a better look and deal with the wound.'

'Very well. You are the doctor. Who am I to disagree?' the guard replied, closing his shutter, the clang of metal swiftly followed by the rattling of keys.

Once admitted through the doors, Polidori led the way along a vaulted corridor. The light was dim, despite the torches in a maze of passages, where – this was Venice after all – many ceilings had been muralled with illustrations from the Bible. On the walls there were paintings of Madonnas and apostles, though being blinkered by his mask Byron could only glimpse brief snatches. With his ears also muffled by his wig he dimly heard some distant voices chanting prayers, and over that the steady tapping of his cane's echoed beat across the marble of the floors. The voices faded as they walked below an arch, along stone flags, through passages with white-washed walls entirely empty of adornment. Here, their shadows were distorted, two elongated silhouettes taking the form of freakish monsters, one of them more erect, his movements swift and elegant, whereas the other lagged behind, his sliding gait as sinister as some predatory beast.

Dismayed by this illusion, Byron feared he might be lost in some underworld of Venice. A place where ghosts were said to walk, and where he heard a nearby groan, and then an awful cry of pain. Suddenly, a door flew open. A nun ran out and scurried past him, her hands clasped tightly to her breast. When Byron turned, she'd disappeared, as if a sprite upon the air – unlike the other troll-like creature sprawled across a narrow bench, lips dribbling and slack, sucking the mouth of a bottle. But at least this sozzled lush marked the end of the tour, for just beyond him were the doors over which a wooden sign with golden letters bore the legend: *THE MORGUE.*

Suddenly beset by doubts as to the sense of such a quest, Byron felt nauseous to smell the rancid alcohol and sweat rising from the drunken man. Even worse was the cloying sweetness of dead bodies seeping through the nearby door, that odour mingled with the chemicals employed for preservation. But, after all, this was the place where autopsies were performed, the ghoulish trade that Polidori seemed to view as quite mundane when he said, 'Do come inside. I'll light the lamps and you can take a better look.'

'Are we alone?' Byron enquired, entering the large square room in which a cloud of freezing air bloomed white before his mask. The chill was palpable.

'Yes, we're alone … apart from Marko.' Polidori pointed back towards the bench as he explained, 'He guards the morgue, but he's no trouble. I often come in here at night when there's no-one else around. The peace allows me time to think, which is impossible by day when there are constant interruptions. You see, I'm musing on the plot of another gothic novel. This time about a scientist who dreams of stirring life into the bodies of the dead.'

'And here you find your inspiration.' Still standing at the doors, Byron replied with wry amusement, before another thought occurred: 'You don't intend on plagiarising the work of Mary Shelley? You heard her tale at Diodati. You've surely read her novel since?'

Polidori shook his head. 'I have not seen the published work, though of course I'm well aware of any themes it may contain. Mary and I spent many hours immersed in private conversations.'

'I think *you* may have fallen a little in love,' Byron teased the younger man.

'We shared a meeting of minds.' Polidori glowered back. 'Discussing life after death, and what was deemed as possible within the bounds of medicine and the developments of science. Not that I had that much to tell. She was already widely read, especially about Galvani. You are aware of his experiments with bioelectricity?'

'The stimulation of dead frogs. All those wretched, lifeless creatures pinned on laboratory boards?'

Polidori nodded. 'The miracle of life as their muscles were pulsated, after which Galvini's nephew did more experiments in London. He bought the body of a man, condemned to hang after he'd drowned his wife and child in a canal … putting on a public freak show, with all observers quite astonished to see the quiver of the jaws and other muscles of the face as the force of the electricity surged through and so contorted them into a mask of horror. One of the eyes was opened wide. A hand was raised. The fingers clenched. Both of the legs began to shuffle, and…' The doctor's voice trailed off. 'I do enjoy our conversations, and have missed them since we parted. But, thinking now of the undead, what did you make of *The Vampyre*? I'm assuming you *have* read it.'

Through the glimmer of the lamplight, Byron saw the desperate gleam in the younger man's dark eyes and decided to be frank, for if asked about the contents he would surely only flounder. 'You must forgive me, Polidori. I've barely read the first few pages. The demands upon my time since we last met have been excessive.'

'But from the opening alone, you must have formed some kind of view. Were you intrigued to carry on? Do you like the narrative? The style of prose. The atmosphere?'

'The overwhelming sense was the impression that the villain had been based on my own person.'

'Ah, but he needs to exude the cold charisma you possess.'

'Like another dead frog!' Byron's patience was frayed, but he tried to sound good-humoured. 'Look, Polidori, when I'm at home again I swear I'll read the rest, and then some time this coming week, I shall invite you to dine, and we'll discuss it properly. But, for now...' Another pause, as he wondered just how far he should go in revealing the real reason for his visit. 'Perhaps we could get on with this tour of the morgue. Once I've made my observations, we'll both be free to find our beds.' He clapped his hands to draw some blood into the freezing fingertips. 'The cold in here is extreme. How do you concentrate to work?'

While asking the question, Byron occupied himself with dragging off the mask and wig, and itching merkin of a beard. Flinging the suffocating items onto the nearest empty table he viewed the room without impairment. The large stone sinks, and marble tables glinting with the sheen of scalpels. The diagrams of dissected human bodies on the walls. The glass in the rooflights set above them, dusted grey with falling snow.

'Cold focuses the mind,' Polidori replied. 'And, of course, it helps preserve the bodies while we need them.'

'And what happens ... afterwards? When you don't need them anymore?' Byron glanced towards a dresser with collections of glass jars containing pickled specimens, and rather wished he hadn't asked.

'We decide the cause of death. Whether it's natural, or self-harm ... or sometimes even murder. The heart in that jar, do you see it is enlarged and engorged with clots of blood? Undoubtedly, it was diseased.'

The doctor's gaze moved on, towards a row of tables where the bodies laid across them were concealed beneath white sheeting, though those cloths still bore the stains of fluids seeping underneath them. As Byron watched, and held his breath in somewhat anxious trepidation, Polidori's fingers plucked at the corner of one sheet, drawing it back to reveal the ravaged features of a woman who looked to be in middle age, with gaping sores through which the bone of cheeks and skull were clearly seen.

'Syphilis,' said Polidori. 'By the progress of these ulcers, I would say she'd been exposed to the disease as a child.'

The doctor heaved another sigh, as if to signal his compassion. But there was something in his voice leaving Byron with the thought that Polidori was enjoying every moment of this drama; especially the fact that here their roles had been reversed. In the morgue's night realm of terrors Polidori played the lead to Byron's lesser acolyte. Here, Polidori held the power.

'Do you know this woman's name? Any of their names?' Byron's voice was somewhat strained, for the sight of the corpse had left him feeling most perturbed.

'A few have family or friends who claim their dead for burial. But most have died alone, often beggars on the streets. And then, there are those who arrive by other means.'

'You mean the resurrectionists?'

'We call them body dealers. They bring us fresh cadavers. Now and then, the headless corpses of a guillotined offender, or people drowned in the canal. It is unsavoury, I know. But how else to train physicians ... to try and ease the suffering of those still living on this earth?'

Oh God, don't let me die and end up in such a hell, my body cut with knives, my organs pickled in a jar. Byron's heart was thudding fast. The sudden dizziness he felt was further heightened as he staggered, almost falling where the floor below his feet began to slope towards a gully where the stone was stained a rusty shade of red, running down into drains that emptied into the canal. It did not bear thinking about. And neither did the question he must ask before his courage was to fail him utterly: 'Have any bodies been delivered in the past twenty-four hours?'

Polidori glanced around, then walked towards another table near some padlocked iron doors. 'Looks like there's one still to be processed. I could go and wake the guard. He'll know who brought it in. Although, that sack, it looks like something you'd dredge up from the canal, only to find a drowned cat.'

Horrified to recall what he'd so recently left lying across a sack of rice in the Alfieri stores, Byron moved a little nearer, towards the bundle tied around with several lengths of knotted string. Whatever lay inside it was much larger than a cat.

As Polidori freed the knots and the cloth was drawn back, Byron gasped in recognition. Time was unnaturally suspended. Trapped in the nightmare of his shock he seemed to fall into a trance, seeing this lovely girl as she'd been when still alive, her neck arched back, her throat as pale and elegant as a gazelle's, the pulsing jugular below the near translucence of the skin. And the rubies of the choker she'd been wearing in the brothel, he imagined them as well. Glistening red, like drops of blood...

Dear God! Was he a monster, to fantasise about such things when she was lying dead before him? Through the thud-thud-thudding beat of living blood in his own temples, he forced himself to look anew, and swallowed back the rise of bile, because in death she looked much younger, so much frailer than in life. And how pitiful it was to see the outline of the ribs jutting through flesh below her breasts. The cage of bones around her heart.

'How did she die?' He couldn't hide the break of anguish in his voice. 'I see no sign of injury.'

Looking down at the corpse, the doctor shook his head, and once again resumed a stance of professional detachment. 'As to when she met her end, there is no sign of putrefaction. She's still stiff, which means she wouldn't have been dead for all that long. Three days at the most, but likely to be less.'

'She was definitely alive when I was with her last night.'

'*You* were acquainted with this girl?'

'I met her in a brothel near Santa Mario Zobenigo.'

'Veronica Lombardo's.' Polidori nodded. 'I have visited myself, but only the once. They threw me out after some petty disagreement with a client. A most unpleasant character.'

'So I was told. That other man presumed you were me. I doubt his vision was that clear. But even so it does surprise me, the way you will keep popping up like a jack-in-the-box in all the places I frequent. There must be at least a hundred other brothels in this city. Why did you have to choose that one?'

Polidori looked affronted. 'When I first arrived in Venice, and without your address, I made enquiries as to where you might most easily be found. But for no other purpose than to ask if you'd be kind enough to read my manuscript. I hoped – indeed, still hope – that if you like it well enough then you might offer some endorsement. The novel was, after all, inspired by your idea.'

'And that's the only reason?'

'What other could there be?' Polidori looked the picture of all blameless innocence.

Yet Byron still experienced a tingling of dread as his eyes scanned the morgue and then returned to face the doctor, silently wondering to himself, *Where were you, Polidori, when a woman had her throat slashed at the Palazzo Alfieri? Is she inside this morgue as well?*

Instead, he asked another question: 'What were you doing last night, when I was visiting the brothel?'

'I was here.'

'And you can prove it?'

'Yes. Of course. Ask the doorman, or the guard out in the passage.'

'You mean the fellow we passed at the entrance to the morgue? Was he as drunk as he is now, more steeped in spirits than the specimens you keep inside your bottles?'

Polidori looked offended. His answer was abrupt. 'Take a look at what's been written on the labels of those jars – what's been listed in the records. Everything I do in here is precisely catalogued, with all the dates and the times when the work was carried out. If nothing else, they should provide you with proof of where I was last night, and exactly what I did.'

Byron, who was generally more focused and astute, rebuked himself for lacking logic and rushing to the wrong conclusions. Polidori had departed from the Alfieri salon at least an hour before the murder. If he'd been guilty then the victim would have surely bled to death long before Byron had found her. The argument was folly, and he must put his thoughts in order, or alienate the only person who was able to assist him in resolving the puzzle of this nightmare he was in – the man he now addressed with urgent passion in his voice. 'Forgive me, Polidori. I am somewhat overwrought. This girl is from Lombardo's, and now it seems the brothel mistress is accusing me of murder. If you could tell me how she died, then I might prove my innocence. Because I am – quite innocent.'

'Are the authorities involved?' Polidori calmly asked, though his eyes belied some panic.

'No, not as yet. But Lombardo is demanding a small fortune to keep her silence on the matter. I confess I came tonight hoping to call the woman's bluff, not believing for one moment that the girl was really dead. And yet, here she is. Here—' Byron broke off, and when he spoke again his voice came hoarse with emotion. 'She showed no signs of any ailment ... was merely sleeping when I woke and left her in the bed this morning ... when I was also rather bleary, which I put down to the wine we'd imbibed some hours before. But now, I wonder. Was it drugged?'

The doctor frowned. 'Were you robbed? Such things are common in the brothels.'

'No. Nothing was stolen.' Byron looked down at his fingers where the rings were glittering, all but the opal he had given to the peasant water seller. 'Unless you count this poor girl's life.'

'Well, there's laudanum, of course.' The doctor's eyes slid Byron's way. 'But then we know your constitution is well used to the effects. Even so, under its spell, you could be prone to acting out the motions of whatever you were dreaming at the time.'

'Are you suggesting I killed this girl while in some sleeping passion?'

'I do recall there was a night when I was still in your employ, when you walked into my room in the middle of night and took away the golden candlestick I'd set beside my bed, leaving a brass one in its place.'

'Must you bring that up again? I swear you dreamed it, Polidori. What awful scenes you made next morning, insisting that I'd played some trick to put you in your place – that I considered myself golden and yourself as baser metal. Well, I did nothing of the sort, so will you drop this foolish grudge. I know we've had our differences, but didn't I forgive you for that time when we went boating at the Villa Diodati, when you devised some argument and struck the oar at my good leg? I am quite sure you realised you could have crippled me for life.'

'I wanted to know if you were capable of pain. If you could feel a single thing beyond your own vain self-importance.'

'And *what* was the conclusion?'

Polidori clenched his fists. 'Let us forget these past disputes. I'm simply trying to consider your dilemma in the present, and somnambulism is not so vague an accusation. You must recall the condition was the subject of my thesis when I studied medicine.' The doctor's chin was proudly tilted. 'For which I gained a distinction.'

'Ah yes, romantic moonlit scenes with sleeping damsels in distress, but...' Byron's nerves were near to breaking as he tried to work it out '...what else could have subdued me, and subdued this girl as well?'

'Without examining the stomach and analysing any contents, it's impossible to know. Although...' Polidori stooped down low and sniffed around the corpse's mouth. 'There is the odour of some spirit, but too faint to recognise. Apart from that, I'd make a guess she may have suffered from consumption. She is thin and very pale, and there are residues of mucus and dried blood around her mouth.' Polidori stood again, tilting his head in contemplation. 'This will only be apparent when I inspect the lungs and heart. Meanwhile, I see no evidence of bruising on the body. Nothing to indicate that violence was employed by anyone. Unless the girl was smothered, dying by asphyxiation? There is a bluish tinge around her lips, and on her cheeks.'

Saying this, the doctor brushed away some hair from her neck, naked now of any rubies she'd been wearing in the brothel. In doing so, he uncovered what till then had been concealed, and loudly exclaimed, 'What's this? Here on her throat? It almost looks...'

'Like marks of teeth.' Byron gasped.

The two wounds were very slight, each one an inch or so in length. But they were clearly visible.

Polidori carried on in a state of agitation, 'They could be the incisions sometimes made by a physician before leeches are applied. But ... leeches on the jugular? The flow of blood would be too fast, all but impossible to stop.'

For some moments neither spoke, until Polidori stammered, 'Perhaps she scratched herself as the result of irritation? A spider? Or a flea bite. Would you say the brothel's clean?'

Byron gave no reply, only stared at the corpse, where the fingers of one hand were closed around a scrap of white. 'What's that?' he asked the doctor.

Polidori removed it. The briefest glance and he replied with a mystified expression, 'It appears to be for you.'

Byron took the paper from him and saw his name penned on the front. As the message was unfolded so he read in abject horror: *I am Leila, in the sack, whose life blood has been drained by the Lord Infidel of Venice.*

Byron felt stunned, as he recalled writing down those words himself. He'd been travelling in Greece when he'd met a group of men dragging a sack that held a woman, screaming and calling out in terror. When asked, one of the men claimed their captive was a woman guilty of adultery, and now her fate was to die by being cast from a cliff down to the rocks and sea below. Byron had been appalled. He'd drawn the pistol from his pocket and threatened to shoot unless they set their captive free. Only when a bribe was offered did they finally agree, and he'd escorted the poor woman to a nearby monastery, her story then immortalised in his description of the slave girl known as Leila in *The Giaour,* which despite all he had said at Countess Alfieri's salon about despising such tales, was an exotic horror romance steeped in vampiric mystery.

Screwing the paper into a ball, Byron clutched it in one hand, knowing he could not take the risk of such a vile condemnation being seen by Polidori. Come to that, by anyone. Certainly not the gnomish guard who had now woken from his stupor to stagger in through the doors.

His rasping voice was slurred with drink, his accent rough, a broad Venetian, as he called in their direction, 'What's going on 'ere, Polidori. Another midnight party, is it? Oh...' The fellow stopped abruptly, rubbing his fists against his eyes. 'It seems my vision's multiplying. Am I really that far gone, or does the doctor 'ave a twin?'

When no answer was forthcoming from either of the dark-haired men, the ogre drew a little nearer and leered with delight at what was lying on the sacking. 'Another pretty one tonight. How I weep to see the lovelies being butchered on the slabs.'

Byron could stand it no longer. He had to get away. Ignoring the guard, he thanked the doctor for his time, then swiftly lurched towards the doors and, somehow – God only knew how – found his way back through the maze of all the winding corridors to reach the exit to the square.

There he saw his gondolier, still waiting at the jetty, though dusted in the fall of snow Tita appeared more like a statue than a man of flesh and blood. But how cheering it had been to see him smile, and then to feel the warmth and weight of bearish fingers as they clutched at Byron's arm and helped him board the boat again. Shielded below the tented covers, Byron watched as Tita freed the mooring ropes from wooden stakes, then used his pole to launch the vessel out onto the Canal Grando. Lulled by the sound of lapping waves, Byron allowed his eyes to close, head falling back on velvet cushions where it was soothing to inhale the floral perfumes and the musk of stale sex lingering from all the nights when he had rocked with different lovers on the water. But instead of being roused and asking Tita to look out for any likely-looking whores touting for business on the bridges, he only wanted solitude. How could he bear to think of pleasure when the fluids of embalming lingered thickly in his nose, as if the spirits of the dead had also followed from the morgue and were now sitting at his side?

On the point of vomiting, he dragged back the heavy fringing of the curtain at one window, sliding open the glass to gulp fresh air into his lungs. How different was this night from many others he had known during the month of Carnevale. No more joy in looking up to see cascades of golden fireworks blooming brightly in black skies as his gondola sailed on. Only the sorrow in his heart as he tore the crumpled paper from the morgue to tiny pieces and mouthed a silent prayer for the soul of the dead girl.

Was there a deity to hear him, or was his offering worth less than the superstitious tossing of a coin into a well? Tears were running from his eyes as the ragged scraps of paper joined the flurries of the ice drifting down from Venice skies.

Nine

The Flesh is frail, and so the soul is undone

Byron. From *Don Juan:* Canto I

Bathed in the corpse light of the dawn, Byron opened bleary eyes and raised his throbbing head. Reaching for the skull cup standing before him on the desk, he gulped down the sour dregs of Madeira in its base, and then exchanged it for the pen dropped from his hand some hours before. Ink had leaked from the nib and stained the linen of his shirt, but he had no care for that – only to finish his recording of what had happened in the morgue with Polidori earlier, and hopefully to exorcise the buzz of demons in his mind...

The wounds on the throat of the girl in the morgue, it looked as if she had been bitten. Could Polidori have been right in suggesting I'd attacked her in some act of dreaming passion? Was it more than fantasy when I envisioned the pulsing of the vein in her throat? Oh, but these are mere delusions that will threaten to unhinge me, with Polidori's wretched novel still so vivid in my mind.

Why does he write me as a villain in the guise of his Lord Ruthven? Last night, he seemed my friend, but sitting here, alone, I see him as a man with a dark shadow in his soul. I cannot help but hanker back to our time at Lake Geneva, especially that fated night of the great storm when the villa creaked & trembled like a ship tossed about on violent seas. Such strange tales we all imagined as we huddled by the fire & sipped on laudanum & wine, our metaphysical constructions inspired to even greater heights by the raging elements. Even after we'd retired, I barely slept for the thought of Polidori's ghoulish tale, in which a woman with no hair or any flesh upon her skull stalked a house's corridors while crouching down to peer through keyholes as she spied upon the living. It was not so much the concept ~ a silly thing, if truth be told ~ but the thought that Polidori was himself a silent voyeur. We all agreed that his sexual & literary frustrations were what lay at the heart of the doctor's violent outbursts, culminating in the most unfortunate affair when Shelley called him a buffoon & a mediocre writer, after which Polidori challenged him to a duel.

That proved to be the final straw, though I admit I was sad to send the doctor on his way. The youthful want of admiration can be a brutalising thing. But could such grudges have inspired the man to acts of murder now? For all his brooding & his sulks, I doubt he's capable of that. But then, I think about the chest of medicines he always carried in his luggage on our travels. Among the manna, & the worm cake, & the jars of turkey rhubarb, there were bottles labelled poison, including one of prussic acid. Kept for what end, he would not say. But, thinking more on that matter, perhaps it's best if, from now on ~ at least until the puzzle of these deaths has been resolved ~ I avoid his company.

As for that witch, Lombardo, with her vicious accusations, do I accede to her demands & pay to stop her tongue from wagging? My reputation goes before me & there are those who would believe her, even relish my destruction. There is also the rumour Polidori mentioned at the Alfieri salon, saying that Shelley & myself have formed some secret sect in which depravities are practised. What did he say it was called? The Society of Ancient Rome? Utter balderdash & rot! Who would devise such a rumour? Perhaps some husband made a cuckold? Or, an even higher source, for I've been told of the existence of a papal report stating that Shelley & myself have been sent to Italy as enemies of the Vatican, working as undercover agents for the Protestant religion.

Oh, what nonsense this is! Why am I torturing myself over a silly piece of gossip? Most likely the idea has come from Polidori's mind. Some petty revenge concocted out of jealousy. Yet, it is hard to deny my frequent nights of dissipation, of which Lombardo has her proof. My name is often listed in the pages of her ledger. The latest date will also tally with the murder of the girl who is now lying in the morgue. Whether or not she met her fate in the bed at my side, there is no doubt that she is dead, & unless I am prepared to unleash the hounds of hell & have my privacy invaded as it was before in London, what choice do I have but to pay the price of silence, & then to hope this living nightmare fades into oblivion? But, if I pay, will Lombardo only ask me for more, & then for more again? This is entirely probable, in light of which I shall ignore her & turn my mind to other things ... such as the changing of my ways. After all, this sort of thing comes from putting it about! I shall become another Paul on the road to his Damascus. I'll say farewell to concubinage & the joys of Carnevale. From this day on, I shall remain as celibate & pure as the monks who reside upon the island of Lazzaro.

So, we'll go no more a roving
So late into the night,
Though the heart be still as loving,
And the moon be still as bright.

For the sword outwears its sheath,
And the soul wears out the breast,
And the heart must pause to breathe,
And love itself have rest.

Though the night was made for loving,
And the day returns too soon,
Yet we'll go no more a roving
By the light of the moon.

THE SECOND ROLL

Ten

Here is the empire of thy perfect bliss,
And here thou art a god indeed divine

Byron. From *Don Juan*: Canto I

It was past ten of the clock, and the first party he'd attended since deciding it was best not to 'put himself about' – though that was proving difficult when it seemed that every female disgorged from London into Venice sought to flow in his direction.

To avoid the worst temptations, he'd gone to sit on his own, staring at the exit doors and wondering how soon to leave without offending his hosts. It was the dullest of nights, though to be fair, on his arrival there'd been some pleasant entertainments. Nine or ten young girls in white, with crowns of pomegranate blossoms, singing ballads while accompanied by flutes and violins. They were as lovely and as innocent as angels sent from heaven but had in fact been provided by a charity that cared for orphans gathered from the streets, of which the Countess Alfieri was a leading luminary.

Once the singing reached its end, so the waltzing started up, and Byron's temper swiftly soured. With his lame foot he could not dance, and it was torture to endure the laughing shrieks and stomping progress of so many clumsy matrons. It would not be too fanciful to imagine a tornado was rampaging through the building, the way the chandeliers were swaying and vibrating on their chains. There was one moment Byron feared that they might all come crashing down and result in general carnage.

Everything was too excessive. Much too loud. Too overwhelming. Since his visit to the morgue some months before, he'd rarely ventured from his house except to swim in the Lagoon or ride his horses on the Lido. The exercise did help to lift his depressed and lagging spirits, but not sufficiently of late, when he and all the staff at the Palazzo Mocenigo had succumbed to hacking coughs and excessive fever sweats. Fletcher's condition was extreme. He'd walked around hallucinating, twice waking Byron in the night to complain of hearing voices and footsteps on the stairs. The valet had convinced himself of ghosts in the palazzo, whereas Byron did his best to explain that what he'd heard was nothing sinister at all. Merely the eerie lap and whisper of the waters as they splashed against the stones of the house.

Or *had* there really been intruders, taking advantage of the fact that everyone was indisposed? When well enough to work again, Byron had been dismayed to discover several stanzas of *Don Juan* lying scattered on the floor beside his desk. He'd called for Fletcher in some panic, but the valet, who'd recovered his more sanguine disposition, suggested it was likely to have been a gust of wind blowing from the balcony. 'Or, perhaps...' he'd pointed out some sluggy turds on the desk, 'one of the seagulls flew inside. Those wretched birds are worse than rats. I wouldn't be the least surprised if they've not also been the source of this pestilence we've suffered.'

One person not affected by the scourge had been Allegra. Still without a nursemaid she'd been left to run quite wild. So, perhaps she'd been the 'ghost' roaming the stairs at dead of night. Perhaps her little hands had rummaged through the papers Byron left on his desk? Either way, he was grateful when the Hoppners paid a visit and suggested that Allegra go with them to the consul. At least, until such a time as her father and his household were sufficiently recovered to care for her again.

And with the Hoppners she remained. He really should have fetched her home. But they had a child of the same age as Allegra, which meant his daughter had a playmate who could keep her company. At the same time, he was relieved to be free of all the babblings and tantrums that his daughter had been prone to these past months. What an impact such a tiny human being could exert on all the lives that spun around her, as if the planets round the sun! It could be thoroughly exhausting, not to mention a continual distraction from his work – which was calling to him now. Yet, here he was, idling his time away at the most desultory party in the history of Venice.

Suddenly disturbed by a tapping on his arm, Byron glanced up and recognised the golden mask always worn by the Countess Alfieri. Having joined him on the chaise she purred Italian in his ear: 'What a delight to find you here. But, I wonder, are my salons out of favour with Lord Byron? I do hope it's not because…' her pause was heavy with suggestion '…of the unfortunate event that occurred when we last met.'

'I do not wish to be reminded.' Byron's eyes locked with those behind the glisten of her mask.

Sitting back, she cocked her head and considered him at length. 'Are you well? You look pale … even more so than usual.'

'I have been ill.'

'Is it the malady that's spreading through the city? What about your little daughter? It can be perilous for infants.'

'She is with the Hoppners. I—'

'Well, this *is* a surprise!' the Contessa interrupted, her

attention now diverted by some movement at the doors. 'Count Guiccioli and his wife, and if my spies have it right she's barely nineteen years of age, and until now most of her life has been spent inside a convent.'

'Hoping to be a nun?'

'Oh, there you go, jesting again! It was for her education, and protection from those men who would defile her in a trice had she not been locked away. But now the girl is safely married, despite the fact that there must be a gap of more than forty years between herself and her Count.' The woman's voice dropped to a murmur. 'She is his third wife. I have heard the first one died of some fatal poisoning when he preferred one of her maids. It *may* be true...' she left a pause '...but people are inclined to gossip, as I have learned to my own cost. When my own husband succumbed—'

'Do they say you murdered him?' Byron interjected and offered her the smile the poet Coleridge once called 'the gateway to heaven'.

When she failed to respond he turned his eyes back to the doors, seeing the Count Guiccioli as a man somewhat more than the average in height, who was well advanced in years, with deeply lined and leathered skin, though he also possessed an air of faded elegance, and below the powdered wig (something that might have been en vogue a good ten years or so before) some sprouting tufts of red afforded him a rakish look, as did the pointed beard neatly barbered on his chin. A velvet jacket had been tailored to his shoulders to perfection. Calfskin breeches exposed a well-made calf and muscled thigh. No doubt, when in his prime he may have turned a host of heads, and it seemed the man believed he still retained that talent now – for as he strode into the room, so his calculating gaze appraised the throng of dancers, and lingered on the more attractive.

At the same time, the Countess arose to greet the new arrivals, blocking all view of anyone but this bluebeard of a count. But when she moved to the one side – when Byron saw the convent wife – it was as if a thunderbolt had struck from Heaven to his heart. So much for any vow of wishing to be celibate, though perhaps he'd paid his penance here in Venice long enough. There'd been no sign of repercussions from Lombardo when he'd chosen to ignore her demands. Not that Byron had forgotten his last visit to her brothel. His dreams were often haunted by the girl in the morgue.

For now, wide awake, the ghastly nightmare was to fade when the Countess Alfieri turned to call, 'My dear Lord Byron, may I introduce the Count and Countess Guiccioli.'

'Please – call me Teresa,' the wife insisted with a smile, though Byron had no voice to answer, only able to stare at the goddess Aphrodite come to life before his eyes. While doing so he decided to devote himself entirely to an affair with this woman. He was already entranced by her burnished auburn hair, adorned at the brow with a band of pearls and diamonds. He also liked the Grecian style of her shell-pink muslin gown, in which the sleeves fell from her shoulders and exposed the flesh of arms quite exquisitely formed.

It was a little disturbing that she should share the very name of the tragic heroine in his poem *Mazeppa* – the narrative of a Cossack and his lover Teresa, whose affair was soon discovered by her husband, an old Count! Consumed by jealousy and rage, the Count demanded that Mazeppa should be stripped and then bound naked to the back of a horse. A horse cruelly flayed by men who brandished whips, sending it mad before it galloped at full speed into a forest, and...

Startled back into the present, Byron felt himself stripped naked when the aged Count Guiccioli offered him a hand in greeting. The man had large, ungainly fingers, and yet the nails were long and filed, tinted pink with some cosmetic substance, buffed until it shone. Such a contrast to his own, ragged and bitten to the quicks, and of which he was too conscious when the wife stepped in between them – when Byron bowed, took her hand and pressed it to his lips.

As the husband turned away and continued with whatever conversation he'd been holding with the Countess Alfieri, Byron glanced through lowered lids, in the way that always seemed to set the women fluttering.

Teresa remained in full possession of her senses when addressing him again: 'What a pleasure to meet with the infamous Lord Byron.' He heard the note of irony in that word 'infamous'. But what did that matter when this woman's large brown eyes held such intelligence and warmth? And then, there was her voice, like music to his ears, being lower than expected and surprisingly melodic as she continued to enquire, 'You must tell me is it true – you have made your home in Venice?'

'I have, and I confess no other city in the world could prove to be as stimulating as it is at this one moment. Standing here, talking to you, I would say it holds the essence of every passion known to man … even to the point of fever.'

Fearing he may have gone too far, Byron paused to take a breath, but could not ignore the fact that he had crossed the Rubicon and must grab at this one chance before it disappeared forever.

'If my manner is too forward then I beg for your forgiveness, but…' inclining his head, he murmured softly in her ear, 'would it be possible to meet somewhere more discreet? If you should be so inclined, you'd be most welcome to visit my Palazzo Mocenigo. It is on the Grand Canal.'

'Is this the fever speaking?' Teresa raised a hand, her fingers trembling as they touched the pure white petals of the rose pinned to the bodice of her gown, over which there swelled a pair of the most perfect breasts.

That little show of her emotion stirred his courage to go on. 'My mind is perfectly clear. I only hope to know you better. It is imperative I do so.'

'Really? Imperative?' Her discomposure was replaced by the

smile of her amusement. 'You are as forward as they say, and perhaps as dangerous?'

She must have heard of his affair with Lady Caroline Lamb, and how that woman had once labelled him 'mad, bad, and dangerous'.

'My reputation goes before me,' Byron hastily explained. 'Whatever you have heard regarding rumours of ill conduct, I won't deny most will be true, though perhaps exaggerated. I had the character you see, of being a rake, but also being famous ... a thing society abhors, but many ladies seem to like. In short, I will confess, I was a man too fond of pleasure, whether given or received. But more lately, I am changed.'

A blush of colour tinged her cheek to hear his sheer audacity – before replying through a sigh, 'You should know, I am with child.'

If she'd been any other woman this would have been a swift deterrent. How odd that it was not, that he simply did not care. He felt like a man who, until that point in time, might have been walking in bare feet over some scorching desert sands, parched and panting with thirst, and on the brink of facing death, when all at once he'd been presented with a shimmering oasis in an Arabian romance. Here were the fronds of lush green palm trees as they swayed in cooling breezes. Here was a man who wept with thanks when he knelt beside the water flowing at Teresa's feet, from which he longed to drink ... and drink, and drink again.

He answered candidly, 'I have two children of my own. Ada will soon be four, and lives in London with the wife from whom I am estranged.' He emphasised the word 'estranged', though he was sure she must have known. Didn't *everybody* know? 'And then, there is Allegra. My illegitimate, in Venice.'

'How old is she, your Allegra?'

'Only two, but very clever. She will prattle in Italian, and even sing a little Mozart. She is, so I am told, the very image of her father. And just like me as a child she finds it hard to say her "r"s. She can be droll, but often frowns. She has the prettiest of pouts. Pale-blue eyes. The whitest skin, quite as fine as porcelain. Her hair from birth was prone to fairness, but grows darker by the day...'

'You seem the proudest of fathers. She sounds to be the perfect child. Perhaps one day I will meet her.'

'Indeed, I hope you will. Although for now she is residing with some friends here in the city.'

'You live alone?' she replied, eyes fused intently on his own, leaving Byron overwhelmed by a jolt of recognition, as if he and this woman had once shared another life, and now they'd been reborn to find each other here in Venice.

I loved her then – I love her still. A line from *Mazeppa* resonated in his mind, just as the real Teresa's husband came to steal her back again, placing a hand upon her arm and speaking somewhat sternly:

'Our hosts will soon get tired of waiting to receive you. Regardless of which, it would be rude to monopolise Lord Byron any longer.'

As Byron dragged his eyes away from the radiant Teresa and saw instead the malevolent expression of her Count, he said as brightly as he could, 'I'm sure we'll speak again. Hopefully, before too long.'

'Perhaps.' The Count was haughty, all but sneering down his nose. 'Though I doubt it will be here. The Countess Alfieri has informed me she's about to perform a recital from some new novel she's been reading. I may enjoy the theatre, but I simply can't abide all these nonsenses of stories being published everywhere. Poetry is even worse. Nothing but self-indulgent nonsense.'

Byron heard Teresa's gasp at this insult from her husband, before she made her own objection. 'Well, I *am* interested in both poetry and novels. I insist we stay and listen.' She turned to Byron, more demurely. 'My father always says I was born with a book already open in my hand. I have several of your own, which I admire quite as much as those by Dante and Petrarch.'

Byron smiled and would have liked to hear her speak a little more about the bards of Italy, but alas, it was too late. The Count had turned on his heel. The wife was spirited away, across the room to where the dancers had now paused to take refreshments, and where the instruments that played for them had fallen into silence.

Amid this lull, and through some gaps among the thronging of the guests, he saw the Countess Alfieri step onto a dais at the salon's farthest end. Once there, she dipped a hand into a beaded reticule dangling from one wrist, and from that bag she then withdrew – was it a Bible Byron saw? The leather black. The letters gilded. *Surely, she's not in preaching mode,* were the first thoughts that sprang to mind, although how slight the volume looked when the woman held it high, calling for 'hush' before exclaiming:

'I have received an early copy of this novella by Lord Byron. Much like his verse, what is held within the covers of this book is an intoxicating mix of the exotic and erotic, along with fascinating elements of autobiography.'

Byron's head began to spin, whether a symptom of the illness from which he'd recently recovered, or the state of his confusion when the Countess next announced, 'I'm sure the author will approve of the extract I've selected, from what is titled as *The Vampyre* – being a thrilling gothic tale in which an Englishman called Aubrey falls in love with a sylph of a girl he meets in Greece. But, alas, their love is doomed, for unknown to our hero, his travelling companion is the vampyre, Lord Ruthven. And *he* has plans of his own for the delectable Ianthe.'

Amid the muted murmurs, the fervent whimpers of excitement from some quarters of the room, an older matron grumbled loudly that such a subject did not seem to be the least appropriate for any decent gathering. But her objections were in vain. The Countess had found her mark and was declaiming from the stage:

'Here is the part of the tale when poor Aubrey must accept it is impossible for him to save the woman he adores.' She took a pause, inhaled a breath, and then recited from the book...

> Aubrey being put to bed was seized with a most violent fever, and was often delirious; in these intervals he would call upon Lord Ruthven and upon Ianthe—by some unaccountable combination he seemed to beg of his former companion to spare the being he loved. At other times he would imprecate maledictions upon his head, and curse him as her destroyer. Lord Ruthven, chanced at this time to arrive at Athens, and, from whatever motive, upon hearing of the state of Aubrey, immediately placed himself in the same house, and became his constant attendant. When the latter recovered from his delirium, he was horrified and startled at the sight of him whose image he had now combined with that of a Vampyre; but Lord Ruthven, by his kind words, implying almost repentance for the fault that had caused their separation, and still more by the attention, anxiety, and care which he showed, soon reconciled him to his presence. His lordship seemed quite changed; he no longer appeared that apathetic being who had so astonished Aubrey; but as soon as his convalescence began to be rapid, he again gradually retired into the same state of mind, and Aubrey perceived no difference from the former man, except that at times he was surprised to meet his gaze fixed intently upon him, with a smile of malicious exultation playing upon his lips: he knew not why, but this smile haunted him. During the last stage of the invalid's recovery, Lord Ruthven was apparently engaged in watching the tideless waves raised by the cooling breeze, or in marking

> the progress of those orbs, circling, like our world, the moveless sun; indeed, he appeared to wish to avoid the eyes of all. Aubrey's mind, by this shock, was much weakened, and that elasticity of spirit which had once so distinguished him now seemed to have fled for ever. He was now as much a lover of solitude and silence as Lord Ruthven; but much as he wished for solitude, his mind could not find it in the neighbourhood of Athens; if he sought it amidst the ruins he had formerly frequented, Ianthe's form stood by his side–if he sought it in the woods, her light step would appear wandering amidst the underwood, in quest of the modest violet; then suddenly turning round, would show, to his wild imagination, her pale face and wounded throat, with a meek smile upon her lips...

Byron had heard enough. Any attempt of the Countess to go on was doomed to silence when he called across the room, 'I'd never write such torpid prose, in this or any other novel. I demand you end this farce and then explain what's going on! It is a dire impersonation. The very crudest passing-off. It will not stand. I shall see the publisher in court.'

The room was filled with buzzing murmurs that seemed to carry on forever, until the Countess replied, 'I'm sure you're very well aware that *The Vampyre* will be published by Henry Colburn in London, and as early as next month. But who'd deny this *is* your style? The overblown and tragic themes. The florid prose. The strong dependence on allusive imagery.'

Why was she damning him in public, where before she'd only praised? Who had sent her this book? It could only be one person, and that was Polidori. Was he also in the room?

Byron spun around, but every face he saw was blurred. Meanwhile, the Contessa demanded people move aside, allowing space as she led him to one corner of the room. 'His Lordship has been ill. He is confused. I fear he'll faint. He must sit down. Can someone please bring the man a glass of wine?'

When he returned to his senses, Byron was in a smaller chamber where some tables had been laid with sets of gambling dice and cards. He all but slumped onto a chair while the Countess stood nearby, still with the copy of *The Vampyre* firmly clutched in her hand. When a maid brought in some wine, the sympathetic-looking smile below the Alfieri's mask did not slip for a moment. But when the servant left again, the expression grew much colder, eyes glittering as hard as steel when she reached out to touch his brow and said, 'MyLord, you are perspiring. It seems to me you have the sheen of the corpse upon your flesh.'

He grabbed her wrist and threw it off. 'What in Hell's name is going on? What you just read is Polidori's. I would never write such drivel, as I am sure you are aware!'

All at once he recalled the dead girl in the morgue. Had she been Greek, like Ianthe, wounded by Ruthven in *The Vampyre*? It was a thing to be forgotten, or else to go insane. And to be sure of the forgetting he had never carried through with his promise of inviting Polidori to his house to discuss the novel further. After all, what was the point when the little he *had* read was unfit for publication? It seemed too cruel to tell the truth and rub more salt into the wounds of disappointment that he knew the doctor nursed already. And, what if Polidori fell into yet another rage and challenged him to a duel?

Rather than risking such dramatics Byron had placed the manuscript in a drawer of his desk, telling himself he'd look again when he was feeling less oppressed. But he'd known he never would, and until tonight's performance by the Countess Alfieri he'd remained in ignorance of how the story might progress.

Meanwhile, the Countess placed the book down on a table at her side, picking up a deck of cards as she innocently asked, 'Why should I think it Polidori's?'

'It was in your own palazzo that he spoke about the story, before he thrust it in my hands … and all beneath your very nose.'

'He may have simply remembered and transcribed your fabrication? The fragment you both spoke of? It seems to me that the character of Aubrey is so obviously based on Polidori, while the vampyric Lord Ruthven is a mirror of yourself. This self-reflection is a theme in so many of your poems.'

'Why on earth would I portray myself as being such a demon?'

'Why would Polidori do so?'

'Because this is the petty vengeance of man who has no hope of attaining his own fame in the literary world.'

'Oh, but this novel *will* be published, and the world will then discover the awful truths that Polidori must have learned when you employed him as your personal physician. I wonder now, did you kill the whore at my palazzo? Why would you enter that alley? It does not lead to the canal where your gondola was waiting.'

'I heard her cries. I tried to save her! But you know all this already.'

'I *did* believe your innocence, but when I came to read *The Vampyre,* how could I not recall seeing the blood smeared round your mouth? The pallid face and wounded throat of that poor woman on the ground?'

Bryon muttered through a growl, 'I've had my fill of this nonsense. I should have gone to the police and reported the crime. If I recall, *you* were the one who wished to keep it concealed. Why was that, I have to ask? What did you do with her body? Sell the corpse to Polidori for dissecting in the morgue? Are you and the doctor bound in some net of private intrigue, its sole intention to disgrace me?'

Her answer was to draw two cards from the pack. She held both up for him to see, then cast them down at his feet. 'The queen of hearts. The queen of spades.' She offered him the saddest smile. 'Two women left to rot in the filth of Venice gutters. How many others in your past? How many yet to come?'

Byron had had enough of the woman's cryptic games. Without another word, he rose from his chair, heading out to the main salon, where the dancing had resumed – and in the middle of the throng was the auburn-haired Teresa.

Had her heart been turned against him, infected by the dart of Countess Alfieri's poison? He had to speak to her again. But how, when she was waltzing in the arms of a man even older than her husband? As if aware of his gaze, Teresa glanced across her shoulder and through the crowd to meet his eyes as she went whirling around the room. When, at last, the music stopped and her partner kissed her hand, about to lead her from the floor, she drew back and shook her head. With both hands clutched to her breast, Teresa sank to her knees, declining all attempts of any help from those around her. Instead, she called out to him: 'Mio Byron! Come to me.'

There were gasps of shocked alarm, for such a term was intimate, and not the way a married woman should address a man in public. Certainly not a man of Lord Byron's reputation.

He gasped himself when he drew close enough to see the bloom of red that stained the muslin at her breast, tinging the petals of the rose from purest white to vivid pink. All but dreading to imagine some assassin had attacked her, he heaved a sigh of relief when she weakly announced, 'I think a corset bone has snapped.'

'Don't move an inch. Let me remove it!' Byron insisted as he knelt at her side to give assistance. What if the bone had punctured flesh? The flesh too near her heart? His fears were heightened even more when she fell into a swoon, collapsing forwards in his arms.

But this was only an act, for the Countess Guiccioli was quite conscious when she whispered, 'It is nothing but a scratch. A gift for us tonight. I must be quick and let you know before my husband comes to find me. Tomorrow, I am free. He will be away on business. I will come to your palazzo.'

There was no time to respond, for another strident voice rang out more loudly in his ears. This time, the Countess Alfieri, who clapped both hands against her mouth before she cried for all to hear – 'The blood! Look at the blood! What has he done to this poor woman? By all the saints, may God preserve her!'

Eleven

Like knots of vipers on a dunghill's soil,
Rage, fear, hate, jealousy, revenge

Byron. From *Don Juan:* Canto II

This memoir has been neglected, but for the very best of reasons. Since Passion week ~ so aptly named ~ I've fallen damnably in love with a countess from Ravenna. I have told Fletcher there's no doubt that she will be my last amour, though he refuses to believe it. He looks at me & shakes his head in that woeful way he has, or else he laughs & says, 'MyLord, have you become the mooniest of all the moon-eyed boys? Is this woman some enchantress who has bound you in a spell?'

I tell him, yes, she has bewitched me, & now I am in Heaven ~ though I thought myself in Hell after the night of our first meeting, tossing and turning in my bed until the dawn as I relived Countess Alfieri's claims that I had penned such utter dross as Polidori's Vampyre novel ~ & then the woman's dreadful scream when she inferred ~ more than inferred ~ that I'd committed some audacious act of bloodlust on Teresa.

How could I ever think to hurt her, a young woman fair as sunrise & as warm as the noon? But was it pitiful to hope she would also be attracted to a man a decade older, whose hair was frosted with grey, with crows' feet etched so lavishly at the corner of each eye?

Early next morn I washed and dressed & in the mirror saw a face somewhat younger & more handsome than the monster I'd imagined in the hours of darkness. With renewed confidence & vigour I left the house in search of flowers from the nearby market stalls. If Teresa failed to come to my palazzo on that day, I'd compose some pretty verse & send the blooms to her instead. But, in the end, I had no need to turn detective & seek out her place of residence.

Returning through the house's kitchen, I chanced on Fletcher, muttering below his breath as he filled a silver pot with steaming coffee, setting out some gilded cups and saucers on a tray.

'Ah, just in time!' I announced, savouring the rich aroma.

'It's for your lady visitors,' the valet glumly announced. 'They would insist on coming in, so I've followed your instructions & installed them in the room that always smells of rot & damp. Nobody lingers there for long.'

'Visitors?' Did I dare hope?

'One says she is a countess. She does have all the airs and graces.'

Could Fletcher mean Teresa? Surely not the Alfieri! Without waiting to ask I hastened to the small reception room I rarely use, due to the stench of the canal, which always seems much stronger there. Not that my visitors appeared to be the least bit oppressed by the atmosphere of dankness which, I hoped, perhaps in vain, might be improved by the perfume of the flowers I was holding ~ & what a glorious relief to find no countess in a mask, only the lovely open face wreathed in smiles while calling out in her low & fluting voice, 'Ah, mio Byron!

You are here. I was just telling my friend that perhaps I was mistaken & you had played me for a fool.'

Only then did I observe the woman perched at her side on the mildewed furnishings, who looked about Teresa's age but without her natural charm, being more serious in manner & with dark eyes below thick brows, deliberately avoiding mine as Teresa carried on:

'This is Eleanora. We first met in the convent, & now she's been escorting me on visits to my friends.'

Eleanor responded dourly, 'Your valet was not friendly. He seemed to think—'

I broke in, 'He can be cautious, but very often with good reason. Sometimes unwelcome visitors have tried to breach my privacy.'

As I said this, I could not help but think of Caroline Lamb. Unwilling to accept that our affair had reached its end, the waif-like young woman with a head of close-cropped hair had masqueraded in the guise of a page who'd come delivering a letter. Fletcher, completely fooled, had let her into my chamber, then had the devil of a struggle when attempting to remove her, sustaining many scratches to his person in the process.

'I do hope I'm not unwelcome.' Suddenly, less assured, Teresa's face was very wan, & was that the purple stain of a bruise below one eye? Surely her husband did not beat her? But, no, the mark was but a shadow. More the look of weariness. Perhaps, like me, she had not slept.

'Never unwelcome!' I assured her. 'I have hoped against all hope that you'd accept my invitation.'

'How could I not, after last night, after those things you said to me? I had to see you, to be sure that...' She faltered on the words. 'That I had found my destiny.'

Hearing such frankness in her voice, did I dare to imagine that this goddess of a woman also shared my own conviction that our love was preordained? In a delirium of joy, I stammered like a fool, 'I ... I bought you these flowers, although the colours fade to nothing more than drabness when compared to your own radiance & beauty.'

Saying this, I thrust the blooms into Teresa's hands, and when our fingers briefly touched was surprised to feel the thrumming of some vital energy running invisible between us. If we had only been alone, I would have reaffirmed my love & said that if I'd had my way I'd never let her leave again. But I was mute as I stared at the rosebud of the lips that briefly twitched in a smile before their owner replied, 'When I arrived at your palazzo ... when you could not be found, I asked your valet if he might at least permit me to see the room in which Lord Byron writes his verses. It was there I meant to leave the gift I brought for you. Alas, he refused. But, I wonder, now you're here, would you perhaps agree ... to show me yourself?'

Before I could respond, she passed the flowers to her friend, rising swiftly to her feet just as Fletcher rattled in with Mutz in his wake. A small commotion then ensued while Mutz growled fiercely at Teresa, during which it seemed to me that Fletcher dallied for longer than was strictly necessary, fussing about with the cups, setting some sweetmeats on the table, before his duties were complete and I ordered the man to take the dog & chain him up in the menagerie below. With some peace again restored, I led Teresa from the room into the passageway beyond. There she paused to draw a package from a pocket of her gown, & her cheeks were blushing red when she said, 'This is my gift to you. Will you open it now?'

The paper held a lock of hair. But not the hair from her head. Knowing exactly what this meant, I held the package to my heart while inclining my head so as to murmur in her ear, 'Sometimes I work in my study. At other times, in my bedchamber. Which would you prefer?'

She preferred to see the bed.

Since that morning, we conspire to meet whenever possible, whether here in my palazzo, rocking in my gondola, or occasionally the chamber of her residence in Venice ~ should her husband be away. How daring we are, with the Guiccioli servants loitering about the doors, & who could say which of them may then tell tales to her Count. In truth, the fonder I become, & I am so very fond, the more I fear for her safety. Her husband is a jealous man, & the rumours will abound that he murdered his first wife. For myself, I never leave my palazzo nowadays without a pistol on my person, for I confess I would not be the least surprised to turn around & find a blade held at my throat.

There is also the problem of the Countess Alfieri & her claim that The Vampyre is nothing less than a thinly veiled confession of my life. Who would believe such utter nonsense? Well, my own publisher, it seems! John Murray plagues me with his letters, often taking me to task for the sale of my work to one of his competitors. It is the most outrageous fraud, & if he'd read one single sentence of The Vampyre he would know those words did not spill from my pen. Meanwhile, I have suggested that he sets his lawyers loose upon this scoundrel publisher, & on Polidori too ~ that is if the imposter ever shows his face again. I have looked everywhere in Venice, meaning to take him to task, but he is nowhere to be found.

Thank heavens for Teresa, who always lightens my mood & finds some seeds of comedy within this all-too sorry farce of confused identities. She does not doubt my innocence & insists that she has read sufficient of my verses to be sure I never wrote such a clumsy piece of fiction...

The chimes of nearby church bells echoed across the Grand Canal. Was it eight o'clock already? Byron set down his pen, stretched his neck from left to right, then raised both arms above his head to draw some blood into muscles grown stiff from lack of exercise.

Normally, his inclination would have been to call for Tita and be ferried to the Lido, where he'd saddle up a horse and gallop through the waves, where the rhythm of the motion between man and animal was, in its own way, another form of poetry. Such an elation of the spirits when, afterwards, sweating and hot, he'd strip off and plunge his body in the coolness of the water, swimming for hours below black skies, or simply floating on his back, staring up in ceaseless wonder at the stars that shone above him in their galaxies of thousands. At least, that *would* have been the case before Teresa came along, since when the pleasures of the bed had eclipsed all other sports.

If only she were with him now, rather than sitting in her box at the Teatro La Fenice, where no doubt she'd be concerned at his failure to arrive. Was it a play tonight, or another operetta? He hadn't thought to ask. No doubt some comedy romance, which the Italians adored. Well, he was in the mood for fun, and better still, by being late should be able to avoid the inconvenience of the crowds who often gathered on the bridge of the canal before the entrance at the start of each performance. Like a ghost, he'd slip inside and make his way on up the stairs, to where the footman at the door of the box would show him in. He'd find his love with Eleanora, her compliant chaperone. After all, what decent woman could be seen alone in public in the company of Byron?

Eleanora was not there. Instead, he entered the box and saw the powdered wig worn by the Count Guiccioli – and the presence of the husband surely scuppered any plans for romancing the wife. Could Byron leave before they saw him, or contrive some excuse about an incident at home that required his attention? Ah well, he was here, and might as well accept the glass of tepid fizz the footman offered before he settled in the chair on Teresa's other side.

He touched her hand, but only briefly. She glanced at him. A worried smile, but then returned her attention to the performance on the stage, from which the voices of the singers soared through strains of violins. Lost in the beauty of the sound, Byron surveyed the baroque glory of the theatre around him. The looming walls were dizzying, containing row upon row of ornately gilded boxes that glittered in the light of candles. In one, directly opposite, he saw another flash of gold, drawing his eye to the mask worn by the Countess Alfieri. Had she noticed his arrival?

She would soon enough, for a woman in the crowd before the stage suddenly screeched: 'Look! Up in that box. Lord Byron with his lover!'

The singing from the stage was drowned by the eruption of resultant boos and hisses – whether they could be for him, or for Teresa, or the woman who had dared to interrupt the performance of the show, Byron could not be sure. More silently, a thousand faces turned to stare in his direction. In response, he dragged his chair behind the box's velvet curtains, hoping to sit there unobserved for what remained of the show. But, disturbed between the folds of brocade and golden tassels, a tiny fly escaped its bondage. There was a high-pitched whining buzz as wings flew close to Byron's face, before he batted it away, though the sound of the insect somehow wormed into his mind, was even humming in his blood. Smoke from the candles on the stage caused his eyes to blur and dazzle. As he blinked to try and clear them, he looked up towards the glimmer of the crystal chandelier, like a great star in the domed and muralled heaven of a ceiling. Below it, plaster figurines appeared to tremble into life. The stuccoed walls throbbed and glowed, as if alight with flames of fire. The air was hot, too thick to breathe, though that was hardly a surprise. It was June, and the Venetian summer months were rarely balmy. In such a crowded space as this the heat could be unbearable.

How Byron endured the next few hours, he did not know. He would usually enjoy *The Marriage of Figaro,* with infidelity, revenge and finally the happy ending. But through the whistles and applause, and then another curtain call, he was increasingly distracted, even more so when he heard the count's barbed comment to his wife – 'I assume such a performance suited your friend to perfection.' The husband's lizard eyes slid Byron's way when he went on, 'But did he notice how my wife has been casting her smiles at every other handsome man in the audience tonight?'

Byron bristled inwardly. Yes, he had failed to notice where Teresa's eyes had drifted, though there had been other nights when her flirtations drove him mad.

'Allessandro!' She frowned as she rebuked her husband's claim. 'You know that is not true. I was acknowledging our friends. Some of them are men, but there are many women too.'

'Such as the Countess Alfieri, although she seems to have more interest in Lord Byron, don't you think?' The count's reply was for Teresa, but all the while his steely gaze remained intent on Byron's face, surely relishing this chance to turn the screw of any scandal regarding Polidori's novel. After all, he had been there, the night when Countess Alfieri recited from the book. He would have heard the woman's words in response to the blood seeping through Teresa's gown.

Who would think a drop of blood could lead to such hysteria! In the first days of their affair, before the wound had chance to heal, Byron had probed it with his tongue, tasting the scab's thick iron tang. He'd called Teresa the witch who had grown another nipple for the pleasure of her devil ... And how he yearned to touch her now, to lie beside her in his bed and feast his eyes on those pale breasts – instead of which he had to face Count Guiccioli's jealous leer, only glad of the distraction when Teresa raised her opera glass to search the other boxes and exclaimed, 'There she is!'

'Shall we call her over here?' Count Guiccioli asked his wife. 'Invite her to share another bottle of champagne?'

'In that case,' Byron stood, 'I think it best I take my leave.'

But his departure was prevented when the Count, very nimble for a man of almost sixty, barred the door of the box and made a lunge for Byron's wrist, which he gripped as if a vice, while muttering below his breath, 'At least, remain long enough for me to explain why I joined my wife tonight.'

The Count glanced back towards Teresa, who was still sitting in her chair, her eyes grown wide with concern, but otherwise she retained an attitude of calm. Only the sudden rise and fall of creamy flesh above her bodice revealed the panic she was feeling, as did the hands that she clasped across her gently swelling belly.

The Count went on, speaking more loudly: 'My dearest wife, I have been patient with regard to your activities in Venice these past months. I know you take me for a fool and will continue to insist that the nature of your friendship with this renowned philanderer is platonic in its nature. If you *had* to take a lover, then at least he is our equal. But I think you are forgetting, I am a man of the world. I know when you are lying, and I've had more than my fill of all the verses being sung of your affair in the streets. I won't be made a laughing stock. It can't continue any longer. Tonight, you'll say goodbye. You'll never see the man again.'

'Alessandro, no!' Teresa stood so hurriedly her chair was tipped and clattered over.

Ignoring her distress, the Count continued to scold. 'A husband has a duty to protect his wife from danger. And, mark me well, you are most certainly in want of my protection.'

'Nonsense!' Byron said. 'I'd never cause Teresa harm. I assure you, Guiccioli, I admire and respect her.'

'And yet...' the Count broke in, still holding fast to Byron's arm, 'this very afternoon I heard from friends that there are people here in Venice who suspect you may have some connection with the deaths of local whores.'

'Deaths ... of whores?' Teresa echoed.

The Count let go of Byron's wrist, and turned to clutch at hers instead, addressing his wife as if she were a wayward child. 'I cannot trust him in your presence for a single moment longer. Tonight, you'll make a start on preparations for our journey back home to Ravenna. We must remove ourselves completely from this city's influence – from this man and all he stands for. If we do not, I doubt we'll ever be allowed to show our faces in good company again. Think of that, if you will, and how dull your life would be without your parties and amusements? Or perhaps you would prefer to take the veil and return to your old convent life again?'

Hearing such a threat, Teresa looked at Byron. Her voice came breathless when she begged, 'Won't you tell him he's wrong? Tell him you're not a murderer? Tell *me* it isn't true!' Snatching her hand away from her husband's gripping claw, she cried out, 'Alessandro, you're a fool to believe that woman's gossip. The countess is deranged! She's—'

'You are growing overwrought, which is not good for our child.' Her husband cut her off, even more daunting when he spoke with such a calm determination. 'Do you think I'd give a single moment's credence to the Countess? Only a dullard would believe that a vampire could exist. But you should have no doubt, the rumours of two whores being murdered are quite true, and...' his lips stretched wide, a slash of red through which he sneered '...Lord Byron knew them both. He is considered the main suspect.'

'Who has told you this?' Byron struggled desperately to contain his rising anger.

'The governor general is my friend, and his own spies have informed him that you also belong to a scandalous club. The Society of—'

'Ancient Rome?' Byron laughed.

'So, you admit it does exist?' the Count replied with satisfaction. 'The club you nurture as a cloak for your base proclivities, though not for so much longer. An arrest is imminent, and before that disgrace I want my wife out of your life! If you have any care for her future happiness, you will agree to set her free from this unfortunate liaison.'

Teresa gazed at Byron through eyes that sparkled bright with tears. She touched a hand to her breast, where tonight the decoration was a rose of darkest red. She made to take a step towards him, but one foot caught on the leg of the chair upturned before. Teresa stumbled forwards. One of her arms struck on the door leading to the corridor. The footman on the other side noticed the knock and presumed he had been summoned to come in.

While the Count was occupied in dealing with the man, Teresa whispered breathlessly, 'Go, my love. You must go. He never makes an idle threat.'

Her warning ended when she turned to face her husband again, and like a mirror of that night when Byron first laid eyes on her, Teresa slumped to her knees. But, had she really swooned, or did she kneel in silent prayer? Was Teresa only begging for her count's forgiveness?

Glancing back one final time, Byron saw the fallen petals of the rose that now resembled stains of blood on the box carpet.

The omen of what was to come.

Twelve

The first dark day of nothingness

Byron. From *The Giaovr*

As his gondola went gliding under arches of stone bridges, Byron sat hunched in his black cloak and resembled nothing less than a villain brooding malice in a Radcliffian romance. He plunged one hand into his jacket and caressed the cold, hard weight of the pistol hidden there, sorely tempted for one moment to press the barrel to his head. But then he thought about the gore staining the boat's upholstery and, well, that was hardly fair on Tita. Worse still, to imagine the pleasure it would bring to his mother-in-law. Instead, he stared in misery at the lamps burning brightly in the windows of palazzos, the walls of buildings so near he could have touched them with his fingers. The crumbling stones were streaked with damp and were stinking of corruption, like oyster shells left out to rot once the pearls had been discarded. Added to that noxious stench was the decaying scum of petals in their thousands on the water. Flowers thrown from the bridges for the ancient ceremony of the Marriage to the Sea, celebrating a time when a doge once cast a golden wedding ring into the waters.

Teresa wears the ring belonging to another man. Byron's mind was fraught with anguish. But then, what choice did he have but to give his lover up? If she stayed with him in Venice, she would most certainly be dragged into the nightmare accusations of his connection with two murders. The wicked lies that surely rose from his own delinquencies.

'Body of Bacchus.' 'Blood of David.' 'Filthy crab.' 'Son of a dog!' He winced to hear the raucous calls of other passing gondoliers. They had a language all their own, insults peculiar to Venice, yet couldn't every shout have been directed straight at him? Wasn't Byron now the dog that had had its final day, his life descended to the level of a paltry fairground farce in which he played the lovelorn fool? Dramas of that type might have amused him in the past. All those happy times in London when he'd relished his involvement with the Theatre Drury Lane, meeting with actors and playwrights over dinners and rehearsals. And what a night it had been when he'd donned a mummer's mask to strut the stage and join the cast for the Christmas pantomime, hearing the audience shriek with laughter when Grimaldi the great clown held out his arms and exclaimed: 'Here we are again!'

And here I am. Byron envisioned the woman in the alley, her throat slashed open with a knife. Had such a vision turned the mind of the Countess Alfieri? Had *she* told Count Guiccioli, or reported her fears to the authorities of Venice? What other fabrications might the woman next come up with? Should he take a detour now? Go and visit her palazzo? If she was back from the theatre, he could insist that she refrain from spreading any further slander. But would that do more harm than good? What if Lombardo was to blame? Or even Polidori? It was peculiar the way he'd materialised in Venice, and then – puff! – he'd disappeared.

Had his novel been a ploy by which to ruin Byron's name? Was Polidori a fiend who revelled in the woes of others? Since the doctor's departure from the Villa Diodati, Byron had heard disturbing tales, though he had shrugged them off as gossip, making light of the events in any letters sent to friends, when he'd recorded them as if the details of a war report:

Lord Guildford – killed – inflammation of the bowels. Mr Horner – killed – diseased lungs. Mrs Hope's son – killed – scarlet fever. Rank and file – killed – forty-five paupers of Pisa – wounded and missing (the last supposed to be dissected). Lady Westmorland – incurable – her disease is not defined, but is most likely to have been a case of unrequited passion for the darkly handsome doctor...

Another darkly handsome man was now suspected as a killer. What a sensation if Lord Byron should be tried and then found guilty! Although a public execution should provide some added value to his verses in the future.

Byron laughed mirthlessly, before recalling the time he'd been in Rome and paid to watch three robbers being guillotined. The memory would never leave him. It had been branded on his eyes. How clearly he had seen the executioners half naked, the dropping rattle of the blade, the ghastly splashing of the blood. What dread he'd felt to hear the scream when one man's skull had proved too large to fit within the guillotine, and so they'd severed off one ear. At least his end was quick enough. The head was gone before the eye could even think to trace the blow, and then held forwards by the hair as crowds below began to cheer. The frenzied throng made such a noise, Byron was sure he'd be deafened. He'd been trembling so badly he could barely hold the opera-glass to watch more scenes unfolding. And yet, he did. Because he must. And by the time the last thief's head had been severed from its neck, the effect upon his nerves had settled to a numb acceptance – which only went to demonstrate how a man can be inured to the sight of blood and death. How horror begets horror.

He woke to find his head remained intact upon his shoulders, but it was aching horribly and still partially immersed in a whirl of vivid dreams. There'd been a forest steeped in shadows. There'd been wolves. The wolves were howling. Byron was howling too. He'd licked his tongue over his teeth. He'd felt the sharpness of incisors, the sticky drool upon his lips...

Mutz was on the bed beside him. The dog's wet tongue was slobbering across its master's mouth.

Fletcher was also in the room, calling out, 'Wake up, MyLord. You must get up, or you will surely end your days here like a hog, grunting and farting in its sty. Will you look at the mess!' The valet tutted as he stared at empty bottles on the floor. 'How one man could have consumed this much wine in just three days is a mystery to me.'

'Three days?' Byron groaned as Fletcher drew the curtains back, and in that special way he had when in a disapproving mood – which was to tug upon the fabric and that way heighten the clatter of the rings against the pole. How it jangled Byron's nerves, even more so when the light came shafting through and left him blinking like the blindest of moles. Shuffling higher on the pillows, he raised a hand to shield his eyes and willed his tongue – so dry and swollen – to ask what time of day it was.

'More like the evening. Well past six,' Fletcher dryly said. 'And now a letter has arrived which may require your attention. Shall I bring it to you here, or...'

'On my desk, if you don't mind. But first, I need some coffee. Will you brew it yourself? No-one else quite has the knack. And make it strong. Very strong. I need to clear my head, or I fear I shall be doomed to the fate of Alexander.'

'You mean he drank himself to death? Well, carry on and you'll succeed. Take a look in the mirror. A proper death's head on a mop stick.' Fletcher scowled as he stooped to gather up the bottles, tutting again to see the spills of dark red wine on sheets and carpets.

Only when he'd left the room to clink his way along the passage did Byron rise from the bed and stagger to the washing bowl. The sudden elevation of his body left him dizzy. His fingers gripped the marble stand until the nausea had passed. Meanwhile, he wondered if Teresa was now back in Ravenna – if the post Fletcher mentioned could be a message from his lover. Or would it be a legal summons connected to her husband's threats? He'd seen more than enough of lawyers' letters in the past, what with the bankruptcy fears before the sale of Newstead Abbey, and then the maze of the logistics for his marriage separation. But that had been in England, not in Venice, where he'd fled to escape such tyranny.

His hands were shaking violently when he took up the shaving brush, working the bristles in the soap and then lathering his face. Three days of stubble took some concentrated effort to remove. The cut-throat blade left several nicks. But the blood was swift to clot and he continued with his toilet, dragging a comb through knotted curls before he took one final glance at his appearance in the glass – and let out a strangled cry when no reflection could be seen.

The comb was dropped to the floor. The dog leapt down from the bed to come and sit at Byron's side, gazing up in mute concern as its master stood in shock, only to draw another breath when Fletcher rattled in again, setting down a tray, before he asked with some concern, 'MyLord, are you well? You look as if you've seen a ghost.'

Byron said, 'Will you come here? Will you look into this glass? Tell me exactly what you see.'

He heard the valet's steps as they approached across the boards. He felt the warmth of Fletcher's breaths tickling against his neck, but in the mirror's gauzy sheen Byron saw nothing but the haze of the furnishings around them; the faintest blurring hints of colour at the edges of the frame in front of which both men were standing.

Byron groaned through his distress. 'There's nothing there. Just silhouettes. Our shadows on the glass. Do we actually exist, or are we dead, the two of us? Doomed to haunt this house as spirits, still believing we are living?'

'Are you still booze-addled, MyLord? Tis but the dazzle of the sunlight on the surface of the glass.' Fletcher reached over Byron's shoulder and altered the angle of the mirror on the stand. For good measure he then rubbed the sleeve of his jacket over the dust that furred its surface – and what a miracle that was. In a trice the room was back, and there was Byron next to Fletcher, with Fletcher shaking his head as he returned to the table and set about the business of the pouring of the coffee.

Byron said nothing, staring hard at the face in the glass, now so much gaunter than before. Fletcher was right. Today he looked more like a corpse than living man.

But the coffee would revive him. It smelled delicious, tasted better. Gritty and black as soil. And even though he could feel the scalding burn against his tongue, he drank it fast and had already poured himself a second cup before the stimulant began to work its magic on his spirits. By the third cup, he had dressed, if somewhat shambolically. His feet were bare, his shirt unfastened, the tails left hanging over trousers as he wandered from his chamber and made his way towards the study.

Once there, he asked the valet to fill his skull cup with Madeira, which made a welcome digestif after the plate of bread and eggs that Fletcher also carried in, insisting that his master should consume every last morsel or face an imminent starvation.

Imminent. That word again. The one Count Guiccioli used at their last meeting in the theatre. *An imminent arrest.*

He glanced about to find the letter Fletcher mentioned earlier. He did not recognise the hand and saw no seal to indicate that its contents were official. But he felt a dark foreboding when, as if in a daze, he picked up it, rose from the desk and walked towards the balcony. Only when standing on that, looking out across the water, did he tear the letter open and reveal the correspondence:

This message brings grave news of our mutual friend, the Countess Guiccioli. Her priest has written to inform me that he believes her hours are numbered and it is her greatest hope to see you one last time. Dear Lord Byron, if you hold Teresa in your heart with even half of the devotion that she holds you in her own, you will grant this last request. After all, you did once say whatever gift she asked of you could never be denied.

I hope you will go, but my advice would be to also take a friend as some protection. Count Guiccioli may permit you a last visit with his wife, but that cannot ensure your personal safety in his house. Teresa's child has been lost. He lays the blame at your door.

Yours in great sadness,
Eleanora

'Teresa. Oh, Teresa!' The letter fell from Byron's hand as his vision blurred with tears. But his thoughts were razor sharp. He must travel to Ravenna, and he must go without delay, though what to take on such a journey? Only the bare essentials, and of course his pair of pistols...

About to go in search of them, he heard the clanging of the doorbell, and when Fletcher reappeared the valet spoke in lowered tones: 'MyLord, there is some gent who calls himself Inspector Russo, from La Forsa here in Venice. Says he needs to speak with you about a serious complaint.'

Fletcher said no more than that, only frowned in consternation. But, knowing him of old, Byron could swear he heard him thinking: *What have you gone and done this time?*

Thirteen

Now crawl from cradle to the grave

Byron. From *The Giaour*

'Don't let him in. Say I'm not here.' Byron declaimed the words so loudly, not a soul in the palazzo could have failed to realise that he *was* definitely present. He wasn't thinking logically. He only knew that he must leave and make the journey to Ravenna. After all, what other upsets in his life were as important as his need to see Teresa?

Having come to his senses and decided it was best to face the inconvenience, two men were duly ushered in. The slighter of the pair had a corny complexion and was prematurely balding. Perched on the end of a snub nose were silver wire-rimmed spectacles, the eyes that peered behind them darting nervously about every corner of the room. His colleague was the taller and altogether more assured, around the age of fifty years and quite the bull calf in his build. His black moustache was ostentatious, as were the slugs of bristled brows above brown eyes that gave the hint of a kindly disposition.

'Gentlemen!' Byron announced, though the effort to affect a tone of welcome was enormous, and he was surely unaware of quite how ghoulish he was looking, baring teeth still stained with red from a less than thorough brushing with the powder earlier. 'You find me in some disarray, the reason being my distress at having only just this moment been informed of the illness of a friend who I hold in the greatest esteem. I'm sure you'll understand my need to go and visit her, though naturally I'd be prepared to speak to you at leisure when I return again to Venice.'

The older man replied in a voice that sounded waspish, and much higher than expected: 'For a gentleman who's said to be a genius with words, you must try a little harder if you are hoping to avoid us.'

Byron's false cheer was replaced by a tarter indignation. 'Who do you think you are, to come into my house and address me in this manner?'

'I am Carlo Russo, inspector superior. And this' – the fellow motioned to the colleague at his side – 'is Signor Tommaso Zanon, a local officer in charge of civil order here in Venice, who's been receiving complaints about your personal conduct. And now...' he left a pause '...as the pleasantries are over, perhaps we may continue with the business of our visit?'

Byron stared at him in panic. What would his character Don Juan have done when faced with such a scene? Too late to hide in any wardrobe. What about the balcony? Could he climb the balustrade as La Fornarina had once done, leaping into the canal, swimming to his liberty?

Instead, he suggested, 'May I show you a letter, to prove the truth of what I say about the illness of a friend?' But where had the letter gone? Had it been taken by a breeze, flying off to join the scum of rotting flowers still floating on the surface of the waters? 'Damn!' Byron exclaimed, casting his eyes about the room. 'I had it here, in my hands only moments ago.'

'Please don't fret,' Russo said. '*If* it exists, then we shall find it.'

'Of course I'm fretting,' Byron snapped, raising his chin pugnaciously, holding his fists as if about to begin a boxing match. It was a sport he'd enjoyed and been adept at in his youth though he'd not practised it in years. Instead, he punched with words. 'I need to leave without delay. Your presence in my house is a flagrant imposition.'

The inspector was much calmer. 'I have a warrant on my person to allow such an intrusion. But, Lord Byron, to be blunt, you should know we are here on the best authority, having spoken to a person who professes to have had an intimate involvement with yourself, and this palazzo. Through her, we have learned of some vital evidence and...'

'What evidence?' Byron demanded. 'Who is this intimate you speak of?'

'Her name is Margarita Cogni.'

Byron sighed. 'Well, I admit La Fornarina was my lover. She has spent time in my palazzo ... though it was never what you'd call a serious affair. However, she did threaten some reprisal at our parting ... so, I suppose this is it.'

'You may soon be reunited.' The inspector smiled back below the bush of his moustache. 'She has agreed to take the stand and testify in court.'

At this point, Fletcher interrupted: 'Mr Russo, hear me out, as one who's had the misfortune to have known this Cogni woman. She is not to be trusted. She is a tyrant and a thief, more suited to be leading a voracious hoard of bandits than any decent occupation. What MyLord could have been thinking, taking up with such a...' The valet stopped mid-sentence, his rheumy eyes glancing back at Byron with regret. 'With such a crafty bob tail. Ask any member of the staff still working in this house. I guarantee they'll say the same.'

The inspector nodded sagely. 'I could tell when we met, she has some fire in her blood. And yet she seems a Godly woman, more than repentant for the sin of her own adultery. I cannot blame her for the wrong. She sought a means of making money to assist her ailing husband. You know he suffers from consumption and may not have long to live? Ah, I deduce from your expression you are ignorant of this. But it is why she played the whore, to pay for medicines and doctors. Hardly her fault if the man who employed her sexual favours' – Russo fixed his gaze on Bryon – 'also forced her to engage in the worst depravities.'

'She asked for everything I gave her,' Byron remonstrated.

Russo shrugged. 'That may be so. I only know the woman wept when describing how you forced her to stand naked while she read to you from pornographic books. Stories of the most sadistic and unnatural couplings. And then there is the fact that you keep a cabinet containing hair that you have taken from the heads of all your victims. Both the living ... and the dead. The trophies that you use for the practising of witchcraft.'

Byron couldn't help but laugh. 'During these private confabulations you have shared with the Signora, did she perhaps forget to tell you that she cannot read or write? She has lied, and you've been fooled. Apart from which, I find it hard to imagine that a man born in such enlightened times could even dream that *I'm* inclined to dabble in black magic.'

As he spoke, he scanned the shelf for his copy of *Justine*, but the De Sade had disappeared, as had the little wooden chest that held his lovers' locks of hair. When had they gone? Byron recalled the time when his entire household had been affected by a fever – when Fletcher had reported hearing footsteps in the house in the middle of the night. So perhaps there *were* intruders. Only not the spirit type.

Against the turmoil of such thoughts, he was vaguely aware of the inspector droning on: 'You may say you have no interest in the art of the occult, but I have also seen the files confirming your connection with a sect of dissolutes, who—'

'The Society of Ancient Rome?' Byron groaned dramatically. 'Utter hogwash and twaddle! Meanwhile, you dilly-dally here, wasting everybody's time with these piffling accusations...'

'Hardly a piffling accusation.' Russo's dark eyes were fused with his. 'Or, indeed a waste of time, to apprehend a murderer before he strikes again. How can a man such as yourself be left to roam at liberty? Oh, you may sneer and deny association with such evils, but...' The inspector raised a hand and gestured round the room: 'Do you consider your nobility and wealth provide a shield? Do you sleep your days away in this glory of a fortress, and then emerge to seek your pleasures in the hours of the darkness while inhabiting the realms of the Venetian underworld? Oh yes, we're well aware of your habits, Lord Byron. We have spies who have observed your every movement in this city, in which it's known you have a weakness for the fairer of the sexes, but not exclusively. Whether male or female, on the whole you prefer the company of whores to those of moral principles. This is no vague accusation. We have the dates and the times of your visits to the brothels, one even listing your age in a visitors' book as being more than one hundred. A strange admission, is it not? We also learned that at some time during the month of Carnevale, two women were killed in a manner that reflects some direct comparisons with your own poetry ... and prose.' Saying this, he turned to nod at the colleague at his side. 'Do you have the documents?'

Byron expected to see the warrant mentioned earlier, instead of which Russo received and then unfolded sheets of paper that looked unnervingly familiar. Was that Polidori's hand? His novel's manuscript? The very sheath of blood-stained pages Byron had previously concealed in a drawer of his desk?

'How do you come to have those papers?' Byron asked in confusion.

'Some of your maids are not averse to taking a bribe.'

Byron could only stand and watch as the inspector's spade-like fingers rummaged through the crumpled leaves and then triumphantly announced, 'Ah, yes! Here we are! The reference to the time of your departure from your homeland ... "Weary of a country in which he had met with such terrible misfortunes, and in which all apparently conspired to heighten that superstitious melancholy that had seized upon his mind, he resolved to leave it—"'

The inspector stopped abruptly and walked across the room to place the papers on the desk. Picking up the Newstead skull, he turned it in his hands and looked for all the world as if he might have been about to soliloquise from Shakespeare. Instead, he peered into the void and exhibited revulsion at the dregs of rusty red congealed in the base, before his thoughts returned again to Polidori's fantasy.

Setting the cup back on the desk, he pleasantly enquired, 'Where do you suggest I take the story up again? I suppose...' he chose a page '...this will serve to demonstrate how your work is very often autobiographical in nature, being both by you, *and* about you:

'"While waiting for a vessel to convey him to Otranto, or to Naples, he occupied himself in arranging those effects he had with him belonging to Lord Ruthven. Amongst other things there was a case containing several weapons of offence, more or less adapted to ensure the death of the victim. There were several daggers and ataghans. Whilst turning them over, and examining their curious forms, what was his surprise at finding a sheath apparently ornamented in the same style as the dagger discovered in the fatal hut — he shuddered — hastening to gain further proof, he found the weapon, and his horror may be imagined when he discovered that it fitted, though peculiarly shaped, the sheath he held in his hand. His eyes seemed to need no further certainty—they seemed gazing to be bound to the dagger; yet still he wished to disbelieve..."'

Byron's teeth wet set on edge to hear such clumsy jarring prose, and he was further discomposed when Russo's eyes moved to the wall on which an ornamental Turkish ataghan had been displayed.

Still with Polidori's scrawl firmly clutched in his hand, the inspector went to take a closer look at the weapon, at the same time asking Fletcher if he would light some candles, for outside the dusk was falling and the room was growing dimmer.

It was several minutes later – due to Fletcher's trembling hands – that several flames were flickering in silver candlesticks and sconces. In such a glow the sabre gleamed, as did Inspector Russo's eyes when he examined the sword as if an insect through a lens. It was with some tenderness he stroked the smoothness of the handle, made of bone and embedded with several tiny bright-blue beads to indicate the 'evil eye', while other symbols were engraved into the steel of the blade, such as the hand of Fatima, or trailing pomegranate fruits. All meant to indicate good luck.

Would they bring luck to Byron now? Somehow that seemed unlikely, especially when the inspector turned to speak to him again:

'A useful sort of object. Not too big to be concealed within the pocket of a great coat. Excellent for slashing throats or, if one preferred, to manipulate the tip and ascertain just the place before one stabbed and gave a twist through the victim's jugular, that way releasing the blood and – as expressed so elegantly in the last line of your novel – to glut the thirst of a vampyre.'

Byron responded angrily: 'There is nothing elegant about that ghastly piece of fiction! What does this sabre prove, only that my lazy maids are less concerned with their duties in cleaning this palazzo than they are in stealing papers. Look at the dust on the handle. It has not been touched in months. I last used it in Athens, cutting the head from a goose to make a roast for myself and my companion, John Cam Hobhouse.'

Inspector Russo smiled. 'I would be curious to know how you came to lay your hands on so exotic a weapon.'

'It was a gift. From Ali Pasha.'

Saying that name, Byron's mind slipped back to a time when he'd enjoyed the sophisticated potentate's attentions, taking coffee, nuts and sweets under the shade of tented awnings, smoking opium from pipes and lying back on silk divans as they'd succumbed to other pleasures. Oh, to fly there this very moment.

'No doubt you've heard of the man?' Byron carried on, pushing away the memories sure to damn him even further in the eyes of this inspector. 'But should that not be the case, he's a famed Albanian warlord who offered me and my companions the kindest hospitality. See that portrait over there. I had it made as a memento.'

The painting of Byron showed him at his most romantic. His face, almost in profile, exposed a strong straight nose, and the narrowest moustache to adorn his upper lip. He wore Albanian national costume, with an embroidered velvet jacket, a turban wound about his head. And, in his arms, the very sabre that had drawn Russo's attention.

Byron stared at the sword and all at once recalled the time when La Fornarina brandished it under the nose of Lady Hoppener. Was that his blood on the steel, from when he'd wrestled it away? How to distract Inspector Russo from noticing as well, sure to reach yet another erroneous conclusion?

He tried to bring the conversation back to Polidori's *Vampyre*. 'The pages you've just read were not written by me, but by another man entirely. Until three years ago he'd been employed as my physician; during which time he took the fragment of a story I'd created but dismissed as being worthless, then reimagined it himself to write the novel that—'

The inspector interrupted, 'So, you admit it arose from your own imagination?'

'Well, yes. I suppose. But only superficially. You can easily compare the style of writing to my own.'

Russo raised black-bristled brows. 'But you *did* compose a poem called *The Giaour*, did you not, about the legend of a vampire? And when you speak of Polidori, would it be so wrong of me to surmise that, as well as being your physician, there were occasions when he also took the role of secretary?'

'He is a man of many talents, and he liked to be of use.'

'So, in certain circumstances, it was you who dictated while he transcribed the words?'

'I did *not* dictate *The Vampyre*! Polidori took the bones and then inflated and conflated. He…' Byron faltered, words trailed off, overcome by the sense that any argument he made was only falling on deaf ears and this inspector was already quite convinced of his guilt.

Russo made his next attack. 'There is also the matter of the Contessa Alfieri. A close acquaintance of the lady has informed us that, one night, after attending her palazzo, you were discovered in the act of devouring – that was their description, not my own – one of your victims in the alleyway connected to her house. They say you lapped at the blood flowing from the woman's throat, before you picked your victim up, and carried her away, no doubt to finish what you'd started in a more secure location. A sordid story is it not? But what it leads me to is this: where is that murdered woman's corpse? Is it, as we believe, concealed within this very house?'

This was a monstrous suggestion. Byron glanced around at Fletcher in the hope of some support but could only see the panic shining through the valet's eyes. Fletcher's cheeks had also taken on a shade of mottled liver more pronounced than usual as the poor man stumbled off and collapsed into a chair, where he looked thoroughly despondent, resting his elbows on his knees, his face cupped in his hands, and the lines of his brow furrowed deep in misery.

It was the sorriest of sights, and Byron only wished to reassure his loyal servant that whatever he had heard was nothing more than fabrication. Instead, he turned to the inspector. 'I have a question myself. Whoever has been spreading Countess Alfieri's lies, why did the woman herself not report this crime to you on the night when it occurred? I'll tell you why: because the truth is that I found an injured woman, and then I did my best to save her. Indeed, I raised the alarm with the Countess's own footman, who later aided me in carrying the victim from the alley to the Alfieri stores. It was there that his mistress demanded silence on the matter, wanting only to preserve her own salon's reputation.'

'And you complied with this request?' The inspector aped

surprise. 'You, a peer of England, and a man of some great substance did not report it for yourself? I find that hard to believe. I tend to think it far more likely that *you* were the one who demanded secrecy.'

Byron batted back. 'Ask her footman. He'll defend me. He'll—' He broke off at the sound of Fletcher's muffled sobs.

The inspector noticed too and dipped a hand into his jacket. A starched white handkerchief was offered to the valet, who blew his nose flamboyantly, dabbing the cloth to reddened eyes.

Byron watched in dismay, but the inspector carried on as if there'd been no interruption: 'As you know full well, that was just the start. Another whore was found dead in a brothel belonging to Veronica Lombardo. She claims that a girl you'd selected was discovered near to death after you'd left her house next morning. She is heartily ashamed of delaying her complaint, the reason being she'd agreed to keep her mouth shut for a bribe. A most considerable amount. But, in the end, even the greediest of women has a conscience.'

Byron remonstrated. 'Yes, I visited her brothel. But the girl I spent the night with, she was sleeping when I left. What's more, no bribe was paid to Veronica Lombardo. *She* did come here demanding money, but...'

He glanced again at Fletcher in the hope of some defence. But hadn't Fletcher been dismissed from the room before Lombardo had begun her accusations? Now, the valet was mute, and Byron felt like a fly trapped in the glue of the threads being so tightly spun around him. Suddenly, he was perspiring, and yet his body felt too cold. As cold as it had been in the morgue where he had seen the dead girl bundled in the sack. Polidori had been with him. Polidori, who had written the story of *The Vampyre*, which seemed deliberately contrived to appear as a confession. But, if that was the case, had the doctor killed the whores? Was he the spider spinning lies at the centre of this web?

Inspector Russo went on talking: 'By good chance when it

came to our own investigations, we found the second victim's body still intact and embalmed at the Venice hospital.' He sadly shook his head. 'A mask was also found. One made of wax. Very expensive. It had a band secured inside with your own name next to the maker's. The guard informed us that you'd left it after visiting one night to view the body of a woman, almost as if you'd wished to relish in the horror of her death. Do you also like to look at the corpse kept in this house? The victim we've been told had unusually fair hair?'

Byron cried out through his frustration, 'Why must you torture me like this? For God's sake, man, leave me in peace and let me travel to Ravenna, where the Countess Guiccioli is lying on her deathbed.'

'Another death?' Russo responded through a pursing of his lips. 'Well, let us hope you are wrong. But perhaps it would be wise for us to take some precautions.'

He nodded to his silent colleague, who in turn opened the doors leading out into the hallway. Almost at once, two other men dressed in military uniforms marched through and came to Bryon's side, swiftly manacling his hands, which were then locked behind his back. Humiliated, shoulders aching, and with his wrists soon growing sore from his struggle to release them, Byron could have howled. But, being so restricted there was little he could do but accept the situation, sitting down upon the chair to which the men had roughly steered him before they left the room again.

Shaking with rage, Byron glared at the inspector and cried out, 'How dare you treat me this way? What danger do I pose, to you or anybody else?'

'You yourself have just alluded to the serious condition of the Countess Guiccioli. Before departing from Venice, her husband lodged his own complaints with regard to your part in the seduction of his wife. He claims you often drugged the woman to a state of such compliance, she could not have resisted your attacks if she had wanted. You then committed acts of violence of so intimate a nature they resulted – as it seems you are already well aware – in the death of her child. Yes, Lord Byron, we have also heard about this tragic news.'

'You are fools. You are deceived by a husband's jealousy!' Byron closed his eyes, letting his chin drop to his breast. Through the breaths that came too fast, he also heard the rising sounds from his menagerie below. The monkeys screeching in distress. Then the deeper growling bark that must be Mutz, before bravado turned into a strangled whimper. Who was hurting his dog?

He all but screamed at the inspector, 'If your men have dared to harm any one of my creatures, I'll make sure to raise complaints with my friend Hoppner at the Consul. I'll—'

Breaking off, he grew aware of other movements in the hallway beyond the study doors, just as Russo's balding friend announced, 'The evidence is here.'

Byron was bemused. What on earth was coming next? He didn't have to wait for long. The doors were opened again and the men in uniforms carried in the coffin-like construction of the box that – he gasped – had once contained his model Venus.

Where had Tita hidden her, and how on earth had La Fornarina come to know of her existence? The gondolier must have told her. As far as Byron was concerned, she'd been forgotten long ago, out of sight and out of mind – until now, when the box was set down on a Persian carpet, and it was obvious to see wherever Tita thought to store her had been a place too prone to dampness. The wood was wet and rotting, blooming black and green with fungus. When the inspector stood above it, the spores brought on a fit of sneezing. But soon enough he was sufficiently recovered to ask for the lid to be removed.

How La Fornarina must have planned this, cooking the dish of her revenge to be served in the way always said to be the best, which was as cold as death itself. But Byron's temper was red hot, an inferno that blazed as fiercely as the flames of Hell, for if this spiteful joke should prevent him from travelling to visit with Teresa then he *would* be a murderer. He would find La Fornarina and strangle her with his own hands, and after that he'd find the snitch of the maid who...

Byron was suddenly distracted, seeing the beggar boy Nicolo creeping out from behind one of the window's heavy curtains, slinking towards the exit doors, through which he slipped before he merged into the shadows of the hall. Nobody else had noticed him. Fletcher was busy sniffling. Inspector Russo and his men were staring down at Venus, who was no longer the immaculate, pale beauty she had been on her arrival here in Venice.

Perhaps a rat had breached the box, teeth gnawing through the wax that formed the model's neck and breasts. Perhaps the rat had also died in the nest it had made between the entrails and the organs of the body's cavity, for such a stink came rising up. The noxious stench of putrid meat. Even worse was the straw in which the model had been packed, and which was now a thick black silage, the verisimilitude of fluids that so often leaked from corpses. The only thing that remained exactly as before was the hair upon her head. Even the keenest of eyes might be deceived into believing this was once the crowning glory of a living, breathing woman.

Byron groaned, 'Surely you see she's a model made of wax!'

The inspector's voice was brusque, far more official than before. 'A desperate man tells desperate lies. Is this not the very whore you attacked in an alley at the Palazzo Alfieri?'

Byron was lost for words as the inspector stepped towards him and placed a hand upon his shoulder. A hand as stiff and as cold as any guillotine might be, the pressure growing only stronger when the man continued talking. 'Personally, I give no credence to ghoulish stories spread of vampyres. But I *do* consider you to be a man who is depraved. One with delusions that then drive him to the bloodlust of a demon. Whether you are destined to end your days in an asylum, or to kneel and lose your head, is a mere formality. This victim's corpse will now be taken away for an autopsy. Meanwhile, you, the murderer, will be incarcerated for the protection of the public, until such time as your case is presented to a judge. But do not worry, Lord Byron, we will ensure that your new chambers are befitting of your status. The Piombi, no less. Is it not somewhat ironic that you once composed a verse to describe that very prison?'

Fourteen

I stood in Venice on a Bridge of Sighs,
A palace and prison on each hand

Byron. From *Childe Harold's Pilgrimage:* Canto IV

Ten years had passed since he'd first seen it – the palace prison of the doges. Afterwards, he'd been inspired to write a verse about those men who'd walked the tunnelled Bridge of Sighs. What emotions had they felt to be entering the jail known locally as The Piombi – or, in English, 'The Leads' – due to the cells that lay directly underneath the metal roofs, where any prisoners would swelter in the hotter summer months or freeze when winter came around.

Inconceivable to think he had joined that fellowship, and for a period of weeks. Or was it even longer? He'd lost all sense of time. All hope of being free again. No more caffé corettos in the city's quiet squares. No riding in his gondola, trailing his fingers through the diamond glints of sunlight as they shone upon the green of the canal. What he would give for the chance to feel those cooling waters now. By day, his cell was like an oven, and not much better in the night. His flesh was sore from being drenched so continually in sweat. The food and water pushed on trays through a hatch in the door was only fit for the rats who scurried through the cell. But he'd soon grown used to them, barely noticing the tickle of their whiskers, or the needle sting of pain when, now and then, one tried nibbling his toes. The same with the bats roosting in rafters overhead, or the swarming buzz of flies hatched from maggots in the buckets full of slops and excrement. He didn't even care when, one morning, he awoke to discover that the rings on his hands had disappeared. It must have been the guard. Ah well. C'est la vie!

Some things remained as before. Every dawn he heard the screeching of the gulls that had once perched on the ledges of windows at the Palazzo Mocenigo. Same sombre tolling of the bells resonating from the churches, though those that rang for him these days were very nearly deafening, with his current residence being much closer to the campanile tower of St Mark's. The midday sun still shone as bright, and often glanced across the stone of winged lions that presided on gleaming domes and cupulas. He'd close his eyes against the dazzle of the light and make a wish that he might sit upon the back of such a lion and fly away to his Teresa in Ravenna. But then, he would remember. It was too late. She would be dead and buried in her grave.

Beset so morbidly with grief, now and then his thoughts went drifting to the model of his Venus in her box, more like a coffin – what had looked so like a corpse in its state of putrefaction. Surely by now Inspector Russo would have known that she was nothing but a doll with human hair? What did it matter anyway, when the Lombardo had reported the murder in her brothel, added to which, hadn't Russo been convinced that the novel with Byron's name upon the cover proved his guilt in the crime? The real story of the lord who murdered prostitutes in Venice would by now have found its way to every ear and conversazione existing in the city, to every shop and restaurant, to every church, and bordello? Even if he was released, would he have a life worth living?

Lying on his pallet in the fast-descending dusk, Byron gave up on every hope of ever finding liberty. Where were the lawyers who would fight to defend his innocence? Where was the valet he had hoped might try and come to visit him, for hadn't Fletcher always proved to be devoted in the past, sticking as firmly as a limpet through the worst of any scandals? But then, a master who had murdered was less easily forgiven. Fletcher could well have decided that enough was enough. He may already be in England, busy setting plans in motion for his pasta factory.

Byron closed his eyes and drifted into sleep. He dreamed the bats above his head were beating leathered wings, as if they clapped for his attention, then that the maggots crawled from buckets and latched themselves to his skin. Like the leeches of physicians, their squirming bodies swelled with blood, so much blood the maggots burst, and Byron woke – or thought he woke – gagging at the noxious stink. Only when nothing remained but the taste of his own bile did he open his eyes and let out a cry of shock.

A man was standing at the window. The man was Doctor Polidori, his body shadowed by the bars through which the eerie, silvered moonlight cast thin nets of radiance. Not that he spoke a single word of a reply when Byron asked, 'Why do you have such a fascination with the dead?'

He only shook his head, and like a ghost his body melted, disappearing into air. An answer came instead from the girl who Byron turned to see beside him on the hay. It was the girl from the morgue, who opened bleached and milky eyes and whispered through her cold blue lips. The very message on the note that had been placed in her hand: *I am Leila, in the sack, whose life blood has been drained by the Lord Infidel of Venice.*

With his hands pressed to his ears, Byron wept, 'Leave me alone! This isn't real. It can't be real.'

Such a relief to look again and to see the corpse's face had been transformed into Teresa's. Teresa lived. Teresa smiled. Teresa sighed and spoke his name, to which he murmured his response:

Ah, sweet lips! that make us sigh. The pale lovely smile of the beauties of the grave. He was about to kiss those lips but then saw worms spilling out, through which she hissed her threat at him: *Thy corpse shall from its tomb be rent...*

Waking to the horror of those lines from *The Giaour*, he was consumed with self-disgust, also afraid of what possessed him to have conjured such a vision. A dream so vivid and so real he was forced to ask himself: *Am I losing my mind?*

In his state of dark dejection, he ignored the heavy rattle of the lock in the door, and then the creaking that more usually announced the arrival of the drudge who fetched the slops. He lay quite still on the bench, his face turned blindly to the wall, when all at once he dared believe he heard the voice of a friend.

'Am I still dreaming?' he croaked, rising stiffly to his feet to see a man walking towards him through the soupy night-time gloom – the man who stretched his arms out wide, drawing Byron to his breast in an asphyxiating hug, before he finally stepped back and exclaimed: 'Byron, my friend! Can this be you?'

Byron had never been so thin, his face a hollow haunted mask below its glaze of perspiration. Whereas before he'd been clean-shaven, now he'd grown a tangled beard, giving him a gypsy look; as did the greasy, knotted hair that straggled down below his collar, where many more strands of grey had grown in among the brown.

The visitor went on, 'Are you ill? I fear you must be. This is worse than I'd expected!'

Byron stared back in slack-mouthed wonder, still unsure of what was real and what the construct of a dream. But this pug-faced and barrel-chested figure standing in his cell was surely made of flesh and blood, just as solid and substantial as in their frenzied student days, or when they'd roamed the Continent. Oh, what adventures they had shared. What scrapes dear Hobhouse saved him from! But there were none in which he'd been quite as compromised as now.

In such a dismal setting, his usually staid friend appeared exotic and flamboyant, with his elaborate cravat, and his hair worn in a quiff in the style of Beau Brummel. A quiff that wilted like a flower in the humid atmosphere as tiny beads of perspiration bubbled like diamonds on his brow, running down across the jowls that framed a plump pink mouth – a mouth that trembled as its owner fought to hold back his emotions.

'Don't pity me, dear Hobby!' Byron glumly remarked. 'You know how much I despise pity. But, oh ... how good it is to see you.'

'Well, I was travelling in Florence and thought I'd visit you in Venice. Though I must say I found it strange when you failed to reply to any of my letters.'

'And then you learned I was here. I suppose the whole wide world knows of my shameful fate by now.'

Hobhouse frowned and shook his head. 'Quite the opposite, I'd say. When I called at your palazzo, the maid who met me at the door assumed you'd gone away on some new travels of your own – although where to, or for how long she was unable to inform me.'

'Fletcher wasn't there?' Byron enquired. A flash of hope, the flame of which was quickly doused.

'I presumed he must be with you, that perhaps you'd flitted off to your villa at La Mira. And who could blame you with the atmosphere in Venice at the moment.? It is unbearably hot. And the stink of the canal! Not good for any constitution.'

Byron lowered his face, hoping to hide his disappointment. 'I fear that Fletcher may have gone back to his family in England, and...' Then he asked with urgency, 'Did you by any chance happen to enquire after my menagerie? I have been worrying the creatures won't be cared for in my absence.'

'I did hear a bark or two coming from somewhere in the house.'

'That would be Mutz. How I have missed him.' Byron's face wore the expression of a man who had already climbed the ladder to the gallows, the noose a necklace at his throat.

Hobhouse considered for a moment. 'To be honest, I'd have thought your first concern would be your daughter?'

'She's safe. With the Hoppners. She's been there for quite some time. Even before my arrest.'

'Well, I hope you're not offended, but as one friend to another, wouldn't the child be better off with her mother back in England? I've heard through mutual acquaintances that Claire Clairmont rues the day she ever sent her daughter here. She fears Allegra is neglected, and it seems she is correct – even if this present circumstance is out of your control.'

Stung by pangs of remorse, Byron asked, 'If you have time, could you visit with the Hoppners ... to ensure Allegra's well?'

'I'll do my best,' Hobhouse replied. 'But, back to your menagerie. I may not have seen the animals you keep at the palazzo, but on the way to the square in which my lodgings are located I was accosted by a veritable bear of a man claiming to be your gondolier, along with some young pup of a tatterdemalion.'

'Tita!' Byron exclaimed. 'And was the boy called Nicolo?'

'Correct, on both counts. At first, I thought they must be thieves, quite prepared to raise my fists and box their ears if they should dare to lay a finger on my person. But the big, black-bearded fellow soon assured me of no harm, only said he wished to tell me more about your whereabouts. He said the child, who he was holding by the scruff of his collar, had told him everything about your unfortunate detainment.'

'Ah yes. He was there at the time of my arrest. He would have heard everything.'

'I would have liked to ask him more, but as soon as the man eased his grip the lad was gone. Scampered off before I'd had a chance to say Jack Robinson.'

'Disappearing is his forte.' Byron smiled bitterly. 'I wish I knew the trick of it. Oh, Hobby, I've been charged with the most horrendous crimes, and...'

Byron could not go on. Much like the night when he'd

discovered the woman in the alley, he felt as if he might be drowning. But despite the degradation of his present situation, he was taken with a need to try and elevate the mood, waving an arm about the cell as he asked, 'Well, now you're here, how do you approve of my new summer residence? Not quite as fancy as I'd like, and there's no promise you won't leave without some extra passengers. The place is riddled with vermin.'

He didn't mention the stench, which he knew must be offensive, though for himself he'd gown inured, which was really just as well. Was it not astonishing, the depths a man could sink to and still desire to preserve a little dignity with friends?

Hobhouse smiled at him benignly. 'Only *you* could have arranged to emulate the fate of history's most famous lover, ending up in the same gaol as Giacomo Casanova!'

'He was here?'

'How rare for me to know something Byron does not. In truth, I only heard the tale from Tita earlier. He would insist it's public knowledge that some fifty years ago Casanova found himself arrested by the Inquisition and promptly charged with outrages against the Holy Religion, after which the man was sentenced by the Council of the Ten to five years of isolation. Right here, in The Leads. This could have been his very cell. But...' Hobhouse grew more serious, 'Tita also told me the police who came along on the night of your arrest are widely known to be corrupt, and yet regarding your own fate, there hasn't been a whiff of scandal. That is to say nothing beyond the repercussions of this vampyre novel doing the rounds, and how the Countess Alfieri is a woman possessed, telling anyone who'll listen that the story is a brazen confession of your crimes.'

Byron glumly interrupted, 'I *absolutely* did not write that travesty of a book. I know my name is on the cover, but it's the work of Polidori!'

'You have no need to convince me.' Hobhouse's voice dropped to a whisper, looking back towards the door as if he feared that someone standing on the other side of it might chance to hear him speak. 'I was told a while ago that he'd composed some trashy novel, widely touted in London as a tale fabricated by yourself and the Shelleys when they came to Lake Geneva. All nonsense, of course. I know your style, and this is nothing but the crudest of impostures. Didn't I say at the time when you employed young Polidori, he would be sure to cause you trouble. Ah well,' Hobhouse sighed, his voice returning to full volume, 'we are beyond such matters now.'

Byron replied, 'Yes, you did. Alas, I didn't listen.' Meanwhile, he stared at the grille of metal bars across the window. The very window where he'd dreamed he'd seen the doctor earlier, but where he now saw nothing more than cloaking shadows of a night in which the moon was fugitive. 'God knows,' he carried on, 'I've sinned enough in the past, but to think it's come to this. And worst of all, did you know Teresa Guiccioli's dead?'

'This I have also heard.' Hobhouse spoke regretfully. 'There is much talk of it in Venice, and of your affair with her.'

'And are they also saying that the fault lies at my door?' In his anger and distress Byron was all but railing. 'It isn't true! I am maligned. But there are times when I do wonder, am I a man who is cursed, who brings unhappiness or death to every woman I've desired?'

Hobhouse frowned. 'Surely not all. A hundred must be still alive, and most of them in the best health! But it is true, you have always been a slave to your passions. I've often found your hedonistic tendencies to be offensive. But, deep down, inside your soul, I know you are an honest man, and as such I have loved you as well as any brother. If you say you're innocent, then I accept that is the truth. Why you've been locked inside this prison remains something of a puzzle.'

'To which I wish I knew the answer.' Byron shook his head. 'You tell me Casanova was left to rot in these cells? Do you expect me to take some consolation from his fate ... to wait five years to be released?'

Hobhouse's smile was enigmatic. 'There is some hope in his escape. Is not the lead of which the roofs above your head have been constructed one of nature's softest metals? Casanova had the sense to pull a nail from the floorboards and employ it as a tool, to scratch a hole between the timbers and...' Hobhouse glanced up towards the cobwebs, and the bats that hung suspended, black wings cloaked round their small dog faces '...soon he was squeezing through the gap, over the rooftops, and then crawling through another of the windows, from where he entered a room in which he found sufficient bedsheets to knot together as a ladder. And, by such ingenuity,' Hobhouse ended on a flourish, 'Casanova was free!'

'So as to fuck another day,' Byron said with little humour.

'Indeed! You may decide to write some verses on his exploits as a companion to *Don Juan,* when you're at liberty to do so.'

'By scratching through the lead, and climbing over the roofs?' Exhausted and weak after the month of his ordeal, Byron doubted he'd be capable of walking half a mile, never mind performing antics like a circus acrobat. But surely, he could try. If Hobhouse had a knife...

Hobhouse pressed a finger to his lips, demanding silence as he walked towards the door and called out to the guard, 'Per favore, consenta alla Signora Leigh di entrare nella cella.'

'Augusta?' Byron gasped. 'My sister's here? She's come from England?'

Hobhouse frowned, shaking his head as if some miming Pantomimus, which was confusing when soon afterwards his voice was loudly booming. 'She been travelling with me. We'd been hoping to surprise you. She's only recently been told that this may be the final chance for the two of you to meet. You must try and understand, she is suffering terribly from the guilt and distress of what *her* actions have caused.'

What on earth could Hobhouse mean? There'd been the scandal of his love for his half-sister back in England, but how could *she* bear any guilt for his present situation? How could *he* not be affected by any chance to see her face after an absence of three years, although he feared she'd be disgusted by his much-reduced appearance. By his existence in this hovel.

Concerned with such vain superficials he was entirely unprepared for the scene that followed on – after the jailor once again unlocked the door and it was opened to reveal a slender woman, a great deal taller than Augusta. And, since when had Augusta had hair as black as jet, a few stray wisps of which were poking out below a wide-brimmed bonnet? Apart from the brown eyes, thickly fringed with long dark lashes, Byron could see no mouth or nose due to the lace-edged handkerchief she was holding up against them. No doubt to block the cell's foul odours.

As she moved closer to his side, Hobhouse removed himself to take her place outside the door, where – unbeknownst to Byron – the gaoler then received his second bribe of the night, and with that business then concluded, Hobhouse stood before the hatch, ensuring no-one else could spy upon the meeting of the siblings. If they had, they would have seen the woman dropping the cloth she'd been holding to her mouth and whispering in Byron's ear. No sweet endearments of affection, only the gruffest of demands that he must do as she instructed – which was to strip off his clothes and then replace them with the items she removed from her own person.

At first too slow to comprehend, Byron was aghast when he realised that this was not his precious sister but the elusive Polidori. Seeing again the leering demon from his nightmare, he demanded, 'What are you doing, dressed like this? Have you come to torment me, to take your pleasure in my ruin?'

Polidori looked offended. 'This whole affair has been depressing. I've done my best to drown my sorrows, lost in gambling and brothels, and all but down to my last coins when I noticed your friend Hobhouse sitting at a pavement cafe. He took pity on my plight, and invited me to dine, only then to recount all the rumours he'd been told of your connection to my novel. As you may imagine, I was not totally surprised after our meeting in the morgue...' The doctor paused for emphasis. 'Where you had a special interest in one of the bodies.'

'I told you why at the time. This talk of murder is all lies. But, I wonder,' Byron mused, his muscles tensed, a sudden note of desperation in his voice, 'did you ever ascertain the reason for her death? What caused those marks on her neck?'

'When you'd gone, when I had chance to take a better look, my thoughts remained as inconclusive. The wounds weren't serious enough to cause a death from loss of blood. But she would certainly be weakened and, as I mentioned at the time, she showed some signs of the consumption. However, while discussing this with Hobhouse I did think of something else I'd overlooked. I said no more to him, and I'll say no more to you. I could easily be wrong. But if the corpse has been preserved and is still stored inside the morgue, I mean to visit it again. Hopefully, my recent absence won't have led to my dismissal.'

'You would do this, for me?'

'I admit I feel obliged. If I had never created my Lord Ruthven in your image—' Polidori's words broke off at the sudden sound of knocking, which was the warning sign from Hobhouse that their time was running out.

'We should get on!' hissed Polidori, whereas Byron stood in panic, feeling dizzy, trembling as fingers fumbled with his shirt studs.

Polidori was much swifter. The shawl he'd wrapped around his shoulders, the high-necked gown, and long white gloves that concealed the pelt of hair growing thickly on his arms, were all discarded in but moments. Standing half naked in his drawers, and exhibiting a muscular and densely furred bare chest – a finer specimen of manhood than Byron ever could aspire to – the doctor helped the prisoner remove his own filthy clothes.

'What to do about your boots?' he asked, looking down.

'They'll have to stay in place. But these long skirts should help to hide them.'

Polidori, who'd now dressed in Byron's own discarded rags (most of the seams about to burst), helped to hide Byron's hair under the brim of the bonnet, securing it in place with several pins and wide pink ribbons firmly tied below his chin.

'My beard!' Byron said, to which the doctor glanced about to find the handkerchief he'd dropped. Screwing his nose in disgust, he picked the item up, shaking it free of raisin turds of bats and rats before he thrust it Byron's way and instructed, 'Hold this against your face, just as you saw me do before. It's dark, and that will help. The prison lamps are very dim, but—' He broke off at the clicking of the key in the lock, and stepping close to Byron's side, hissed once more into his ear, 'I'll lie on the bed and keep my face averted. You must affect to be distressed and fall into a swoon. Hobhouse will come inside. He'll lift you in his arms and then he'll carry you out. There is no other way to avoid your limping gait.'

How long did it take? It could have barely been five minutes before they left the prison's doors and climbed aboard the rowing boat, where Tita helped conceal them under mounds of nets and canvas. The stink of fish was suffocating. Some small relief when Hobhouse pulled a miniature of brandy from the pocket of his jacket and pressed it into Byron's hand:

'Drink this! God knows, you need it. You're little more than skin and bone, but even so, having lugged you down those stairs was more demanding than I thought it would be. I'm not so young or so fit as I was in our youth. All those times I heaved you home from drunken revelries in Cambridge. I dare say I shall awake in fits of agony tomorrow.'

'You can rest at my palazzo,' Byron murmured to his friend, before he took a greedy gulp from the bottle he'd been given. Having offered it back, he closed his eyes and lost himself in the hypnotic lap and splash of Tita's oars in the canal – until both he and Hobhouse tensed, hearing the shouts of carousers, which for a moment they'd mistaken for the dreaded hue and cry of prison guards in hot pursuit.

But soon enough the noises faded, and with no sign of any chase, they began to feel at ease. Certainly relaxed enough for Hobhouse to push the fishing nets aside, breathing in less fetid air before he finally announced, 'You can't return to your palazzo. The very first place they would look. You haven't jumped from the pan only to fall back in the fire.'

'Where else am I to go? And what of Polidori? He will surely be in danger.' Byron's voice came slow and slurred. A combination of his fever, of exhaustion, and the numbing effect of alcohol.

Hobhouse considered for a moment. 'When it comes to Polidori, there are risks in the plan, but to be honest, I don't think I could have stopped him if I'd tried. He seems to me to be a man who no longer has a care if he should live or die ... though *this* new escapade of yours appeared to fire him with some purpose. He feels responsible, you see. As indeed he ought to do. But, by the time the morning comes, when it's discovered that Lord Byron has miraculously grown two perfect feet in the night, there'll be no doubt that the cat is out of the bag. Polidori will claim to have been kidnapped and then forced into the cell by the same rogues who enabled your escape. If his story's not convincing, I've taken some precautions. I did at first consider Hoppner, in his role as British consul. But I assumed you would prefer your friend remained in ignorance of this unfortunate affair. Instead, I wrote, anonymously, to this Inspector Russo man, the letter lodged at the headquarters of La Forsa of Venice. I said it was outrageous that a man of noble birth, and an Englishman at that, should be subjected to such treatment, with no adherence to the natural procedures of the law. I also said I was prepared to take the story to the press, both here in Italy and England, although,' Hobhouse bit his lip, 'that would mean publicity. For myself as well as you.

And these days I have to think of my political ambitions.' Hobhouse continued through a frown: 'If your abductors really are as corrupt as Tita says, the very last thing they will want is the risk of such exposure. Of course, there is no guarantee they won't come after you again. But Tita says he knows a place where you'll be safe. Somewhere he's sure no-one will ever think to look.'

Hearing no reply, Hobhouse turned through the gloom to see that Byron was asleep, a greasy coil of rope forming the pillow for his head.

With the grimmest of smiles, he raised the bottle to his lips, briefly wincing at the burn before he muttered to himself, 'My old friend, let's hope you are as innocent as you profess.'

Fifteen

And all my sins, and half my woe,
But talk no more of penitence...

Byron. From *The Giaovr*

What a joy to hold a pen & set down words upon a page. The nightmare time of my confinement in The Leads was all the worse for such a wicked deprivation, whereas here on the monastery island of Lazzaro I may write at liberty.

I must confess I have no memory at all of my arrival. When I first woke, I imagined I was in another prison. But then, what prison smells of incense? What prison bed has laundered sheets, which I pushed back to see the sunlight streaming through an unbarred window? How it glimmered on the golden crucifix above a prayer desk, then shafted in through the door, when it was suddenly opened & there was Hobby, smiling broadly to discover I was conscious.

He said I'd been asleep for days & this our fourth upon the island. He'd been so anxious for my life the herbalist had been called in to offer potions of sedation, for I'd been raving like a madman, shouting out Teresa's name & insisting I must die so as to be with her again.

How her fate oppressed my heart, with yet more sadness to bear when Hobhouse said it was now time for him to journey back to Venice & from thence return to England. He only wished he'd had more time to enjoy my company, but this visit was not one he'd be forgetting in a hurry, having exceeded all adventures & excitements of the past. 'Byron...' he concluded, 'when will you settle to a life more predictable & dull?'

The man himself is the embodiment of staid dependability, though how incongruous he looked in that monastery cell, with his flattened coxcomb quiff & both his thumbs hooked in the pockets of his gilt-embroidered waistcoat. Was he aware of the smell of rancid fish he was exuding? Hobby does like to be well groomed, to the point of stuffiness. Even as a student he presented the demeanour of a man a great deal older than his natural years. So often people have remarked on the oddness of our bond, but I don't think it accidental. Without a father in my life, Hobhouse was ~ indeed still is ~ the paternalistic friend who has supplied the heavy hand too often needed on my shoulder. He may aspire to politics, but I believe his character is better suited to the clergy. An amiable village vicar, forgiving sinners of his parish, just as he's always had the grace to forgive me in the past, or else to fabricate the stories that excuse my bad behaviour.

With this particular scrape, he said he'd told the monks who'd received us on the island that he'd placed me in their care in the strictest confidence, for I had suffered from the illness of ~ this was the gist of it ~ 'a transient insanity brought on by melancholia'. I suppose what he said held some element of truth. But how ridiculous it sounded, & I told him so as well. Still, Hobhouse was proud of his ad hoc diagnosis, rocking on his heels & puffing out his barrel chest before he said he'd hit the bull's eye, with my arrival being made in the guise of women's clothing which, if nothing else, proved I'd not been quite myself. With regard to my sojourn in The Leads, he insisted I say nothing of the matter, for even here among the monks there may be men who would betray me to my enemies in Venice.

Just as this conversation ended, a heavy knock came at the door & I received what was to be the morning's second visitor ~ being Father Paschal Aucher, the monk historian with whom I'd grown acquainted in the days after I'd first arrived in Venice. Back then, I'd often visited the monastery to study, learning the basics of his language with the intention of compiling a grammar that translated English to Armenian. Sadly, these laudable ambitions were to fail when I succumbed to the more carnal temptations the city had to offer, & now I felt some trepidation, for would my tutor & friend hold some grudge at that betrayal?

I had no need to fear. The small Armenian's dark eyes gleamed bright with warmth & welcome. In his simple long black habit, a flat black cap placed on his head & silver cross upon his breast, his calming presence filled the cell, as did the most formidable of beards grown on his chin, its oiled blackness barred with white suddenly bringing to mind the badger I'd once kept as a pet when a child. I raised a hand to my own chin. Whatever beard I might have grown made a poor comparison. What's more, I feared it full of lice that I had carried from The Leads.

Striving for some dignity, I struggled up from the bed & dragged the sheet around my body in the manner of a toga, only to hear Aucher laugh. In the gravelly deep voice stressed with the accents of his homeland, he said I'd need to find a crown if it was now my intention to walk about the monastery as if some Roman emperor. In return I then informed him of the time I'd spent in Rome, when I'd commissioned a bust to be made of my head, though having seen the laurel wreath the sculptor placed on top of it I came to rue my vanity, for I looked less a man & more like a Christmas pudding.

Still, the question had been raised. What was I to wear?

The answer came when Hobhouse stooped to lift a bag full of clothes that Tita had collected from my own palazzo closet. The two of them had considered everything that might be needed, & with more kindness to come when Father Aucher then suggested I might like to take a bath before a breakfast in the gardens.

At that, he left, & Hobhouse followed, leaving me alone again, until some other monks arrived, lugging a wooden tub between them. The water poured from large stone jugs was but lukewarm & barely deep enough to rise more than an inch above my buttocks. But what bliss to soap my skin, lying back as one young man began to wash my hair & beard, even the growth between my legs, afterwards applying oils of some concoction he assured me would eradicate all vermin. I must admit there was a time when those caresses would most certainly have led to the arousal of what no amount of scum upon the water could conceal. But I was feeble & exhausted. In no mood for new affections.

Dressed & clean, I left the cell & made my way towards the courtyard, finding Hobhouse at a table underneath some trailing vines. Glad of the shade & of the breeze blowing in from the lagoon, I soon devoured every item of the food set out before us ~ which left my friend with mouth agape, being more used to see me pick & then discard most of my meals. I also savoured the coffee, though it was a little thin & nothing like the perfect brew that Fletcher always makes. (I should say 'used' to make. His absence is the greatest loss.) The oranges were sweet as sugar. The bread could not be fresher, still steaming from the ovens. There was also the preserve which is a speciality of the island of Lazzaro, being made by the monks from the petals of the roses growing here in abundance. They mix them into water steeped with lemon juice & sugar to make a jam called Vartanush. It tastes of Turkish Delight & Hobby liked it very much; so much so that by the time Tita came to ferry him back to Venice again, he'd stuffed two jars into his pockets to sustain him on his travels ...

Byron walked the dusk-lit island as the monks attended Vespers, chanting prayers below the stars of the cerulean-blue heaven in their jewel box of a chapel. He liked to hear their mournful voices drift towards him on the jetty where, several weeks ago, Hobhouse had clutched at Tita's arm and launched his bulk onto a boat. The craft had dipped alarmingly, but Hobby soon regained his natural equilibrium, waving at Byron as he'd called, 'Rest assured, I'll pay a visit to the Hoppners at the Consul. I'll enquire about Allegra. Tita will bring you word.'

'And my menagerie...' Byron began, but did not finish, seeing the scowl on Hobby's face as he settled on the bench of the shrimp-tailed batela, a boat more stable than a gondola for crossing rougher waters.

Tita sat holding the oars, as immobile as a statue. Squinting against the sun, his eyes fixed firmly on Byron's as if the gondolier already had some news to impart. But, for then, nothing was said. Tita turned his head away and manoeuvred the boat out to the blue of the lagoon.

Every evening after that, Byron stared through the distant haze in which the domes and spires of Venice rose as if a desert mirage. He'd watch them disappear as the skies fell into darkness, after which he would retire to his cell to read alone. It mattered not what it was. Any words and any subject to distract his mind from turning to events over which he had no hope of control.

But, on this night, he realised he'd left the book he wished to read in the island's library. Deciding to retrieve it, he found the building steeped in gloom, though the moon was almost full and ample light shone through the windows to illuminate the aisles running between tall racks of shelving. Even if it had been darker, he was familiar with this maze. He could have walked with both eyes closed across the polished wooden boards, below the ornate plaster ceilings, between the cabinets that held, not only rare and ancient books, but an eclectic mix of treasures brought to Lazzaro by the monks when they'd first made the place their home. This museum of their past contained the stumps of marble columns and fractured porticos from temples. There were fading painted murals, statues of saints and pottery of the most intricate designs. And, of course, there were Bibles. Some enormous specimens. Many on stands with covers open to show illuminated texts.

He paused before one page of parchment adorned with gilded capitals above cramped lines of black-inked words, and underneath the somewhat primitive rendition of a man who was plunging down head-first through skies of stars and meteors.

'Is this Satan, being cast out of Heaven into Hell?' Byron spoke the words aloud and was surprised to hear an answer:

'An understandable mistake, but if you read the script below, it tells of quite a different story.' Father Aucher made his way along the aisle to Byron's side, where he continued to explain, 'That's not another Holy Gospel, but a medieval record of every demon known to man. It was used by exorcists who wished to name the evil spirits driving men to acts of madness.'

'I don't remember seeing it in the library before.'

'It is a recent acquisition.'

'Well, if this isn't Lucifer...' Byron looked puzzled as he asked, 'Who is it meant to be?'

'Another fallen angel,' Aucher bluntly replied, as if this was a truth as indisputable to know as the beard upon his chin. 'Don't they say a host of them followed the Devil into Hell?'

Byron looked back at the page. In the bottom right-hand corner was another illustration. It showed two men who were lying in the strangest of positions, both reclining on the ground in such a way that each appeared to be the mirror of the other.

Their heads and upper torsos were quite whole and independent, but where their legs were entwined, they looked like stumps, no feet to see. Did the picture represent some unnatural freak of nature? A pair of twins whose flesh had fused while still inside the mother's womb? Byron had witnessed travesties of such a kind in circus shows, with the poor afflicted souls being mocked, abused and prodded at with sticks by hell-born babes who lacked all common decency. Or – his head tipped to one side – were the two of them engaged in some act of carnal passion?

Aucher disturbed his reverie: 'We keep the remains of such a creature on Lazzaro. Would you like to see?'

'A freak of nature?' Byron asked.

'No. Some mummified remains.'

Byron's interest was piqued. At the same time memories flashed bright before his eyes. Polidori in the morgue. The racks of pickled specimens. The dead girl lying on the sacking. What *had* happened to her corpse?

The awful vision dissolved when Father Aucher raised both hands and gently cupped Byron's chin. Byron himself remained quite still, not knowing how he should respond or what the monk's intention was. After all, why had he followed Byron to the library? Why had he left the other monks to their chanting in the chapel? Had Byron misconstrued the true foundation of their friendship? Yes, they'd formed a mutual bond during their studies in the past. But the brothers of Lazzaro were very different to those he'd once befriended while in Greece, where any sexual attraction between two men was deemed as natural and not considered a sin – which was appealing to a youth who'd been so eager to explore every delight that life could offer. Still, it came as a relief when Father Aucher dropped his hands and asked again, with some concern, 'Are you sure you wish to see? It is not for the faint of heart.'

A lamp was found to light their way through the night-time library. At last, they reached one corridor, narrower than the rest, and where the books stacked on the shelves on either side exuded pungent scents of leather and vanilla, and under that the faintest scent of something acrid. The smell of burning?

Father Aucher dipped a hand into the folds of his habit, drawing out an iron key to unlock a hidden door, ingeniously disguised as a panel in the wall. There was a scraping of metal and then a click, and with one push the door whined open on its hinges to expose another chamber; a room no more than ten feet square, and lacking any windows to draw in fresh ventilation. The smell of burning came again as Aucher walked ahead of Byron, the light of his lantern flickering on grey stone walls, and then a simple wooden box resting on a metal stand in the centre of the room.

Aucher set the lantern down on the casket's long glass lid. Light shimmered on the body of the mummy underneath it. As far as Byron could see, the corpse's flesh was well preserved, though somewhat blackened by the years. A set of withered genitals proved that it had been a male, as did the well-developed chest. The face had striking eyes, both being opened wide. The whites were clear, irises blue, which made a vivid contrast to the darker flesh around them.

'Uncanny, isn't it?' Father Aucher turned to Byron. 'The way those eyes look almost real. Like the portraits in some paintings, they seem to follow when you move. But...' Here Aucher paused, beckoning for Byron to come closer, 'what you see is an illusion formed by artistry and pigment. These eyes are painted on the lids, which I assure you are closed. Although, what lies underneath them...?'

As Aucher let the question hang, Byron remained some feet away, but still quite able to observe the body in sufficient detail. The head was bald. The ears each side of it appeared to be intact. Where shrunken flesh stretched tight across them, the angles of the cheek bones were prominent to see. But, even in such a state, who could deny that this had been a handsome man when still alive. No-one who looked at these remains could not be moved by the allure and the sense of mystery. So, why did Byron feel afraid?

He'd once viewed the Sloane collection in the British Museum – something strangely alien in the spells and the paintings that adorned the golden caskets, the scents of cinnamon and myrrh rising from the linen wrappings in which the bodies were preserved. In Italy, he'd visited the famous mummies of Palermo, the catacombs containing corpses of the dead in their thousands. How grotesque some had been, suspended from the walls, dressed in decaying silks and lace. How desperately affecting were the withered husks of children. But none of them appeared as living, whereas this mummy at Lazzaro looked as if it was but sleeping; that it might wake at any moment.

Byron moved a little closer, and only then observed the way the neck, the wrists and the ankles had been secured by metal chains fixed to the casket's wooden base. 'Why would you manacle a corpse?' he asked in some surprise.

Aucher considered for a moment. 'As you know, the first monks who came to settle on this island brought with them sacred objects saved from looting or destruction. Most of them are on display. But where this relic was concerned something unexpected happened, after which the monks decided to conceal the body here, warning all who were to follow that it should never be released.'

'How does one release the dead?'

Aucher shrugged. 'There are records of a young librarian who'd once worked here in the museum, where the mummy was displayed. First, he'd complained of a fever, and then debilitating headaches. He grew to be lethargic, whereas before he'd always had the heartiest of constitutions. From the description of his illness, I have occasionally wondered if he'd suffered from typhoid ... if that condition could have caused the bruising rashes on his neck. He also had hallucinations, afterwards saying he had seen the mummy opening its eyes so as to stare at him directly, as if the very Lazarus who Jesus raised from the dead, and after whom this island's named.

'Believing he had seen the holiest of miracles, the monk first fell to his knees, whereupon, or so he claimed, the mummy spoke to him. None of these words are recorded, being in an unknown language, but they were said to exert a most powerful seduction. Some form of spell or arcane magic that caused the monk to be entranced, only waking again to find that he was lying in the arms of the mummy as it nuzzled at his neck. Almost as if – and I repeat only what's written in the annals – as if the corpse had been reborn a human child driven by instinct to suckle at its mother's breast.

'When this perverse, unnatural hunger to feed had been assuaged, the creature seemed content. The monk returned it to its case, where once again it grew so still it appeared to be dead. But recovered from his daze, the man grew mortally afraid, and so much so that, at first, he dared not tell another soul of what he had experienced. He feared his brothers would assume he'd gone insane, or else been driven by the lust of mortal sins too horrible for him to speak of. But, unable to forget the glamour of the spell, he was beguiled to return. In the end, the loss of blood resulted in his death. Only in his final hours did he confess to this unnatural communion he'd shared, after which he begged his brothers to destroy the evil creature or risk the danger of more men being enticed in the same way.'

Father Aucher heaved a sigh.

'As you can imagine not everyone believed the story, but some monks who were present at the time of this confession were convinced he spoke the truth, which was why it was decided that his body should be burned instead of being buried. In case his soul had been infected with the blood of the undead and he also rose again.'

'Hmm.' Byron sounded dubious. 'I myself may have been ravished more than any other soul since the Trojan wars began, and yet I find it near impossible to imagine a man being seduced by a corpse. Could it be that these delusions led to a mass hysteria? Why burn the body of the monk, but leave the mummy still intact?'

'Ah, but they *did* try to burn it. What you see here today is somewhat changed from the specimen delivered to the island.'

'Changed? In what way?' Only now did Byron notice what looked like blisters on the skin, many more around the mouth, where lips were plumper than expected and slightly parted to show the tips of white incisors, with not a hint of the darkness discolouring the flesh. Perhaps the black was natural?

'Could this man have been a Moor? There are many here in Venice. Could he have been a slave?'

Father Aucher shook his head. 'No slave would be preserved like this. Embalming is expensive. And then there is the fact that all surviving records state the mummy was not black on the day of its arrival. Quite the opposite in fact. They describe the corpse's skin being as pale as alabaster, and so translucent that the veins were visible below the surface. It also had a head of abundant golden hair.'

Father Aucher looked perturbed, lifting both hands to clasp the cross that was hanging at his chest. 'You need to understand. This was a less enlightened age. To see a corpse so beautiful, and with no signs of decay after many centuries was attributed to powers beyond our human comprehension. Such was the fear that an ancient evil curse had been awakened, it was agreed by everyone that the body should be doused in holy oils and then cremated on the pyre beside their brother. But the mummy would not burn. It remained entirely whole.'

'Another sort of miracle,' Byron murmured to himself while continuing to stare at what lay below the glass.

Whether sacred or profane, the flesh still looked quite pliant, even rubbery in texture. *Almost* – Byron considered – *as if it is alive, or like my doomed model Venus, an effigy of wax.*

'I suppose...' he carried on, moving close to Aucher's side, 'the lack of hair on the head and around the genitals must have resulted from the fire. But the eyes – don't you think the paint would have dissolved? And the lids – are lashes growing? And here,' he touched a finger to the glass above the face, 'are those bristles on the chin?'

Aucher inclined his head to take a closer look. 'I don't recall them there before. But then, regretfully, my sight has been failing for some years.'

'Hair can still grow after death.' Byron spoke with confidence, but seeds of doubt were niggling. 'Would that still be the case with a body that's been burned, that's been dead so many years?'

'Didn't your Shakespeare once claim there are stranger things in Heaven and on earth than may be dreamed of in mankind's philosophy?'

'And you?' Byron asked. 'What do *you* dream of or believe in?'

'What I believe in does not matter. But I confess there is a motive in me bringing you here.'

'Which is?'

'Lazzaro is an island, but not so very far from Venice that we do not hear the rumours and the scandals of the city. Recently, there has been news of a novel you have written. The story of an undead soul, or what Armenians would name as a dakhanavar.'

'What can I say? It isn't true. A man called Polidori wrote it.'

'And yet *you* flee from the city, seeking sanctuary here. Why is that, my friend? I see the sorrow in your face. I see how every night you walk the boundaries of this island, staring back towards the place that was your home till recently. Are you mourning the life and the lovers left behind? I do not judge, but I must ask why it is you don't return? You are not ill. You are not mad. What has made you so afraid?'

If only I could say, Byron thought before repeating what Aucher had just uttered, 'Dakhanavar? Tell me more.' His eyes flicked back towards the corpse as Father Aucher carried on:

'There is a myth told by my people that among the fallen angels who followed Satan to his doom, there was one who'd seen the nakedness of Eve when she'd been lured by the serpent to eat from the tree of good and evil – the fruit with which she then beguiled the first man from innocence. From that time on, the demon yearned to know the pleasures of the flesh as enjoyed by mortal men who lived upon the earth. As the millennia then passed, his desire kept on increasing, until, at last, he found a way to manifest in human form. Cloaked in a spell of radiant beauty, charming all who were to meet him, he seduced countless lovers, and in this way his seed was spread, leading in turn to the birth of the monstrous half-breed creatures that are called the dakhanavars. These, the first-spawned of the vampyres, were feral in their nature, but much like their demon father they possessed unearthly beauty and a dislike of natural light. Also like him, they had to feed their mortal bodies to survive. And the food they came to crave – the one that satisfied them most – was that of human blood.

'As the slaughtering began, and very soon grew more intense, most assumed that the sudden rise in deaths was the result of a new plague in the land. But when the truth was discovered, many men gathered together so as to track the demons down. Realising that the vampires were afraid of light or fire, they drove them out from the villages and towns with burning torches. Those they caught were staked and burned, but it was said some dakhanavar still survived, even thrived in the mountains and the forests, living in caves like animals, from which they sometimes crept at night to stalk unwary travellers. Waiting until their prey was sleeping, they would attack and plunge their teeth into the ankles or the feet...' Father Aucher snorted loudly. 'I'm sure it can't be very pleasant, but for some reason I have always found that detail comical.'

'I suppose a neck or breast would be a little more romantic,' Byron suggested with a smile.

'This is true,' Aucher agreed. 'And why, as time went by, the demons were said to have evolved more cunning ways of luring their prey, and why their victims had to find some alternative protection. As in the tales from other cultures, it seems the dakhanavar are averse to smells of garlic. That's why Armenians who travel in the wilderness today carry the bulbs or the flowers of the plant inside their pockets. At night, they mash them to a paste which they rub over their feet. They toss what's left onto their fires, hoping the stench as it burns will drive the predators away. There is also an old folk tale about two shepherds in the mountains who deceived one of the demons, each of the men hiding his feet underneath the other's head.'

'Not the cleverest of souls then, these so-called dakhanavars?' Byron said, as he recalled the illustration he'd seen, in which two men lay end to end and appeared to have no feet.

Father Aucher shook his head. 'Who can say, when so many of these tales are based on nothing more than fear and ignorance? But there are those who believe that demons walk upon the earth, and as I mentioned before, there were monks here on the island who trusted the monk who said this corpse had sucked his blood. They also believed' – Aucher's next words spilled out much faster – 'that *this* is not a dakhanavar, but the demon who first spawned them. That's why the body would not burn, being already well inured to the blazing fires of Hell. The charring of the skin had not been caused by any pyre the monks created to destroy it, but only happened afterwards when the flames had all burned out and a new day began to rise. It was exposure to the sunlight that caused the flesh to crack and blacken. I dare say Hades is hot, but the sun in the sky is still too near to God in Heaven for any demon to endure. Ah well...' Aucher sighed. 'Perhaps they should have left it and permitted God to finish what his banishment had started. But fearing what might happen when the dark of night returned, the corpse was chained within this tomb.'

This narrative was too extreme for any sane man to believe in, but Byron felt a chilling frisson of excitement when he asked, 'Do *you* think it is true? What about the other monks in the monastery today?'

'Until tonight, I've been the only man alive to know this secret. As such, I sometimes visit to ensure that nothing here has...' He glanced down at the corpse. 'That nothing has changed. And yet,' his voice became more earnest, 'there have been times when I have sensed the essence of some other spirit also with me in this chamber. I'm sure there has to be some natural explanation, but my reaction's always been to place my trust in God. To stand and pray for any soul that once inhabited this body to find eternal rest.'

'A form of exorcism?'

'Perhaps you'd call it that. But much stronger is my instinct to see it driven back to Hell, or, failing that, wrapped up in chains and carried out to sea, discarded where the water is so deep it could never hope to rise back up again.'

With that, Father Aucher retrieved his lantern from the case, leading Byron from the chamber and securing the door before they left the library. As they emerged into the night Byron stared across the lawns that lay beyond the pillared walkway, where their shadows looked like phantoms trapped by the bars of a cage. For a moment he forced himself to think of nothing more than inhaling the sweetness of the roses that were clambering about the garden walls. Another intake of breath and he heard the sombre sounds of male voices chanting Latin: '*Deus in adiutorium meum intende. Domine, ad adiuvandum me festina. Gloria Patri, et Filio, et Spiritui Sancto.*' – Oh God, come to my aid. Oh Lord, make haste to help me.

'Shouldn't you be praying too?' he turned to ask Father Aucher. 'Not squandering your time with the Lord Infidel of Venice?'

Aucher's expression was benign. 'I do not judge why you are here. Such confessions may be saved for the ears of He who does. He who absolves the worst of sinners, *if* they are willing to repent.'

'Father, I am no saint, but when I first came to this island, I was inspired by your example to spend my life in studying and the writing of my verses, to try and be a better man than the one who'd fled from England. As you know, that didn't last. I am weak, and much too fond of the pleasures of the flesh, although this year I did resign myself to being more restrained. But—'

'There is always a "but",' Father Aucher interrupted. 'I'm guessing that the object of your passion has turned out to be a married woman. Someone who's unavailable?'

'She *was* married, but no longer. Now...'

Before he could continue, the monk attempted to console him, but with no real understanding of the tragic circumstances at the heart of Byron's sadness: 'You are a man lost in romance, who falls in love three times a year. But, in the eyes of God, and by the law of this land, a married woman must be loyal to her husband in this life or face damnation in the next. You should think of her soul. You will find some other lover. And let us hope the next is free of any sacred obligations.'

'Father, she is dead! Our love was doomed from the start, not least because of the lies being spread all over Venice.'

'Lies?' the monk enquired.

'The Countess Alfieri read this wretched vampyre novel and I fear it's turned her mind, confusing Polidori's fiction with an unfortunate event that happened earlier this year ... a night when I was present at the scene of a crime that sadly ended in a death. Now she slanders me in public. She and a vicious brothel keeper are both claiming I'm a man whose lust for blood has led to murder. Thanks to them, I was arrested and imprisoned in The Leads. That is until Hobhouse devised the means of my escape, after which he brought me here, and...'

'Slow down. You go too fast.' Father Aucher raised a hand to stroke his fingers through his beard. 'I know a little myself about this Countess Alfieri. Is she not a patron of a charity that cares for children from the streets? Ah yes,' the monk went on. 'The scandals of the city often fly on wings of gulls that come to shit here on Lazzaro. You see, around five years ago, one of our monks became involved with this woman and her work. His name was Petros. He was young, and he doubted his vocation. So, we sent him to the city, where his talents could be used in other less restrictive ways, such as gathering alms for the convents where the orphans could be housed and educated. At the same time, regretfully, he grew suspicious of wrong-doings, writing to tell us of some children being sold into the brothels. With that letter, Petros also sent his crucifix to us – to prove the message came from him. Since then, I've often wondered if the Countess Alfieri might have learned of his plans to go to the authorities, and—' Aucher broke off, mulling over his next words for several moments. 'On the other hand, it *may be* that, just like you, the woman was the victim of some idle city gossip, that whatever Petros heard was nothing other than conjecture. As you know only too well, things are not always what they seem, and jealous tongues can be malicious. The only thing of which I'm certain is that he sent us no more letters. To all intents and purposes, Petros vanished from this world.'

Byron sounded dubious. 'I can't imagine the Countess spending time with a monk, but then again she is obsessed with Matthew Lewis and his novel. Do you happen to know it? A tedious gothic romp, at times grotesque and quite horrific. A fevered plot with bleeding nuns and the corruption of—'

'I do not know or wish to know it,' Father Aucher answered sternly, before a sigh of resignation. 'What are we to do with you? I would like to offer help, but for the sake of the monks who continue living here, I must also be aware of any future repercussions. If it is known that a man so recently accused of murder is concealed within our midst, can you not see the dilemma? We are settled. We are safe. But if we were forced to flee...'

'I would be mortified to think my presence here should lead to that!' The blood roared loud in Byron's ears as he babbled out the rest. 'I can see you've been placed in an impossible position. If you could only spare a boat, then I can sail to the Lido. If not, then I could swim. It's not so far away. I have my horses stabled there. I'll go...'

Where could he go?

'No!' Aucher answered firmly. 'Not that I doubt your ability to swim that stretch of water, at least in times of better health. But...' he took hold of Byron's hand to accentuate his point, 'you are too hasty with presumptions. I *do* fear for my brothers, knowing full well that this countess has many influential friends. If she wished, she could make our lives impossible. But, when it comes to your dilemma, *if* you are truly innocent, then my advice is that you hasten back to Venice to defend your name and reputation. If, as you say, you're innocent, then trust in God. He'll guide your path.' Aucher dropped Byron's hand, 'What is the alternative? This is a sinister affair. If you have lied to me then I am foolish and naive. But, as your friend, and for the sake of my long-lost brother Petros, who I fear to be dead, I want the truth to be exposed. You should also seek some justice for these murdered prostitutes – if not by yours, then by whose hands? Are you prepared to close your eyes and turn away, to leave the killer free to slay another victim?'

As Father Aucher finished speaking Byron realised the chanting of the monks had also ended. The chapel doors were opening, releasing wafts of burning incense as several men in long black robes wandered out of them like ghosts. Heads were bowed. Hands were held to breasts in silent prayer. Their serenity in faith was something Byron greatly envied. But, even now, without Teresa, could he tolerate a life fettered by prayers and promises of abstinence from sexual pleasures, or was he likely to embody the abbot as portrayed in Matthew Lewis's *The Monk*. A man who shuddered with desire whenever kneeling to pray before a beautiful Madonna, never able to detach the allure of mortal flesh from the spiritual divine?

Apart from which, Aucher was right. He should not shy away

from justice. He was not a hunted fox, run to ground and cowering while the howling dogs of Venice came snapping at his heels. He would leave the monastery and return to his palazzo. He would seek justice from all those who had conspired to destroy him.

The mind that broods o'er guilty woes
Is like the Scorpion girt by fire

Byron. From *The Giaovr*

A night of ghastly dreams lingered on in Byron's mind. Even when he'd left his cell to eat a solitary breakfast in the monastery courtyard, he was still haunted by the thought of Father Aucher's demon mummy – so much so his muscles tensed in a dread anticipation when he was suddenly aware of a presence close behind him. A figure blocking out the sun, its shadow falling long and dark across the table's pure white linen.

He turned to see no risen corpse, only his burly gondolier. Tita's abundant oiled black hair fell in ringlets to his shoulders. Golden medallions were glinting on the tanned and naked breast below a ruffled open shirt. It was a look accentuating his piratical demeanour. The cocky confidence and swagger so often echoed by Byron in his verses of *Don Juan*.

'Tita!' Bryon inhaled the musky masculinity of the sweat the man exuded. 'What brings you to the island, and at this hour of the morning?'

'Where do I begin?'

'Is there so much to tell?' Byron's anxiety was rising. 'Is all well at my palazzo? What of my daughter at the Hoppners?'

'It's to do with La Fornarina. She's been visiting again.'

Hearing the woman's name, Byron spoke through gritted teeth, 'How dare she show her face again after the trouble she has caused? Does the woman know no shame?'

'She wanted to apologise.' Tita looked a little shifty. 'And I should do the same. That model made of wax, the one you asked me to hide, I showed it to her once. A big mistake. I see that now. And then, when Margarita heard about your vampyre novel, well, that's what gave her the idea. How was she supposed to know those officers would go and think they'd found a real body, or that you'd end up in The Leads? Now, she insists she's still your friend and will do everything she can to put things right for you again.'

'It was never my novel! And hasn't this come rather late?' Byron snapped angrily, but then grew philosophical. 'After this, she and I can never be friends. Even without her treachery, an affair between the sexes rarely subsides to such a bond. It is different with men. In the main, they hold less grudges.'

There was a pause during which his eyes locked with the gondolier's before he carried on again.

'Do you have reason to resent me? It was never my intention to involve you in the turmoil of these recent events. If you have the slightest doubt – I mean about my innocence – I don't expect you to remain in my employment any longer. I suppose what I am asking is, are you still a friend or an enemy of Byron? Do you believe I am a man who is capable of murder? Because, if you do...'

He broke off as he recalled the fair-haired woman in the alley, nagged yet again by the fact that it had been the very night when Tita's disappearance from his post beside the boat fitted exactly with the moments when the crime had been committed. But hadn't Tita been grogged and busy with another whore, which was not unusual. He seemed to know most of the women of the night-time trade in Venice, and in turn had introduced Byron to the other half. As La Fornarina had once said, Tita was a rogue. But a rogue was one thing, a cut-throat murderer another.

As if he'd heard Byron's thoughts, Tita fixed him with a look, not of a servant, but an equal. 'If you are guilty, so am I.'

'Which means you think I am!'

Tita shrugged. 'Of many things, but not of killing anyone.'

'Well, others do, and here I am.' Byron mused on his dilemma. 'Could Nicolo be involved? I saw him hiding in my study the night I was arrested. But why? What was he doing?'

'Only watching. Listening. He is devoted to you. He also knows those officers who turned up at your palazzo were already bought and paid for by your enemies in Venice, and—'

'I guessed they were corrupt,' Byron interrupted. 'But did you know La Fornarina had the nerve to tell that Russo man I'd forced her to strip naked and read from pornographic books? It is quite ridiculous. The woman is illiterate! At least…' all at once he was overcome by doubt, 'she told me she was.'

Suddenly, it seemed that everything he'd known or once believed in had foundations built on sand. He was glad of the distraction when Tita reached into a pocket and pulled out an envelope.

'For you, from Signor Hobhouse. Wrote it before he left the city. Said he was glad to be off, that all the water made him seasick.'

'Let me see!' Byron said, snatching the envelope. At the same time, he indicated to the food left on the table. 'If you're hungry, go ahead. I have no appetite today.'

As if he'd not been fed in weeks, Tita grabbed an orange, biting through the skin and slurping at the juice in the most disgusting manner. For one horrible moment Byron pictured his servant kneeling over a woman, sucking the blood from her throat. But, shaking his head to dispel such awful thoughts, he forced his mind to concentrate on nothing more than the words on the page held in his hand.

My dearest B,

I write in haste as I make the preparations for my journey back to London. But rest assured what little time I've had to spare these past few days has not been spent in idleness.

First, the news of Polidori, for whom you need have no concerns. Indeed, he came to visit my hotel this very day. He wasn't in the best of health. Somewhat feverish and pale after his stay in The Leads, though the doctor would insist his affliction was no more than a mild summer cold. In between his coughs and sniffles, which I assure you were not mild, he then explained how he'd been freed. It took no more than a shout at the cell door to fetch the guard, though that was not the end of it. Polidori was subjected to several hours of questioning, during which he denied any knowledge whatsoever of your present whereabouts (which is quite true – I did not tell him). Whether or not he was believed is neither here nor there. In the end he was released and is at liberty again.

However, your own fate still weighs heavy on his conscience, which leads me to believe I may have judged the man unfairly after meetings in the past. Yes, he is arrogant and vain, but he does have a moral compass. Having aided your escape, he now insists he'll do his best to put right all this confusion over his novel's authorship. Well, we shall see what comes of that, for I doubt the fellow wields one single ounce of influence. I only wish he did.

The other news I have to tell concerns your daughter, Allegra. When I visited the consul to enquire about the child, I was informed that the Hoppners have upped and gone to Switzerland, where they will spend the summer months. But, not knowing where you were, and receiving no replies to any letters they'd directed to the Palazzo Mocenigo, it seemed they thought it for the best to leave Allegra in the care of other friends here in the city. She now resides with Mrs Martens, the Danish consul's wife. I paid the woman a visit and saw Allegra for myself. I thought the child a little thin and rather wan in her complexion, but remarkably erudite in speech and comprehension.

Byron set the letter down. This news of his daughter came as something of a shock. The Hoppners may have acted in Allegra's best interest, but when it came to the wife of the Venetian Danish consul, he possessed not one clue about the woman's character.

More cheerful was the news of Polidori's release. It could be clutching at straws, but at their meeting in The Leads the doctor *had* suggested there was something he'd neglected to consider when it came to the girl in the morgue.

'I have to hope,' Byron murmured, all at once growing aware of the music emanating from the monastery chapel. A hymn to mark the hour of Terce. Soothed by the beauty of the voices, he raised his eyes to the skies, where darker clouds were gathering. A storm was surely brewing, but for then, when another shaft of sunlight pierced the grey, it seemed as if a glaring spotlight filled the stage on which he played – not himself, but a shadow of the man he used to be. Byron could feel his body blurring, his life fragmenting, so diminished he'd be sure to disappear if he remained another day on the island of Lazzaro.

His mind was quite resolved when he asked more urgently, 'Tita, do you think my palazzo's being watched? Is it safe to return?'

There was a pause while Tita swallowed down his final mouth of food, then fastidiously brushed at breadcrumbs tangled in his beard. 'Well, I'd say their game of cat-and-mouse has come to an end since your escape from The Leads. And La Fornarina's been busy spreading the word that you've gone off on some new exotic travels. India's what she came up with. The furthest place she could imagine. By now the whole of Venice will have heard the story too. Nobody will imagine you'll be back there in a hurry.'

'Well, perhaps I should surprise them.'

'You want to come with me now?' Tita raised a brow in question as he scraped back his chair in preparation for departure.

'No,' Byron replied. 'Best I travel alone. And later on, when it's dark. When there's less risk of spying eyes.'

Seventeen

The sky is changed–and such a change! O night,
And storm, and darkness...

Byron. From *Childe Harold's Pilgrimage*, Canto III

Below the cover of black clouds, of gusting winds and heavy rain, Byron fought to keep a grip on the oars of a boat. Soaked to the skin, in constant fear of being dragged below the waves, his over-riding instinct was to pray to God to save him. But for a man who conjured verses from the air as if confetti, he failed to think of any words to offer up as supplication. And he was not entirely lost. Although the rain obscured the towers and the cupulas of Venice, he could hear the muted bells chiming out the hour of two, all sounding deeper and more sonorous than any he'd grown used to on the island of Lazzaro. How he smiled to hear their welcome, for they sang to him of courage, and though his muscles ached and burned, the steady rhythm of the rowing drove him on until, at last, he reached the Grand Canal, and sometime after that the rain-blurred facade of the Palazzo Mocenigo.

Smiling with relief, he steered the boat towards its steps, then placed the oars in their locks and raised his hands to wipe his eyes. Now, with clearer vision, he realised no gondola was moored to any of the posts. Had Tita taken it somewhere, or gone out whoring for the night? If only Fletcher was around to provide the checks and balances required to contain the gondolier's worst inclinations. Not that Byron ever dreamed the day would come when he would miss the valet's grumbling complaints.

Over his sigh of remorse came the screeching of timbers. The boat collided with stone walls. The stern was breached. Water rushed in as Byron tried to disembark but was hindered by his clothes – having decided that the habit of a monk would help deter any interest if he passed other boats on the lagoon. But then, who else was mad enough to be out on such a night?

Safe and panting on the jetty, with only bubbles on the surface of the water where the boat was sinking rapidly below it, Byron lifted a hand to push the cowl back from his brow. Squinting up at the house, he saw no sign of any life. Every window was in darkness. But when a sudden bolt of lightning lit the world, as bright as day, he clearly saw the rain cascading through the gutters that discharged across stone lions on the walls. Water that flowed like silver hair. Water that ran like drools of spittle through the lions' open jaws.

And they had hair as the hair of women, and their teeth were as the teeth of lions. He recalled what he'd once read from the Book of Revelations. It hadn't soothed him at the time, and now he shuddered as more doubts began to seed inside his mind. Was he about to throw himself into the lion's den?

As heavy gloom reclaimed the skies and thunder rolled some distance off, he heard the sound of frantic whimpers, and then a scratching that was coming from within the palazzo. Was it Mutz, sensing his presence, waiting eagerly to greet him?

Byron approached the doors, his face up close against the grilles through which he murmured, 'Mutz ... good boy. Try and open the doors!'

Would the dog recall the trick? Hoping for a miracle, Byron heard the scrape of metal. Well, if Mutz had managed that, could his master force the mortice locks by flinging the weight of his body hard against them? Instead, he heard the clink of chains, and then both the doors swung wide before him – as if he was some Ali Baba calling 'open sesame' at the mouth of the cave in which his treasure had been stored.

For a moment he was dumbstruck. Mutz was undoubtedly a dog a good deal cleverer than most, but could he really turn a key as well as drawing back a bolt? The question faded from his mind when the creature bounded out and almost knocked him off his feet. Byron laughed in delight – and just as quickly bit his tongue. He didn't want to draw attention from anyone still awake in the neighbouring palazzos, where several windows glimmered gold with the lights of lamps or candles.

He and the dog entered the house, just as a sudden blast of wind flung the doors against the jambs. Alarmed at the sound, but feeling safer thus concealed, Byron crouched and pressed his face into the warmth of Mutz's fur. The dog responded with successions of small yelps and yet more whimpers as his master rubbed his flanks and caressed his underbelly. Mutz was plump, if anything a little more so than before. He had clearly been well cared for in the time of Byron's absence. Hopefully, it was the same with the other animals.

The odours of fresh hay and natural musk were reassuring. There was no rancid stink of waste to indicate neglect, but the first euphoria of returning to his home may have clouded Byron's judgement. Now, he sensed something amiss. He held his breath and cocked his head. Why were the animals so quiet, especially when another spear of lightning flashed to life and cracked the Venice skies in two? Within that stark illumination he saw the gleam of several eyes staring back in his direction. One of the monkeys grunted softly between small squeaks, almost like hiccoughs. The feathers of the crow rustled and snapped against its bars. And what was that other sound? Above the steady susurration of the rain against the windows, he was aware of something moving, near the stairs to the upper floors.

Gripping onto Mutz's collar, Byron turned and saw a figure dart between two arching pillars. Remembering the night when he'd last been in the palazzo – when Russo's men had dragged him off to be imprisoned in The Leads – he shouted angrily, 'Who's that? Why are you hiding? Come out and let me see your face. If you don't, then be assured I shall set my dog on you!'

It was nothing but bravado. Mutz was panting in panic, pressing his flank to Byron's thigh. And how could Byron think to fight, when his muscles were still heavy from the exertion of his journey? But adrenaline was pumping through his veins to spur him on, only heightened by the eerie, keening whines of the dog; though as the whimpering subsided, he decided Mutz was frightened by the storm and nothing more. No-one was hiding by the stairs. The flash of lightning had caused an optical illusion, with the shadows of the house dancing about in a manner that resembled something living. Something, or someone, that had now melted into the air, never really being there.

The sense of peace was not to last. Another flash illuminated the white marble of the staircase, where a rope was dangling from the balustrade above. Letting go of Mutz's collar, Byron's feet began to move as if of their own accord – although forgetting the long hems of the habit he was wearing, he tripped and fell against the newel post. Once his balance was restored, he used the column as the leverage to push his body on, lifting the skirts of the robe above his calves to climb the stairs, until he reached the small half-landing where the rope had been secured.

He had no knife with which to cut, and shaking hands rendered him clumsy as he fought to drag the rope across the rail and free the knot, and by that means perhaps to save what was tied upon its end. Alas, it was an empty whim. His arrival came too late to make the blindest bit of difference. The corpse was soft and pliable, but already growing cold. Byron could only moan to see the pity of this death as he cast his eyes around for a shroud to cover it. A tapestry on the wall would do as well as anything. But before he tore it down, he dared to take another look at what was lying at his feet. The neck was obviously broken. The eyes were bulging, dull and glazed. And what was that, something pale and bloody clamped between the teeth? At first, he thought it might have been a tattered remnant of some fabric, but when he touched it, he recoiled. It was flesh. Human flesh. Whoever killed his monkey had picked the one more prone to biting.

His gasp of shock was interrupted. Was that the sound of someone laughing? Could it be the other monkey? Byron looked down. Saw only Mutz. At the same time, he realised that what he'd heard was more like sobbing. Slowly, descending the stairs, he ducked his head to try and see who was cowering below them – and was startled by the shrill, despairing cry that met his ears: 'Madre di Dio, salvami da questo fantasma!' – Mother in Heaven, save me from the ghost!

Byron recognised the voice, and responded in Italian, in a tone that he hoped might help to offer reassurance: 'Nicolo. Come out of there! You mustn't be afraid. Even if I was a ghost, why would I be haunting you?'

Stepping closer to the void, he pushed the cowl back from his head, though hard to say if Nicolo was in a state to recognise him. There came no answer but the rasp of frightened breaths above the lashing of the rain against the windows.

Byron tried another tack. 'Nicolo, you must tell me – who murdered my monkey?'

The child's voice was croaked with tears. 'It was after Tita left. After he told me to wait and open the doors if you came back here tonight.'

'But then, you had no need,' Byron interrupted. 'Not with Mutz having opened the bolts to let me in.' He motioned to the dog, for the first time noticing that the hinges of the doors were hanging loose from splintered wood. Mutz hadn't opened them at all. Someone else had used brute force.

The boy rushed on. 'When they'd gone, I pushed a chest against the doors. I didn't know what else to do.'

'So, the scraping I heard ... that was you, dragging the chest away from them again? But if you knew it was me, why did you run away and hide?'

'I heard your voice. I knew your voice. But then I saw you coming in, and you ... you didn't look like you. I thought it was the Devil who...' The child broke off, words muffled sobs. 'The thing they said would come to kill me, if I...'

'Who said these things?' Byron demanded, at the same time looking back towards the cages draped in shadows. 'Are the bastards still here?'

'No. They've gone.'

'How many were there?'

'Just two. They both wore masks. I couldn't see their faces.'

'Well, whoever they were, they must have known I was returning.' Byron was speaking to himself. He was thinking now of Tita, wondering where the man could be, and where his loyalty might lie. What could have made him disappear, and on the very night Byron had told him he'd back? But worse than that, had Tita known this child would be forced to watch the monkey being killed? And what about the other horror Nicolo witnessed weeks before, when he'd been lurking in the study on the night the model Venus was displayed in her box, looking so like a rotting corpse?

Suspicions whirled in Byron's mind: *Why was Nicolo there, in his study on that night? Could he be another traitor, perhaps employed as Russo's spy?*

Meanwhile, the boy crawled towards him from the shelter of the stairs, below which Byron was surprised to see a mound of crumpled blankets.

'Is this where you sleep?'

'I like it near the animals. And Mutz, he keeps me safe.'

Byron looked at the dog and shook his head in dismay. 'He didn't do so well tonight.'

'He did his best. He guarded me when I was hiding, while they did ... the thing they did.' Nicolo's eyes momentarily glanced back towards the marble stairs. 'They said they'd string me up there too, until the woman – I think I heard the voice of a woman – told the man let me live, so that I could tell you...'

'Tell me what?' Byron's temper was at the point of breaking.

'That they knew you'd escaped from the prison of The Leads, and now wherever you were they would find you in the end. They said what happened to the monkey was a calling card for Byron. Next time, it would be me. And, if not me, the little pet made of your own flesh and blood.'

'Allegra!' Byron froze. *They could only mean Allegra.* He had to take some calming breaths before he carried on again. 'Don't worry, Nicolo. If they return, I shall be ready, and...' He spoke more gently to the boy, 'never be afraid of ghosts. They don't exist, and just as well, when those alive on this earth can behave so wickedly. But now I'm back, and I'll ensure these villains pay for what they've done.'

Braver now, Nicolo stood, reaching out for Byron's hand. Earnest, dark eyes were shining up through his narrow pallid face. 'I never did believe you'd gone and murdered anyone. When I was in your study, when they carried in that box, I knew the thing you kept inside it wasn't real, only wax. But that inspector man was fooled, just like me when I first saw it – when Tita played a joke one night and called me over there.' Nicolo pointed to an empty arching recess where the walls bubbled up with beads of moisture and were sprouting blooms of fungi. The same black mould that had blighted what remained of Byron's Venus.

While that ghastly memory played anew in Byron's mind, Nicolo carried on: 'Tita said there was something in the box he'd like to show me, and when he opened the lid, I...' Despite all his bravado, the child was clearly still affected. The fingers of one hand grasped the sleeve of his shirt, the knuckles clenched so very tightly that even in the murky light Byron could see the white of bone prominent below the skin.

'It seems that Tita made a habit of displaying my Venus!' Byron's voice held a new sharpness, 'Was he drunk at the time? Even so, that's no excuse. He takes too many liberties.' Silently, Byron now wondered if the gondolier had aided La Fornarina in her vengeance. If the plan to disgrace him was not hers, and hers alone.

His thoughts were broken by the boy, who spoke in Tita's defence. 'He likes his wine, and there are times when he will jest, or be too rough. But it was nothing more than that. He was as shocked as me to see your Venus in that state. He said he'd only meant to show me what a naked woman looked like.'

'How old are you, Nicolo?' Byron's voice was terse. 'Twelve. Maybe thirteen? What was Tita thinking of?'

Byron felt sick to recall his own childhood in Scotland – when his nursemaid, May Gray, professed her Calvinistic faith to everyone she met in public, whereas in private she'd be drunk and prone to violent tendencies. Before too long her evil tongue took on a form more physical. If not her tongue, it was her hand. If not her hand ... how could he bear to recollect the shame of it? At the age of only nine, he'd all but fainted with the exquisite, searing pleasure of an orgasm, since when the burning fires of Hell and the delights of Heaven's pleasures became confused in his young mind – as did the lasting consequence of an excessive desire to engage in carnal acts. Byron the man had gone on to seduce a host of lovers, leaving a string of broken hearts and ruined hopes in his wake, but he was not a murderer and he would prove his innocence – though far more pressing at that moment was the question as to where his gondolier might have gone.

He stared intently at the boy. 'Did Tita say when he'd be back?'

When Nicolo shook his head, Byron let go of his hand and turned to make a start on creating a new barricade to block the broken doors. For at least the next ten minutes there was no sound but that of objects being dragged across stone floors. Some of the larger sacks of grain ordered in for his pets. Boxes filled with candles. An antique sedan chair left by a tenant in the past. It was folly to imagine he could really hope to stop any brutes hell-bent on entry, but at least he could prevent the doors from banging on the jambs.

Wearily, he began to ascend the stairs again. Reaching the landing with the monkey, he glanced back down at the boy. 'You are sure about the numbers? There were only two of them? No-one else who'd still be lurking in the rooms of the palazzo?'

'I'm sure,' Nicolo said.

'Then come with me – and bring the dog. You'll share my chamber tonight.'

Eighteen

The freed inheritors of Hell ...
So curst the tyrants that destroy!

Byron. From *The Giaour*

Nicolo fell asleep almost immediately, and on the very sopha where Byron had first glanced at the pages of *The Vampyre*. How many months ago was that? It seemed a lifetime since the story took on a life all its own, and ruined his in the process.

His own rest, so deeply needed, proved to be more elusive. Lying on his bed, his muscles ached, his body tensed at every creaking of the boards. Or was it rats from the canal, having invaded the palazzo in the weeks of his absence, now all too vivid a reminder of those that plagued him in The Leads? He knew his mind was playing tricks but thought the sounds would drive him mad. Finally, he succumbed to the temptation of the black drop, almost swooning at the taste of the syrup on his tongue, and then the welcome rush of warmth as it went coursing through his veins.

Waking to the tolling of the bells of five o'clock, Byron blinked against the light already creeping through the windows. *What will this new day hold for me*? he thought while staring blankly at the cobwebs draped like lace from the curtains of the bed posts, screwing his nose against the stench of the dog's meaty breath as it lay snoring at his side. Apart from that, all was serene. No rush of wind or blasting rain, which meant the weather must have changed, although the air was very humid. He'd like to open the casements, let a breeze flow through the room. But there was little chance of that when the house's upper floors must be kept well secured, in case the villains returned.

If they did, they'd face a fight. The night before he'd removed the sabre from his study wall. Odd to think Inspector Russo had not taken it away to use as evidence against him, if nothing else because the weapon was an object of great value. Also undisturbed were the pistols Byron kept in the stand beside his bed, both of them primed, ready to shoot at any villain who might think to threaten him or Nicolo.

He glanced at the boy. How beautiful he was. He might have been a little prince born to some sultan potentate, his hair so glossy and dark against the sopha's brocade cushions. That hair – only now did Byron see what it was about the boy that had touched him at the time of their first meeting. Nicolo could have been himself at that same age, so like a painted miniature Byron's mother always carried – and which she'd held in her hands when he'd last seen her on her deathbed. Now it was buried with her too.

She did not lie beside her husband, which was fitting as they'd rarely shared a bed during their marriage. The man they'd called Mad Jack had abandoned his wife and baby son in infancy, leaving a mountain of debts from gambling and dissipation before meeting his doom while living on the continent. Some said it was consumption. Others claimed he took a knife and slashed his own throat in a drug-fuelled despair. Whatever the truth, it proved to be the final scandal to crown a litany of sins, including an affair with a beautiful half-sister.

Like father like son? The failings weighed on Byron's soul, as heavy as the albatross in Coleridge's poem. Not that he'd ever contemplate seeking death as an escape. His life would carry on, and he would strive to be the father Allegra needed him to be. He might even raise Nicolo as her companion and brother. Or was that thought too fanciful? After all, what did he know about the boy's own past life? Perhaps he'd ask when he awoke. There might be a verse in it...

Byron suddenly lurched up. Was that some movement in the house? Still a little muddled from the opiates he'd taken, he now remembered Fletcher's fears of the palazzo being haunted. Was Byron also hearing the voices of the dead, for if those sounds were made by mortals, surely Mutz would have responded? But the dog continued snoring, and Nicolo did no more than briefly sigh in his sleep.

Shaking his head to try and clear it, Byron chastised himself. There were no ghosts in this house. But there were servants, and the servants would be up and about. Should he call them to his study and demand to know which one had riffled through his desk and stolen Polidori's novel? It might be best to do something about the monkey before that, or he could only imagine the hysteria to follow. Imperative to find a way to deal with the corpse, and as soon as possible in this humidity and heat. But first, he'd need a cup of coffee. Something to stimulate his brain and clear the fog of laudanum.

Yawning, rubbing the knots of aching muscles in his shoulders, he left his bed and stepped across the crumpled habit from Lazzaro left discarded on the floor. Naked but for his drawers, Byron walked towards his washstand but didn't panic as before when he saw a blurred reflection on the surface of the mirror. Now, he knew that weird illusion was only due to the furring of dust upon its surface. Smearing a palm across the glass he saw his image reappear, though barely recognisable. His beard was long. So was his hair, straggling about his shoulders. He could have shaved and cut it off during his stay with the monks, but he quite liked this newer Byron, a little wild and dangerous, and with yet more strands of grey growing in around his temples, he considered the impression altogether more befitting for a poet of his standing – or so he mused before the serpent of reality struck back with the sting of poisoned fangs.

What standing did he have? And whatever Hobby said, how could he ever return to his homeland again? Feeling unsteady on his feet, he touched the silver crucifix on a chain around his neck. Lighter than an albatross, it felt too cold against his breast but was oddly reassuring, being a gift from Father Aucher when they'd said their last goodbyes: *A token of protection for the trials to be endured. Send this to me ... when the time comes.*

Byron grimaced as he drank from a cup of lukewarm coffee. The food he'd scavenged from the kitchen, where no staff were in attendance, was equally unappetising. Sitting at his study desk, he peeled the skin from an orange, half of which was green with mould. It made him think anew of Tita, slurping the fruit on Lazzaro. The crust of bread he next bit into proved so hard he feared his teeth might not survive the assault. The cheese was good though, despite some maggots squirming on the surface. The cake was moist, seemed freshly made, which allowed him to hope that the cook had not entirely abandoned the house. He feared the other servants had though. And really, who could blame them? During the time he'd been away, and with Fletcher also absent, who had been there to pay their wages? Only Nicolo, and Tita—

Tita, whose booming *basso profundo* echoed up through the building: 'Che bastardi sono stati qui. Se a Nico è statto fatto del male, gli spacco le fottute teste!'

The words translated as a threat to any bastards who might have dared to hurt Nicolo, with this explosion being followed by some deeper grunting sounds amid the scraping back of objects Byron had used the night before to barricade the canal doors.

Ah well, he supposed he'd have to face the gondolier and demand an explanation for his absence soon enough. But should he fetch a pistol first? How could he be sure this response to any danger for Nicolo was not simply another bluff? But if that was the case, how could Tita know that Byron was back in the house, not with the boat from Lazzaro having sunk in the canal?

As he pondered over this, Byron heard another voice that caused a surge of sudden happiness to swell in his breast. He had no doubt those gritty, northern tones belonged to his valet, still in Venice after all, not gone to England as he'd feared.

'Fletcher. My dear Fletcher!' Byron rose from his desk and hastened from the study. Once on the staircase he ignored the ripening odour of the monkey as he leaned across the rail to see his beaming gondolier.

'Eh, Byron!' Tita laughed. 'Safely home after all.'

'And where exactly have you been?' Byron called imperiously.

'Had a message from your valet.' The gondolier turned his head, addressing Fletcher, who emerged through the doors to stand behind him. 'Didn't I tell you he'd be here, home from that island full of eunuchs!' Suddenly more serious, Tita glanced back up at Byron. 'Who broke the locks? Where's Nicolo?'

'He's here, and in my chamber. He let me in when I arrived in the middle of the night, but not before some intruders...' Byron paused, looking back at the tapestry lying on the floor just behind him. How to tell what it concealed? But why delay, when there could be no disguising the odour of decay that filled his nose: 'They killed one of my monkeys.'

'What the hell?' Tita said, looking genuinely surprised.

'Could it be Inspector Russo?' Fletcher's voice was edged with panic. 'That man who carted you away?'

Byron sighed, 'Oh my dear Fletcher, to think you witnessed

such a thing. That ghastly box, and what it held. I swear to you—'

'There is no explanation needed.' Fletcher raised a hand, as if demanding his master hold his tongue on the matter. 'It was a shock at the time, and I confess I've spent long hours wondering how I could ever be so deaf and blind to your worst depravities. I even feared there was a risk I'd be accused as an accomplice. After all, I'd seen the blood staining your clothes after the night of the Alfieri party. The ones I went and laundered to remove the evidence. The worry laid me very low. The sorrow too, for your own plight. But before the night was out Nicolo came to my room, and he told me the truth about that model made of wax – how the thing I'd thought was real was nothing but an imitation. Next day, Tita assured me that the child spoke the truth, and then went off to confront that wicked menace, La Fornarina.'

'As I told you yesterday,' Tita butted in, 'La Fornarina is sorry.'

Fletcher sneered his response: 'Oh, how she blows with the wind. We all know her tongue is forked.'

'Let's speak no more of that woman! What's done is done, and here I am.' Byron was not in any mood to hear his servants' bickering. Far more important at that moment was the happiness he felt to see his valet home again. Limping on down the stairs, he extended his arms and called out, 'My trusted Fletcher! Thank God you are well. And I confess, more selfishly, I shall be glad to have some element of order reimposed on my shambles of a life.'

Fletcher quickly reverted to his habitual gruff manner. 'I can see you need a shave. And ... shouldn't you be dressed?'

Byron, now so much nearer, observed how careworn Fletcher looked. His eyes were bagged. His ruddy jowls were hanging flaccid round his mouth, looking at least a decade older than on the night when he'd last seen him.

'Where have you been?' Byron asked. 'I feared you might have left for England. Those plans you had—'

Tita broke in, and clapped one muscled arm around the valet's shoulders. 'He's been in Ravenna! Can you believe this dull old frog ever got there on his own? Your Fletcher has more spunk in his body than we thought.'

'Ravenna?' Byron said, his mood again becoming dismal. 'Teresa went there with her husband.'

'And that is why I followed,' Fletcher swiftly interjected. 'To visit your amour after finding the letter telling you about her illness. The one you'd dropped to the floor when that Russo man arrived. I wanted to inform her that you would have gone yourself ... if only you could.'

'Did you see her?' Byron asked with a note of urgency. 'Did she know who you were, or speak of me at all? You didn't tell her...' He broke off, too horrified to imagine Teresa going to her death hearing the news of his arrest – during which he was distracted to observe a wraith-like figure emerging on the steps where the gondola was moored.

A slender youth wore crumpled clothing, too large and ragged on his frame – or deliberately contrived to make him look like a beggar and draw the least attention? For when this stranger proceeded to approach the canal doors, when both Tita and Fletcher moved aside to let him pass, despite the shadows born of illness, Byron immediately knew the large brown eyes raised to his own, the same with cheeks that before had been full but were now wasted and too pale, and – oh, the smile that opened up the flower of the face could belong to no-one else.

'Teresa!' He wasn't sure if he should laugh aloud for the sheer joy her arrival, or to weep when the cap upon her head was removed and he could see that her lovely auburn hair had been cropped short.

'Ah, *mio* Byron.' She must have been aware of where he focused. 'They cut it off when I was ill. They said it sapped my strength. But it has helped with my disguise ... to resemble a boy for my journey here to Venice. It was Fletcher's idea. He said one of your lovers in the past had done the same and he had been completely fooled.'

'Indeed.' Byron paused, never so glad to be reminded of the thorn in his side known as Caroline Lamb. 'But...' his smile turned to a frown, 'I was told—'

'That I would die? The doctors say I nearly did. It is a miracle I'm here after the loss of so much blood. I am still weak, but every day I grow a little stronger. And when your Fletcher came to see me – when he told what had happened, I *knew* I had to live, to come back to Venice and do my best to save you. But there's no need. You're free already!'

As he descended the last of the stairs to reach her side, Teresa's eyes swam bright with tears, hands reaching up to touch the cross hanging at his naked breast, then higher still to the beard growing thickly on his chin. 'I like you like this. You look as wild as a satyr.'

What a knife to pierce his heart as he remembered the girl in the brothel calling him the Star and Satyr of all Venice. His voice was near to breaking when he clutched Teresa's hands. 'A satyr no longer. I am changed, and for the better. You have changed me, Teresa.'

Frozen in that pose, Teresa grew more serious. 'When I think my own husband may have had some influence over all you have suffered. All those dreadful things he said, when we last met at La Fenice. I thought it was a bluff from the jealous hypocrite who beds his whores and mistresses while expecting me to live in his house like a nun. I don't want his palaces, his high society or riches. I am happy to remain in this beggar's disguise, if that means that I can spend a little time with you again.'

'Only a little? How long?'

'A week. Maybe less. My Count believes I'm with my father. Gone to his home to convalesce, after...' Teresa's words broke off, but Byron had heard the pain that lay beneath them.

What could he offer in response? She was bound to be affected by the loss of her child. As for the rest, she had not died. She was in Venice and alive.

But for how long, if her husband came to know of her betrayal?

Nineteen

The devil's so very sly ...

Byron. From *Don Juan:* Canto I

Tita had been charged with the disposal of the monkey, and after that to find a locksmith to repair the broken doors. Higher up in the palazzo, Fletcher's duties were resumed, with Nicolo and the dog rudely woken from their slumbers and expelled from Byron's chamber.

Alone in there with Teresa, Byron tenderly removed his lover's male disguise, peeling away the cotton bindings she had wound about her breasts, perhaps to flatten them, perhaps to stem the flow of milk from her recent pregnancy – which made him feel yet more regret to think she'd suffered such distress. Ah, but this was not the time for any bitter self-reflection, only the rush of warm contentment when he surveyed the slender woman lying naked on his bed. Kneeling on the floor beside her, his fingers traced the ghostly silver of the scar that still remained from the broken corset bone. Such a sacred memento of the night of their first meeting, and all the other days and nights of sublime passion that had followed. But for now, he did no more than hold Teresa in his arms, wiping away the beads of sweat that sometimes bubbled on her brow. Was she fighting an infection, or was it nothing more than the oppressive Venice heat? Whatever the cause, there would be no making love. She was too fragile. Too exhausted. It was enough to feel the softness of her breaths upon his cheek.

As that day passed into night, and then another dawn arose, pleasure was found in other ways, through kisses, tongues and soft caresses. He helped her bathe and then to dress her in the feminine attire she had carried in her luggage. They drank wine from the cellars, and ate the fruit, bread and cheese Fletcher bought from market stalls. The cook occasionally appeared, but had still not been told of Byron's return, or the arrival of Teresa. Who knew if she might blab into the ears of enemies? And what if Count Guiccioli knew Teresa was in Venice? Would he come to claim her back? Would she be forced to obey and find herself in some new danger? She swore she would not, and that her husband never harmed her; that he had only ever wished to ensure her protection, being unduly influenced by the wickedness of rumours spread by Countess Alfieri. But was Teresa too naive? Had Guiccioli poisoned her? Was Byron too complicit in the fantasies she wove as she nestled at his side, kissing his cheeks, his nose, his lips, whispering into his ear, 'We could elope, and go away. Somewhere my Count will never find us.'

'We could...' Byron began, but knew it was impossible. His was a face that would be recognised in almost any place remotely civilised enough for them to try and make a home. And what of Fletcher? Would his valet agree to new adventures? There'd been a time, in the past, when Byron could have asked. But, even then, the older man had not been keen on travelling, not only being sick at sea, but very often when he rode in the back of any carriage. Whereas Byron was content to take the rough with the smooth, Fletcher's need of coddling led to tedious complaints. He could be stubborn as a mule. A mule who had arthritic bones. And even *if* he did agree to assist in an elopement, he was not the only member of the household to consider.

Turning over on his side, Byron's eyes locked with Teresa's. 'Have you considered my daughter? I won't leave Venice without her.'

'I would never have expected you to leave Allegra here. I shall love her as my own. How could I not, when she is yours? Fetch her soon ... then we can go.'

Hearing her desperation, he sealed her lips with a kiss. He understood just how precarious her presence was in Venice. More silently, he also pondered on his own burning desire for some measure of revenge on Alfieri and Lombardo.

With the house still steeped in silence, Byron left his lover sleeping, threw on a gown and made his way along the passage to his study. There, on a sheet of plain white paper he scribbled down the first of the two letters in his mind:

> *A mutual acquaintance has informed me of the news of your recent liberation. Should there be further information linked to your medical profession at the Venice hospital, another friend who has but recently returned to the city would be grateful to be told.*

The cryptic note was left unsigned. It was better that way. But Polidori could not fail to understand the gist of it.

The second message was quite different, drafted this time on headed paper, and signed with a flourish:

> *Mrs Martens,*
>
> *We have not met, but it has come to my attention that the Hoppners have deposited my daughter in your care. I must thank you for your kindness & should there be any need for*

reparation for your troubles, you must only send me word. All expenses will be honoured, just as soon as I return to my palazzo in Venice. I cannot say exactly when, but it should be within the month, at which time my intention is to settle all accounts still outstanding in the city before embarking on new travels. When that departure date arrives, I mean to take Allegra with me. In the meantime, my daughter will be cared for by my valet at the Palazzo Mocenigo. His name is William Fletcher. He goes on ahead of me with these instructions in his hand...

'What do you think?' Byron asked, when Fletcher stood beside his desk around a half an hour later, listening to his master read as he poured a cup of coffee from a steaming silver jug. Byron paused to take a sip, sighed and closed his eyes so as to savour the perfection, thinking if Fletcher ever mentioned a wish to retire or, God forbid, return to England, he would gladly pay a pension consummate with all his years of loyal service in the past – if *only* he would stay and perform one daily task.

When his eyes had been reopened from the folly of this notion, Byron asked, 'What do you think? Could you deliver this note to the Venice hospital, and then present the other letter to the Danish Consul's wife, who – so I'm told – is now caring for my daughter.'

'I heard of this from Tita.' Fletcher nodded gravely. 'Also, how he and Mr Hobhouse helped you escape from that gaol. My, oh my!' The valet tutted. 'All your trials and tribulations since I headed for Ravenna. Well, we must pray and thank the Lord for Mr Hobhouse and his brain. How many times has he saved you from pertikuler adventures since your days as stripling students. So many now, I have lost count! At least the monastery explains that costume I discovered in your closet yesterday. For a moment I did wonder if you might be harking back to your party days at Newstead. When you and your friends got yourself togged up as monks, cavorting till the early hours. And on the matter of bad habits, that dog's been on your bed again. The hairs and slobber can't be healthy, not with the Countess Guiccioli in a state of convalescing.'

Byron had missed his valet, but not his pious condemnations. 'Where is it now?' he curtly asked.

'The dog?' Fletcher frowned. 'Off with Tita, or Nicolo. Or perhaps he's being fed with the other animals?'

'No, not the dog. The monk's habit.'

'Drying out on a peg, though let us hope you'll never have the need to put it on again.'

'Never say never!' Byron smiled. 'It might be just the thing, if I decide to venture out. We could say one of the monks from Lazzaro is my guest while on some business here in Venice.'

'Hmph!' Fletcher gave a snort. Apart from that he made no comment, his main train of concentration now returning to the letter regarding Allegra. 'I wonder, MyLord...' He paused and chewed the cud inside one of his cheeks. 'If you could be a tad contrite. A little less of the spikey. And then, I have to wonder, will Allegra even know me? A child of that age can so easily forget. Should Nicolo come along when I go to make enquiries? She played with the boy when he first came to the palazzo. He might be able to oil the wheels of her return. Or, forgive me speaking out, for I dare say you will not like this, but what about La Fornarina? For all her sins, she always showed a fondness for the child. And Allegra liked her too, so...'

'After her lies and what they led to? Is La Fornarina a witch? Has she cast you in some spell? Tita too, for that matter?' No sooner had the words tumbled from his tongue than Byron paused in self-reflection. 'I know full well it's been too long since Allegra left this house, and I alone am at fault for her present situation. It's also true that La Fornarina has been kind to the child, but she's as sly as a fox. How can I trust a thing she says, or risk her coming here again? What if she grabs another knife and tries to murder Teresa? No!' He shook his head, 'Such a plan would never work. Take Nicolo if you must. But, either way, do hurry up.'

Waiting for Fletcher to return, and for Teresa to awake, Byron entered his closet and saw the habit from Lazzaro hanging before him on a peg. He took it down and drew damp folds across his head and arms, staring long at his appearance in the shimmer of a mirror. With the cloth of the cowl falling low across his brow, and with his shoulders hunching forwards, could he pass unrecognised and walk about the city? But this was only a delusion. There was his foot. Always, his foot. His wretched limp to mark him out.

There was the old sedan. Could Tita and Fletcher be persuaded to ferry him about in the chair? On second thoughts, it was not the least bit likely that his valet would agree to such an effort. He'd have the sullens for a week. No, Byron's only choice was to remain in his palazzo, to discard these monkish robes and dress again in his own clothes. He must endeavour to be patient, spending the time here with Teresa while awaiting any news that might arrive from Polidori. And, of even more importance, he must be here to greet his child when Fletcher brought her back again.

More than two hours were to pass before the valet reappeared. Byron was standing in the bedroom, reciting verses to Teresa. She was reclining on the sopha, her elfin face still much too pallid, but she smiled ethereally and looked delectably sweet, clad as she was in nothing more than one of Byron's fine silk nightshirts.

By contrast, Fletcher's face was red, and wore the grimmest of expressions as he breathlessly announced, 'MyLord ... the oddest thing. I don't know what to make of it. But Mrs Martens, who's been caring for Allegra these past weeks, she will insist the child has gone. Only yesterday, she said, after receiving a letter with instructions for the girl to go off with some woman.'

'Some woman? What woman? Who has taken Allegra?'

'Apparently, she gave no name, but insisted you'd employed her for the care of the child. All this Danish woman offered me as proof was a letter with your signature and crest. I must say, had I not been so acquainted with your hand I might have been deceived myself.'

'This is an outrage. It's deception. It is nothing less than kidnap!' Byron's voice, an angry shout, became more plaintive when he asked, 'What can I do? If I approach the authorities for help, will they seek to rearrest me? What good is that to Allegra? Where *can* my daughter be?'

Meanwhile, Teresa, who'd been listening to this exchange in silence, looked past the valet to where Nicolo lurked outside the door. 'Who is this?' she enquired.

Fletcher followed her gaze and addressed the child directly, 'Oh, there you are, Nicolo. Where on earth did you run off to?'

Nicolo opened his mouth, but in lieu of any words only trembling breaths were heard, which immediately alerted Byron's mind to more suspicion. Had Fletcher and Nicolo been followed through the city? Why would Nicolo run away?

'Nicolo, where did you go?' Byron asked impatiently as the boy entered the room, standing close at Fletcher's side. 'Did you see them again. Did you recognise the rogues who broke in here, and...' He bit down on his tongue. Best not to speak about the monkey and upset the boy yet further.

'No.' Nicolo shook his head. 'I went to try and find Allegra.'

'Yes, we know. She wasn't there. Or so this Mrs Martens claims.'

'But I know where she is. That's why I went...'

'Where did you go?' Byron fired off his demand like the bullets from a gun. At the same time a chill of dread began to prickle through his veins. The spirit of some prophecy. The sudden knowledge of exactly what Nicolo would reply – and that reply would surely be the House of Lombardo.

Nicolo carried on. 'I didn't see her for myself, but I asked someone who would know.'

'Get to the point,' Fletcher growled, grown as impatient as his master.

'Please, Nicolo,' Teresa said as she rose from the sopha and made her way to Byron's side, her fingers twining through her lover's as she stared at the boy. 'We have to find Allegra.'

Nicolo stood there gaping, blushing with embarrassment when sunlight shining through the window further highlighted the fact that underneath Byron's shift Teresa stood entirely naked. But, at last, he found his tongue, looking at Byron when he said, 'She's with the Countess Alfieri.'

Twenty

What from this barren being do we reap?
Our senses narrow, and our reason frail,
Life short, and truth a gem which loves the deep,
And all things weighed in Custom's falsest scale.

Byron. From *Child Harold's Pilgrimage:* Canto IV

Byron stood frozen in a trance. When he spoke he sounded like a clockwork automaton. 'I must go and fetch my child. I must bring Allegra home.'

'Wait!' Teresa dropped his hand, walking closer to Nicolo and kneeling down beside the boy before she implored, 'You're sure Allegra's still in Venice? You don't think the Contessa might have taken her away?'

'I … I believe she's still here,' Nicolo stammered nervously, just as Mutz entered the room, his hackles up, licking his lips, his yellow eyes glaring fiercely in the direction of Teresa.

Fletcher looked alarmed. 'MyLord, control your dog!'

Over the low vibrating hum of the threat in Mutz's throat, Byron reassured the valet, 'As you know perfectly well, he is all bark and little bite. What has he ever done but stare and growl at anyone? More's the pity.' Byron frowned, thinking again of the dead monkey. But even so it was not worth the risk of Mutz's jealousy, which was why he went to stand between his lover and the dog, pulling Teresa to her feet before suggesting she return to the sopha again.

The situation thus diffused, Byron continued with the questioning Teresa had begun. 'Nicolo, you are sure about Allegra's whereabouts?'

'Come on, lad. Spill the beans,' Fletcher urged in kinder tones. 'The more we know, the better chance we have to get her back again.'

It was as if he'd cast the spell to free a tongue that had been bound, its secrets locked for far too long. Nicolo took a long deep breath, and his story began:

'I know one of the maids in the Alfieri kitchens. That's who I went to see. She said she'd seen a little girl in the Contessa's private rooms. She'd been called to go upstairs, to take a plate of sugared almonds. The girl was crying, you see, and the Contessa thought she'd like them. Anyway, my friend, this maid, she was alone with the bambina long enough to ask her name, and she was told it was Allegra, and that her papa was Lord Byron.'

Byron muttered in amazement, 'Is it possible that during the course of just one summer Allegra could have learned to speak as coherently as this?' His voice came louder when he asked, 'What is the name of this servant?'

Nicolo shook his head, 'I won't say. She could be punished for telling me this. But I'd swear she wasn't lying. And I've seen them for myself. The Contessa's special children. The ones she takes to live upstairs, to sleep in feather beds and be dressed like china dolls when she walks them through the city. That's as long as they last. Before they disappear again.'

As this statement bluntly ended, Byron remembered the singers and musicians at the party where he'd first chanced upon Teresa.

And now, with the knowledge of his daughter's whereabouts – thinking of Father Aucher's story of the monk who'd developed such concerns about the Countess and the children in her care – it was all he could do to swallow back the rise of bile when he asked, 'How do you know so much about the Alfieri?'

'My father knew her ... when he lived. He was a merchant, selling jewellery, and other antique ornaments. She used to be a customer.'

'What did she buy?'

'Murano glass. Only the rarest. Most expensive.' Nicolo hung his head, and looked disturbingly familiar, though try as he might Byron couldn't think where he had seen that pose before, not with his mind so engrossed in what Nicolo had to say. 'The Countess always paid, but there were times when another older woman placed her orders. She was never so polite, always insisting on credit, and my father did his best to find the special things she wanted. But that left him in debt. He grew so sick with the worry, he collapsed in a fit. A week later he was dead. After that, me and my sister were thrown out, onto the streets. We didn't know what to do. We had no other family. Our only hope was that the Countess might still pay what was owed. My sister found out where she lived. One day she knocked on the door, and...' Nicolo paused; a trembling breath '...the Countess saw us and she listened when we begged for her to help. But she said we must be lying. She said she'd paid for everything and had receipts to show as proof. She did ask to see the ledgers – the other orders we had mentioned but,' Nicolo shook his head, 'we didn't know where they were. We supposed the bailiffs took them.' Nicolo's features crumpled as he fought back the tears.

In the empty space that followed, Teresa gently asked, 'Did she do anything to help? Anything at all?'

'She hired my sister as a maid, working in her private quarters, and sometimes caring for the orphans. That's why I mentioned her to Fletcher, after you thought I was a beggar and took me into your own household. That first morning when he said Allegra's nurse had run away, I thought, if this Lord Byron has kindly offered me a home might there also be a chance that he'd employ my sister here, but...' Nicolo shrugged. His words broke off, fingers plucking at the buttons of his jacket. 'It was only a dream. I hadn't seen her in so long. She was kept upstairs. I went no further than the kitchens, forced to sleep on sacks of rice in the stores with the rats.

Hearing this, Byron thought of the body of the woman he'd once left in such a place. The very night he'd met Nicolo and sent him off to his palazzo – where it seemed the boy's propensity for sleeping in rough places was a habit that continued. He must ask Fletcher to find the boy a proper bed. At least, for as long as they all remained in Venice.

Meanwhile, Nicolo carried on: 'I was fed and I had shelter, and in return I was to look for other children on the streets, to take them back for the Countess, and...'

'The Alfieri's Pied Piper!' Byron spoke in disbelief.

In response Nicolo frowned, having failed to understand such a literary allusion. 'I only thought I was helping. But then, one night when the kitchen staff supposed I was asleep, I heard them talk about what happened to many of the children when they left the palazzo. They said the luckiest were taken for adoption by the wealthy. Some went to monasteries or convents, especially the ones who were gifted musically. But others disappeared, never heard about again. Perhaps they'd run away and returned to their old lives. I know that some of them did. I often thought of going with them. But, you see, I had to stay, because that's where my sister was. And I was useful to the Countess.'

'Useful? In what way?' Fletcher intervened.

'She asked me to spy.' Guilty dark eyes glanced Byron's way.

'On me?' Byron asked, recalling the times he'd had the sense of being followed as he walked the night-time streets.

'The Countess wanted information. Who you saw. What you did. If I could, I was to find some way to enter your palazzo.'

'Which is exactly what you did, when I invited you in, being foolish enough to take pity on a beggar! But why? What was the reason? None of this makes any sense.'

'She wanted to see your poems. To know if there were any that might mention her by name.'

'How very fortunate to find a little thief who could read!' Byron's tone was scathing.

Nicolo blushed and looked away. 'One night, when you were ill, I found some verses on your desk. I took them back to the Countess in the hope she'd be glad, and then she'd let me see my sister. But I was wrong. She barely looked at the papers before she threw them on the fire, and then she told me to go. I haven't seen the woman since. But even if I did, I swear I'd never steal a thing from you again. It was the first and only time.'

Fletcher grabbed Nicolo's arm. 'What a little ingrate! I hope by now you will have learned which side your bread is buttered on. That's if you've got any sense in the space between your lugholes.'

Byron's hands were clenched to fists. He well remembered the Countess asking if he could recite the latest verses of *Don Juan* for the amusement of her guests, and how he'd foolishly confessed that she had featured in one stanza. It was merely a few lines, never intended for the public. But anyone who chanced to read them would have been in little doubt as to who he'd referenced...

A Venetian arista known as much
For her lascivious pursuing of Don Juan,
As she was for the mask that concealed her poxed visage...

While these words played in his mind, Nicolo looked at him again, cheeks flushing red and stammering as his apology continued:

'I ... I knew it was wrong. I didn't want to steal the verses. But can't you see, I had to do it for the sake of my sister. And when I saw what you'd written – what you thought of the Contessa – I wanted her to see it too. I *wanted* her to be hurt.'

Byron responded angrily, throwing his arms out in despair. 'Little wonder she has come to despise me with such vigour, why she's determined to destroy my existence here in Venice. And now, she trumps me again with the abduction of my daughter!'

Teresa spoke more evenly. 'Where is your sister now, Nicolo? Do you think she could help us to get Allegra back?'

'I don't know. Some of the servants said she'd run away. But would she go – and not take me?' Again, Nicolo hung his head – which was exactly the moment Byron knew where he had seen such an attitude before. The girl in the brothel. The girl who had wanted no reminders of a past she'd said was lost. Hadn't she mentioned a brother? Hadn't she had the same black hair and sultry looks as Nicolo? The very same exotic eyes that Byron had supposed to hail from Turkey or Greece.

Whatever blood flowed in their veins, it hit him like a hammer's blow. The mirrored symmetry of facts was far too strong to be denied. But how had the girl come to be in the brothel? Had Father Aucher been right when he'd suggested that the Countess Alfieri was corrupt, selling children into vice? But whatever the connection with the underworld of Venice, it was clear that Nicolo still remained in ignorance of his sister's tragic fate. What on earth would he think if he knew the truth of it? *How* could Byron think to tell him? Certainly not with Fletcher and Teresa in the room.

Thinking again of the children he had seen in the brothel, the ones whose lips were smeared with rouge, and who wore the wings of cherubs while attending to the pleasures of the gentlemen of Venice, Byron turned to Nicolo. 'What is your sister's name?'

'Eva. It is Eva.'

'Meaning "life"', Byron said, almost choking on the words. 'And now...' he blinked back tears, 'I have another name for you. On those occasions when you've been in the Palazzo Alfieri, have you ever heard a mention of Veronica Lombardo?'

'No,' Nicolo replied, but then appeared to change his mind. 'There *might* be someone of that name who sometimes visits the Contessa. I've never seen her myself, but I've heard the servants talking.'

Byron struggled to suppress the volcano of rage that might burst forth at any moment. 'This is exactly as I thought. Nicolo, my friend, for your honesty tonight I am forever in your debt – especially this news of my daughter's whereabouts. When the time comes, I may ask for your assistance again. But, in the meantime, rest assured...' Byron glanced back towards Teresa, as if he sought her reassurance, 'wherever I live, here in Venice or elsewhere, you will always have a home.'

'My sister too?' Nicolo asked.

His pleading gaze broke Byron's heart. What could he say in reply?

'For Eva's sake, and for your father's, I swear the Countess Alfieri will pay *every* debt she owes.'

Twenty-one

Cut to his heart again with the keen knife
Of silent, sharp endurance ...

Byron. From *Childe Harold*. Canto III

I wished to think. I had to plan. But on arriving at my desk, I was immediately distracted by a packet from John Murray which contained the first edition of my verses of Mazeppa. Idly flicking through the pages, to my horror I discovered that the fragment I'd composed while at the Villa Diodati had been included in the text. The very words that Polidori since developed for the novel that has proved my nemesis. Had I accidently sent my scraps of paper back to London, bundled up with other writing I'd intended to be published? It was admittedly my habit to pass most work by Murray's eyes, both the good & the bad. But why on earth would he decide to print these words, at such a time?

My temper reached its boiling point. I tore the page from the book and flung it to the floor. But now, I have retrieved it & shall paste it in this memoir. Let it be the stark reminder of how one scribbled page of prose ~ which Polidori emulated more precisely than imagined ~ could lead to such a dire outcome. Oh, the power found in words! How the smallest drop of ink may fall like dew upon a thought, which may then reach the minds of thousands.

A FRAGMENT.

June 17, 1816

In the year 17 -, having for some time determined on a journey through countries not hitherto much frequented by travellers, I set out, accompanied by a friend, whom I shall designate by the name of Augustus Darvell. He was a few years my elder, and a man of considerable fortune and ancient family - advantages which an extensive capacity prevented him alike from undervaluing or overrating. Some peculiar circumstances in his private history had rendered him to me an object of attention, of interest, and even of regard, which neither the reserve of his manners, nor occasional indications of an inquietude at times nearly approaching to alienation of mind, could extinguish...

However short this text may be, it is plain enough to see why I decided the project was only fit to be buried, & long before Polidori raised the nonsense from its grave. As to the gist of Murray's letter, it seems that having failed to prevent The Vampyre *novel being published with my name upon the cover, he then decided to print this Fragment publicly, to prove that Polidori was a plagiarist & liar. I would much rather he had dealt with the dissembling publishers & their rogue impersonation.*

Oh, I must leave this irritation, for the present, anyway. I must attempt to be more sanguine & concentrate on the decisions to be made nearer to home. In short, the ones involving the Countess Alfieri & her abduction of my daughter. I intend to take revenge, & my revenge now has a name. It is Eva. Eva. Eva. I write it here three times as if to conjure up a spell in which the spirits of the dead will rise to join me in seeking some justice from the living. But as I have no expectations of assistance from that quarter, I must endeavour instead to make full use of the advantages I have at my disposal. First of all, my loyal servants, Tita, Fletcher, & Nicolo. There is also Teresa, who, despite her ailing health, has suggested going off to make a solitary visit to the Palazzo Alfieri. Her intention is to plead on my behalf with the Countess for the return of Allegrina. But is my daughter a pawn to be so easily relinquished? On top of which, there is the risk to Teresa herself. If the Countess Alfieri knows Teresa is in Venice, she may then send a message to her husband in Ravenna. I think again of Mazeppa, flying to me on wings of warning. I may not have been stripped naked & then bound to the back of a maniacal horse, but I have been incarcerated & threatened with the guillotine. Is that not a wild ride to call my very own? Yet, I am here. I have survived, just like Mazeppa in my poem, and though the hero of my verses never learns his lover's fate, I am determined to try and keep my own Teresa safe.

Meanwhile, with every passing moment I grow more fearful for my daughter. The Countess Alfieri must have some intimate involvement with Veronica Lombardo. If not, then how did Eva come to be in the brothel?

The images that fill my mind. I cannot begin...

Disturbed by some knocking coming on the study door, Byron looked up to see it open, and a shadowy figure looming close behind the valet.

'Polidori, MyLord.'

Fletcher barely had the chance to begin an introduction before the visitor announced: 'I came as soon as I could after receiving your letter!'

Polidori sounded harassed and looked decidedly unwell. Hobhouse had been right. The doctor must be ailing from some form of sweating fever, perhaps contracted in The Leads. If not that, was it the after-throes of taking opiates? Byron well knew the effects and had often seen the doctor in this state when the two of them had shared a common household – and smoked a common pipe.

'Sit down, before you drop!' Byron gestured to a chair.

'I'd rather stand. I must be brief,' Polidori said abruptly, coming closer to the desk while glancing back across his shoulder in a most suspicious manner. 'I fear I've been followed. Hopefully, I threw them off, but...'

'Well, if you have it's rather late to be showing concern,' Byron replied tetchily, at the same time wondering how Polidori always managed to exude such an air of despondency and gloom, dimming the light of any room, sucking the energy away. Already feeling exhausted after no more than a few moments in the doctor's company, he continued questioning: 'Did you see who it was?'

'Oh, who can say, when there are eyes staring out from every window and alley in this city? I cannot sleep for the worry. I keep a candle by my bed, the flame alight all through the night. But even then the fluttering will form such shadows on the walls, like the wings of a bat. Gigantic wings. I hear their snapping.'

'You are not well,' Byron replied with some compassion in his voice as he recalled the fearful nightmares that he had also suffered since his time in The Leads. But this reference to bats, with their vampiric connotations – it was distinctly irritating.

'Are you surprised if I'm laid low?' Polidori's tone was fractious, before he spoke more levelly. 'But that is not why I'm here. I've come to inform you of something I've discovered, and when you know what it is, I'm sure you'll understand why I'm cautious for my life.'

'As serious as that? Well hurry up. I have some other urgent matters to attend to. I really must get on, and—'

'Indeed, it is, most serious!' the doctor interjected. 'And stemming back to the time when I was still unaware of your own imprisonment, when I attended another of the Alfieri salons.'

'Why on earth would you go *there*?' Byron was bemused. 'Surely the last place on this earth you would be seen, paying court to the woman who's been telling all of Venice I'm the author of the novel you wrote – even though I can recall her being present at my side when you first mentioned it. For God's sake, man! She saw the manuscript pass from your hand to mine.'

'Which is why I returned, to insist she stop her lies. To try and make her understand that she's destroyed my every hope for a literary career.'

'Not only yours! My life is ruined by the connection with such...' Byron broke off before the insult could be spilled from his tongue. 'Why should the woman listen now, when she has lied for so long? And, with regard to the publishers you chose for this debacle, I wouldn't be the least surprised if the Countess Alfieri had not been generously imbursed to drive the sales of the book.'

'That could be so,' said Polidori. 'She had the gall to laugh at me when I asked her to desist. She said she hadn't thought the words of a countess who resided quite so far away from London could ever hope to influence what was printed on a cover. But then, she seemed to relent and said she'd try to set things right, if I would only agree to come and read from my book at her next conversazione, when she would publicly announce that we had all been deceived by Lord Byron's wicked claims – at which point she'd introduce me to her guests as the true author.'

Byron tried, but could not hide the disgust in his voice. 'What do you gain from this appearance? Would you also take the mantle of the murderer she claims to be *my* true identity? You are too easily seduced. Believe me, Polidori, she won't be doing anything out of the goodness of her heart. She'll have some trick up her sleeve.'

For the second time that day, Byron stopped himself from slurring Polidori's writing talent.

Meanwhile his doppelganger guest drove the conversation on. 'My sole intention now is to travel back to England. I hope to meet the publishers and put an end to the fiasco. But with regard to that, it is embarrassing to ask, but my funds are much depleted, and I was hoping you'd assist with the expenses of the journey. There is also the matter of a testimonial which you might write so as to swear *The Vampyre* novel is my own.'

Byron happily agreed. 'I'll pen a letter right now. And Fletcher' – he nodded to the valet at the doors – 'can countersign it as a witness. He will also make arrangements to supply you with some money. It's the least I can do. I hope you know that despite our differences in the past, I only wish you success in any future you have planned. You are young and still have your whole life ahead of you, although...' he paused, considering how much more he should reveal when Polidori was already in a state of distress, 'I'm not sure how this will help, but I did write to John Murray, requesting he take measures to sue these upstart publishers. Sadly, he's met with no success, at least as far as I'm aware. Still, perhaps you could take the reprobates to court yourself, at least to gain what you are due of any monetary profits.'

Polidori's smile was bitter. 'But not respect for my work, when any fame still comes to you. Byron, the genius!'

'Oh,' Byron blithely replied. 'I'm very often hailed as one, and willing to put up with it. But it's a status dearly bought, and not necessarily one that brings a man any contentment. These days I've come to realise that fame and immortality are nothing more than empty dreams pursued by idiots and fools. How futile is the one, and how undefined the other!'

Polidori heaved a sigh. 'Imagine how I felt when the publishers replied to my complaints by sending cuttings of appalling reviews? Not that they're the least concerned. They say if everyone believes *you* are the author of the novel that's the only thing that matters. It will sell immensely well, regardless of what piffle might exist between the covers. Piffle!' The doctor winced. 'They called my novel piffle!'

'That was rather cruel of them.'

'Indeed it was. I cannot bear the insults any longer. I have grown sick with disappointment, vomiting and almost fainting from the disruption to my humours. I rage against the inequality received by those of us who are divided by our births from the light of adulation – those of us who are condemned to always fester in the shadows. Well, let the darkness of obscurity enfold me in its wings! Let it carry me away. From now on I yearn for nothing more than anonymity.'

Byron fought against the urge to inform Polidori that this overblown complaint was everything that had been wrong with his novel in the first place, instead of which he attempted to draw the conversation back to his own personal concerns. 'I sympathise. I really do. But you will write another book, and find another publisher. One who will treat you with respect. But all that is for the future. In the present...' Byron's nerves were poised upon a cliff edge; he only wished the doctor gone, but he still had another question he must ask before that happened: 'Would it be too impudent to enquire a little more about our meeting in The Leads, when you suspected there may be new information with regard to the girl in the morgue?'

'Yes. Yes,' Polidori was swift to reply. 'There was a clue I'd overlooked. Or should I say I'd failed to notice the evidence of any weapons used to bring about her death. I've brought one specimen to show you. The other one, I left in situ – in case my honesty is questioned. Regardless of which, it is all there in my report.'

'Your report?' Byron repeated, wondering where this was leading. 'Who is it for? Inspector Russo?'

Polidori looked confused. 'I know no-one of that name.' Saying this, he removed some folded papers from his pocket and placed them down on Byron's desk. 'I could have left this at the morgue, but things so easily get lost among the other record-keeping. Really, the system is shambolic, and I presumed that what I'd found would be better lodged with you. That is to say, it may suffice if there's a new investigation.'

Byron picked up the little package, although it seemed to take an age before the knot of the string that held the papers in place had been released to expose ... a splinter of glass?

Whatever is it? Byron wondered as the object caught the sunlight. It wasn't very large. Perhaps three inches in length, and in width much narrower, tapering towards a point. The jagged edge was also stained with what appeared to be dried blood.

Polidori explained: 'It's not been cleaned in any way. This is exactly as it looked when first extracted from the body. But you can see what it is, recognise its provenance?'

Byron frowned and shook his head.

'Think of the Countess's display of Murano ornaments at the Palazzo Alfieri.'

'Well, now you come to mention them...' Byron mused in some confusion. 'But, what on earth have they to do with what's in front of me right now?'

'This is the blade of a knife. When still attached, it had a handle that was also made of glass, something elaborately turned and stained with coloured pigments. Can't you see?' Polidori stabbed a finger at the object. 'The fracture line along this edge is as sharp as any razor. Clearly, it's very small. Larger versions are more commonly acquired for cutting cakes. You know, for marriages, or birthdays ... or for the opening of letters. But, now and then, they are commissioned for a darker enterprise. When thrust into a victim's flesh, the assailant only needs to give a twist of the handle, and...' Polidori raised his hand and deftly circled the wrist as if to demonstrate the act '...off it snaps, leaving the blade still embedded in the body, all but invisible to see but for the breaching of the flesh. In the case of your dead whore, two such knives were employed.'

Byron cried, 'Polidori, you *are* indeed a genius. So, those incisions in her throat, they were deliberately formed to make it look as if she'd suffered from the bite of a vampyre?'

There were still questions in his mind. The Countess Alfieri might have contrived such a crime – one that mirrored the horrors in Polidori's novel – but could she act the violence out? What woman of her standing would frequent a Venice brothel? And yet, men did, and of all sorts, many among them being noblemen invited to her salons. And then there were the servants who were loyal to their mistress, such as the footman who had helped conceal the truth about the woman who'd been murdered in the alley.

Byron shook his head again. 'I cannot work the puzzle out, but seeing what you've brought me...' he peered more closely at the glass, 'I see the splinters of depravity that run as black as gall through the heart of Alfieri and Veronica Lombardo. What I need to understand is how the two of them conspired to bring about that poor girl's death. I was with her all night. Surely, I would have noticed, if...' He bristled at the thought of someone else in the room. Someone attacking the girl while he was sleeping at her side. 'If these knives were used to kill her, why did I fail to see the blood?'

'Could her neck have been turned in such a way that any blood drained down, onto the floor?'

As Polidori mulled it over with professional detachment, Byron recalled the iron tang that he had noticed when he woke. But it was faint. Very faint. A great deal stronger was the perfume tinged with something animal. Something like civet and rose. Something very like the perfume always worn by Alfieri.

As Byron sat in a stunned silence, Polidori carried on: 'The intention may have been only to injure the girl in such a way as to tarnish your name and reputation. The jugular is superficial, with all too little protection from any bone or cartilage. Linking with the venous structure, the artery collects the blood as it is drained from the brain and then dispersed through other veins into the heart's right atrium. If there's a tear, or a cut caused by the blade of a knife, the rapidly declining pressure will cause a failure of the heart. If the carotid artery is also damaged, as it was, it would immediately result in a loss of consciousness. Death would follow. Very quickly.'

'How quickly?' Byron asked.

'A minute. Maybe seconds. But either way the haemorrhage could well have been internal. And if the blood was fast to clot it's not so inconceivable that you'd fail to be aware of anything untoward.'

'I see,' Byron said, a hesitation in his voice as he took in this information. At the same time, he understood that he *should* go to the law and report everything Polidori had revealed. But what if he came face to face with that Russo man again? Would he be rearrested? Would he be sent back to The Leads? And what would happen to Allegra, now caught up in this debacle?

Twenty-two

To feel the poison of her spirit creeping

Byron. From *Don Juan:* Canto III

'One more thing,' said Polidori as he was standing by the door, clutching the letter in which Byron had explicitly denied being the author of *The Vampyre*. 'There may be other evidence pointing to Countess Alfieri. Among the ornaments she keeps on display in her palazzo, during the time of my last visit I saw what looked suspiciously like glass handles that could once have been attached to knives. Very small. A perfect match for what I've given you today. She may keep them there as trophies. Perhaps she takes some perverse pleasure in displaying them in public?'

So went the doctor's last farewell, before Fletcher led him off to find the money to be used for his immediate travel needs, that in addition to the bank draft to be cashed at the time of his arrival back in London.

Alone once again, Byron stared at the shard of broken glass that might yet be the key to prove his innocence. But, before that, he must settle to composing some new letters.

The first was short and addressed to Father Aucher on Lazzaro. It began with enquiries for the welfare of the man and the promise that the monastery would soon be reimbursed for the value of the boat Byron had used to come to Venice, and which was now forever lost on the floor of the canal. The final lines reminded Aucher of the last words they'd exchanged, and if his friend also remembered, could he give a 'yay' or a 'nay' to the letter's messenger, which in turn would then be carried back to Byron's waiting ear?

The second missive was intended for the Countess Alfieri and needed more deliberation. But after several attempts, with many papers screwed to balls on the floor around his feet, Byron had the thing completed:

> *For some time, I have been meaning to express my deepest sorrow with regard to events that have sullied our friendship over the course of these past months. I was further inspired after a recent meeting with Doctor Polidori, when he told me you are willing to admit to his claim to be the author of* The Vampyre. *For this, we are both grateful. As you know, such a confession would greatly aid what has become my present sorry situation, beset as I have been by false threats & ghastly rumours. Still, I cannot deny some element of guilt that has led us to this point. Please believe me when I say I have been piqued beyond all measure since discovering the theft of some pages of my verses. What can I do but reassure you that such lines were never meant for any eyes but my own? Even so, I have no doubt they were construed as being mercilessly cruel in their description of one, who, until then, had shown me nothing more than kindness. Of all the gracious, learned women I have met with here in Venice, you are by far the least deserving of such cruel humiliation. I bow my head in abject shame for what was scribbled by a man who'd dipped too deep into his cups. Can you find it in your heart to extend*

benevolence, for having fled the shores of England I am eternally indebted to have found such a haven and a solace in your salon? How I have missed those gilded nights.

May we attempt to put the bitterness of differences behind us, resuming what was shared before that fated hour when Polidori placed a copy of The Vampyre *in my hand? Will you write back & give me hope that my name & reputation are redeemed in your mind? If not, I may accost you in the streets, kneel at your feet & beg forgiveness ~ for I am recently returned to my palazzo here in Venice, and shall soon collect my daughter from the temporary care of the Danish consul's wife.*

It is with her, so I have learned from other friends here in the city, that Allegra was left when the Hoppners departed on some travels of their own. But, for the moment, & before I bring the child home again, my palazzo is serene & I should like to take advantage of the freedom I possess by inviting you to dine. Tomorrow night, if possible? Only the two of us ~ when we shall speak more openly than it is possible to do in the constrictions of a letter.

I await your response with agitation in my heart.

Your most repentant friend & servant,

Lord B

To fawn in such a manner left him sick to his craw. But appealing to the Countess Alfieri's vanity was the surest way he knew to lure her to his house, and he'd deliberately cloaked any knowledge he might have as to Allegra's whereabouts. Forementioned was forewarned, and if the woman realised she'd been discovered in her theft, then – who could tell – she might decide to hide the child somewhere else.

As to the mention of Nicolo, it added credence to the story but also placed the boy in peril. This was why, as soon as Byron had completed his letters, asking Fletcher and Tita to make haste in their dispatching, he'd returned to his chamber and suggested that Teresa take the boy along with her when she set out on the journey to visit with her father in his castle near Ravenna.

She'd looked confused to hear those words. Her body trembled. Cheeks flushed red. Was that the blooming of a fever? Byron fretted as his fingers stroked her brow and then caressed Teresa's fine cropped hair, which shone as bright as burnished gold, and could not have been more different from the longer darker tresses of Eva in the brothel. How her image haunted him.

Meanwhile, he swore to Teresa that as soon as possible he would find a way to join her, but for now she must make haste and leave his house before the dawn. What if her Count had gone to visit her father's residence only to find she had deceived him? If he had ventured there already, she could explain her delay as being due to ailing health, being forced to stop and rest at some inns along the way. He'd tried to think of every option. All except the one remaining. What if Teresa insisted on staying here in Venice? How could he have her in the house when the Countess Alfieri was invited to his bed?

Later that night, when it was dark – when the Countess Alfieri had responded favourably to the morrow's invitation, and when Tita had returned from the island of Lazzaro, bringing with him the 'yay' of a reply from Father Aucher – Teresa finally agreed to don her male disguise and then to board the gondola in preparation for her journey.

'She isn't happy with this,' Tita had dourly remarked when Byron finally emerged from the embrace of their goodbyes beneath the gondola's black awnings.

'She understands,' Byron had answered with a crack in his voice, for any man who felt no pain after seeing the tears flowing down Teresa's cheeks would surely have a heart of stone. To hear her ask, 'Mio Byron, say this is not the end? I know you're tired of me. I'm not the same anymore. I'm...'

'Ssshh.' He'd touched a finger to her lips and was inclined to do much more, for how alluring she had looked, dressed as a boy, eyes shining bright below the shadows of the awnings. But this was not the time for love, and instead he'd only muttered, 'None of this is true. You are as dear to me as ever. I'll come and find you very soon. But only when I have Allegra.'

One final kiss, and he'd emerged into the open air. After the brief exchange with Tita, he'd looked past the gondolier, towards where Fletcher and Nicolo stood by the doors of the palazzo, both as sombre as two judges passing their sentences of death. Moving to one side, that way allowing them to board and join Teresa in the boat, Byron reached out to place a hand on Nicolo's narrow shoulder, squeezing gently when he said, 'I'm trusting you to help Fletcher, and to keep Teresa safe. Will you promise to do that?'

Before the boy had even nodded, Byron turned away in haste and disappeared beyond the doors, where he immediately began to make his plans for the next day.

Twenty-three

Alas, the love of women! It is known
To be a lovely and a fearful thing.

Byron: From letters.

She was late. Well past ten when Byron stood beside a window overlooking the canal to see a gondolier attired in Alfieri livery assist the Countess from a boat onto the steps of his palazzo. From there he heard her tell the man, 'There is no need for you to wait. I'll find my own way home again.'

So, she intended to stay, just as Byron hoped she would. Hoped, but also dreaded. Not for the first time that night he felt a stab of panic, only increased by what was seen of the face beyond her mask. The skin that shimmered silver-white beneath the lanterns at the door seemed to belong to a ghost more than one of flesh and blood. Such a vision was heightened – quite literally heightened – by her gown of pale-grey silk, and the very same white hairpiece she'd been wearing on the night when he'd last visited her house, what he'd conflated in his mind with the doomed Marie Antoinette. Not that his plans were murderous where the Countess was concerned, but even so, what on earth was he getting himself into? More to the point, at that one moment, what was she holding in her hand? It looked to be a golden cage, which she set down upon the stones before she tugged at the chain to set the doorbell jangling.

How the insistence of that sound frayed already straining nerves. He took a sharp intake of breath, then paused to glance at his reflection in a glass on the wall. With his face freshly shaved, he looked much younger than he had on his return from Lazzaro. This altogether more 'Byronic' version of himself wore his usual black suit, and a crisp, white linen shirt, while hanging from his neck was a rope of lustred pearls, and the heavy silver cross gifted to him by Father Aucher. The metal's gleam seemed to catch the sparkle in his eyes. And yet, how weary he appeared. How he longed for nothing more than to sleep and put the nightmares of this city far behind him.

Please God, let this one night prove to be an end of it. Steeling himself to head downstairs and welcome in his guest, his progress was not swift due to the hinderance of his foot, dragging more than usual. But once on the lower floor, he drew back new sets of bolts, and the doors were opened wide for the Countess Alfieri to come drifting in-between them.

Her perfume filled his nose. How noxious it was, forevermore to be equated with the death of the girl at the House of Lombardo. It was hard to force a smile when the Countess exclaimed, 'What a surprise to see you greet me at the door personally! Is there no butler or maid?'

'My valet's otherwise engaged. The cook and any servants have been dismissed for the night. I wanted to be sure we had the utmost privacy.'

His reply was in Italian, in preference to the English she more often liked to practise, for tonight it was imperative that every nuance from his lips, and from her own in return, was entirely understood. As he spoke, he also reached to take the hand she offered him. He pressed it to his lips, though it was all he could do to conceal his inner loathing. But it was vital to be mannered, to do his best to charm this woman, who must be utterly convinced that tonight he was prepared to grovel at her feet, and possibly to do much more.

Letting go of her hand, he saw her throat adorned with rubies and a string of coloured gems to match the grape-like clusters also dangling from her ears. Although perhaps they were not jewels, but beads of glass? Murano glass? Byron felt sick when he recalled the weapons used to murder Eva. And hadn't Eva also worn a ruby necklace in the brothel? He momentarily wondered how he'd find the self-control to carry on with this charade. But find it he must.

His thoughts were interrupted by the sound of pretty trilling. Looking down he saw the cage with a lovebird on its perch.

'What have we here?' he enquired.

'A gift for your daughter ... when you bring her home again.'

How brazen she is! Byron considered silently. *This crude pretence of ignorance as to Allegra's whereabouts!*

Meanwhile the woman carried on: 'Did she not once have such a pet, before it chanced to escape through a window in this house?'

'That was a parakeet.' Byron's voice remained quite measured, despite the fact that what she'd said filled him with even more suspicion. The feathers' colours were the same. A vivid yellow. Emerald green. But lovebirds also had that blood-red splash around their faces, at their throats and over their breasts – apart from which, how could the Countess Alfieri have known about the other bird's existence? Hadn't it been the very morning when he'd left Lombardo's brothel? Had Nicolo been around? Who else could it have been? Who else was present when Allegra tumbled through the study doors with the birdcage in her hands? Ah, yes! The brothel mistress and her guard, they'd been here too, having arrived sometime before to issue blackmailing demands. Had the Lombardo left his house to make a visit with the Countess?

With these questions in his mind, Byron stooped to lift the cage and place it on a nearby shelf, leaving it there when he led his guest on up the stairs. Was it coincidence again, the way she paused on the small landing from where the monkey had been hung, looking down into the shadows as she innocently asked, 'Are your animals all well?' She sniffed the air, as if the creatures' musky odour was offensive. 'No new losses to endure? I know how fond you are of them. I do remember your pain at the death of a badger.'

Byron's flesh was prickling as he recalled the conversation on this subject at her salon, when she'd referred to the arrival of Allegra in his house, as if the child had been no more than another acquisition meant for his menagerie. But it was more, much more than that. Did she know about the monkey?

I must be careful, Byron mused, as he steered her through the doors to the piano nobile, leading the woman to his chamber where the table had been laid in readiness for their meal. 'I hope this is appropriate.' He offered her a sideways glance. 'So much less formal and more intimate than any dining room.'

Content with the arrangement, she was soon nibbling cicchetti freshly made that afternoon, after Byron had announced his return to the cook and she'd rushed out to buy the makings of his very favourite dishes. Arranged on gilded plates, the polpette, tramezzini, and crostini looked delicious, although Byron was too nervous to eat a single thing.

Still, attempting to ensure a natural flow of conversation, he said, 'I must apologise to offer such thin pickings. But I assure you' – he motioned to the marble mantlepiece on which some bottles had been placed – 'the wine we have to drink is of the finest quality.'

His Newstead skull cup had already been filled to the brim, having uncorked one of the bottles hours before his guest's arrival. Now, with his back turned to the Countess, he mimicked filling it again, while in another empty glass he poured the wine he'd earlier decanted into a carafe. In the glimmer of the candles in a silver candelabra, the claret in her glass took on a viscous quality, shimmering, as dark as blood. Not that this put the woman off. Far from it – she drank deeply, replying with a smile as it was lowered from her lips, 'Your wine *is* very good. And, after all, it is not food that draws me here to you tonight, as if the moth to your flame.'

Byron sipped from his cup. 'We are both too cynical and worldly for pretence.'

'Indeed.' She nodded slowly. 'We are alike in many ways. I sometimes feel as if we knew each other in another life.'

As he recalled the way he'd felt on his first meeting with Teresa, the Countess pursed her full, rouged lips before she carried on again. 'A shame our friendship had to sour ... and for me it was much harder to accept than you might think.' She took another sip of wine. 'Like an arrow to my heart to see those verses you'd composed. At least you had the good grace to refuse to recite them at my last conversazione.' Here the woman began to quote the dreadful lines: '"A Venetian arista—"'

'Stop!' Byron interrupted. 'You must have read the explanation I offered in my letter?'

The Countess laughed, her head thrown back to expose her pale white throat. In the candlelight the rubies she had wound there gleamed like blood against the flesh, entirely smooth and with no scarring of the pox. But that was not the only reason Byron's eyes became transfixed. How did the woman have the gall to wear those jewels, unless to flaunt her own involvement in the murder at the brothel?

Oblivious of the emotion so apparent on his features, she smiled seductively. 'I have always been ambitious, greedy for knowledge, beauty ... love.'

And death? Byron mused, before he archly replied, 'All aspirations easier for men than women to achieve.'

'Which is vexing for those women who *know* they are their

equals. Very often, more than equals, despite society's restrictions.' The eyes behind her mask became two calculating slits. 'This is why I've tried my best to live as independently as any man in this city. On top of which, one needs to find something unique to set a style, to be assured of being noticed and achieving recognition. Beauty is ephemeral. Here today and gone tomorrow.' She waved her hand in the air to demonstrate futility. 'Venice is full of lovely faces. So many two-a-penny whores, as you've discovered for yourself. A woman like myself must seek to offer something else if she's to have any hope to keep her place in the world.'

'You are still beautiful today, just as I'm sure you've always been,' Byron charmed outrageously, but then he only spoke the truth, before alluding cryptically to her past friendship with a monk from the island of Lazzaro. 'Some would say that if you set your cap towards the pope in Rome, even he would be tempted to break his vows of abstinence.'

Her chin formed dimples as she frowned – and they were very pretty dimples – before she drained her glass of every drop of wine remaining. 'Oh,' she sighed. 'You'd be surprised, but your jest does hold some truth. There was a time, too long ago, but the memory still haunts me, of a lover whose status was so much greater than my own. Alas, he broke my heart.'

'The dreadful torments of our passions. We are rarely in control of the cards Fate has to play. But...' Byron knew this was his chance to raise the matter of *The Vampyre*, 'although the scandals of my past mostly pass as unregretted, the one you seeded here in Venice went on to cause me untold pain.'

She turned away. The briefest nod. 'You've been punished long enough.' Her eyes were smoky and dark when she looked at him again. 'I believe you may have come to know your place a little better.'

'*If* that place is at your side.' He was now fully in the mode of an actor on the stage, almost relishing his part as he rose from his chair to fill her glass again, although he felt somewhat concerned to see what glimmered like the flint of hard suspicion in her eyes. Had she guessed the wine was drugged? No. This was not the case. She took the glass he returned without the slightest hesitation, drinking again, cocking her head as she suddenly enquired, 'Who did you love the most – when you still lived in England?'

A strange question to ask. Byron leaned low across the table, his voice now bearing all the guile of the seducer set to pounce. 'You must never ask for details, for I am not so indiscreet. Perhaps, another day.'

He broke off as she extended a hand to touch his cheek, and from there one of her fingers traced the outline of his lips. Meanwhile, her voice came low, her words were barely more than whispers. 'For longer than you know I have looked forward to this moment. To kiss your mouth once again.'

Was she mad? He'd never kissed more than the fingers of her hand. Byron retreated from her touch to sit erect in his chair. Even if he had not known of her involvement with Lombardo, or the abduction of his daughter, the thought of sleeping with a woman infected with the pox caused any blood that might be stirred to sink like lead within his veins.

At last, he managed a riposte. 'I believe that, here in Venice, the women kiss in more erotic ways than those of other nations. It is somewhat notorious, and I think may be due to worshipping religious icons, which always seem to invite the most ardent osculation.'

'You mean we like to kiss and fuck and venerate those we love! Or do you worship something more than your own pleasure nowadays?' Her eyes were fixed on the cross Byron wore around his neck, while the hand that had so recently reached out to touch his lips fell clumsily against her glass. It toppled over and it smashed, the contents soaking wet and red across the table's fine white linen.

Looking down at the stain, she seemed to find it hard to focus. She blinked and screwed her eyes, before they fluttered closed.

She shook her head from side to side as if that way to try and force herself to stay fully alert, and when she spoke to him again her voice became a slurring drawl. 'The air in here ... it's very warm. Do you have some water?'

He offered her another glass. Water mixed with laudanum. He hoped she wouldn't notice the viscous strings of brown as yet not fully dissolved, or the bitterness the wine may have previously disguised. It was vital to ensure the sedation was complete, that she would sleep a good six hours, or perchance for even longer. Sufficient time for him to execute the plan he had in mind. To leave her here in his palazzo while he travelled to her own to claim the daughter she had stolen.

Only the thought of Allegra drove him in the enterprise as he sat and watched the Countess lift the water to her lips. When she had swallowed most of it, he breathed a sigh of relief, then rang the bell, which would alert his gondolier that the next act in the drama was beginning.

The moments following were tense. *Would she never fall asleep?* At least she seemed oblivious to the sounds of slamming doors from elsewhere in the palazzo. What on earth was Tita doing? Hadn't the man already sorted out the props that were required for The Great Humiliation of the Countess Alfieri?

With her chin propped in one palm, she began to complain: 'Why do I feel so hot? This dress. This wig ... my head is thudding.' Her voice sounded peculiar, and it was more than just the slurring. There was something in its tone Byron did not quite recognise, and yet he felt as if he should. Meanwhile, she sat a little straighter in her chair, lifting her hands, trying to rearrange the lambs' wool of the wig stuck on her head. But her fingers were too clumsy. The wig began to slip and so revealed the natural hue of the brown that lay beneath it. Some lustrous strands, as sleek as silk, fell in coils around her shoulders.

'Bother! Where are the pins?' she muttered to herself. 'Your wine is good, but very strong, and I have had too much of it.'

'I suppose you must have done...' Byron broke off at the sound of heavy feet out in the passage. Preparing himself for the arrival of Tita, he now offered the suggestion, 'Countess, would you perhaps be more relaxed if lying down?'

She shook her head, let out a groan, after which she fell unconscious, head lolling forwards on her breast just as the chamber door was opened to reveal the gondolier, who laughed out loud as he exclaimed, 'Looks like your visitor is good and ready for her bed.'

Once they'd dragged her to the mattress, Tita gruffly asked, 'This wig and mask? On or off?' The man was grinning as he twirled a soft white ringlet through his fingers.

'Leave her with some dignity!' Byron was adamant. He did not wish to expose whatever blight might be seen beneath the mask of her disguise.

'Dignity?' Tita hissed. 'I'd like to see her dangling in a cage at San Clemente.'

San Clemente was the isle in the lagoon where the insane were sent to hang above the water as exhibits for the tourists, and she did look somewhat deranged, now that she'd finally succumbed to the embrace of laudanum, the faintest glisten of drool spilled from one corner of her mouth.

Instead of triumph, Byron found his heart was stung by sympathy, about to call the whole thing off. But every ounce of compassion disappeared when he recalled the reason she was there. She had abducted his daughter. She had claimed *The Vampyre* novel to be his own confession of the most audacious bloodlust. And that necklace she was wearing. He should tear it from her throat. He should—

Tita broke through his reverie. 'You're looking green about the gills. Go and sit down. I'll set this up. Make it all fit for the bride on the night of her wedding. That's if the groom's up to the task?'

As Tita laughed salaciously, Byron replied with some force,

'No! Let the woman be.' His voice was softening. 'But you could do the ... other thing.'

Tita obliged and made his way through the door into the closet, from where there flowed the wafting scents of camphor, cinnamon, and myrrh, all being somewhat overwhelmed by a darker, danker fragrance mingled with the smell of burning – which only increased when Tita re-emerged, when he was holding in his arms a roll of cloth that corresponded to the size of a man.

Byron averted his eyes when Tita laid his burden down at the side of the Countess, before the gondolier looked back and asked, 'Funereal enough?'

'Well,' Byron said, when he'd recovered his composure, 'the Countess always did enjoy the gothic horrors as performed by favoured authors at her salons.'

As the candles on the table began to fizz and sputter, casting the room in heavy gloom, Byron turned to enquire, 'Is all of this not too excessive?'

Tita laughed. 'Don't spoil the fun before it's even started!'

'Oh, I don't know,' Byron persisted. 'Has the passion of revenge made me as bad a fiend as she?'

Tita shrugged and turned away, heading towards an open window overlooking the canal, staring out in brooding silence at a world illuminated by the moon's thin silver light.

Suddenly, growing anxious to see the plan through to fruition, Byron called impatiently, 'What you doing over there? We should leave without delay.'

Tita ignored him for a moment, busy wiping both his hands across the ruffles of his shirt, smearing the white of them with dust that looked like ash, and was no doubt some residue that had fallen from the bundle he'd been holding. Only then did he look back below his darkly beetled brows. 'I think we should stay put. Even if Helen of Troy was sailing down the Canale Grando, calling for me to go and fuck her, not even *she* could persuade me to the miss the final scene of this performance tonight.'

He waved a hand towards the bed where the Countess lay immobile, only the snuffling of faint breaths to indicate she was still living.

'What do you mean, "stay put"?' Byron was greatly irritated by Tita's state of laissez-faire. 'What about Allegra?'

The big man smirked, inscrutable. 'Your little girl's already home.'

What was this madness Tita spouted? Apart from the Countess, and the menagerie below, they were the only living souls in the palazzo at that moment.

Or, so Byron had presumed, before a knock came on the door.

Twenty-four

It was no monk, but lo! a monk array'd
In cowl and beads and dusky garb ...

Byron. From *Don Juan:* Canto XVI

'Who's there? What do you want?' Byron called uncertainly.

'It's me. It's Nicolo.'

'Nicolo?' Byron echoed as he opened the doors – only a little, not so much that the boy could observe what lay behind him on the bed.

'Why are you here?' Byron was brusque. 'Aren't you supposed to be with Fletcher?'

'I was,' the boy replied. 'But Fletcher thought it best if Tita brought me back to Venice. He said I'd be more useful if—'

'Don't be angry with the boy,' another voice now interrupted. This time it was a woman's – husky, low and confident. 'Without his help, where would you be? After all, he is the reason your Allegra's home again.'

Stepping out into the passage, Byron saw the dark Madonna who'd emerged from the curtain that concealed the servant stairs.

'La Fornarina!' It was all he could do to gasp her name. And was that flour from making bread, or new-grown grey that he could see frosting the woman's loose black hair? Could he believe that she was real, for with no light by which to see her but the flicker of the candles emanating from his chamber, she did not seem corporeal, and neither did the child the woman carried in her arms, and which he stared at so intently as he made his way towards them. But then what child of any dream could look so like his infant daughter, her pale skin soft as a peach when he touched it with his fingers? What illusion of the night possessed such eyes, just like his own, being that unique shade of blue that sometimes shifted into violet, the dark-lashed lids fluttering against the apples of her cheeks. Did he hear her say *Papa*? Did she still remember him, or was that only wishful thinking? After all, it had been – how long? He'd lost all track. Far more weeks than he could count since he'd last paid a visit with his daughter at the Hoppners.

His own eyes closed for a moment, pricked with the tears of his regret. When he opened them again it was to see that Allegra's were focused on the cross he was wearing at his breast. Her dimpled hands reached out to grasp the glimmer of the metal. From her pretty cherub mouth came a string of lisping words spoken in Italian: 'Allegra likes it. Pretty. Pretty. Allegra wants...'

Her voice trailed off. The arm fell back. The child was barely conscious, much too docile and lethargic as her face was turned from his, nestled instead against the softness of La Fornarina's breast. And now, from La Fornarina's lips came the sharper remonstration: 'Well, are you going to stand there staring, mouth gaping open like a fountain with no water left to spout! If you lack the grace to thank me, you could at least find the manners to invite me to sit down. As you can see, your daughter's grown since I was last in your house. I am worn out from holding her.'

'Come to my study,' Byron said, responding like a lackey to her strident demands. *As if she'd never been away,* he thought to himself, at the same time looking back and calling out for Nicolo to go ahead and light some candles.

While the boy took care of that, Byron busied himself, fussing like a mother hen, plumping the cushions of the chair on which La Fornarina settled, and where she looked like a queen presiding on a throne as she cradled the squirming Allegrina in her lap.

Unsure of what to do when the child began to whine, Bryon meekly enquired, 'What do you need, La Fornarina? Tell me and you shall have it. Some milk or water for Allegra? A glass of wine for yourself?' All at once, he was inspired and removed the silver cross that was hanging at his neck, placing that as if a trinket in his daughter's curling fingers.

Meanwhile, La Fornarina snorted, 'Since when were *you* religious? Is this some token of protection?'

'I hope she'll always be protected, by any gods in existence,' Byron airily replied, but it was quite the miracle the way Allegra grew more placid, as if the crucifix exuded some magic power of sedation. Or was it something else? Something wrong with the girl? He grew more anxious, muttering, 'Should I send for a doctor? Could she be ill? The sleeping fever?'

'She has no fever. She is cool.' La Fornarina stroked the hair falling across Allegra's brow, then carried on more warily: 'She had a bottle in that house. Milk and grappa by the smell. I'd say your daughter's drunk. But, in a way, that was a help. She didn't cry or make a sound to alert anyone when Nicolo went to find her. And now, as you can see, she is beginning to revive. I think ... by the morning ... we will see.'

We will see. We must hope. Byron's thoughts ran on ahead to complete the sentiment. But in his mind, he saw *Gin Lane*, the famous etching made by Hogarth, in which inebriated wretches dosed their offspring from the bottles of the spirit they'd imbibed, lying sprawled in filth and squalor in communal drunken stupors. At the same time, he looked around, searching to find Nicolo who was standing half concealed behind the curtains of one window, almost as he tried to hide from the candles' grasping flicker.

'Don't cower there! Why are you hiding?' Byron called out, thinking again of the night of Russo's visit. 'Come and tell me all that happened at the Palazzo Alfieri.'

'You won't be angry with the boy, for leaving your Teresa,' Tita's gruff voice came in reply as he ambled through the doors. Slumping in another chair, and looking perfectly at home, the gondolier crossed both his arms behind his head and raised his legs upon a small silk footstool.

Does he do this when I'm not here? Byron wondered to himself, for the first time noticing dried streaks of mud upon the silk. But he had no chance to ask, for Tita's mouth was opened wide in an ostentatious yawn through which he brazenly went on, 'Blame me, if you must. I'm the one who convinced Fletcher to let the boy come back with me. You see, I got to do some thinking as I took them to the mainland. It's the rhythm of the rowing. That, and the freshness of the breezes rising up from the water. If I'm pissed, I sober up. If I'm sad, I—'

'Oh, do get on!' Byron sighed. 'We can discuss the finer blunders of your poetic exculpations on some other day. Isn't tonight better served in you returning to my chamber ... to watch the Countess Alfieri?'

'She won't be waking for hours,' Tita said defiantly. 'But, back to earlier tonight, when I had time to do some mulling on the plans we'd been discussing and, well, it seemed a thorny problem, how you and I would get our feet across the Alfieri's doorstep. But then I thought about Nicolo, and I knew we had the key. After all, he's well acquainted with the staff and their routines.'

Stepping into the light, Nicolo carried on the thread. 'The Countess Alfieri always keeps at least one footman by the doors of her front hall, whatever hour of the clock. The ground-floor windows are all barred. The rest are shuttered up at night. The only way to get inside is through the alley, then the stairs leading up into the kitchens—'

'What we needed to find' – Tita's turn to interrupt – 'was a servant we could trust, to help with getting your girl out.'

'My friend, the maid,' Nicolo said, gaining more confidence each moment. 'The one who told me before, about Allegra being there. I went to see her just as soon as we arrived back in Venice, and she agreed to sneak me in, and...'

'Nicolo, you have triumphed!' Tita beamed at the boy. 'Now, every housebreaker in Venice will be offering you employment.'

Byron groaned at the vagaries of Tita's moral compass. 'The boy may have succeeded, but what if he'd been caught? What protection did he have, or Allegra come to that?'

Nicolo glanced at La Fornarina. 'Tita didn't think it wise for me to carry Allegra through the city on my own. If she'd cried, she might be heard, and that would only draw attention. But a woman with a child, no-one would think to bat an eye, only assume she was the mother. That's why, when we got back from the mainland again, Tita stopped by the house of Signor Cogni the baker, where—'

'You found the baker's wife,' Byron exclaimed with a rush of affection for the woman. The way she smiled. The way she tilted back her head in that proud way before she joined the conversation:

'Well, how could I say no, when Tita asked me to help? But more than that, I had to do something to show you I was sorry. Something to make you forgive me, after I told the police about the coffin in your house.'

'It was a box, not a coffin!' Byron sullenly protested, before continuing to ask, 'What made you lie, La Fornarina?'

'I wanted you to suffer, and if *I* couldn't break your heart then I would hurt your reputation. Something to cause embarrassment. A little gossip that was sure to blow over in a week. How could I know they'd be so stupid as to think a lump of wax was an actual dead body? When Tita told me about it, how they'd dragged you off in chains, I was so sorry, I wept.' She raised a hand to rub her eyes. 'As I am weeping for it now.' She cried a crocodile's tears, but how could Byron not be moved when she finally concluded, 'It was the least I could do – to bring Allegra back to you. Will you let me stay here with her? If you don't want me as a lover, then why not hire me as her nursemaid? That's if you're still in need of one.'

It seemed she'd worked the whole thing out. Byron was silent for a moment, taken aback by this request and by the pleading in her voice. A while before he could reply, 'Ah, La Fornarina, if only that were possible, but we both know it wouldn't work.'

'You're right!' She tossed her head again. Small puffs of flour – yes, it was flour, not streaks of silver in her hair – floated down to fall like flakes of winter snow around her shoulders. 'Anyway,' she mocked a smile and waved a hand dismissively. 'How could you ever resist me, living here in the same house, and in a bed not far away? Apart from which, it is too late. I have found another lover. Someone who's kind and generous, who does not rile me as you did. And, unlike you, he really means it when he tells me that he loves me.'

'Is this true?' Byron asked, somewhat deflated by the news, although he had no right to be so.

It was Tita who replied, at the same time lowering his arms to fold them loosely at his chest. 'She's found herself some Austrian. One of those officers you see strutting about the city as if they think they own the place. I would have woo'd her myself, but it seems I am too late.'

La Fornarina laughed at him, back to her old brash self again. 'Do you think I am so desperate as to bed a gondolier? I'd be sharing you with every other whore who works in Venice.'

Tita shrugged. 'What can I say? Except, so far, no-one's complained about my skills with an oar.' In the midst of such crude banter, Byron looked at his old lover and earnestly enquired, 'And do you also care for him? This Austrian of yours?'

Her smile disappeared. 'This baker's wife will never find her satisfaction with one man. Not unless he is the one she knows that she can never have.'

Just as Byron was relenting, wondering if he could bring this woman back into his household – specifically into his bed – the irrational train of thought came to meet its natural end when he remembered the scene in the room along the passage. How long could it have been since the Countess fell asleep? When had the bells last chimed the hour? Such an eerie sense of stillness suffused the rooms of his palazzo. It seemed to cradle all of Venice – until the calm abruptly ended, being shattered by a scream.

Byron froze and held his breath, dreading there was more to come. La Fornarina gasped out loud and clutched Allegra to her breast, although the child was lost in dozing and did not seem the least affected. Not so far off, Nicolo's face drained to a shade of ashen white.

Only Tita did not seem to be daunted by the sound but rose sedately from his chair as he cheerfully announced, 'Ey up! Our Sleeping Beauty must have woken from her dreaming. Me and Lord B should go and see what's going on back in his chamber. The rest of you, stay quiet here.' His voice grew sterner with the warning. 'That's if you know what's good for you.'

Byron agreed. How could he think to take the risk of Nicolo or Allegra being witness to the horror in his bed? Turning again to La Fornarina, he gave his brisk command: 'Take the children to the nursery rooms upstairs, then lock the doors. Don't move an inch until I come myself to tell you it is safe.'

Walking through the passage door leading directly to his closet, Byron spied into the chamber where the Countess Alfieri cowered underneath the table at which earlier that night she'd sat so graciously to dine. Despite her state of dishabille, her mask half-skewed upon her face, the woman must have had the constitution of an ox to have revived so rapidly from the sedation of the black drop. And now, seeing Tita standing in the room before her, she gave a whimper of relief and crawled towards him on all fours.

Her progress was slow, her hands and feet becoming tangled in the skirts of her gown, as well as lengths of frayed black cloth that had previously formed a denser roll upon the bed. But having reached the gondolier she pointed back towards the source, her voice a whispered trembling: 'Look! Look there. Do you see?'

'I can see ... very well!' Tita's growl of an answer was edged with his amusement. 'Looks to me as if you've gone and drained poor Byron dry of any blood in his veins. I have to say, it's not attractive. I much preferred the man's appearance when he had a better colour.'

Though these words were in poor taste, they were nothing if not valid. How much more hideous the mummy from Lazzaro looked to be now that its windings were unravelled. How macabre were the features, although the charring of the flesh looked somewhat paler than before, and the dim shimmer of the few remaining candles rendered it as a vision quite uncanny. It was the oddest illusion to see those bright-blue eyes that had been painted on the lids almost as they were real, as if the corpse was now 'alive', however strange that contradiction. Certainly, the Alfieri, in her opiate-muddled haze, believed it to be so.

'It tried to bite me!' She shuddered, her own eyes wide and round with shock. Meanwhile, her fingers touched the rubies that had snagged against her throat, and where some blood was visible as it trickled through the settings.

Should Byron make his presence known and ask to see the woman's ankles; the extraction method favoured by the feral dakhanavar? Oh, how ridiculous that he should even contemplate the thought. Just as well Tita was there, boots planted firmly on the ground when he casually replied, 'You must have had those cuts already. Scratched yourself while in a stupor. Or...' he glanced across the room, 'from that pile of broken glass.'

The Countess squinted at the table and the shattered shards of crystal. 'I can't remember. Oh, my head!'

Byron no longer had the stomach to prolong this agony. 'Enough!' he called as he stepped from the closet to the room. But if he'd hoped to calm the woman, the very opposite occurred. When she turned to see him there, she let out an anguished groan. Who would think the living man could achieve the same reaction as the corpse upon the bed? But it seemed that Byron had.

'Countess...' he addressed her. 'I'm sure by now you realise that tonight has been my chance to seek revenge for all the damage you've inflicted on my person. The lies you've spread have proved to be the greatest inconvenience. But if that was not enough, you had the gall to steal my daughter. I dare not think what you had planned for so innocent a child.'

The woman visibly flinched. She looked bewildered when she said, 'Only to tell you where she was. To invite you to my house, and—'

'Bit late for that, isn't it, when Allegra's here already!' Tita announced triumphantly.

'But how?' the Countess asked. 'When I last saw her, she was—'

'Dosed liberally with alcohol so as to render her unconscious.' Byron growled his interruption. 'Is this what you do with other children from the streets? The orphans sold as slaves? The ones condemned to work in brothels?'

The woman protested, 'I ... No! What do you mean? The Danish consul's wife – she was planning to adopt her, telling any who would listen that the child had been abandoned.' The Countess took a gulping breath, shook her head and carried on. 'To try and stop that happening, I had your crest forged on some paper ... copied from your own responses to my salon invitations. I only took Allegra to give her back to *you*! I thought you would be happy. That you would thank me, and—'

Byron interrupted: 'Why should I thank the very woman who's been telling all of Venice that I am a murderer? Though if you thought that to be true, why did you come here to dine? Alone and unprotected?'

She looked back towards the bed and pressed her knuckles to her mask, rubbing the eyes that lay beneath as if a child who hopes to wipe away the terrors of a nightmare. 'How could you do this monstrous thing? Did your doctor friend supply you with a body from his morgue?'

Byron spoke impatiently. 'And yet you had no such qualms about the woman in your alley.'

The Countess dropped her hands. 'What had *she* to do with me? Whatever villain slashed her throat, it was a mere coincidence that—'

'That *I* was there to find her dying. That you accused me of the crime? And what about the brothel? You must have thought yourself so clever to implicate me there as well. How imaginatively done! How you do relish your obsession with Doctor Polidori's *Vampyre*. But you should know, you are not quite as cunning as you think. Your lies have wounded the true author just as they have my reputation, and now, while working in the morgue, he has discovered evidence that leads directly back to you.'

Byron feared he'd said too much, that at this juncture in time it was unwise for him to speak about the daggers made of glass. She was nothing if not wily. Might she not fabricate some story to extricate herself – as her response was now to prove.

'What brothel do you speak of?'

'As you are very well aware, it is Veronica Lombardo's.'

The Countess looked yet more perplexed. Her brow was furrowed in confusion that appeared so genuine he could almost half believe it. As before, he felt some pity for her state of dishabille. And that preposterous white wig still balanced on her head, it was like a comic tribute to the leaning tower of Pisa. How mortified she would have been if she had looked into a mirror. And yet, some natural poise remained as she turned towards the bed, where the mummy still lay.

'Want to see more?' Tita asked. 'Shall I remove the other wrappings?'

Byron was just about to say that would not be necessary, when the Countess Alfieri took the initiative herself. Crawling back towards bed, she tugged at what was left of the windings and revealed, not more charred and naked flesh, but a fine black woollen robe, such as those worn by the monks on the island of Lazzaro.

Byron wondered if the gondolier had dressed the mummy up in the habit from his closet. Or, perhaps Father Aucher had decided it was best to send the corpse fully attired. There may have been some element of method in this madness, for the Countess Alfieri recoiled in alarm, turning to Byron as she gasped, 'Is this Brother Petros? There is something so like...'

Byron could make no sense of the mutterings that followed, watching mutely as the woman dragged herself onto the mattress and lay down beside the mummy, gently fondling a rosary of beads around its neck. The cross was turned in her hands to reveal a small inscription. Too far away for him to read, but whatever it could be she was clearly much affected, and like a woman possessed she cried out through ragged breaths, 'It is *his* crucifix. His name's engraved on the back. And under that, my own initials. The ones he added there himself.'

'As a token of love?' Byron asked.

'Ah,' she smiled bitterly. 'Petros was beautiful. He had the face of a saint, and I did love him in my way. We first developed a friendship through our charity work, but soon enough he was accepting invitations to my house. Not that any affair was fated to last. Petros was a troubled man, often weeping in my arms as he was torn between two worlds. In the end, his love for God proved to be stronger than the pleasures of the flesh we'd enjoyed.'

The woman heaved a sigh, staring into Byron's eyes as she plaintively enquired, 'How did he die? I cannot bear to think he might have suffered. Petros was the best of men. I was told ... I believed he'd returned to his vocation on the island monastery. But would he really have gone without a word of goodbye? He would have given me that. I always wondered if she'd lied.'

'She? Who is this she? Is it Veronica Lombardo?' Byron asked as the Countess lifted the mummy's blackened hand, pressing near skeletal fingers to the roundness of her cheek, as if the carcass was alive and acting through its own volition.

Oh, *how* cruelly he had tricked her. But now, to see her suffering, how could he find it in his heart to tell the Countess these remains did not belong to any monk she might have known in the past? He could only stand and stare as tears were spilled from her eyes to glisten on her mask, dripping from there to fall like rain across the mummy's parched grey face – until she gave the briefest nod and looked back at him again.

'Tell Veronica Lombardo to come here to your palazzo. Tell her I need to know the truth.'

Twenty-five

As cursing thee, thou cursing them,
The flowers are withered on the stem.
But one that for thy crime must fall,
The youngest, most beloved of all...

Byron. From *The Giaovr*

I have tried so many times to wipe the horror from my mind ~ the awful image of the Countess when she returned to the bed & lay down beside the mummy, when she entwined her living hands about the dead thing's brittle fingers & closed her eyes as if to sleep. She would not speak. She almost looked as if she was another corpse. I was happy to comply when Tita said we should both go, leaving the woman to wallow in her misery alone.

Having secured any means by which she might escape, we also sought some hours of sleep before the morrow came around. Wherever Tita disappeared to, I settled in a study chair. However, rest remained elusive & my thoughts continued turning. Was there a possibility that, even now, she might be standing beside the bedroom window, breaking the glass & screaming down to any souls already out & about on the canal? But was that likely when I had the upper hand with regard to the murder in the brothel? I may not yet have understood what evil led her to that crime & she may still be unsure as to what proof I claimed to hold, but the woman was not stupid. What could it be but her glass daggers?

How then to play the final round of this Venetian masquerade? Should I do as I had threatened & report her to La Forsa? But if they were in her pay, I could be trumped & rearrested before I've even had the chance to place my cards upon the table? As for the Lombardo, what new truths might she reveal? I had to know, & so I wrote: ~

I believe you may have recently misplaced a certain friend. She is not lost, but is with me at the Palazzo Mocenigo, where she has now expressed a wish that you might also come & visit. Should you accede to this request, do ensure you are alone. If you are not, my spies shall see & report your whereabouts to my colleagues at the consul, taking with them certain items that will undoubtedly prove the Countess Alfieri's role in a murder that occurred at your brothel recently ~ the crime for which you were content to see me charged and locked away.

When you last came to my palazzo you demanded compensation for the loss of your 'investment'. Now, I seek to do the same. I seek justice for the shame you have cast upon my name, & for the boy called Nicolo, who is now in my employ after suffering the loss of both his father & his sister, with the latter being lured into the cage of your house.

Feeling imprisoned himself, wishing to savour the warmth of morning sunlight on his face, Byron signed and sealed the letter, and delivered it in person. Knowing his daughter's whereabouts, and that the Countess Alfieri was the most barbed and dangerous of the two thorns that scratched his flesh, he did not fear being seen or recognised by the Venetians busy bustling around him. Indeed, his mood was oddly light as he inhaled the salty air. Air that glistened like tiaras above the cupulas and towers. He gazed up at them in wonder as if it was for the first time, as something glorious and eternal but, for himself – he smiled sadly – only ever transient. It was as if he had already departed from this city, seeing the beauty laid before him as a ghost, a thing half formed. He barely heard the slip-slop echoes of the waters all around him. The screams of seagulls overhead. The bawdy songs of gondoliers. Ah, what a glory of a dream Venice had been these past few years, and she would never be forgotten. But already she was drifting into realms of nostalgia...

Don't look. This life is over, he told himself as eyes were lowered, limping onwards through the warren of the lanes, the cold damp stones on which his cane was echoing. Finally, the tapping stopped. Had time itself also ceased? The House of Lombardo oozed a dank and eerie silence. Windows and shutters were all closed, and had those stems of foliage always sprouted through the cracks unrepaired in crumbling walls? Where was the thug of a guard?

He knocked three times to no avail, so pushed his letter through a gap between the door and step below it. If the Lombardo was inside, she would be certain to receive it.

Arriving back at his palazzo through the entrance to the garden, Byron listened out for any sounds to indicate that his menagerie was waking – and heard instead the bell-like laughter of his daughter, Allegra. She was sitting on a bench below a vine, where leaves were scorched and any fruits on them had withered. Clearly no watering went on during the months of his absence. Not that such things concerned him now. Far more important was his joy to see Allegra awake, with La Fornarina at her side. Both were chewing on some bread, watching Nicolo throwing twigs across the yard for Mutz to chase.

So much for doing as I asked and staying locked inside the nursery, Byron sighed. But then again, how could he possibly complain when he'd become so immersed in his own business of revenge that, for a while, he had forgotten their existence in his house? To see them now though, what sweet frisson of delight filled his heart. This scene of domesticity was all too real and in his grasp. *If* he could love La Fornarina. *If* Nicolo was his son. And, the daughter he'd neglected, how enchanting and angelic she appeared when she looked up and called, 'Look! My papa. My papa Birron is here!'

Letting his cane drop to the ground as she came gambolling towards him, he swept her up into his arms. He held her high above his head and swung her round, and round, and round, until he felt quite overwhelmed by a sudden giddiness. Forced to sit upon the bench, he watched Allegra scamper off to join Nicolo and the dog. Meanwhile, he took La Fornarina's hand in his own and softly said, 'These precious moments will be crystallised like amber in my heart. If only things could have been different. If *I* had been a different man.'

La Fornarina laughed at him. 'But you are Byron. You won't change.'

'Oh, but I have. In many ways. And I am grateful to you. Not simply because you brought Allegra back to me...'

He left a lengthy pause.

'There are still things I need to do here, and with those actions comes the risk of yet more danger for Allegra. Will you take her somewhere else? Please, La Fornarina, won't you say that you'll do me this last favour?'

'What do you want?'

'Do you recall the time I took you to my villa at La Mira?'

'Your summer house?' She nodded sadly. 'We fucked for days on end. It is a happy memory.'

Byron struggled to ignore the sudden stirring in his loins. 'Indeed, it is. But, for now, if I gave you some money, would you take Allegra there? It wouldn't be for very long. Perhaps a day, no more than three. If it is...' He paused again while reflecting on the fact that that would be because he'd failed, that Alfieri and Lombardo had somehow triumphed over him. 'Then I'll make sure Tita knows what to do for the best. Ideally, he or Fletcher will take Allegra back to England, to the care of her mother. If not, there is my sister.'

'Do not speak in such a way!' La Fornarina objected with a violent cry of passion. 'What do I care for anyone you might have known before in England? Next thing you will be asking me to plan your funeral, and *that's* the job for a wife. And not one married to a baker!'

'I must account for every outcome. Even the worst of them.' Byron turned to meet the sparkle of her animated eyes.

'Oh, mio Georgio,' she sighed. 'If I could raise your Allegrina as my own then I would. But there's my husband to consider, and I believe he is dying.'

'So Inspector Russo told me, though I'd presumed it must have been another of your lies.'

La Fornarina's eyes took on a sad and distant look and her voice was near to breaking. 'Very soon I could be widowed, and though my Austrian is kind it's not a serious affair. Would he still want me with a child tied to the hems of my skirts? With you ... it could be happier.'

When he failed to respond her words took on a harsher tone:

'But now you have another lover, and *she* is your grand amour. You will take your child to her and play your happy families. I could sit here at your side and try to tell you you're mistaken, that in time you will regret this Guiccioli affair. I could tell you that one day you will wake up and you will wish you had never seen her face. But I know it is no use. Tita says you are besotted. In so deep you'd sooner drown than think to give the woman up.'

Byron had no regrets. Whatever else she might have been, La Fornarina did not possess the gift of prophecy, although he did believe in fate and that a future in Ravenna with his mistress and his daughter was already preordained. As to being in love, he'd made mistakes in the past, but from now on he would endeavour to be better in the future. What was love anyway? Perhaps little more than the power of the spirit to imagine something beautiful and then to make it real. If it *was* real, it should be cherished. Love made this life worth living for. Worth dying for as well. Love. Only love. Nothing mattered any more.

He looked up to see Allegra. She was too pale and too thin for a child so very young. But she was happy enough, crouching down on the ground, where she appeared to be entranced with a pile of small round stones. But were they stones, or something else?

Byron rose from the bench and stepped a little closer – seeing the swirl of vibrant colours encased in spherical glass marbles. 'Who gave you these?' he asked abruptly, though he already knew the answer, being certain that he'd seen some baubles just the same in the Palazzo Alfieri.

Allegra lifted one to show him, but noticing her father's frown she quickly snatched it back again. There was the clacking of hard edges as she deposited the marbles in the pocket of her dress, before she said with a pout, 'The lady. The nice lady. She lets me play with them.'

Life's harsh realities could no longer be ignored. Allegra's 'nice lady' was now lying in his bed, and at her side was the mummy from the island of Lazzaro.

Good God, what have I done? Byron's mind was all a panic, over which he heard the clucking of the hen from nearby cages, swiftly followed by the chatter of the one surviving monkey.

After calling for Nicolo to go and feed the animals and then to meet him in his study, he leaned down to plant a kiss on Allegrina's head, rising back to his full height before he turned to La Fornarina. 'I think … the time has come.'

She said nothing, only nodded to convey her understanding. It was the quietest farewell. Both knew it was their last.

Twenty-six

Remorse and shame shall cling to thee,
And haunt thee like a feverish dream!

Byron. From *Remember Thee! Remember Thee!*

He waited and he waited for Veronica Lombardo, well into the afternoon, which grew extremely hot and humid. Sitting at his desk, he heard no sounds from the menagerie of creatures down below. Only the gurgling and slap of the canal against house walls, or the clouds of black mosquitos flying through his study window. Their high-pitched buzzing made him tense. He would prefer the pretty music of his daughter's prattling.

As for the woman on his bed, all was serenity and calm. He'd listened at the door and heard her breathing evenly. A little later Tita told him that he'd taken in some water, but as far as he could tell the Countess was still asleep.

Thinking again of the mummy on the bed with the Contessa, he felt distinctly nauseous, despite the fact that everything had more or less gone to plan – with Alfieri being drugged, and then awaking to imagine that the husk at her side had been himself in vampyre guise.

What was the term Aucher had used? Ah yes, the dakhanavar. Well, whatever the truth of the mummy's genesis – whether a demon raised from Hell to slake its lust through drinking blood, or the desiccated carcass of a mortal, long since dead – Byron wished for nothing more than to see the monster gone. And he *had* promised Father Aucher that when he'd finished with the prop, the mummy would be rolled into its winding cloths again and ferried out to the Lagoon. It would be weighed down with chains. It would be cast into the water. The ocean bed would be the grave from which the corpse would never rise.

So vividly did he imagine such a scene in his mind's eye, Byron started with a gasp when he heard the sudden clanging of the doorbell down below.

The Lombardo had arrived.

She'd come alone, which surprised him. Even more of a shock to find the woman quite so altered from the time of her last visit. Her usually pristine black robes were creased and caked with filth. Had she walked through the streets rather than travelling by water? She must have done. She looked exhausted – too diminutive and frail against the bulky gondolier who'd let her in and then escorted her upstairs to Byron's study.

Was she afraid? The way she'd yelped when Tita grabbed her by the arm and pushed her through the doors? However much Byron despised her, Tita's manners were appalling. Still, needs must. He would suffice, at least till Fletcher could return from Ravenna to resume his normal duties. Not that Byron himself showed the Lombardo more respect. He did not stand to greet her, only lifted his head as he frostily announced, 'So, Signora, you condescend to come and bless us with your presence.'

She said nothing for a while, seeming to struggle as she used only one hand to lift the veils that were covering her face. As the fabric fluttered back across her head Byron caught the vaguest odour of the perfume worn by Countess Alfieri. Did the Lombardo use it too?

Meanwhile, he was transfixed by the bare face he'd never seen. Denuded of its thick white paint, or any other potions she might normally apply to form a doll-like countenance, the Lombardo's wrinkled skin was grey and marred by sores. There was no blackened arch of brows to emulate the hair she'd lost. No imitation of good health in spots of rouge applied to cheeks. Without the tint of any carmine, her lips were barely visible below the criss-cross nets of lines that ran on up towards her nose – the lines accentuated more when she announced, 'Well, here I am! What do you want? Spit it out.'

'How impatient you are,' Byron casually replied, while also stifling a yawn, though this was not an affectation to demonstrate his tedium. Despite consuming endless cups of strong black coffee through the day – and Tita's skills in brewing beans were very poor compared to Fletcher's – exhaustion seeped into his bones. He hardly had the strength to speak. And yet he must, for only when this meeting was completed could he hope to reclaim some vestige of normality.

When she spoke her voice was breathless. 'Your note only arrived with me an hour ago. I've been spending some time at the house of a friend. That's where I also met your daughter. What a pretty child she is. How we enjoyed our games of marbles. But alas…' She held his eye. 'Now all such joys have been denied.'

Byron curtly replied, 'You'll never see my child again.'

Lombardo snorted. 'I heard that boy carried her off. The one they call Nicolo. Some of the other servants saw him. What a turncoat he is, lacking all sense of gratitude for the kindness he's received from the Countess Alfieri. What do they say – a thankless child is sharper than a serpent's tooth? But I have told her more than once, she was a fool to ever think of helping him, or his sister.' She glanced around, and then enquired, a note of caution in her voice, 'Is he here with us now?'

Byron shook his head. He'd sent Nicolo off on errands, taking the dog along as well to give the semblance of a guard. There'd been a third and final letter to deliver in the city. One that concerned this day's events. And, when that task had been completed, Byron had asked the boy to visit his favourite bookshop. He wanted guidebooks on Ravenna, and a velvet-bound edition of the poetry of Dante that he'd seen some weeks before and which he'd thought would make the perfect present for Teresa. After that came medications, and other practicalities – all of which should be sure to keep Nicolo occupied until events at the Palazzo Mocenigo were concluded.

But, for now, forced to address the situation in his house, he felt a moment of confusion. Whatever their connection, why would the Countess Alfieri invite a woman of Lombardo's reputation to her house? And why was the brothel keeper clutching at her arm, holding it rigid at her side almost as if the limb was splinted.

'Are you in pain?' he asked abruptly.

'A bite from a mosquito. There are so many zanzara buzzing about the canals.'

'Also in this room,' Byron replied, seeing more insects hovering around the woman – who suddenly appeared somewhat unsteady on her feet, so much so he was convinced she might have been about to faint.

At Bryon's sign, Tita stepped forwards from the door and helped direct the woman to a chair, to which the swarm of flies then followed. As she slumped down, a billowing bag made of black silk and froths of lace from which the air swiftly deflated, he caught the scent of something sour. Something that smelled like vinegar. And then, the riper stench of rot, the cause of which was emanating from the arm she was still holding, and which – when she tried to bat the insects away – was all too clearly visible due to the sleeve of her gown falling back towards her elbow.

'Well, well. And what is this?' Tita asked, holding the stick of her wrist between his fingers. No matter how she struggled to escape his iron grip, she was locked tight while he used his other hand to tug away the soiled edges of a bandage, and thus reveal the injury where a section of skin had been torn from her arm.

Byron could not speak, only observe the crusting scabs around the surface of the wound. The jagged puncture marks of teeth, from which there oozed a fetid mixture of green pus and clotted blood, with streaks of veins too visible, running through her sagging flesh as if the branches of a tree.

'Call that an insect bite? What a load of steaming bull shit!' Tita dropped the woman's wrist. 'Not unless it's a fly as big as a dog.'

'Or a monkey…' Byron muttered through a growing mist of rage.

'That evil creature!' she hissed. 'It escaped from its cage and viciously attacked me. My guard was also injured when he tried to pull it off. And now, this wound, it will not heal. I fear the beast has poisoned me.' Her laugh was filled with bitterness. 'Killed by the teeth of Byron's monkey! What an inscription for my gravestone.'

Byron's eyes were narrowed, his voice devoid of sympathy. '*You* broke into my house. *You* terrorised my staff!'

'By staff, you mean the boy … no better than a rat. I should have strung him up that night and let him dangle with your ape. Hopefully, he understands that there are always consequences for those who choose to betray us.'

'Us?' Byron asked. 'By which you mean yourself and the Countess Alfieri?'

'We have a certain bond.'

'I know she passes on the orphans she professes to have saved to be enslaved in your brothel. I can only assume she is paid handsomely for that, or does she do it for no more than a perverse gratification? Whatever the reason, you are both steeped to your necks in depravity and sin.'

'So says the Satyr of Venice!' The Lombardo's breaths came faster. She tried to rise and leave her chair, but Tita pushed her down again, grunting back through gritted teeth, 'Sit down, you bitch. You won't be leaving till you've told us everything.'

'And after that?' she enquired.

'Lord B will decide. His is the life you've tried to ruin. His decision on the penance.'

'You owe Nicolo, too. For the sister who was murdered...' Byron began, but had to pause to stifle his emotions. At last, he carried on: 'Why did the Countess do it? Why did you connive to help her?'

The Lombardo listened mutely, wincing as she pulled her sleeve back down across the wound. Apart from that, her features were fixed, more like a carving made of stone until, with concentrated effort she raised her head and started laughing. It was a sound quite hideous, and how it grated Byron's nerves. But, at last, the woman calmed and seemed to savour her reply. 'For all your cleverness and wit, you still don't see what's going on.'

At this point another voice was heard to join the conversation. The Countess Alfieri had unexpectedly appeared to stand between the study doors, from where she now addressed Lombardo. 'So, you came. I hoped you would.'

Byron glanced askance at Tita. 'I thought you'd locked her in my chamber.'

'She was asleep. She wasn't moving,' the gondolier replied as he stared past the Countess to the passageway beyond.

Byron followed his gaze. Was someone there, behind the woman? Someone lurking in the darkness? A stench of mouldering as well, which, for the very briefest moment overwhelmed the riper odours emanating from Lombardo. But soon enough he realised the stink was carried on a breeze, from outside, from the canal. Any shadow in the passage had been thrown by no-one else but the Countess Alfieri. Though it was strange, when she walked on, passing through the study doors, the way the darkness seemed to separate and veer away from her in quite the opposite direction. Byron could swear he'd heard some footsteps, dragged and sliding on the marble.

No, it wasn't possible. His senses were unbalanced. The strange distortions of exhaustion. The only sounds of walking feet belonged to those of the Countess, who now came nearer to his desk, and what a sight the woman made, bathed in the watery light shafting through the open windows. With the wig she'd been wearing now removed and firmly clutched in the fingers of one hand, her own dishevelled mane of hair was hanging loose around her shoulders. Hair like the mane of a lion. A lion newly fed, with the red of her cosmetics streaked like blood upon her chin. Same with the skin of her throat, where the choker had chaffed. Her pale-grey gown was also stained, but with a darker gritty ash. All in all, the woman looked, as Fletcher might have said, as if she'd fallen in a hedge and then been dragged out of it backwards.

The Lombardo heaved a sigh as she addressed this apparition. 'You could be some tawdry whore parading drunk on the streets. Well, whatever you've been doing in this house, did you know he sent his lackies to your own, to fetch his daughter away?'

The Countess barely murmured, 'I left her in your care.'

The older woman hissed, 'It was the middle of the night! Do you deny me any sleep? You know how I've been suffering. Look to your staff! They are to blame, specifically one of your maids. She's a friend of that Nicolo and was obviously involved in the abduction of the girl. You are a fool!' She drew a breath, before her insults carried on. 'In the daughter you held the key to Byron's silence. While he was in The Leads, we were safe and he was doomed. But now the lock has been unpicked and the door is opened wide for the truth to be exposed. You have invited ruin in.'

Byron asked, 'Is there no crime the pair of you have not devised? Slander and libel. Murders. Kidnap? I confess I am bemused that a few lines of worthless verse should result in fostering such extreme degrees of hatred. Lines that were only ever destined to be cast upon a fire.'

The Lombardo batted back, 'Most of your verse deserves that fate. You strut about this city like a pompous emperor, but in truth you are not fit to lick the Countess's feet. You *never* saw her worth. But I did ... only too well.' The older woman's serpent smile was as cold as winter ice, her stumps of blackened teeth exposed aggressively. 'She was the best of my investments, having captured the heart of the old Count who often came to visit at my brothel. A man so riddled with disease that not a soul was surprised when he expired but a month after their wedding celebrations ... leaving *her* at liberty.'

'And how I paid for that freedom!' the Countess cried angrily. 'I am still paying to this day. Did you poison the man – with the contract you drew up to release me from your house, also allowing you a share of my own inheritance? And what of Brother Petros? Did you murder him as well? Last night, I dreamed ... such awful dreams, and yet they seemed to be so real. He was lying at my side, but he was dead and mouldering. I smelled the rotting of his corpse. It was blackened and charred, as if his body had been burned.'

While Byron wondered if the Countess had indeed been driven mad by the vision of the mummy placed beside her on the bed – which she spoke of as a nightmare, not a real, solid thing – the Lombardo blasted back:

'That monk was about to bring disaster on my head. Do you imagine I'd stand back and simply wait for that to happen? Yes, I had him killed. There was no alternative. He was nosing around. Much too suspicious of my business. But Petros did not burn. I had him gutted like a fish, his body dumped in the lagoon.' The woman chuckled to herself. 'I let him swim back to the nets of his Jesus fisherman.'

'How could you be so wicked? He was my friend. He was...' The Countess Alfieri's words trailed off in a sob.

'What choice did I have?' the Lombardo snapped at her. 'I would have been destroyed if that meddler survived.'

Unnerved to hear this frank exchange, Byron stood, scraping the legs of his chair across the floor. 'So, Countess, you were once a common prostitute. You were pimped to your Count, and through this charity of yours you then provided this woman with more children for her brothel. The very brothel where Nicolo's sister was forced...' His words trailed off as once again he imagined the scene. He and the girl, both drugged and dreaming. Unaware of the flashing of glass daggers in the darkness.

'It isn't true!' the Countess cried. 'Nicolo's sister was employed in my house as a maid. I believed she'd run away. I never knew where she'd gone.'

'Or do you *choose* to believe that?' Byron's tone was cynical. 'If you did, you are a fool.'

'Byron is the fool who believes he is wise.' Lombardo cackled her response. 'But his eyes, they are still blind.'

'Not so blind that I don't see the rubies at the neck of the Countess Alfieri. The very jewels the girl was wearing when she died inside your brothel. What more proof do I need of her involvement in the crime?'

The Lombardo smiled with malice. 'I gave those gems to the Countess, some weeks after the event. Call it payment for the girl I abducted from her house. But it is true, she did not know, and it is mere coincidence she chose to wear them here tonight. But then, she suits them, does she not? And she's deserving of their worth, unlike that thankless little whore.'

'That girl had a name, and it was Eva!' Byron snarled. 'Do you not possess one ounce of guilt within your rotting heart?'

The Lombardo glared at him. 'Whatever she'd been called in her past life, her name was Trouble from the moment she arrived through the doors of my brothel. She was too surly by far, always bemoaning her fate. She even threatened to escape and tell the Countess what I'd done. Failing that, to run off to La Forsa with complaints. What a fool, when so many of those men are in my pocket, the very highest in their ranks among my most devoted patrons.' The old woman heaved a sigh, her face a picture of remorse. 'I did consider selling her to another of the brothels, but to pass on shoddy goods would only stain my reputation. And reputation is all, as you know yourself, Lord Byron. When that is lost our lives can change … and sometimes change beyond all measure.'

When the woman paused for breath, her mouth was opened so wide he could see her teeth again. Teeth striated black and grey but looking strong enough to bite. *Teeth as were the teeth of lions.*

Inwardly, he shuddered. Meanwhile, Lombardo carried on. 'I suppose, in the end, I simply made her wish come true. Now, she is dead and rests in peace. Maybe in another world, though of that I have my doubts. I envy her in a way. No more worries. No more pain. The sweet oblivion of death.'

'Hardly at peace. She's in the morgue, killed by two daggers made of glass. Murano glass, like the collection at the Palazzo Alfieri.'

'The palazzo where I go whenever I desire, and where the Countess often spoke of her friendship with Lord Byron.'

'And how that friendship has since soured.'

'Was it ever sweet?' The old woman smiled slyly as she glanced towards the Countess. 'When she informed me that you'd recently inspired another friend to write the story of a vampyre, I suggested she might play a little game of revenge by implying that the tale was autobiographical. A confession of your own unnatural lust for blood and death.'

Byron turned in alarm to the Countess Alfieri. 'You knew full well that I had nothing to do with any murders! What offence can I have caused? Surely it cannot be because I scribbled a few lines of some crude and worthless verse?'

The Lombardo interrupted: 'You will rant on about your verses! It is so very tedious. And yes, no doubt you're innocent of the murder in the alley. That would have been a common cut-throat. But what a serendipity when you deigned to show your face at the House of Lombardo, allowing me to contrive the perfect crime to seal your fate. I suppose you could say I killed two birds with the one stone. The hen, anyway ... though I'll be honest, my intention was to wound rather than kill her. I was shocked when I first found her lying cold in the bed. But it worked out for the best. If the girl refused to work and earn her keep in my house, then she could do another job on her back in the morgue. At the same time, I might reclaim my investment by demanding compensation for her death, and when that failed ... well, I suppose I did not think to see the cock escape the prison of The Leads so as to crow another day.'

'This can't be true!' The Alfieri's face had turned as white as parchment. She dropped her wig to the floor. Both hands were raised to her throat, the fingers twisting back and forth as she tried to unclasp the ruby necklace fastened there. It was as if, only then, she had truly grasped the horror of what the other was recounting, staring at Byron in distress. 'You must believe me. I knew nothing of this death in the brothel.'

He was wary. She was cunning. Hadn't she wanted to destroy him, so cruelly taunting him in public? No, he refused to be deluded, stabbing back, 'Oh, how you lie, though I'll admit it was clever, making it look as if the girl had been ravaged by a vampyre. But Polidori's clever too, and he's discovered what you used. One blade is now in my possession while the other one remains within the body of your victim. It will stand as evidence.'

The Lombardo batted back, 'Anyone with half a mind would suspect *you* stole those knives from the Palazzo Alfieri. You were last there, after all, when the murders first began.'

As the Lombardo spoke these words, the Countess Alfieri took a few more steps towards him, only a yard or so away when she suddenly cried out, 'Would you care for these deaths if your name was not connected? Did you ever think of me? The cruel fate I had to face when *you* so blithely cast me out from the only happy home that I had ever known, reduced to begging on the streets, and even labelled as a thief?'

Hearing these bitter accusations, Byron could only stand and stare in a state of mute confusion as he registered the fact that all at once the woman's voice sounded entirely different. She still addressed him in English, but with a mournful lilting tone. The unmistakable Welsh accent that had surely once belonged to a maid at Newstead Abbey.

'Susan? Susan Vaughan?' He gasped the name just as the Countess dragged the mask from her face.

Twenty-seven

Mournful but mournful of another's crime,
She look'd as if she sat by Eden's door.
And grieved for those who could return no more.

Byron. From *Don Juan:* Canto XV

At last, recovered from the shock, Byron was able to ask, 'How do you come to be in Venice? The last I heard, you were in London.'

'When I wrote you a letter, begging for your help after I'd been accused of theft – having tried to sell the gown you once gave to me at Newstead, the only thing of any value I possessed in all the world...'

Byron remembered the gown. How beautiful she'd looked in it. The lustrous green of the velvet against the cream of her complexion. Was she so different today, even after seven years? What the Lombardo said was true. He had been blind, only seeing the woman's fuller figure, the cosmetics that concealed the milky clearness of her skin. The ornate wigs. The golden mask – which, now it was removed, revealed no sign of any pox. And those eyes!

Those rose-red lips. How had he failed to know them? Was it because he'd never dreamt that a maidservant from Newstead could have risen to such wealth and influence in the world?

Unconsciously, he touched the lid of the box on his desk. The one that held a handkerchief embroidered with their two initials. The token she'd once sent along with a letter. Something she knew he'd recognise to prove her plea was genuine.

Such was his state of discomposure, he could barely raise his eyes when Susan spoke to him again. 'Can you imagine what it's like, to be that desperate for money? To have no job, no home, no family or friends to take me in after you'd cast me out of Newstead? I used to think our love was fated, something written in the stars, like *Romeo and Juliet.* I couldn't count how many times I took that play down from your shelves. Every spare moment I possessed was spent inside your library. All I hoped for was the chance to impress you with my learning, emulating the airs and the graces of the ladies who visited the house as guests. How naive I was back then, my head too dizzy with romance and foolish possibilities, when I would never be the rose smelling sweet enough for Byron. For you, I was the same as any other maid who'd lift her skirts at your command, blow you a kiss and then return to her skivvying again.'

Susan looked down, voice trembling. 'I often think about that winter, when you said you'd come to Newstead for the night of your birthday. My birthday as well. How excited I was. For days before, I went out searching through the woods and gathered ivy for the walls of the stone parlour. If only you had seen the garlands draped around the pillar in the middle of the hall, just like a Jack in the Green. In the glimmer of the candles, it was a fairy-tale palace. And in your dress, I was its queen. But a queen without her king. Dear Mr Murray, the old butler, he took the empty chair beside me. He even gave a speech and raised a glass to your good health, and after that to my own. But how could I drink, when I felt sure the wine would choke me? Why...' All at once her voice was plaintive as she stretched her hands towards him. 'Why didn't you come?'

'I sent Robert, my page, to explain I'd been detained on some business in London.'

'So I learned later that night, when I'd gone tipsy to my bed, and Robert crept beneath the covers. His hands were calloused, rough and clumsy, whereas yours...' She closed her eyes. 'Oh, I know I was stupid to do what I did. But I was angry. I was jealous. How did I know that in the cold, hard light of day he would betray me, running back to you in London and confiding everything? And then, that poem you sent...' Susan began declaiming words, much like the Countess Alfieri when reciting at her salons: –

'Adieu fair thing! without upbraiding
I fain would take a decent leave,
Thy beauty still survives unfading
And undeceived may long deceive.'

Byron took up the verse –

'Oh thou! for whom my heart must bleed,
From whom this anguish springs...'

He broke off with a groan. 'Susan, you must forgive me! My pride was wounded. I was hurt. That's why I had you dismissed. But I should have talked to you. I should have let you explain.'

'You *should* have answered the letter I wrote to you in London. You *should* at least have come to see me when I was living in the squalor of those rooms in Pimlico.'

'I did! I was too late. When I arrived at the house no-one could tell me where you'd gone. It was as if your existence had been banished from the earth.'

'And in a way it was, all thanks to a visit from your lover, Lady Lamb. She'd seen my letter in your rooms and noted down the address. She gave me money, made me swear never to contact you again.'

'Dear God. What a minx!'

'I won't deny I was amused to read her novel some years later, when the path she'd strewn with rosebuds turned to one of weeds and thistles. But she was generous to me, whatever motive lay behind it. At least she saved me from the gallows, or transportation to some hell-hole.'

'For which I'm grateful too,' croaked Veronica Lombardo, who had been sitting in silence, listening to every word. 'She bought a passage on a boat, not knowing where it might end up. I found her wandering the docks where I was walking one day, looking out for pretty faces. For the lost and the lonely.'

The Lombardo flinched with pain when she rose from her chair. Her eyes were narrowed to slits, appraising Byron with disdain.

'She wasn't much to look at then. Skinny and bedraggled from the ordeal of her travels. But I saw the potential. I cared for her as if a daughter, and though she took some polishing, my clever little jewel was soon speaking Italian as if she was native – and oh so eager when it came to music, art, and literature. Not for her the common clients. She always drew the more discerning, and finally the nobleman who wished to make her his wife. So, you see, where England failed my blessed Venice has prevailed.'

Lombardo's laughter was replaced by a fit of phlegmy coughing. Only when that had abated did Susan speak to fill the silence:

'All those books I'd read at Newstead, they were what opened the doors to the splendour of this world, free to host conversaziones when I was made a widow. But then, one day, I was told of your arrival in the city and...' She broke off. Her eyes were glassed. 'I feared you'd see my face and expose me as a fraud, that everything I'd come to own you would steal from me again. At the same time, I must confess, I was curious to see the literary god who had been exiled from his homeland and with such scandals in his wake. And, for myself, that was the time when I let the rumours spread that my syphilitic Count had infected me as well. A convenient lie, as lies so often are. But it allowed me the excuse to always wear a mask in public. Even so, when we first met, when you arrived at my door – as sooner or later all of London's outcasts do – I couldn't help but believe you'd see straight through the disguise. Instead, you were fooled, never suspecting a thing. All I needed to do was bide my time and, when it came, to grab the chance for my revenge.'

'When Polidori arrived with his story of a vampyre?' Byron remarked with a frown.

'It was a gift, but...' Susan turned to stare at the Lombardo. 'Things went too far. *She* went too far. I swear I had no part in any murder in her brothel. As to the kidnap of your daughter...' She swallowed down a sob. 'I told you before, my sole intention was to save her from the woman making plans to adopt her as her own.'

'For which I owe you some thanks.'

Her eyes were glittering with tears. 'Indeed you do!' She spat the words. 'What did you ever do for me? Only take my innocence and treat me like the whore I was later to become. For many years I hated you. But, in the end...' her voice was breaking, 'the love I'd felt for you in Newstead proved to be the stronger. I'd grown too tired of the game of hide-and-seek I'd been playing. When I arrived here last night, it was to tell you who I was, and then to give Allegra back.'

'Well, he beat you to that!' the Lombardo interrupted. 'And now you must forget him. You must let me take you home.'

Byron protested forcibly: 'Susan, tell me what to do, what to say to make amends?'

'Pah!' Lombard laughed. 'Your conscience strikes a little late. I was the one who offered help when she needed it the most, even disposing of that corpse you carried into her stores. There's nothing you can think to give her that I haven't done already, although I wonder would a man such as yourself label me as her guardian angel or the Devil who has damned the woman's mortal soul? Well, in return I would say that if not for men like you, women like me would not exist.' Her finger shook as she pointed scornfully in his direction. 'In the future, should you think about Veronica Lombardo, go and stand before a mirror. Ask yourself where lies the source of the true evil in this world? Is it you, or is it me?' Although the day was still as sultry, just as oppressive as before, when her words came to an end the Lombardo was taken with a fit of shivering. Even when those tremors passed, the woman looked exhausted. Her voice was barely audible:

'My time to die is not far off. I'm here to give you my confession. But in return I ask one thing. Leave my countess out of this. Let her live her life in freedom, as I leave you to live your own.'

She was true to her word. Another knocking at the door announced the lawyer to whom Nicolo had been tasked to take a letter earlier that afternoon. This was the man who'd previously dealt with the settlement of money offered to La Fornarina, and who now carried in some papers set out as Byron had instructed, clearly stating that the Countess and Veronica Lombardo conspired to slander his name, but now agreed that accusations regarding Byron's connection with the novel called *The Vampyre* were entirely spurious. A coda was then added in which Veronica Lombardo dictated her confession of the murder in the brothel, saying she'd taken the glass knives from the Palazzo Alfieri, only afterwards returning the handles that remained to the mantle-shelf display.

Once the papers had been signed, the older woman shuffled off and stood a while before the console with the relics that had drawn her attention on the morning she'd first visited his house. There she nearly collapsed, bending over with a gasp. But how to summon up compassion for this embodiment on earth of the

Greek goddess Apate, the witch of darkness who had revelled in concealments of truths?

Now, Byron would do the same. Before the lawyer had departed, he'd already made his mind up to say nothing of the crime. What would it mean for Susan Vaughan, with the exposure of the lies on which she'd based her present life? Not that he cared if the Lombardo faced a death by execution. It was the least she deserved. But the black widow spider might take the stand in any court and spin yet more of her poison to ensnare him in her web. He already saw the headlines that could finally destroy him, trumping every other scandal that had ever gone before – 'Lord Byron Accused of Killing Whore in Venice Brothel'.

Anyway, hadn't Fate contrived her punishment already? The brothel keeper's arm was obviously infected. If a sepsis had set in, as he believed it must have done, she could be dead within a week. Even at this very moment Byron doubted she would have the strength to walk through the doors and make her way back down the stairs. Oh, how he wished she would depart. What if the woman died this moment, right here in his palazzo? She was the colour of cold porridge, and such a rattle in her throat. The very last thing he needed was a body to dispose of...

Another body to dispose of – for only then did he recall what was lying on his bed.

Desperately trying to rid the horror from his mind, he looked at Susan and implored, 'Will you stay, talk with me, if only for a little while?'

Susan's voice held an edge of cold finality: 'What more is there to say? You have built the gilded cage in which you've chosen to live, and I have built my own.'

This was no longer the maid who'd worn a dress of dark-green velvet. Green as the leaves on the trees under which they'd once made love. This was the Countess Alfieri, and she was quite a different woman.

From the balcony above, Byron watched as the two women stepped aboard his gondola. The ailing Lombardo all but crawled below the awnings, as if she entered her own coffin. How apt that was, and Byron wished her every ounce of suffering. But, seeing Susan there as well, and how she called back up to him with that echo of his verse – 'Adieu! I take my leave' – he could not speak for the grief lodged like a stone in his throat. Yes, she had betrayed him all those years ago at Newstead, but it would never have happened if he'd been there as he had promised, instead of which he'd stayed in London, immersed in the abyss of other sexual affairs. As a man of wealth and fame, the rules were always in his favour with little consequence or danger, whereas for her – one careless night, and a young woman was abandoned to a world of pain and sorrow. Little wonder she had sought to destroy him here in Venice. But, in the end, who was the winner in this game of retribution?

The gondola went gliding off. Only when it turned a bend and was entirely lost from view did he leave the balcony and head towards the study doors. It would be several hours before he saw Tita again. After this trip, he'd be heading to La Mira for Allegra. Before the child was back in Venice, Byron himself must ensure that the mummy from Lazzaro was removed from his bed.

But when he entered his chamber, nothing lay upon the mattress. The only proof of its existence was a residue of ash left across the linen sheets.

Where can it be? A silent scream of panic and alarm – until he suddenly recalled Tita having said that he'd gone into Byron's chamber earlier that afternoon, taking a glass of water in case the Countess had been thirsty. He must have grasped at that chance to wrap the body in its windings, and then he'd carried it downstairs in readiness to be ferried to its grave in the lagoon. Yes, that would be it. And that explained Susan imagining that what she'd seen in the night had been nothing but a dream – for when she woke a second time and found herself to be alone it was quite natural to presume that in her state of drugged sedation she had been hallucinating. For her, the mummy from Lazzaro simply did not exist.

Sweet hour of twilight! - in the solitude
Of the pine forest, and the silent shore
Which bounds Ravenna's immemorial wood..
Evergreen forest! which Boccaccio's lore
And Dryden's lay made haunted ground to me,
How have I loved the twilight hour and thee!

Byron. From *Don Juan:* Canto III

Since I last wrote in this memoir my life has changed beyond all measure. Where I am sitting now is the Italianate version of the Arabian oasis I imagined on the night of my first meeting with Teresa. No scene could less resemble the crumbling gothic splendour of my palazzo back in Venice. No summer stench from the canal. No raucous screeching of the gulls that had begun to oppress me as the harbingers of doom. Such was my guilt for Susan Vaughan...

Byron inhaled the pine-fresh air and smiled to hear the sweet cicadas of the songbirds in the branches. The forest's dappled light gleamed like emeralds as it shafted through the canopy above. How charmed was his life to find this paradise on earth. And yet, he almost hadn't come.

When Tita returned with Allegra from La Mira, she was already sickening with the summer pestilence. By the next dawn she'd grown so ill, his only thoughts were of his child, giving her bark to ease the symptoms, and making sure she imbibed sufficient quantities of water. He suffered many sleepless nights on a pallet by her cot, but that was better than his chamber, where the smell of burning flesh was still so pungent in his nose – even stronger when he fell into delirium as well.

Was it real or imagined when he awoke one dead of night while sprawled across the study chaise, with Tita kneeling at his side, telling Byron that he'd rowed the mummy out to the lagoon, then watched it sink below the waves? They never spoke of it again, even though the gondolier would remain in Byron's service when he finally left Venice. Theirs was a secret shared till death.

Nicolo followed him as well, despite the boy being torn at the prospect of abandoning the sister he believed to still be living in the city. He never knew of Eva's fate. Enough that Byron alone was continually haunted by the thought of her body wrapped in sacking in the morgue. Was she still there? He sometimes wondered...

As to his passion for Teresa, meeting Susan again had left his mind in turmoil. Not that they could share a future. Too much pain in Susan's past. Too much resentment in her heart. But was he doing the right thing, both for himself and for Allegra? Might it be best if Teresa reconciled with her Count and continued with a life devoid of any further scandals? But, *if* she agreed to that, should he remain in Italy or settle in a different land? He increasingly imagined setting sail upon a boat that was wrecked and washed ashore some isolated desert island, where he might walk across the foam that formed a lace on golden shores, much like Defoe's Robinson Crusoe, or his own Don Juan.

Where would his desert island be? Perhaps the New Americas.

He began to learn the basics of the Spanish language, making lists of all provisions he would need for such a journey. To cover any costs, he'd sell his Rochdale estates, which would surely raise enough to form his own small personal empire. It amused him to imagine calling it Byromania. How that would rile the wife who had once labelled his admirers as the Byromaniacs. He even wrote to Hobhouse and enquired if his friend could sort the finance with his bank. But Hobhouse soon replied with stark reminders of the fates of other Englishmen who'd hoped to settle in such lands: '*Didn't Monk Lewis succumb to a death from yellow fever after visiting Jamaica? In light of which* <u>*you*</u> *should be careful to choose a place more temperate. Even if you could survive, surely Allegra is too young to risk her life on such adventures.*'

Hobhouse was right. He always was, even if Byron rarely listened. And, in the end, Fate intervened. The day when Fletcher reappeared at the Palazzo Mocenigo.

Only just dawn, and Allegra was still sleeping in her cot. Byron was sitting at his desk, mulling over yet more lists he'd been compiling for his trip. 'Ah, Fletcher!' He beamed to see the valet in the doorway. 'Come! Sit down and let me run you through the plans I have in mind. I was thinking of Peru…'

'Peru?' Fletcher looked queasy. 'Have you not had enough of all your dramas and high dudgeons? If you don't mind me saying, you're looking very wan. Very grey around the gills. Tita was telling me, downstairs, how both you and Allegra have been stricken with the fever. Perhaps it's left you somewhat addled.'

'My mind is perfectly clear,' Byron responded airily. 'I simply need a change of scene.'

'Would that be something to do with the Countess Alfieri? Her being the young maid you once dallied with at Newstead?'

'How do you know?'

'Tita told me.'

Byron hoped Tita had shown a little more discretion where

the mummy was concerned, for how on earth could he explain *that* adventure to his valet?

Fletcher looked yet more disgruntled as he enquired, 'Well, are you ever going to ask about Teresa?'

'Is she well?' Byron asked.

'She *was*, when we arrived at the castle of her father, but soon after she relapsed, coughing blood and feared by all to be on the point of dying. It may be consumption, though she has rallied somewhat since and gone on with the plan to return to her Count, where she awaits your own arrival, but…' Fletcher left the threat to hang, 'it isn't looking good.'

What a shock to hear such news, and how miraculous the way it helped to clear Byron's mind of any recent indecision. How could his conscience bear the weight of yet another tragedy?

'I must write to her at once and insist she stays alive. The moment Allegra has regained sufficient strength, we will travel to Ravenna.'

And in Ravenna I remain. Byron's pencil scratched the page, *Here, Destiny has smiled on me, for Teresa recovered within days of my arrival ~ which I confess did make me wonder if the illness was contrived as a test of my devotion. Her powers of persuasion are really quite remarkable, even convincing her Count that from now on she be allowed to keep her lover near at hand. More conveniently still, he has donated one whole floor of his palazzo for my use. I cannot make the fellow out. It could be to do with money. He's always tapping me for loans, or to support his ambitions for political advancement. From despising me in Venice, he now accepts me as Teresa's cavalier servente. (In a land where the faith makes divorce impossible, this is the formal acceptance of a male companion who may escort a wife in public & not be damned by idle gossip.) I find the role convenient, being as formal as a marriage, but without the dreariness or chains of domesticity.*

Not that I claim to have arrived here in Ravenna as some

Caesar spouting 'Veni, Vidi, Vici'. It seems to me that Teresa is the ruler of the hearts of both myself & her Count. But in my lover's company all dark clouds are blown away, especially when we're out riding, though she has little natural talent for controlling a horse. Hers will keep running after mine, trying to bite his tail. Today, when mine kicked back, Teresa screamed alarmingly. The grooms then had the Devil's work to try and stop her tumbling from her saddle into brambles. She lost her hat, but otherwise only suffered a few scratches. Indeed, so winsome did she look with her hair snagged through with leaves, I asked the grooms to take the horses and dally at a distance, leaving me free to dab her wounds & kiss the drops of blood away.

Now she is lying on the grass, reading from a book of the poetry of Dante. Earlier, we passed the spot where they say his bones are laid, & she asked if I'd compose a verse of my own, alluding to the poet's great devotion for his Beatrice. Of course, it goes unsaid that what Teresa really means is that I should be inspired to write about my love for her. What a vain coquette she is to seek such immortality! How can I resist?

If there is anyone who currently disturbs my peace of mind, then it is Fletcher, who complains about my menage-à-trois. It is a mystery to me, considering what he has witnessed in all the years we've been together. But I believe at the heart of this latest diatribe is the offence the fellow took when I invested in a suit of livery for him to wear. I thought it made him rather handsome, suiting his features to perfection. A uniform of striking blue with golden buttons & fringed epaulettes sewn over both the shoulders. But Fletcher would insist I'd 'tricked him out like a monkey performing in a circus'. The uniform was thrown away.

Now, his main bone of contention is the hours that I keep, which he insists are topsy turvy & do not suit his constitution. However, here I won't be bullied into changing what has come to suit my temperament so well. Unless invited out to dine, I eat alone at eight or nine, then deal with any correspondence.

When that is done, I work or read, or else seek night-time entertainments till the coming of the dawn, when I retire to my bed & sleep remarkably well. Better than ever in the past. I will rise mid-afternoon, when I may eat a frugal meal before I visit with Teresa ~ with those illicit stolen moments often enabled by the help of her priest & chambermaid. Well, yes, I will admit that when described in such a way I do see Fletcher's point of view. If dramatized, my current life could well be turned into a farce in the style of Goldini. But, the air of subterfuge only heightens the excitement as I creep through corridors, with bedroom doors devoid of locks, knowing full well we could be caught in the act at any moment.

I don't forget my other mistress. My little queen of creation is remarkably well, and she is cared for by the maid who helped enable her escape from the Palazzo Alfieri. However, I confess the demands of a child so very young are often vexing, especially when I am writing. Still, <u>when</u> she is behaving, not mischievous & too headstrong, she can be extremely droll. At the Ravenna carnival she danced & clapped her little hands as she shared her papa's love for all the noise & joy & colour. She also likes to come with me when I am visiting the stables, where Nicolo has full charge of my menagerie of pets. Here Mutz, now in his dotage, is permanently kennelled, due to the menace of his jealousy & growling at Teresa. But he will tolerate no end of attention from my daughter, who likes to crawl upon his back, her fingers clinging to his fur as he takes her for a ride. If not Mutz, she is besotted by the lovebird in its cage. It is most curious & playful. But was I right to bring it here?

I may have spread my own wings and flown away from Venice, but there are still too many days when I awake from wine-drenched dreams & stand before my mirror to see a shadow running dark across the corners of my vision, as the Lombardo said I would. Could it be a premonition of some danger in my future, or the stain of a past I've never truly left behind? Deep in my soul I've always known it could be no accident when Polidori created his 'vampyre' in my image. I am a creature set apart. Grown too heavy is the burden of my life of dissipation. There has to be a reckoning. I fear that time is drawing near. Even now, as I write in this green palace of a forest, I hear the sudden raucous cries as crows go flying overhead, so many crows that, for one moment, they form a cloud that blocks the sun. Is it not said that such birds are often found in cemeteries, scavenging upon the dead?

I think again of the time when a fortune-teller took my hand in hers & said that I would be sure to meet my end in my thirty-seventh year. As that day grows ever nearer, I must endeavour to leave something of value this world. Something more meaningful & concrete than my works of poetry. But, how to seek the world's approval after a life of self-indulgence & fitful passions, never lasting? What is this calling, always nagging, for which as yet I have no answer? Only these lines from Don Juan*...*

He thought about himself, and the whole Earth
Of Man the wonderful, and of the Stars,
And how the deuce they ever could have birth;
And then he thought of Earthquakes and of Wars,
How many miles the Moon might have in girth,
Of Air-balloons, and of the many bars
To perfect Knowledge of the boundless Skies;
And then, he thought of Donna Julia's eyes...

I think of Susan Vaughan. How I once gazed into her eyes below an oak at Newstead Abbey.

Twenty-nine

THE CHURCH OF SAINT MARY MAGDALENE

June 16th, 1938

The Reverend Barber is startled by the screeching of crows coming from the church's graveyard. *The strangest synchronicity*, he is thinking as he stares across the rows of empty pews towards the entrance to the crypt. Beyond that pit of blurring darkness, the arched stained-glass above the altar fills with shafts of golden light.

'This is the miracle of God. The promise of the day reborn,' Barber mutters to himself. But there are no more days for Byron, and Barber feels the weight of grief while staring down at the last roll on the pew at his side. He knows too well what is to come. The tragedies that occurred between the time of the poet's arrival in Ravenna and his final days in Greece.

This is why his fingers tremble as he frees the last black binding – and sees the handwriting is different. It is more rounded. Feminine. And the ink appears less faded. The pages have a textured surface with expensive scalloped edges. There is an envelope attached, fixed with a rusted metal clip. When he tries to pull it free, the metal fractures and the package slips to fall beside his feet.

Much like Byron's valet Fletcher, the Reverend suffers from arthritis, not much improved from having spent so many hours of the night on this unforgiving pew. With a groan, he reaches down, past the lamp no longer burning, on through the cobwebs and the mouse turds where, at last, he grips one corner of the paper he is seeking and inhales its musty odour – and over that another fragrance, somewhat stale, but does he recognise the notes of rose and civet? The blood runs cold in Barber's veins when he recalls Byron's description of the perfume always worn by the Countess Alfieri, and Veronica Lombardo. At the same time, the tower bell begins to toll the morning hour. One, two, three, four, five ... and six. And under that there is the rumble of an engine, growing louder in the lane beyond the church, which means the builders have arrived to seal the tomb back up again. None of them will be surprised to find the Reverend at the doors, after all he has the keys needed to let them in again. But does he have sufficient time to take the rolls to the crypt?

His decision is made. 'I will return,' the Reverend murmurs, as if addressing someone living, leaving the papers still concealed in shadows underneath the pew.

Some months have passed. The seasons turn beyond the vicarage's windows. The winter nights are drawing in. The air is chill, and there's a fire burning brightly in the grate. It throws a gentle radiance around the room, across the desk on which the Reverend Cannon Barber is transcribing the last of the rolls into the pages of a notebook. Finally, his work is done, and with a sigh of deep contentment he sits back in his chair to read it through again ...

London. 1866

I, Countess Alfieri am now old and cannot be so very far away from death. More than forty years have passed since I heard of Byron's end, having left Italy to fight in the Greek War of Independence. There, he was hailed as a hero but then succumbed to a fever in the swamps of Missolonghi, where the doctors placed their leeches on his temples and then failed to stem the flow of blood. Oh, what an irony that was for the man I had once slandered as the Vampyre of Venice.

Before he left Italy, he sent a gift to me in Venice. It was a little silver box, the Byron crest on the lid, inside a lace-edged handkerchief and in its folds a single acorn. Under that, two rolls of papers held the personal reflections that could so easily have brought my house of mirrors crashing down ~ had he chosen to expose me. But he did not, and for that I shall be forever grateful.

In a brief note he sent his warning. Be careful. Always remember.

Remember what? That night of horror in the Palazzo Mocenigo? Or the brief love we two once shared?

For all my comforts and wealth, I've always missed my life in Newstead, that mausoleum of a house in which a young and foolish maid once dreamed of standing at an altar in a dress of dark green velvet. And now, I have returned, and tonight an aged countess will walk the aisle of Hucknall church where she will kneel to say a prayer, and then descend into the crypt below the chancel steps. (If there's sufficient money offered, most any door can be opened. Even the houses of the dead.) This is where I mean to leave Byron's memories of Venice. I have considered burning them, but I find I cannot do it, even though the gossip vultures will be gathering to swoop and peck my flesh when I am dead. But if I leave them in the crypt, perhaps the secrets will be safe. If, in time, they are discovered and all the scandals are exposed, I doubt that Susan Vaughan or the Countess Alfieri will still be alive to care.

Fletcher and Tita would care, if either one of them is still living today. I know they travelled with the coffin on its journey back to England. Did Fletcher ever build his macaroni factory?

Teresa, she still lives, but Byron never married her, despite her Count being persuaded to agree to an annulment of their marriage in the end. Now she has discovered another wealthy husband, who, so I've heard at my salons, always takes the greatest pleasure in introducing his wife to any new acquaintances as 'Madame la Marquise de Boissy, autrefois la Maitresse de Milord Byron'.

And then, there is the baker's wife. Not very long before I made this journey back to England, I was walking through the city when I found a beggar woman selling oysters from a basket – the aged wretch who I had heard the locals called La Fornarina, because Lord Byron used to say she resembled a portrait by the painter, Raphael. I have seen that very painting. The youth and beauty of the model. But I could only stare in shock at this old woman's coarse white hair and her sagging leathered skin. Impossible to think that she could ever have been young, or that Byron was seduced. But when she suddenly glanced up through her remarkable black eyes, I knew. It was true. This was his Harlequina.

The shock, it left me trembling. I felt compelled to walk away, but pity stopped me in my tracks. I dropped my purse into her lap and every coin it might have held. I did not tell her who I was, but when she smiled, 'Thank you, Contessa', I realised she knew me too.

Of those in Byron's memoirs now consigned to their graves, the first of them was Lombardo. She died by her own hand, shortly after that last meeting at the Palazzo Mocenigo. Had Byron noticed when she stole the attic hemlock from his house?

Her corpse was taken to the morgue and there, for all I know it remains to this day. I did not claim her body. I did not mourn her loss, though I still weep to think of Petros. As for Nicolo's murdered sister, there is a stone that bears her name on the cemetery island of San Cristoforo della Pace. I pay for flowers to be placed upon her grave every day. If Nicolo, her brother, ever comes back home to Venice, maybe he'll find his way to her.

What a ghastly symmetry when Doctor Polidori died by drinking prussic acid after going back to London. One of my English salon guests wrote to tell me at the time, speculating that the man had been haunted by his failures; most of all by the fact that people still believed Lord Byron had been the author of The Vampyre. *I must accept my own blame in the spreading of that lie. It is a stain on my conscience that can never be erased. But no matter how I wept, my sorrow for his death was as nothing when compared to what I felt for Allegra.*

Many say that Byron failed her, sending his child to be raised and educated in a convent. But in the note sent with his memoirs he said he feared that his daughter might be kidnapped by the bandits running wild in Ravenna – the callous men demanding money, who dragged dead bodies through the streets, and sometimes into his own home. He also wrote of the times when he'd been walking through the city and had noticed a dark figure peering out from shadowed alleys. He'd supposed it must have been another admirer. There were so many at the time. Men and women alike who would follow him about, and all obsessed with the most trivial occupations of Lord Byron. But then, there came the afternoon when he'd been sitting in a cafe with Allegra, eating pastries, and he'd seen a hooded man staring in through the window. He could have been mistaken, with all the steam blurring the glass, but at the time he felt quite sure. It was the mummy from Lazzaro.

I always knew it was real. I told myself it was a dream, because to think of it existing is to welcome madness in. But, for more than a year after the Palazzo Mocenigo had been abandoned and left empty, many who passed on the canal claimed to see a shadowed figure staring out through the upper windows. There were times when I awoke in my own bed to the smell of musky herbs and burning flesh. I became very pale and lacked all energy. To this day there is a sore on my throat that resembles a pair of wounds, like puncture marks. None of the doctors I've consulted have the salve to make it heal. Some seem to think it the result of a virulent disease that, for a while, spread through the city and for which they have no name. But then, my ailment is as nothing when compared to those poor souls murdered while plying their trade in the shadowed night-time alleys. Unlike the prostitute attacked and left for dead at my own house, not one of these had an ounce of blood remaining in their bodies.

The deaths all stopped. It would have been around the time when Byron thought he saw the mummy in Ravenna. Because of this, I understand why he decided to place Allegra in the care of the nuns at Bagnacavallo – even when her natural mother wrote and begged to be allowed to take her daughter away, claiming she'd had a premonition that her child was sure to die if she remained in the convent.

Allegra's mother was right. Among my friends, the tragedy was only spoken of in whispers – of how the girl had died from typhus, or perhaps a recurrence of an illness she'd once suffered from while living in Venice. I have since read an account by Teresa Guiccioli, saying that when the news arrived such a dreadful mortal paleness spread over Byron's features. He attempted to stand, but only sank back down again, and remained in that position for an hour or even more. No amount of consolation seemed enough to reach his ear, far less to ease his broken heart. When he finally spoke, it was to say that only then could he appreciate how vital his daughter was to his existence, for no sooner had she gone than he knew that he could never live in happiness again.

Is that why he went to Greece to join the fight for independence? To escape the curse of grief, only to meet with his own death?

A little time before embarking on my journey back to England, I wrote to Countess Guiccioli to ask if Allegra had been buried with her father in the crypt at Hucknall Torkard. I only had the vaguest hope that the woman would reply. But she did, and in her letter she informed me that he'd hoped for his daughter's remains to be buried in the garden of the church very near to his childhood school of Harrow. It was a place where he'd been happy and where he used to say he'd one day like to take Allegra. Instead, he left instructions for her stone to be inscribed with some words that he'd chosen from the book of Samuel – I shall go to her, but she shall not return to me. He'd also asked for her coffin to be laid beside the footpath, below the branches of an elm where he'd so often sat himself, and afterwards immortalised in these lines of poetry ...

Spot of my youth! whose hoary branches sigh,
Swept by the breeze that fans the cloudless sky;
Where now alone I muse, who oft have trod,
With those I loved, thy soft and verdant sod;
With those who, scattered far, perchance deplore,
Like me, the happy scenes they knew before:
O, as I trace again thy winding hill,
Mine eyes admire, my heart adores thee still,
Thou drooping elm! beneath whose boughs I lay,
And frequent mused the twilight hours away ...

I wonder does his spirit ever leave its resting place and return in twilight hours to lie in peace beneath that elm? If so, he will have found no stone to mark Allegra's grave. When her coffin was delivered to the church it was decided that no bastard of the infidel Lord Byron could deserve to have a Christian burial. She lies within an unmarked grave.

Still, I shall visit Harrow church before I travel back to Venice and, if that elm tree still exists, I'll place some flowers in its shade.

EPILOGUE

The Vicarage
HUCKNALL TORKARD
October 16th, 1938

The Reverend rises from his chair and murmurs the prayer: 'Suffer the little children to come unto me. Forbid them not, for of such is the Kingdom of Heaven.'

Wiping a tear from his eye with the back of his hand, he bitterly regrets the actions of his fellow church men. Who could discard the earthly memory of one so innocent? If he could only believe the rumours to be true, that Allegra hadn't died in the convent after all, but was removed by her mother with the collusion of the abbess, and the coffin that arrived at the doors of Harrow church contained no more than empty air. But hadn't people said the same of Byron's casket in the crypt?

Where do these stories even come from? Barber heaves a sigh while staring down at the roll penned by the Countess Alfieri. Did she ever have the chance to meet Nicolo again and take him to his sister's grave, or had he lived in ignorance of Eva's death until the end? The Reverend hopes it was the latter.

What to do about these memoirs? Should they be passed to

some official institute, which could then verify the text as genuine? *If* authentic, what comes next? The publication of a book? What purpose would it serve? In opening the crypt, Barber had only ever hoped to dispel any doubts regarding Byron's resting place, and then to draw more admirers of the poet to the church. But it's one thing to welcome those who come to pay their respects, quite another to invite unwanted notoriety.

Barber glances at the window, where there is nothing to see but the ghost of his reflection against the blackness of the night. In its place he imagines a hoard of journalists, their knuckles banging on the glass, demanding interviews while seeking yet more scandal and sensation. Hadn't there been enough of that during the course of Byron's lifetime?

He thinks again of the night when the church was steeped in silence, only the rasp of his own breaths as he'd descended the steps to the shadows of the crypt. There he'd seen the poet's face, and quite exquisitely preserved. But even with the embalming, was that natural for a corpse after a century or more? And had it merely been a trick of the lantern's eerie light, or had the Reverend really seen the faintest twitching of the muscles either side of the mouth?

There is one long, expanding moment during which he lifts a hand to the scar on his throat, being all that now remains of a cut he sustained when he'd tripped and hit his head, and for a while lost consciousness. For many weeks it had been bruised, oozing blood, and slow to heal. He thinks again of the wound on Countess Alfieri's throat. He wonders if Polidori, as Byron's personal physician, had been privy to some supernatural secrets then disguised in the fiction of his novel. Byron himself may have lied, or only written down half-truths with regard to what unfolded in the pages of his memoir. And, as to Father Aucher's tales on the island of Lazzaro, if the Reverend's Christian faith believes in angels up in heaven, is it so improbable that Hell might vomit out its demons? In which case, it is as well that the stone that seals the crypt is now securely back in place...

Oh, this is ridiculous! the Reverend chides himself. He is exhausted, that is all. But, if he, a man of God, and hopefully in his right mind, could think to foster such delusions, who knows what levels of hysteria would follow if the contents of these memoirs were made public.

There is no longer any doubt as to what he has to do. Slowly, methodically, he gathers up the rolls and his own notebooks of transcriptions. He carries them across the room and heaves a groan as he kneels on the rug before the fire.

He feeds the papers to the flames.

Author's Notes

Having been contemplating working on a story about vampires, it seemed to me that every aspect of the genre had been covered. What could I offer that was new?

I started reading other novels that were based around this subject, and when I came to *The Vampyre* by John Polidori, I discovered that events surrounding his fiction were themselves a potent mix to inspire my own creation. What could be more atmospheric than the setting of Venice? What central character could be at once as problematical, but also as alluring as the infamous Lord Byron?

For all the faults and contradictions related to his character, Byron was undoubtedly a charismatic man. He was deformed, but beautiful. He could be surly and withdrawn, or gregarious and charming. He died too young, but what a life! – from the theatrical adventures encountered on his early travels, the fame and adulation after *Childe Harold* was first published, and then the debts, the sexual scandals and failed marriage that would see him being exiled from his homeland, until the final tragic act as the hero in Greece.

With such a wealth of historical material to draw on, the roots of *Dangerous* were firmly planted in the time Byron spent at Lake Geneva, where he was joined by the Shelleys, Mary's half-sister Claire Clairmont, and his personal physician, Dr John Polidori. With that summer being blighted by the eruption of Mount Tambora, with eerily dark skies and unseasonably bad weather, the group amused themselves by reading the ghost stories found in a *Fantasmagoria*, after which Byron suggested they write some horrors of their own. What resulted from that challenge was quite remarkable. Mary Shelley started work on her novel *Frankenstein,* and Byron's own discarded words would go on to inspire *The Vampyre* by Polidori.

Both of those gothic novels still have influence today. But when *The Vampyre* was first published, the fame it brought to its author was not due so much to the words within the book, more the controversy caused when the rogue publishers named Byron as the author on the cover. Byron denied any involvement, but the belief would persist, and as his poetry was often autobiographical in nature, the subsequent confusion over the novel's authorship offered me the perfect chance to connect him to some murders with vampiric connotations. However, I must stress, though accused of many things, Byron was never involved with the deaths of prostitutes.

How much of what I've written in this novel is the truth?

The prologue is based on an actual event – a day in 1938 when the Reverend Cannon Barber arranged to open the crypt in the Hucknall parish church, hoping to prove that Byron's body was still lying in its coffin and had not been, as was believed by many at the time, stolen by resurrectionists. He did discover that some jewels were missing from the coronet on top of the coffin, and some brassware had been taken. Perhaps these things had been pilfered at the original internment, or at the time when his daughter, Ada Lovelace, was laid to rest beside her father. Meanwhile, Byron's body was still lying in its casket, and remarkably preserved after more than a hundred years. However, my own details of the Reverend descending to the crypt at dead of night, and what he subsequently finds in the form of secret memoirs, are entirely fictional.

If you wish to read the Reverend's own account of this event, it is published in a book. ***Byron and Where He Is Buried,*** by Thomas Gerrard Barber.

CHARACTERS

Many of my novel's characters have been based on real people in Byron's life at the time. Byron himself lived in Venice for three years before he left for a more settled existence with **Teresa Guiccioli**, and after that to find his fate in the Greek War of Independence. During his stay in the city, he was known as 'Star and Satyr', due to his literary renown, but also because of his sexually voracious and liberated lifestyle, often reflected in the action of his *Beppo* and *Don Juan*.

Teresa Guiccioli was married to an older Count, and also pregnant with his child, which she later miscarried. None of this deterred Byron, who fell madly in love from the moment they first met, and in a scene very much like the one I have described. However, I have played fast and loose with the timelines of this grand affair, just as I have with the existence of the **Countess Alfieri**, who is entirely fictional, and therefore definitely not present at the party to read from the pages of *The Vampyre*. Neither was Teresa injured by a broken corset bone. This injury was inspired by an event back in London when Byron's thwarted lover, **Lady Caroline Lamb**, was so jealous that she caused a scene at a ball with a knife or broken glass. Whatever it had been, the result was much blood, though little risk to her life.

Caroline Lamb is mentioned very briefly in this novel, specifically with her coining the description of Byron as being 'mad, bad and dangerous', but also through my allusion to her own roman-á-clef which was titled *Glenarvon* and was written as revenge after the end of their affair. As with Polidori's *The Vampyre*, this novel is still available to read today, but all ideas of Caroline ever meeting Susan Vaughan are entirely fictional.

Susan Vaughan also existed in Byron's real world. Like other servants at Newstead, the pretty, clever Welsh maid had a romance with the young lord, around the time of his return from his first Continental travels. When *Childe Harold* was then published and led to such success, Byron spent more time in London being pursued by ardent fans and indulging in affairs. Oblivious of this, Susan planned to celebrate their two joint birthdays at Newstead, and how poignant is the letter she wrote to her lover, describing her joy in going out to choose the greenery to decorate the hall – which sounds more fitting for a wedding and was perhaps why Byron feared she might have plans above her station. Later, when he heard she'd ended the party by sleeping with his page, he – somewhat hypocritically – claimed to be so distressed by the infidelity that Susan was punished with the loss of job and home. Sometime after that she was arrested in London on suspicion of selling a dress that had been stolen, during which time she wrote to Byron and appealed for his help; and then there is her sad goodbye: –

> *'I should have been exceedingly pleased to have seen you before I had sailed. Indeed I take it very unkind I never saw any one else ashamed at me. It is impossible to say how happy it would make me to see you again at sweet Newstead or anywhere else.'*

Where did Susan go? Was she convicted and transported to the colonies? From that point on, no more is known. However, such a void gave me the chance to create a whole new life for the maid, not least the opportunity to seek revenge on her old lover in the fictional guise of my Countess Alfieri. She and the brothel keeper, **Veronica Lombardo**, only exist in this novel.

Another real person is **Margarita Cogni**, known as **La Fornarina** because she so reminded Byron of a portrait by Raphael that is generally known as *The Baker's Daughter*. Margarita was indeed the wife of such a man. But in this novel I have melded her character with that of another Venetian. Margarita's predecessor,

Marianna, was the wife of a draper Byron lodged with when he first arrived in Venice before taking on the lease of the Palazzo Mocenigo. It was she, not Margarita, who pawned a necklace Byron gave her.

La Fornarina would have known Byron's daughter Allegra, but not for very long before the woman was dismissed. Prone to jealousy and rage, she did indeed attack a visitor one night with a knife. On another occasion she threw herself in the canal.

When it comes to **Allegra**, most allusions to the child in this book are based on truth. She was sent to live in Venice with her father by Claire Clairmont, with whom he'd had a brief affair. But despite his promises to keep Allegra at his side, he often left her with the Hoppners at the British consulate. Later, in Ravenna, the child was placed in a convent. When Claire Clairmont learned of this, she had a dreadful premonition that her daughter would die if she remained with the nuns; which is exactly what did happen when the child contracted typhus, or perhaps malaria. The little girl was five years old.

It is such a tragic story. But I believe that Byron cared – in his own way – for Allegra. It is important to remember his own treatment as a child and how that may have affected his own style of parenting. Byron's father, 'Mad Jack', was mostly absent from his life, gambling his wife's inheritance, whoring around the Continent, and also indulging in an affair with a half-sister. Byron and his mother, who was widowed when her son was only three years old, had a stormy relationship. She was at times affectionate, but often prone to violent tempers, calling her son a 'Byron dog', and mocking his lame foot. A nursemaid, **May Gray**, introduced the child to sex at a very early age, and then quoted from the Bible about hell and damnation. Little wonder Byron grew to be distrustful of women and often scorned the Christian faith.

As for Allegra's happiness, when Shelley visited the convent in which her father placed her, he found the child a little shy, but in good health and obviously indulged by the nuns. There is also the fact that Teresa Guiccioli enjoyed her convent education. She no doubt had influence over the fate of Byron's daughter. Another thing often ignored by those who vilify the man for the treatment of his child is the political upheaval and dangers in Ravenna. Teresa's family were members of the Carbonari, a group of militants who sought to free Italy from the rule of foreigners, in this case the Austrians. Meanwhile, bandits roamed the streets, and the daughter of a man as famed and wealthy as Lord Byron would need protection from the very real risk of being kidnapped.

Fletcher was Byron's loyal valet, who remained in his employ until the time of his death. I don't know about his skills with brewing a cup of coffee, but when the man returned to London he did indeed invest his money in a pasta factory. Information is scarce, but from what I can gather it was not a great success.

Tita was Byron's gondolier, who also followed his master when he left Venice for Ravenna. Physically, he was said to be somewhat piratical, and may well have been a model for some of Byron's verses. He was a gift for the imagined scenes he plays in my own novel.

John Cam Hobhouse first met Byron during their student days at Cambridge, after which the two of them travelled on the Continent and formed a friendship for life. However, Hobhouse never rescued Byron from any prison or transported him to safety on the island of Lazzaro. Those scenes are purely fictional.

John Polidori was the son of an Italian scholar who'd settled in London and married an English wife. A child prodigy, John qualified as a doctor at the age of just nineteen. He was then hired by Byron as his personal physician when the poet left England for his voluntary exile. The darkly handsome young doctor was asked by Byron's publisher to keep a diary of their travels, and that no doubt gave Polidori hopes for literary success. In truth he lacked his employer's natural wit or writing talent, but the two of them did share something of a resemblance. This doppelganger theme became essential to my story, with its confused identities. And Polidori did indeed take to dressing like Byron. It is also true that Polidori became very fond of Mary Shelley during the time they all spent at the Villa Diodati, and that he subsequently challenged Percy Shelley to a duel.

Three years later *The Vampyre* novella was published during Byron's time in Venice. However, all encounters with Polidori in the city are entirely fictional. Polidori never worked in the hospital morgue.

It is also true that Byron's publisher decided to print the 'fragment' of the tale that first inspired the doctor's novel, thereby implying Polidori was a shameless plagiarist. Having travelled back to England, Polidori grew depressed and lost himself in drink and gambling. He also suffered a fall that caused a head injury. In 1821 at the age of twenty-five he died, most probably by drinking prussic acid, although his family denied any claims of suicide. (Though not of relevance here, it may also be of interest that Polidori's sister was the mother of the artist Dante Gabriel Rossetti.)

Augusta – Byron's half-sister – plays little part in this plot, but the affair with her brother was undoubtedly one reason for his exile and disgrace. Their relationship deserves a novel of its own, but I did take the liberty of having Polidori pretending to be her in the fictional scene that takes place in The Leads.

The **anatomical wax Venus,** one of which Byron did buy while on a visit to Rome, must surely be included in this list of characters as she plays such a part in the plot's development. These models were rare and expensive works of art: life-sized, often bejewelled, with heads of human hair and reclining in a pose as if they'd just engaged in sex. Whatever uses they were made for – as educational devices, or more carnal purposes – they were perfectly formed, as were the inner organs, which could be seen by removing the panelled abdomen.

As to the **mummy from Lazzaro**, I have played very freely with the basis of some truth. The monastery island near to Venice does exist. Byron visited there often and along with **Father Aucher** had worked on the creation of an Armenian-to-English dictionary. He would have seen the many fascinating artefacts the monks brought to the island when they fled from persecution by the Turks, but not an Egyptian mummy, which did not arrive until a year after his death. My reference to dakhanavars is based on research of Armenian vampire tales. *The Book of Demons* is a figment of my own imagination ... though perhaps one does exist.

Byron's **menagerie** must also have a mention. He had the greatest fondness for the animals he kept. As a student in Cambridge, when not allowed to have a dog, he stabled a tame bear. Boatswain, a Newfoundland dog that died from rabies while at Newstead, was so beloved that his death was immortalised in verse. The younger Byron even wished to be buried with the dog in the ruins of the abbey.

Whether the animals described in my novel truly tally with those that Byron kept at the Palazzo Mocenigo, in 1819 he wrote to a friend with the mention of some monkeys, a fox, and two new mastiffs – one of which was known as Mutz. He also wrote to his half-sister: *'My dog (Mutz by name and Swiss by nation) shuts a door when he is told – there – that's more than Tip can do.'*

When he'd moved to Ravenna, and Shelley visited, his friend then wrote that he'd been greeted on the stairs of Byron's home by *'five peacocks, two guinea hens and an Egyptian crane'.*

Another animal that really did exist is the elephant described in the early pages of this novel. I echo Byron's own account of the creature breaking free and then rampaging through the city. Such a vivid metaphor reflects Byron's own experience of leaving England's constraints before a time of wild abandonment while living in Venice.

SETTINGS

As to the settings in the story, most are based on real places.

I have already mentioned the **monastery of Lazzaro**, which can be visited by taking a boat ride from Venice.

The **Palazzo Mocenigo** that Byron leased while in Venice still exists to this day. I have had to imagine most of the interior, researching photographs and paintings, and descriptions of the objects Byron kept at the time – such as the model of the hermaphrodite goddess Flora, the gilded skulls and attic hemlock, and the ornamental sabre that was hanging on one wall. But I have taken a boat on the canal and seen the steps and mooring posts before the doors, the ironwork of the grilles fronting the house's lower windows, the balconies, and the stone lions' heads that feature in the novel.

The theatre Byron visits, the **Teatro La Fenice**, is open for tours and many grand performances. Sadly, it's not quite the same as the theatre I've described, because the building has burned down on more than one occasion. But the architectural style has been faithfully retained, just as ornate and majestic as in 1819.

The prison of **The Leads** beside the Bridge of Sighs – in which Byron never stayed, but Casanova really did – is also open to the public in a limited capacity. When I visited myself, it was to find an exhibition with many instruments of torture, and on the second floor some rather realistic models of prisoners in cells.

Countess Alfieri's salon in a palazzo near St Mark's is drawn from my imagination, as is the brothel that belongs to **Veronica Lombardo**. But walk any of the streets, crossing over arched stone bridges, weaving your way through the dark warrens of the calles and sotoportegos, and you will certainly find houses that those women could have owned. If you happen to visit during the time of Carnival you'll undoubtedly see versions of my Countess Alfieri, with many women in gold masks and tall white wigs on their heads, dressed in the lace and silk damasks of Georgian-era clothes. Or are there real ghosts who haunt the city's night-time streets, still so unchanged from the time of Lord Byron's residence?

I must confess, whenever there, I often look over my shoulder hoping to catch a glimpse of him.

Acknowledgments

My sincerest thanks go to my literary agent, David H Headley, my publisher, Karen Sullivan, editorial director West Camel and all the other employees of Orenda Books. Without your belief, this book would never have existed. Also, thanks to Mark Swan, who has designed such a suitably brooding gothic cover.

I am forever grateful to my writing-group mentors, Linda Buckley-Archer, Susannah Cherry, and M. L. Steadman. Wise heads, and much-loved friends.

To my extremely talented fellow historical novelists, Kate Griffin and Anna Mazzola. You both took the time to read an early first chapter and give the nod of your approval. I am so lucky to know you.

There are so many other authors whose friendship and support has come to mean the world to me. Thank you, to *everyone* who plays a part in my life, whether in reality, or in the online world – especially the WhatsApp Queen, J.A. Corrigan.

Thinking of social media, I must acknowledge inspiration found in the X accounts belonging to Jed Pumblechook – @JedPumblechook, The Romanticism Blog – @Wordsworthians, The Byron Society – @byron_society, and Dr Sam Hirst – @RomGothSam.

Thank you to all the early readers who spend their precious time in reviewing a book at the time of publication. And here a special mention to the indefatigable Anne Cater, who organises the best blog tours.

To all the librarians, and the passionate booksellers who

recommend my work to readers, or who invite me to events, I cannot say how much it means. Without you all, where would I be?

To everyone who organises literary festivals, connecting me with my readers – you are so appreciated. In addition, to the chairs of these events who take such care and time in preparation. It is an honour to have met you and have new friends in my life – especially Tim Rideout, whose support has helped to give me self-belief at a time when I needed it the most.

And, finally, to my husband, who is so patient and supportive when I lose myself in work and forget the real world. I do come back ... in the end.

Bibliography

Lord Byron, the Major Works by George Gordon,
pub. Oxford World's Classics

The Vampyre by John Polidori,
pub. Project Gutenberg

The Monk by Matthew Lewis,
pub. Oxford World's Classics

The Story of My Life by Giacomo Casanova,
pub. Penguin Classics

Byron and Where He Is Buried by Thomas Gerrard Barber,
pub. Hucknall Parish Church

Byron, A Life in Ten Letters by Andrew Stauffer,
pub. Cambridge University Press

Byron's Letters & Journals by Richard Landsown,
pub. Oxford University Press

Byron, Life and Legend by Fiona MacCarthy,
pub. John Murray

Lord Byron Accounts Rendered by Doris Langely Moore,
pub. John Murray

Byron's Women by Alexander Larman,
pub, Head of Zeus

Byron in Love by Edna O'Brien,
pub, Weidenfeld & Nicolson

Young Romantics by Daisy Hay,
pub. Bloomsbury

The Fall of the House of Byron by Emily Brand,
pub. John Murray

Summer of Shadow and Myth by Andrew McConnell Stott,
pub. Canongate

The Rise of the Vampire by Erik Butler,
pub. Reaktion Books

The History of the Vampire in Popular Culture by Violet Fenn,
pub. Pen and Sword

In Search of Dracula by Raymond T. McNally and Radu Florescu,
pub. Houghton Mifflin

Venice Pure City by Peter Ackroyd,
pub. Vintage Books

Films/TV I have enjoyed as part of my research

Gothic, film directed by Ken Russell, 1986

Byron, written by Nick Dear. BBC drama
directed by Julian Farino, 2003

The Bad Lord Byron, film directed
by David MacDonald, 1949